THE Hideout

MELISSA TEREZE

First Edition April 2023
Published by GPC Publishing
Copyright © 2023 Melissa Tereze
ISBN: 978-1-915242-22-8

Cover Design: Melissa Tereze
Editor: Charlie Knight

Find out more at: www.melissaterezeauthor.com
Follow me on Twitter: @MelissaTereze
Follow me on Instagram: @melissatereze_author

All rights reserved. This book is for your personal enjoyment only. This book or any portion thereof may not be reproduced or used in any manner without the express permission of the author.

This is a work of fiction. All characters & happenings in this publication are fictitious and any resemblance to real persons (living or dead), locales or events is purely coincidental.

CONTENT GUIDANCE - THIS NOVEL DEALS WITH THE DISCUSSION OF DOMESTIC VIOLENCE.

Also by Melissa Tereze

Another Love Series

The Arrangement (Book One)

The Call (Book Two)

Before You Go (Book Three)

Mrs Middleton Novels

Mrs Middleton

Teach Me (Co-write with Jourdyn Kelly)

Vanessa

The Ashforth Series

Playing For Her Heart (Book One)

Holding Her Heart (Book Two)

Other Novels

Discovery

The Stepmother

Behind Her Eyes

At First Glance

Always Allie

Breaking Routine

In Her Arms

Forever Yours

The Heat of Summer

Forget Me Not

More Than A Feeling

Where We Belong: Love Returns

Naked

Titles under L.M Croft (Erotica)

Pieces of Me

You're afraid of leaving because you don't want to be alone.
But baby, you're ready.

THE HIDEOUT PLAYLIST

1. Keep Climbing – Delta Goodrem
2. Not Me, Not I – Delta Goodrem
3. Gravity – Sara Bareilles
4. Falling – The Civil Wars
5. Like I Can – Sam Smith
6. Distant Dreamer – Duffy
7. Give Me A Little More Time – Gabrielle
8. Alone – Jessie Ware
9. 1000 Times – Sara Bareilles
10. Hate To See Your Heart Break – Hayley Williams ft Joy Williams
11. All I Ask – Adele
12. Love In The Dark – Adele
13. Wherever You Will Go – Charlene Soraia
14. Last Of The True Believers – Jessie Ware
15. I Won't Let You Go – James Morrison
16. In My Own Time – Delta Goodrem
17. Kiss Me (Acoustic) – Dermot Kennedy
18. Yours – Ella Henderson
19. Promise Me – Beverley Craven
20. Hold On – Adele
21. All For You – Cian Ducrot
22. To Be Loved – Adele
23. Forever – Lewis Capaldi
24. Run To You – Whitney Houston
25. Pointless – Lewis Capaldi
26. True Colours – Micky
27. California King Bed – Rihanna
28. XO – John Mayer
29. Roots – Grace Davies
30. The Nearness Of You – Nora Jones

EPILOGUE – Ruelle – I Get To Love You

CHAPTER 1
KEEP CLIMBING

Well, this is a huge change.

Juliet Saunders stepped out from behind the bar she'd recently purchased, stopping in the middle of the tiny room. What the hell had she been thinking when she'd turned her back on law…only to walk into this?

The Hideout.

And yes, that's exactly what it was. A hideout. A place for people—*members*—to rest and reset after a hard day's work. A space that provided a friendly atmosphere. After today, Juliet would look to introduce impressive signature cocktails. Although, she wasn't sure she'd last the duration here. She'd never owned a bar before, but when her mother passed away six months ago—work continuing to do very little for her—she knew the choice she'd been thinking of making for a while was the right one.

She'd made the decision to quit while she was ahead.

The problem Juliet had was that the higher her profile, the more likely the criminals with the dirty money sought her out. They wanted the best to keep them on the outside, and Juliet's name often came into play in order for that to happen. While she believed everyone was innocent until proven guilty, some of her cases had become too much.

She'd left the profession with a mark on her back, almost accepting a bribe to keep her safe, so now here she was…as far away from the criminal justice system as she possibly could be. Of course, she'd miss aspects of her former life, but in the long run, she planned to fade into the background and live a quiet existence.

Surely The Hideout was the place to do that?

Juliet shoved her hands in the pockets of her suit pants, her heels echoing through the empty room as she turned and eyed the piano in the corner. With only seven tables dotted around, the bar in the opposite corner, this surely couldn't be hard to maintain.

All members had been given the information they required; they were aware that The Hideout had a new owner, and none of them had turned down the renewal of their memberships. Really, Juliet was lucky that the place had been set up from the get-go. It certainly made *her* life easier.

Startled when the bell to the side of the staircase jingled, she placed a hand to her chest, exhaling a breath. Juliet approached the bar and checked the system, smiling when she saw her new mixologist standing outside. She was a few minutes late, but Juliet could forgive her. She pressed the switch under the counter, granting access, and waited patiently.

Footsteps rushing down the stairs had Juliet quirking a brow, and then a beautiful blonde woman stopped just inside the doorway. She wore low-rise black jeans, a white shirt tucked into them with the sleeves rolled up her forearms. "Hi. Sorry I'm late. I know it's called The Hideout, but telling me to look for the old Victorian oil lamp above the green door wasn't much help."

Juliet offered a beaming smile, inspecting her mixologist as she stepped further into the room. If she'd known this woman was going to be coming in for an interview, she'd have contacted her days earlier. Wow, she was stunning.

"Paige Harrison. Again, sorry I'm late." Paige extended a hand that Juliet took. She allowed the reaction her body had, a reaction she didn't often accept and waited for the next words to fall from such a perfect mouth. Her lips…her voice. *Oh, dear.* Paige lifted her eyes slowly up Juliet's body, smiling when she reached her face. "You must be Juliet?"

"Correct. That's me."

Paige turned and walked slowly around the bar, whistling as she jammed her hands in her back pockets. "Gorgeous place. Very unusual."

"Thank you. I haven't changed anything yet—just given it a lick of paint here and there."

"It's definitely unique. But," Paige said as she turned, those eyes just as intriguing as the first time. Greyish green, "how does this place make any money? Most of the city likely doesn't know it exists."

"It's members only." Juliet rearranged a few glasses on the counter, trying to keep her hands busy while watching how Paige moved around with such ease. It wasn't often people seemed so relaxed in Juliet's presence. But then again, they were usually looking at jail time, and their life was in her hands. "Where is it you've come from?"

"Oh, other end of the country. Kent," Paige spoke over her shoulder, stepping towards the piano. She ran her hand over the flat top of it. "Do you play?"

"Me? God, no. I wouldn't know the first thing about it." Juliet wished she was that talented. "I was told by an old friend that you were worth contacting. That you're one of the best mixologists around." Juliet wouldn't mention the fact that

Paige didn't stay at one particular bar for too long. She could get into that with her employee if or when they had more conversation under their belts. "And that your smoked Old Fashioned is *the* best around..."

Paige grinned as she held Juliet's gaze. Not what she'd expected, but she could always appreciate a beautiful woman... and the pull Juliet seemed to have when it came to that beautiful woman. *You've still got it, J.* "And I hear you were the best criminal defence lawyer around."

Impressive. Paige had done her background work. The question was...why? "I'm not sure why you felt compelled to check me out, but yes, that's the rumour."

"I recognised the name on your email. I figured you were someone entirely different, but then I dug a little deeper to find that I was right the first time."

"Well, I'm no longer the shit hot lawyer I once was, so please...leave any issues you have at the door."

Paige frowned. "What makes you think I have issues?"

"Most people do these days." Juliet turned with a shrug. If she was going to hire this woman, she had to see what she had to offer. "So, how about you mix me a few drinks, and we get this show on the road?"

Paige lifted a shoulder, confidence oozing from her. "Sure. Let's do it."

As Paige joined Juliet behind the bar, she squeezed past her. Juliet wasn't sure why her body reacted *again*, she was having sex more often than not lately, but then Paige cleared her throat and said, "Maybe you should take a seat on the *other* side of the bar. Then you can see *exactly* what I have to offer."

Oh. Okay. Paige was one of those women. A flirt. *Perfect.* Juliet had always liked to have a little fun whenever the chance presented itself. "Oh, I see exactly what you offer already, Miss Harrison."

But Paige stalked towards Juliet, encouraging her back and out from behind the bar. She wore a smirk, one Juliet noted immediately. "Trust me. You have no idea."

Juliet chose to take that seat Paige had suggested, shedding her suit jacket and throwing it over the back of an empty chair. When Paige looked up at her, Juliet's bare arms exposed in her royal blue sleeveless blouse, the younger woman swallowed.

"Also, you should know that if I hire you, you'll be handling the bar alone. We have a select clientele, and it won't be likely that you'd be run off your feet."

"And where will you be?" Paige asked as she took a cocktail shaker from beneath the bar, her body bent forward but her eyes firmly on Juliet's.

Juliet's eyes drifted lower to Paige's cleavage. "Sitting back while I enjoy the view."

"I got it!"

Paige smacked a hand to her mouth as she landed outside The Hideout. She didn't know why she was yelling down the phone to her best friend, but Paige hadn't expected a new job today. It couldn't have come at a better time. When she needed to stay away from her hometown for an extended break, Juliet had come calling. Or emailing. But it really didn't matter how. It was the fact that Juliet Saunders had just offered her a job in a place that was far superior to anywhere she'd worked before. And that woman...God, she was hot. But she'd known that when she Googled 'Juliet Saunders.' Still, in person, she was off-the-scale gorgeous. It hadn't been her finest moment when Paige decided to flirt her way through the cocktail-making process, but Juliet seemed easy-going enough to humour her. She'd appreciated that. It made this morning far less daunting.

"Can you believe I got it?"

"I can. Because you're brilliant like that!" Harriet squealed. "Bloody fantastic!"

"It's a really cool place, too."

"Oh, I can't wait to come and see you working there. When do you start?"

"Tonight. But it's not the sort of bar you can just show up to. It's private, you know?" Paige hated being so secretive. She wasn't sure she could always trust Harriet. Paige was probably being overly paranoid, but Harriet *adored* the ground James walked on.

"Where the hell are you working, Paige? It's not some swingers club thing, is it?"

"Not that I know of. It's just…different. I love it. And the owner is really nice, too."

Really nice. Paige's stomach flipped at the mere thought of Juliet. But that's all it could be. A stomach flip. A thought.

"Well, look. I'm really happy for you. How does James feel about you moving to Liverpool? Can he change offices so he can be there with you?"

"Oh, sure. I'm sure we'll figure it out." Just the mention of James had Paige's stomach turning, but not in the way it did for Juliet. Life wasn't good at home, hence Paige's desire to travel for work if she could. "I should go. I'd better call him and tell him the good news."

Ha! Good news? Paige knew he was going to have an aneurysm about this. At first, she'd explained how there was a lack of opportunities where they lived down south. It was a small village with a local pub. Nobody was looking for mixologists there. It was no use travelling into London. That place was overrun with people making fancy cocktails. So, she'd slowly started to find work that little bit further away each time.

Truth be told, Paige hadn't even told James she was in

Liverpool. As far as he knew, she was only an hour or so from home. Not the 240 miles away where she currently resided.

"Give me a ring through the week. And I want pictures of the new digs you have! You haven't said much about it." Harriet sighed. "God, I'm so jealous that you can just live your life in a new city whenever you like. James is *so good* for you."

"Yeah. Catch up with you soon. Bye."

Paige looked down at her phone, the idea of calling James leaving a heavy dread in her stomach. There was going to be a huge fallout from this. But at least Paige wasn't at home to deal with it this time. When she'd foolishly gone back six weeks ago, her welcome home had resulted in her being locked in the house for the following eight days. Still, being locked in was far less harrowing than the time before that. And…the time before that. Paige had lost count of the number of times James had raised his hand to her.

She shuddered, her hand shaking as she continued to stare at the dim screen of her phone. She didn't know how she'd convinced James to let her look for a job, but the moment he'd agreed—believing she was working somewhere local this time—Paige had booked a train ticket. Using cash only, hoping he didn't follow her, she took a trip up north. So now, she was basically running from the man she'd married five years ago. And he was entirely unaware. Though, Paige didn't know how. James *had* to know he treated Paige terribly. She scoffed. He thrived off it.

She scrolled her contact list—leaving the street The Hideout was situated on—and called his number.

"Paige! Where the hell are you?"

"H-hi, James. How are things?"

"What kind of question is that? Where are you, Paige? You've been gone for five weeks!"

Paige dragged a hand through her hair, no longer feeling

that happiness she'd felt downstairs in the bar with Juliet. James' voice, the anger in it, always left her wondering what he'd do when they came face to face again. "Yeah, about that. I've just been hired for a new job."

"No. This stops now."

Paige cleared her throat. "I enjoy working the bars. Why can't you be happy for me? Isn't that how marriage is supposed to be? Supporting one another. I've always supported you, James."

"Because it means you're not here with me! You're my fucking wife, Paige. You're meant to be at home with me. Why can't *you* understand that?" When James said that, Paige knew what he meant. He didn't want her to work. *He* wanted to be the one bringing in the income. He wanted Paige to stay at home and do nothing. She hadn't been raised that way, and she wouldn't change for anyone.

"Because that place sucks the life out of me every time I come back. I don't want to be there. I told you I needed something more than that town, to be my own person with my own job, but you laughed in my face and told me my job didn't mean shit. That it wasn't important."

"Because it *doesn't* mean shit. It's just a bar job. Or are you out there trying to get someone to pick you up with that *supposed* singing talent of yours?"

Paige slumped, lowering herself to the floor. She brought her knees to her chest, tears in her eyes. "No. You've made it quite clear that I'd be wasting my time trying to sing in clubs."

"Then I'm glad you've seen sense with that stupid idea. Fucking pub singer."

"B-but I'd be doing what I love."

"Yeah, well, doing what you love doesn't pay the bills, sweetheart." Why was James so concerned about Paige paying the bills? He never allowed her to pay. *Just another way to take that control from me.* "Stop with this nonsense and come home. I'll expect you back tonight at some point. Call me if you need picking up from the station."

"I'm...not coming home. I have my first shift tonight."

"Where?"

Oh, Paige wouldn't make the mistake of telling James where she was working. She'd done that before and he'd turned up, caused a scene...which resulted in Paige being asked to leave the job she'd just secured.

"Just a bar up north."

"Up north? You've got to be fucking joking!"

"No, I'm not. And now I have to go so I can get ready for my shift. Bye, James."

With her head pressed back against the wall and her eyes closed, Paige calmed every emotion and thought she possessed. James didn't know where she was, and she prayed he wouldn't find out any time soon. Paige had a real chance here to enjoy her job. The pay wasn't half bad...and the owner? Well, she was just the icing on the cake.

CHAPTER 2
NOT ME, NOT I

"I'm impressed." Rachel dragged her fingertip along the bar counter, stopping in front of Juliet. Her platinum blonde hair shone against the lights, those crystal blue eyes drawing Juliet in as they usually did. Rachel was one of those women who didn't need to try hard to catch anyone's attention. She simply had to show up, and she turned heads. "*Very* impressed."

"Did you think I'd invite you to somewhere that was less than good enough?"

Rachel took her bottom lip between her teeth, and then she quirked a brow. "Why *have* you invited me here? We're usually at your apartment."

"Because this place"—Juliet held her arms out either side of her, proud that she had done what she'd set out to do—"belongs to me."

"No way!" Rachel's eyes widened, one arm now wrapped around Juliet's waist. "I have to say, I could get used to 'being yours' in here. It's beautiful. Just like the owner."

Juliet drew Rachel into a kiss, smiling against her lips. "If only I wasn't paying you to say those things to me."

"Oh no. Payment or not, I'd still say the same thing. This is great, Juliet. It's so different. But I have to ask...what's the catch?"

"The catch?"

"A place like this *has* to be doing some dodgy dealings. How the hell does it stay open? You can just about swing a cat in here!"

"Excuse me!" Juliet feigned shock, pressing a hand to Rachel's chest. "Are you implying that I'm doing illegal things down here?"

"I'd like to do illegal things to *you* down here." Rachel grinned, dropping light kisses along Juliet's jaw until she reached her ear. "I'd certainly love to fuck you against that piano."

God. Rachel was too much. But that was exactly why she paid top price for her escort. It didn't matter what Rachel's rules said—the fact that sex wasn't usually a part of her service—Juliet was having some damn good sex lately. So what if it came via a hefty payment. "You're bad. But I need you to tame those thoughts for a while longer. I'm about to open the doors, and my new mixologist doesn't need to walk in on us in a compromising position. I'd like to keep her around for a while, not scare her away."

And Juliet really didn't want to scare Paige away. She'd watched her mixing drinks for thirty minutes today, and as Juliet had returned to the office once Paige left, it was all she thought about. Paige's delicate fingers, her wrists, and how she handled the shaker. Why was she suddenly so turned on by a simple cocktail? Because it wasn't the cocktail, it was the woman behind it.

"Is she hot?" Rachel asked, her eyes narrowed. "Please tell me she's hot. At least then we have something to look at around here. I'll be disappointed if it's full of old businessmen."

"She's...yes. She's gorgeous." *Leave it at that. The less Rachel knows, the better.*

Juliet wasn't stupid. She'd noticed how Rachel was around more often than the other escorts she'd been with in the past. And even though Juliet was careful to remind Rachel of their arrangement, their relationship was beginning to blur the lines.

Rachel winked, taking a step back. "I see. You've already been checking her out."

"Well, not exactly. She was in earlier for an interview. It was hard *not* to notice how beautiful she is."

That wasn't a lie. Juliet had found it hard to look anywhere other than at Paige Harrison. There was something incredibly attractive about her natural beauty. While Rachel spent a small fortune on her false eyelashes and semi-permanent makeup, Paige had walked through the door with a breathtaking presence about her. Confident but quiet. There was nothing there to indicate she knew how gorgeous she was, and sometimes, that only made a woman even more attractive.

"So long as she doesn't get in my way, I'm not worried."

Get in her way? Rachel ought to remember that, at the end of the day, this was nothing more than an arrangement. A transaction. If Juliet wanted to dip her toe—amongst other things—into other places, she would do that. And nobody, Rachel included, would stop her.

Juliet lifted a hand, patting Rachel's cheek lightly. "Just don't forget why you're here, honey."

Rolling her eyes, Rachel turned and moved towards the end of the bar. "I'll have a large glass of wine."

Okay, that was something Juliet could do. If it took the emphasis off Rachel and what they could be—had she not come into Juliet's life as her escort—she would offer her all the wine she could. She lifted a glass, holding it up to the light and giving it a final check. She'd spent the entire morning polishing them to perfection. "This place is membership only, you know."

"Then you'd better fix me up a membership."

Juliet considered that for a moment but quickly decided against it. Rachel was great, she really knew what Juliet wanted and needed, but she wasn't her partner. And Juliet *did* prefer time to herself now and then. If she handed a membership to Rachel, that would be less likely than usual. "It's fine. When you want to come in, just let me know."

"Free entry," Rachel whispered as she leant over the bar slightly. "Be careful. Anyone would think you were a little bit in love with me."

Juliet set a glass of wine down on the counter, saved by the bell as it rang at the entrance. "You're too much." She eyed the security screen, giving Paige access immediately. "Now, behave yourself. My staff is here." Juliet straightened her suit jacket, stepping out from behind the bar as Paige walked in. She held out an arm and smiled. Paige looked just as good, if not better, than she had this morning. "The bar is all yours."

"Thanks." Paige switched between Juliet and Rachel. "Are you looking forward to your first opening night?"

"I am. And since this one is going to be around now and then, this is Rachel." Juliet introduced them to one another. "Rachel, meet my new mixologist, Paige."

Rachel lifted a hand. "Hi, babe. Great to have you here."

"Yeah, thanks. Nice to meet you."

"I don't know how busy opening night will be, but let's hope for the best. If you need me, I'll be in the office for a while. But don't worry, I'll be out here with you once it picks up a little."

"Sure. No problem. I'll get my things laid out and ready."

Juliet side-eyed Rachel, surprised to find her escort sizing Paige up. She appraised her, her head cocked, and then she offered a sarcastic smile in Paige's direction as her new bartender turned around.

When Rachel finally drew her eyes away from Paige, Juliet said, "Come on you. You can come with me since you can't be trusted out here."

"Charming." Rachel laughed, slipping off her stool. When she reached Juliet at the side of the bar, she held her waist, and leaned in for a kiss. "It's a good job I'm fond of you."

Juliet took Rachel's hand, guiding her towards the back of the building and through the office door. Once she was safely inside, Rachel pushed her against the door, flicked the lock, and pressed her knee between Juliet's legs. "Someone...seems jealous."

Rachel scoffed, dragging her nails up Juliet's inner thigh. "Not jealous, baby. Just reminding you that you have *everything* you need in me."

"Rachel, I don't have time for this."

Rachel kissed her way down Juliet's throat, moaning lightly. "You know I can have you coming *all over* my tongue in minutes."

Fuck. This woman... It was hard to say no to Rachel, especially when she gazed into Juliet's eyes with a hunger and passion that was such a turn-on, Juliet was unaware of what day it was. "Then I suggest you get on your knees and get to work."

"Mm. Gladly." Rachel lowered herself down Juliet's body, unbuttoning her pants and dragging them down her legs. When her underwear followed, Juliet pressed her head back against the door, the nerves she'd initially had about tonight no longer present. Rachel *always* took her mind off things. "Fuck," Rachel whispered, sinking the flat of her tongue between Juliet's lips. "You taste so good."

When Rachel sucked Juliet's clit into her mouth, she

gripped the back of her head and rode Rachel's face. "Oh, God. *Yes.*"

Rachel eased a finger inside Juliet, pushing deeper as her tongue lashed Juliet's clit. "Let me taste you, baby. Show me what you've got."

Juliet trembled, her nails digging into Rachel's scalp. "Oh, fuck. M-more."

With a second finger filling her, Juliet felt her walls tighten. Rachel certainly knew how to work that beautiful mouth of hers. "That's it, baby. Come for me."

Juliet released around Rachel's fingers and against her tongue. "O-oh, Rachel."

Rachel looked up at Juliet with hooded eyes, licking her lips as she smirked. But Juliet had to remember that this woman was here for her pleasure. Nothing more. Whether that was intimate pleasure or general conversation, Rachel was paid to do this. The only difference between Juliet and Rachel's other clients was that Rachel didn't have sex with anyone else. It had been concerning to Juliet at first—it felt as though Rachel was becoming attached—but then Juliet reminded herself of the number of times Rachel had turned down her booking if she had another client arranged. "I expect a good tip for that."

Juliet barked a laugh, pulling Rachel back up to her feet. "Don't worry. You'll get one."

When she pressed Juliet to the door, Rachel lifted a hand and brushed Juliet's hair from her face. "Part of me knows I'd taste you for free given half the chance. Over and over again." Rachel guided Juliet into a soft, lingering kiss. "But then the other part of me prefers the thrill of not knowing the next time I'll have the pleasure of being inside you."

"This works the way it is."

"It does. And now you have a bar to launch, so get out there and show them what you're capable of."

"Stay a while. I'll pay you to the end of the night."

Rachel nodded, offering a final chaste kiss. "I'm not going anywhere, gorgeous."

Paige felt her phone buzz in the back pocket of her jeans for the third time in only minutes. She knew it would be James, but she needed him out of her headspace tonight. He'd called repeatedly once she got back to the apartment she was staying at for the next month, and that was beginning to tip over into the night. The last thing Paige wanted was for Juliet to think she had problems to take care of. She really didn't...unless James made himself one.

Forget about James. You have a job to do here. Focus on your gorgeous boss instead.

Paige knew it was a mistake to do that; she was, unfortunately, a married woman. But thinking about it wouldn't do any harm. After all, her husband hated her. He had to for the way he spoke to her, treated her, and didn't support her. But really, life with James had never been good. Because Paige didn't love him. Her late mother had been so happy when Paige told her she was engaged that she didn't have the heart to back out. She only *ever* wanted her mum to be proud of her—they'd been through a lot together. She already had very little in the way of family and friends. If she were to leave James and tell those around her who she really was...Paige knew she'd be left with nobody. While living her authentic life was all she wanted to do, she couldn't handle a life where she was shunned by those she'd considered a huge part of her life. Paige wouldn't even have Harriet at the end. She knew that deep down. Her best friend had always been Team James.

How was that? A man who beat her...was loved by everyone.

A clearing of the throat kicked Paige out of her thoughts. When she turned around, Rachel was watching her. Rachel...the woman in Juliet's life. *Damn.*

"Hey, what can I get you?" Paige asked as Rachel pulled herself up onto a stool, clasping her hands under her chin and regarding Paige with a sweet yet fake smile. She was just as much of a looker as Juliet was. But there was something about the way she'd watched Paige all night, how she had that cocky smile plastered on her mouth whenever Paige made eye contact. She wasn't fond of that kind of woman. Kind to your face but a bitch behind your back. Paige preferred to know where she stood with people from the outset.

"Large white wine and a large red wine, please."

"Coming up." Paige turned, taking two wine glasses and setting them down in front of Rachel. "Great place here. I bet you're really proud of Juliet."

"I am. Considering she's spent the last twenty-odd years as a lawyer, I was surprised when she told me she'd bought this place."

"You...didn't decide on this together?"

Rachel laughed. "Oh, no. We're not exclusive. We're just friends."

Huh. Friends. Paige didn't have friends who fucked her behind the closed door of offices. But this information only proved to make Paige's life more difficult. Because if Juliet was technically single, it meant Paige *could* daydream about her. At least if she'd had a partner, it would have deterred Paige from feeling an attraction towards her. "Right. Well, as her friend, you must be proud."

"Immensely. And I'm *very* protective of her. She means the world to me."

Hmm. That was some kind of warning. Paige felt it in Rachel's tone.

Paige pushed the two glasses of wine towards Rachel, resting one arm on the counter. "Am I taking payment for these...or?"

"Nah. Juliet will cover it later."

"Okay." Not willing to get into the whole free drinks thing, Paige turned away and cleared the back counter. It was almost midnight, and if she recalled the closing time correctly, it was coming up.

"So, where have you come from, Paige?"

Paige half-turned, groaning internally. Why did Rachel need to ask questions? Had Juliet sent her over to do so? "Down south."

"Husband and kids in tow?"

"No. Not quite," Paige said, clearing her throat. The less she gave away, the better. "I'm here in Liverpool alone."

"Well, you've got a friend in me and Juliet. Don't forget that."

Paige softened at those words. She wasn't quite sure about Rachel, but maybe she'd got her wrong. "Thanks. I appreciate that."

Rachel slid from her stool, winking in Paige's direction. Paige watched her head back towards the low table Juliet sat at, the chairs that were there this morning now replaced with a luxurious black leather couch. She guessed that was going to become Juliet's 'spot.'

Paige gathered the few cocktail shakers from behind the bar, some drip trays, and a few other implements and placed them at the end. She would clear away so Juliet could lock up and get gone once the bar closed. She leaned over the opposite end of the bar, catching Juliet's attention. "Hey, if you need me, I'll be in the back clearing up."

Juliet lifted Rachel's hand from high up her thigh and sat forward. "Would you like some help?"

"No, it's fine. You stay there. You have company." Paige would love nothing more than to take Juliet's attention away from Rachel. Even if only to see the response from Juliet's 'friend.' If Paige had so much as looked at her boss this evening, Rachel was on high alert, taking over the conversation before Juliet had the chance to reply.

Juliet nodded, her huge brown eyes soft. "If you need anything, just let me know."

"Really, I'm good." Paige tapped the bar as she walked away, gathering what she could in her arms.

And then she took off into the back of the bar, thankful for the time alone. Maybe she could deal with James while she had a moment to herself.

Paige looked up at the door, then quickly took her phone from her pocket.

Eleven missed calls...followed by the usual text messages.

Don't piss me off, Paige!

Delete.

I will find out where you are!

Delete.

Deep breath.

You'll be sorry when I do! Pack your shit up and come home. Make this easier!

Paige pressed reply on James' last message. She hated this. She wanted out.

You really think I'm going to come home when you speak to me like that? Or when you treat me the way you do? Why would I? I'll be back when I'm ready to come back.

She wasn't going back. Paige just didn't have the energy to deal with *that* conversation right now. But the time would come. James would know soon that Paige wouldn't return home. She rested back against the sink, seeing that her message had been read the moment it went through to James. Her heart thumped that little bit harder, but that was standard in her life. Since she'd met James, anyway.

You'd better hope I don't find you! Because I am coming, Paige. I'll bring you home!!!!!

"Oh, fuck off!!" she spat with anger into the silence of the kitchen.

"Everything okay?" Juliet's voice startled her, and Paige dropped her phone. "Oh, I'm sorry. I didn't mean to scare you."

Paige reached down for her phone, shaking the tension she felt from her body. "No, it's fine. And yes, everything is okay."

"Just…you seemed angry." Juliet's dark eyes held concern, but that glint was ever-present. The very same glint she'd witnessed this morning when she was flirting.

Stop. No more flirting. Just work. "Bloody cold callers ringing me. I get at least five calls a day."

"After midnight? That's unusual."

Paige cleared her throat. "Probably international or something. It looked like a weird number."

"Okay, well, I was wondering if you could hang around for a little while once you've finished in here?"

Paige's stomach sank. She hadn't impressed Juliet enough. "Sure. Yeah. I'll just be a few minutes."

"No rush." Juliet regarded her with a gorgeous smile as she ran a hand through her silky dark hair. There was something about her that made Paige feel calm. "I'll see you out in the bar, okay?"

Paige nodded and got to work with the clearing up so she didn't keep Juliet waiting too long. It was late; she surely wanted to get home soon.

Paige finished up in the kitchen, stacking her 'tools' ready for tomorrow, and headed back out into the bar. Juliet was waiting for her on the serving side, two stools set out together on the opposite side. Rachel…not in sight.

"So…" Paige puffed out her cheeks, drying her hands on her thighs.

"Drink?"

"Um, sure. Can I get a honey JD, please?"

Juliet nodded, pouring a large measure for Paige. And then she poured a bourbon for herself and brought both glasses with her. "Let's sit."

Paige was about to sit on a stool when Juliet pointed her towards the couch she'd just shared with Rachel and placed their drinks on the table.

"Before I forget," Paige said as she sat down. "I've counted the tips out and left them behind the bar. You just need to take whatever your percentage is."

Juliet took an envelope from her pants pocket, placing it down next to Paige's drink. "The tips are yours. All of them."

"Wha—how?" Paige couldn't possibly take all of the tips from tonight. The 'clients' here really did throw their money about. There had to be at least two hundred pounds laid out by the cash register.

"You worked the bar, yes?" Paige nodded, dumbfounded that she'd made 100% tips. That rarely happened in bars these days. "Then the tips are yours."

"Thanks. I appreciate that."

"You've not had a great time in some bars, have you?" Juliet relaxed back on the couch, encouraging Paige to do the same.

She took her drink and held it on her thigh, sinking into the soft leather. "Some have been okay, but others haven't. Mostly because they've been chain bars and not independent. The management think they can just help themselves to whatever they want. Us minions don't have a say."

"Well, that won't happen here."

"I really enjoyed tonight. You guys are much friendlier up

here. It's been lovely." Paige studied Juliet's face. She couldn't picture her as a brutal lawyer. She seemed far too laid back.

"I'm glad you enjoyed it. I'm assuming this means you'll return tomorrow?"

"Absolutely. Same time?"

Juliet sipped her bourbon slowly, those eyes quite intense when they held your gaze. "I have somewhere I need to be tomorrow, and I'm not sure I'll be back to open up at the usual time. Is there any chance I can ask you to do it for me?"

Paige had never been given that responsibility before. She usually came and went without a fuss. But from what she could gather, Juliet hadn't employed anyone else yet. "Sure. That's no problem for me. Whatever I can do to help."

"Thank you. It *would* be a huge help." Juliet placed a hand to Paige's knee, surprising Paige, to say the least. She felt the warmth in Juliet's touch, the sincerity too. "I'll let you finish your drink and get home. Can I call you a cab?"

"No. The walk will do me good. I've been lounging around too much lately."

Juliet's hand fell away, disappointing Paige. But it didn't matter how disappointed she felt; she still had a husband at home.

"How long have you been in Liverpool?"

"Only a week or so. Since I moved on from my last place." Paige didn't make eye contact with Juliet. She didn't want her to ask anything Paige didn't want to answer.

"So, not many friends around here yet?"

Paige smiled weakly. "None whatsoever."

"That won't last long. I'll make sure of it." Juliet finished her drink and got to her feet. "Let's talk tomorrow about what plans I have for this place, okay?"

"Yeah, that sounds great."

Juliet offered a slight wink. "Goodnight, Paige. Great shift tonight."

Paige watched Juliet walk away, taken aback by just how beautiful she was. Paige had a long way to go in terms of settling down as her true self, but Juliet was going to make it far too easy to daydream about the future.

It was the hand on her knee, that glint in Juliet's eye...the looks. Paige knew it was a huge mistake to even consider Juliet for a moment, but for once...someone appreciated her for what she was doing.

That was huge for Paige.

CHAPTER 3
GRAVITY

Juliet strode down the street, excited for another evening at The Hideout. That was quite sad, really, being excited about work, but Juliet had always been married to the job. She supposed it was good to see some things never changed. Only this time around, she could spend an hour eating lunch without being interrupted. She could call in on friends without her phone dragging her out the door no sooner than she'd sat down.

All in all, The Hideout offered her more of a social life than court cases did.

Her phone pinged in her pocket. It was probably Rachel, but Juliet had no plans to book her this evening. She wanted to watch Paige work, to get a feel for the woman she'd hired. Okay, she wanted to admire her. As she had tried to do last night. Only Rachel didn't stop talking for one second, and every time Paige came over, or Juliet approached Paige, Rachel wanted to know every last word they'd spoken to one another.

Basically, tonight, she wanted no interruptions.

Because Juliet knew what Rachel was doing last night. She was actively going out of her way to hold Juliet's attention.

While her escort didn't need to do that ninety percent of the time, she'd made sure of it last night.

Whenever Rachel turned her attention to Juliet, Juliet was busy watching every move Paige made. Paige hadn't noticed, thankfully, but it didn't change the fact that Juliet was slightly enamoured by her. She couldn't put her finger on why, but time would tell. Undoubtedly it would.

Juliet took her phone and unlocked it.

I've been asked if I'm available tonight. What should I tell my other client? Rach x

She smiled. Rachel often tried to make her jealous with the knowledge that she had more than Juliet as a client. But Juliet wasn't the kind of woman who played those games. Rachel was an escort. Juliet would be worried if she *didn't* have other clients.

Tell them you're available and have a great evening. J x

Really? You don't want me to sit looking pretty with you at your exclusive bar? Rach x

Juliet laughed, stopping on the pavement close to the bar.

I think I can manage. I have some plans to run by Paige anyway so I won't have much of a chance to spend time with you. J x

But I could sit and watch you. You know I love watching you. Rach x

Wow. Rachel was *really* trying tonight. Were her other clients not paying her well enough?

Call me if your client is a let down and you're not having fun. I'll buy you a drink. J x

Not waiting for a response, Juliet let herself into the bar with her master key. Paige would likely be here already—Juliet got the impression Paige was on the ball when it came to her job—so with a couple of hours to spare before the doors opened, maybe she could run some of those plans by her. While gazing into those greyish eyes. Inconspicuously, of course. Juliet had no idea who this woman was. She couldn't be certain of Paige's sexuality, but she had a fairly good idea that she wasn't entirely wrong in thinking that Paige enjoyed attention... amongst other things...from the ladies.

She frowned as she took the stairs slowly. There was music playing loud down in the bar. While Juliet didn't mind that exactly when the bar was closed, Paige had no way of knowing if someone unsuspecting was lurking around the building. And if by chance they managed to gain access, Paige would be alone and unaware. She'd have to speak to her about that.

As she took the remaining stairs, Juliet noted just how perfect the acoustics were down here. Perhaps she could bring in some music for an evening or two through the week. She didn't know if her clients would be into that, but it wouldn't hurt to mention it to a few of them. If it entertained them, it would keep them coming back.

But then Juliet stopped before she turned the corner into the bar. She knew this song. It was one of her favourites. Sara Bareilles' *Gravity*. Except it wasn't Sara Bareilles singing it. It seemed...live. Raw.

Then she caught the key change, followed by the clearing of a throat.

Juliet held her breath when the most beautiful sound floated around the bar and out into the corridor. This wasn't a CD playing. No, it was a person. But who? Nobody knew about this place. She didn't have any women on her books. And that was definitely a woman's voice.

She wanted to peer around the corner, but she was fearful that the sound would stop. Whoever this was...she *never* wanted them to stop. It was too extraordinary. Too meaningful. Too...full of emotion.

So she took a seat on the stairs and quietly lowered her

handbag to the floor beside her. As they reached the chorus, Juliet fought back tears. This person...had the voice of an angel. How they held the notes, how their fingers worked so effortlessly with the piano, God...she wanted to sob for them. *With* them.

Juliet clasped her hands under her chin, resting her elbows on her knees. This...was special. It was enough to tip her entirely over the edge. Paige must have brought someone in who knew how to play, and right now, Juliet wanted to offer her a pay rise just for directing them to this bar. It didn't matter if she hadn't run it by Juliet first. Paige clearly had connections.

She allowed her mind to empty of everything and enjoyed the moment. Because soon, it would all be over. That voice, the melody, would be gone and all Juliet would have left to face was a night in an underground bar she'd acquired on a whim.

When the song reached a prolonged high note, Juliet's breath caught in her throat. How was it possible for another human being to sound so perfect? Juliet knew of *many* people with incredible voices, but to be faced with it so head-on, so unexpectedly, it had knocked the wind out of her.

Brushing her hand across her cheeks as the song ended, Juliet puffed out her cheeks and fought back a sniffle. Something had been brought out in her this evening. Emotions she didn't know she had. A love for a voice so beautiful and raw.

Juliet got to her feet and took her bag from the floor. She held it loosely at her side, clearing her throat as she turned the corner into the bar.

But what she found in front of her confused her. Paige sat at the piano, her eyes closed, her cheeks tear-stained.

"Paige?"

Paige's eyes opened suddenly, and then she got up and stumbled away from the piano. "Sorry. I was just fucking about. Back to work."

Fucking about? Oh, it was far more than that. Juliet wanted to speak up, to praise Paige for such a performance, but Paige had already left the bar and was in the back. She heard things clattering, and then Paige reappeared.

"You've had five calls since I got here. People looking at memberships. I told them you'd call them back. But then I realised I didn't know if you wanted that, so I took their emails too. It's easier to let people down that way if you're not interested in having them here." Paige busied herself behind the bar, putting drip trays in place as she spaced out her tools where she wanted them. "Oh, and Rachel came by. I let her in, but she left five minutes later when I told her you weren't here yet."

Rachel had been here? That was surprising since she had only just texted her and hadn't mentioned calling into the bar. But she couldn't focus on Rachel right now. Juliet stared, quite shocked by the sudden change in Paige.

"Can...I get you some coffee? Or a cocktail? Wine?" Paige stood in place, a slight crease to her brow. "Juliet?"

Juliet strode across the floor, stopping at the counter. "Do you have *any* idea how talented you are?"

Paige frowned further. "I don't—"

"Was that you? The piano...the voice?"

"Oh, yeah." Paige laughed, waving Juliet off. "But it's nothing more than karaoke. It's a bit of fun when I have a minute to myself."

"A...bit of fun?" Juliet quirked a brow. Maybe Paige was being humble, but that wouldn't wash with her. No way. Not in this lifetime. "Is that what they call amazing talent these days?"

"I, uh...I have stuff to do, sorry." Paige turned and left the bar again, but Juliet followed her this time. Mostly because her office was back here, but also because she wasn't quite finished yet.

"I'll make that coffee. What's yours?"

Paige turned suddenly, holding the cocktail shakers to her chest. "Oh, um…I'm okay, thanks. I don't get paid to sit around drinking coffee. But thank you."

"You do in *this* bar. So, cappuccino? Latte? What's it to be?"

Paige smiled, lowering her eyes. "I'll take a black coffee, please."

Juliet nodded, stepping to the side and offering Paige the exit to the bar. Her subtle perfume wafted towards Juliet, the hairs on the back of her neck standing to attention. "I'll meet you out there in a second. I'll just put my things in the office."

"Cool. Yeah. See you in a few."

Juliet noted the tension in Paige's shoulders as she passed her by, but she'd let it go for a few more minutes. Paige looked like a deer caught in headlights this evening.

A deer with the most beautiful voice in the world…

Paige felt like a complete fool this evening. Not only had she made the stupid decision to unleash the pent-up musician in her, but Juliet had walked in on it. How the hell did she explain and apologise? How did she convince her boss that she wouldn't fool around again with the piano in the corner of the bar? She wanted to run, to hide from the way she was feeling, but she couldn't. She had a job to do. A commitment to Juliet.

Paige hadn't been able to control herself, plain and simple. That piano had been calling her name since the moment she'd laid eyes on it…and knowing she was alone earlier, Paige had craved to stroke the keys. To remind herself what it felt like to sing. To be in her happy place.

She pulled her shoulders back and approached Juliet's table. Two coffees sat waiting, along with Juliet. "Hey, I can just drink this while I work. It's no problem. I have a few things to set up before we open."

"Sit down, Paige."

Here it came. The telling off for fucking around with things that didn't belong to Paige. She slowly lowered herself to the couch, her hands clasped in her lap. "I...want to apologise. Before you say anything, I really want to apologise."

Juliet crossed her legs. Those long, slender, silky legs. Paige could barely focus. "Apologise for what?"

"Playing around with the piano. It's just...I haven't had the chance to play in a while, and it was just sitting there. But it won't happen again. Please, give me a chance to show you that I can be the staff you need. I won't let you down again."

"Let me down? Paige, you haven't let me down. What I walked into...I have no words."

"Like I said, it doesn't mean anything. I had a few minutes to myself, so I thought I'd play. But I know I'm here to work the bar; you don't have to worry about that."

Juliet must have noted how Paige wrung her hands in her lap, sitting forward and placing a hand to Paige's bouncing knee. "Hey. What's going on?"

"Nothing. Why?"

"Because you're a nervous wreck, and I don't understand why." Juliet squeezed Paige's knee, her hand remaining. "I walked in today to the most beautiful sound I've ever heard. Your voice is astounding, Paige. You surely know that."

"It's just a pub singer pipedream thing. Everyone always tells me I'm wasting my time, and they're right. It's a hobby. Something I enjoy when nobody is around."

"Look, I don't know who is telling you that you're wasting your time, but they're talking shit." Juliet held up a hand when Paige tried to protest. "I'm sorry, but they are. They're talking complete shit. You have a talent, and I'm sorry if you can't see it in yourself, but I do."

"Thanks." Paige focused on her now still hands. And then her eyes darted towards the hand on her knee, rubbing soothing circles against Paige's black fitted pants. "Just a bit of fun, you know?"

"It's more than fun. It has to be. If I could convince you to sing for me right this moment, I would."

Paige turned her watch towards herself. "Yeah, we have to open soon. And whatever you heard, it must have been the acoustics playing with your ears. I'm nothing more than a pub singer, trust me."

"Who told you that?" Juliet asked.

James, Paige wanted to answer…but didn't.

"A few people over the years." Paige lifted a shoulder, enjoying the caffeine relief Juliet had placed in front of her. "Hey, I was wondering if I could whip up some signature cocktails? Maybe something that represents you? Something for the bar, you know?"

Juliet's brows drew together. "Something that represents me?"

"Yeah. Something classy. Intelligent. Something that screams Juliet Saunders."

Paige caught the blush as it worked up Juliet's neck. "You want to make a cocktail based on me?"

"Why not? This is your bar, and people love that kind of thing. Think about it and get back to me. I'll do my research in the mornings when I'm lying in bed with a coffee."

"I've started doing that. Lying in bed with coffee."

"Feels good, doesn't it? I love the morning. When it's early enough that it's quiet. Before people have started going about their day. There's something about the stillness of a morning coffee in bed."

"I have to agree."

"I'm sure it's far more enjoyable for you. You have someone to share your mornings with."

Juliet smiled against the rim of her coffee cup. "You mean Rachel?"

"Mm. What *is* the deal with that?"

"You really want to know?"

"I mean, you don't have to explain. We don't know one another from Adam. But she's very fond of you...as she put it last night."

Juliet rolled her eyes playfully. "I pay her to be here, okay?"

"She's...staff?" Why the hell would Juliet pay anyone to sit around drinking in a fancy dress?

Juliet laughed from deep within her belly. God, it was a sound Paige would memorise. "No, Paige. I pay her to be with me. She's an escort."

Paige's eyes widened. "O-oh!"

"Mmhmm."

"Shit, I'm sorry. It's none of my business." Why did Paige have to go and ask about Juliet's personal life? It was never going to be plain sailing. Paige wasn't that lucky. She was the queen of creating awkward conversations. "Forget I asked."

"Paige," Juliet said, shifting closer as she placed her coffee cup down. Their thighs touched, an unfamiliar ache settling deep within Paige. "I'm not someone who hides who I am. I enjoy my time with Rachel, but she's an escort. Nothing more."

"I admire that, I really do."

"But never mind Rachel." Juliet turned side-on, propping her head in her hand. "I want to know all about that voice of yours. You're a bit of a mystery to me, Paige."

"I'm really not. Just a girl from down south who has very little going for her except for her cocktail skills."

"Mm. I'm not so sure of that. But I will get to the bottom of it." Juliet spoke with a playful tone, but it unnerved Paige slightly. She didn't want people digging into her life. Because then, the disappointing truth would be revealed.

Paige didn't want it to be this way. She hated the thought of Juliet thinking she was being secretive. It was just...the only way to survive. "If that's your plan, if you hope to uncover some kind of hidden aspect of my life, then I can't continue working for you. I love it here, this has been the one place I've felt appreciated since I started...and it's only been two days. To think you're wary of me, I couldn't stay, Juliet."

"Oh, I don't think anything of the kind. Not at all."

"Then why do you want to know more about me? It was just a song. No different to someone who sings karaoke at the weekend in a local dive bar."

"Okay." Juliet held up a hand. "I'm sorry. I won't pry anymore."

"It's not that. I just...I'm trying to start over here, and I'd like to do so with a clean slate."

Juliet sat forward, squeezing Paige's shoulder. "Got it. I'll leave you be. I was just enamoured by my beautiful bartender who has an extraordinary voice."

"E-enamoured?" Paige frowned. "By me?"

Juliet got to her feet, taking their empty coffee cups. "What can I say? I'm a lesbian, Paige. I don't often throw myself at women, but the moment you walked through my door...yes, I noticed you. And then you sang thinking nobody was listening, and I only wanted to know you better. Forgive me. It won't happen again."

Damn it. Paige wanted that to happen again. Ten times over. All the moments of the day.

But Juliet stared back at her, those brown eyes sad. "I am sorry. It wasn't my intention to make you feel uncomfortable."

"Y-you haven't." Paige felt bad. Juliet was looking at her as though she'd just done something very wrong. But the truth was, Paige was scared about her future. Juliet knew her only as this woman sitting here right now. To uncover the truth—the husband who couldn't keep his fists to himself...she didn't want Juliet to know *that* Paige. Not if she was enamoured by this one.

"Let's open. Have another great night. What do you say?"

"Yes." Paige forced a deep exhale, smiling. "Let's open."

CHAPTER 4
FALLING

Juliet sat up in bed, propped against the headboard while she cradled a large cup of coffee. Last night had been another successful night at the bar, with more members dropping by to introduce themselves to Juliet and Paige. She truly couldn't fathom how a bar so small and so hidden away could be so successful. But the previous owner—a guy who'd had the place for ten years—had promised Juliet that he wasn't selling her a sinking pit. And he'd been right. Juliet was only two nights open, and she'd had three new confirmed members, with more to contact today.

She smiled, looking out at the river from her floor-to-ceiling bedroom window. Rachel usually woke her up on a midweek morning, but not today. Today, Juliet was taking stock of the path her life was on now. An exciting path. Something entirely different. Something that wouldn't have her being bribed by a local gangland boss or someone else unsavoury.

Really, Juliet had done the right thing. And her stress levels were far less than they had once been. She didn't spend her life in court or on constant work calls. The only people who called her now were suppliers or members of The Hideout.

Her phone buzzed on her crisp, white Egyptian cotton sheets to the side of her. She eyed the device and then took it in her hand.

I'm really sorry about last night. Paige.

Juliet reread the words a couple of times, chewing her bottom lip. Why was Paige so intent on apologising for last night? Quite frankly, she'd made Juliet's *entire* night before it had even begun.

Please, don't apologise. J x

Have a great day. See you tonight! Paige.

Juliet considered her next move. She didn't want Paige to feel uncomfortable here. She didn't want her to worry that she'd done the wrong thing. Juliet just wanted them both to succeed in this venture. It may have been Juliet's bar, but Paige was playing a role just as important there.

Would you like to join me for lunch around 1? J x

She watched the read receipt, then the lack of reply, and then her heart settled when the bubble appeared beneath her message.

Sure. If you needed to speak to me. Where? Paige.

I don't need to speak to you. But up here, we invite new friends to lunch unexpectedly. So, I'll see you at 1, at the bistro on the corner of Raven Street. J x

Juliet lowered her phone to the bed, climbing from it and stretching her body. The sun was shining today, and that could only be a good thing. The sun always brought people's mood up when it was required.

As she wrapped her robe around herself, her phone started to ring. She reached for it and cleared her throat. "Hi, Rachel."

"Good morning, gorgeous."

Juliet smiled, stepping towards the window and leaning against the frame. "Lovely day, isn't it? Any plans?"

"Well, I was hoping I'd get to see you at some point..."

"Not today, I'm afraid. I'm out for lunch and then at the bar." Juliet looked out towards the dock. It was busier than usual, but she loved to see that. Now that she wasn't run off her feet, she could stroll around it more often. "But maybe…this weekend? I'm not entirely sure of my plans yet."

"The weekend? It's only Tuesday."

Juliet's brow creased. Why did Rachel want to spend so much time with her? When they'd first met, it was almost a week before she could meet with Juliet. She was the top escort at the company, hence the waiting time. "You surely can't be free this week. You're always busy."

"Maybe I prefer some clients over others."

"Well, I appreciate that, but I have work to do. The Hideout was really busy last night. I still have to follow up on calls today once I get there."

"I'm really happy it's busy. Considering it doesn't exist anywhere on social media, it must be doing something right."

Juliet stepped back and sat on the edge of the bed. "I understand why people like it. When I used to finish work for the day, the last thing I wanted was a rowdy bar full of young people who were starting their night early. I just wanted to enjoy a glass of good wine with some peace and quiet."

"Yeah, it does have a good vibe."

"So, I'll call you towards the end of the week, okay?"

"You know, I'm available to come over unexpectedly. Maybe…as you're climbing into bed?"

Juliet sighed. "Don't tempt me." She was trying to get out of the habit of having Rachel over each night. Juliet was finally in a position to date, to find someone she could perhaps settle down with. If she relied on Rachel while she wanted those things, it would only end with heartbreak. Because regardless of the fact that Juliet really enjoyed her time with her escort, she couldn't allow herself to see a future with her. It simply wasn't possible.

"Call me, Juliet. Whenever you need *anything*."

And then the line went dead.

Juliet exhaled a breath, leaving her bedroom. It would be the easiest thing in the world to call Rachel to come over, and maybe she'd cave in and do that before the weekend, but Juliet was at least going to try not to.

She had been content with her own company for a long time. Why the change of heart now?

Her phone buzzed in her hand. She was certainly in demand this morning.

Hello, stranger. How's retirement going? Hannah x

Juliet instantly smiled when she read Hannah's message. She didn't plan to keep in touch with her old assistant too heavily—Hannah was thriving in her personal and professional life now—but she would admit that it was lovely to hear from her.

Very well. Busy, as always! Hope you, Caz and Edie are keeping well. J x

We are! Maybe we could catch up soon and I'll tell you all about it. Hannah x

Yes, they should do that. Once Juliet was on top of everything at the bar, she would make plans to see Hannah. Maybe Caz too if she was available. Juliet still got the impression that Caz was a little wary around her, but that was okay. Hannah *had* been Juliet's escort before she gave her a job.

Yes. I'd love that. Let me get my life in order and I'll be in touch. J x

I'll be waiting. It would be lovely to see you. Hannah x

"Enough of that," Juliet said as she pondered the rest of her day. "Time to get ready for lunch with a beautiful woman." *Oh, no.* Juliet had to remember that Paige was her employee. That was where it should start *and* end. *But her voice...* Juliet allowed herself a moment to daydream about last night. Once she'd gotten it out of her system, she could carry on with her day. With Paige. *Fuck!*

Paige checked her hair in the window of a parked car, fixing her sleeves where they were rolled up her forearms. Last night had happened, and now she was moving forward. She was also meeting Juliet for lunch, so she'd made an effort to look good. It wasn't often she had the opportunity to eat out with friends or people she was fond of, so Paige had spent the entire morning looking through the few outfits she had.

Unfortunately, she wasn't in a position to have a wardrobe full of clothes. Depending on the mood of the city she was in, she would settle, or she would move on. But not before she'd revamped some drinks menus. That was her sole purpose when she walked into a job at a new bar.

She checked her phone, praying Juliet hadn't cancelled on her. While she hadn't received a message from her new boss, she *had* received one from her husband.

Harriet says you're in Liverpool. What the fuck are you doing there? It's like you're putting more and more distance between us!

Yeah, that was exactly what Paige was trying to do. Maybe if James realised that, he'd let her go. Paige was hoping for it, but she'd wanted out for a long time, and he continuously told her he would try, only to fail harder the next time. Paige would love her marriage to work. Just not her marriage to James. Because whether he became a 'changed man' or not was irrelevant. Paige didn't love him. She didn't enjoy their life together. She wanted to move on.

This was all a façade. A show for friends and family. The love and marriage Paige craved wasn't with an abusive man. No, it was with a loving and considerate woman. The fact that James threw his weight—and his fists—around wasn't the only reason for her hiding from him. The fact that she was gay played a monumental role, too. If he got wind of that information, Paige likely wouldn't see the light of day again.

It's a great job opportunity with brilliant pay. I'd be a fool to turn it down.

Paige held her phone and looked up at the bistro. It appeared to be a lovely place, she just hoped it didn't cost a fortune to eat here. After last night, she owed Juliet lunch.

As she stepped inside, catching Juliet's attention where she sat away from the bustle of the bar, she smiled.

And once again, her phone pinged.

What do you want from me, Paige? Am I supposed to chase you there and stay with you? Are you in love with someone else? Are you even in love with me anymore?

Was this her opportunity to be honest?

Yes. Yes, it was.

I mostly fell out of love with you when you 'accidentally' opened the cupboard door and hit me in the face with it three days after we got married. Then what tiny bit of respect I had left for you...that faded when you locked me in the house for a week. I won't go into detail about the other times. You know all about them. I think you can see where this is going, though. I don't want to live my life that way anymore. It's not healthy. We clearly don't love one another.

No longer willing to entertain James, Paige locked her phone and strode towards Juliet. Juliet stood and leaned in to hug her, a hug which Paige readily accepted.

"Hi. Glad you could make it."

They sat down, and Paige instantly picked up a menu. Her anxiety was through the roof. Between Juliet hugging her—that supple body against her—and being brutally honest with James, she suddenly felt lightheaded.

"Sorry. I just need a minute." Paige lowered her menu, gripping the table as she closed her eyes. The room was spinning, but as Paige rested back against the chair, she felt Juliet cover her hand. She instantly settled. When she opened her eyes again, Juliet was looking at her with concern.

"Are you okay?"

"Yes, I'm fine. Thank you. A little lightheaded. Probably because I didn't have breakfast."

Juliet squeezed her hand and then drew her own away. "Always eat breakfast."

"I will in the future." Paige smiled as she relaxed further, captured by Juliet's beautiful eyes. Her stunning smile. The warmth of her hand still remained even though they weren't touching. Paige had to get out of her head. "Busy morning?"

"Actually, no. I've had a lovely quiet morning doing very little."

"Sounds perfect."

"Oh, it is. You wouldn't believe how good it feels to *not* worry about work. An upcoming case. The thought of spending all day in court. The planning and the long hours."

"You must have liked your job at one time, though. That's a long career with some...dubious characters to represent. Which, by the way, I'm not judging you for."

"Everyone is entitled to representation."

"Can I ask why you decided to leave your career behind?" Paige quickly eyed the menu when she saw a server approaching. Once she got talking to Juliet, she didn't particularly want to stop.

"What can I get you ladies?" The server stood with an iPad in their palm, looking between Juliet and Paige.

"I'll have the chicken slider and a side of fries, please." Paige handed her menu over, watching Juliet as she perused her own.

"And I'll have the same. Who cares if I'm in a carb coma after it? I can nap before work if I choose to now." Juliet winked in Paige's direction. God, she had to stop doing little things like that.

The server smiled and left the table. Paige took the coffee Juliet had already ordered for her before she arrived and sipped. "So, the job…"

"Ah, yes. Honestly, I'd had enough. My mother passed away six months ago, and I barely had time to attend her funeral. It was then that I realised I was far too committed to my job rather than my life. I had all these plans when I was growing up. I always wanted to be in law, but I wanted to do so with a family and a wife at home. I wanted to be settled down whilst *enjoying* my job." Juliet lowered her eyes, a faint smile painted on her lips. "But it never worked out that way. And though it's no longer possible for me to have the things I dreamed of, it doesn't mean I should work myself into an early grave."

"Oh, I'm sure there's plenty of time."

"That's sweet, but the dating pool is non-existent for women my age. I'm almost fifty." Paige opened her mouth to argue, but Juliet held up a hand. "And that's not me degrading myself, it's really not, but there's *nothing* out there. Escorts, yes. Women who will happily spend the night with you for one hell of a fee, yes. But something real and meaningful? That time has passed for me."

God, that was sad. Would Paige meet the same fate if she didn't take ownership of who she was and what she wanted soon? Probably. But James was constantly at the back of her mind. There was no way he was going to walk away from Paige. That would be far too humiliating for him. And then there was the idea that Paige was into women. Oh, all hell would break loose when he found out that information.

Maybe it was just easier to go back to him. Their life together. A life Paige loathed.

A life she hadn't felt safe in for some time.

"I...lost you for a moment then." Juliet dipped her head, finding Paige's eyes. "All good?"

"Oh, yes. Just...thinking about the changes in my own life."

"I'd say you're doing well at the moment. You've moved to a new city, you have a great job...*and* a great boss."

"Yeah, I do. Thank you again for hiring me."

"I liked what I saw. Why wouldn't I hire you?"

Paige puffed out her cheeks. "I'm sure you've noticed that I don't stay in one place for too long. It's been an issue on the odd occasion. People want someone reliable and long-term. I'm not always in a position to offer that."

"Well, I was hoping I could entice you with *at least* a six-month contract..." Juliet sat back, allowing her offer to hang over them. Paige would love to commit to that, she'd love to stay in Liverpool, but James already knew she was here. Chances were, he'd find her within those six months. Probably a lot sooner. "Say you'll think about it. I think we could be a great team, Paige."

"I will. I've only rented the place I'm staying at for a month, but the owner is in Dubai for the next two years, so six months would probably be fine. I know them."

"Where is it you're staying?" Juliet asked, those brown eyes pinning Paige to her chair. God, why did women have to have such beautiful faces? Why did *Juliet*, in particular, have to be so good-looking? And kind, and sweet, and fucking hot! "You don't have to tell me."

"Sorry. Um, by the river. An apartment block on East Street."

"Not...Alexander Tower?"

"Yeah. That's the one. Gorgeous place. I got really lucky. One of my old bosses owns it, and she doesn't even want any rent from me. Said she'd rather it was lived in than sat empty."

"Alexander Tower is where I live."

Paige laughed and shook her head. "No way."

"It is. What number are you staying in?"

"3...19."

Juliet grinned. "Impressive. I'm two doors down from you. The corner apartment with the best views in the building."

Whoa. How had that happened? Fate, maybe? "Really?"

"Honest to God." Juliet placed a hand to her chest. "You should come over one evening when neither of us are working. Have dinner. A drink. Whatever."

"I'd really like that." Paige smiled, a blush creeping up her neck when Juliet continued to stare. "But I doubt we'll be off on the same day. You don't even have any other bar staff yet."

"The bar will be closed every Thursday," Juliet explained. "Not this week or next because I'm trying to get a feel for the place, but starting the week after, you'll be off every Thursday. As will I."

"Oh, well, then sure. We should do that sometime." Was that the best decision Paige could make? No. But if she could remain neutral here, only see Juliet as her boss, then everything would go to plan. The same as it did in every other city when she kept herself to herself...then disappeared.

"Maybe then you'll trust me enough to tell me all about yourself." Juliet winked, filling their glasses with water from the table. "And if not, I'll have to keep working on that."

CHAPTER 5
LIKE I CAN

Lifting her legs onto the footstool in the window, Juliet sunk back into her reading chair, fresh coffee cooling on the side table. This morning, she had everything she needed. A good romance novel, time to herself, and a reminder of Paige's beautiful voice. What more could she possibly need in her life? Well, a woman to love. That would be a dream.

She rested her head back, sighing as she reached blindly for her coffee.

Paige had been right when she had spoken about the stillness of the morning. Coffee in hand. The chance to just be. Juliet wondered if Paige was doing the very same thing this morning. Was she resting two doors away, taking her time to start her own day?

That woman really was a mystery.

There was a gentle knock at the door. So gentle that Juliet wondered if she'd imagined it. She lowered her novel to the table, took her coffee with her, and approached the door. Another quiet knock, and Juliet reached for the handle.

"Oh, hi." Juliet frowned, confused as to why Rachel was

standing outside her door, no booking arranged. "Is everything okay?"

"Sure. I was wondering if we could talk?"

Juliet glanced down her body, aware she was only wearing a robe. It wasn't ideal, but she'd known Rachel long enough that early morning dress was okay. She'd seen her many times in far less. "Yes. Come in."

"I didn't wake you, did I?"

"No. I was just drinking my coffee and getting some reading in."

Rachel's brows rose as she crossed the threshold. She moved towards the island in the kitchen, placing her handbag down. "I didn't know you read."

There's a lot you don't know about me. Juliet thought.

"Who doesn't read?" She laughed, closing the door and following Rachel into the kitchen. "Cuppa?"

"No. I won't keep you long."

Juliet studied Rachel, aware that her escort seemed moody, perhaps upset. Rachel rarely brought her emotions through the door with her; it was one of the reasons she was such a good escort. Her sole focus was her client. Still, Juliet understood that she was only human and may need someone to talk to from time to time. "Is everything okay? You don't seem yourself."

"I could say the same about you," Rachel said, a weak smile on her lips as she tapped her fingernails against Juliet's marble counter. "You've been very distant lately."

"That'll be the new bar. I'm sorry." That wasn't entirely the truth, but Juliet didn't know how to let Rachel down gently. They'd spent a lot of time together over the last six months. "And I hate demanding your time so much. You have other clients, Rachel."

"You think I care about my other clients? You're the one I enjoy being with."

Juliet nodded slowly, sitting up on a stool. She motioned for Rachel to do the same, her hands wrapped around her coffee cup. "Rachel, you know I think a lot of you, but this is just an arrangement. If it's becoming a problem for you, maybe we need to see less of each other."

Rachel's bottom lip quivered as she said, "Am I not offering the service you want? Am I slacking?"

"Oh, no. Far from it. You've gone above and beyond for me. You really have." Juliet reached a hand across the island, settling it over Rachel's. "Don't think this is about you. You know I love having you over. I just think it needs to be less."

"I don't understand why..."

"Rachel, are you in trouble? Do you need the money? Because I can help you out." It was the only conclusion she could come to as to why Rachel would be so intent on needing to see Juliet so often.

"No. I'm more than stable financially."

Juliet cocked her head, unable to understand why Rachel was so desperate to be here. "Then what's the issue?"

"I...it's just, I really love being with you, Juliet. I know I'm not supposed to cross the line, but I think I have. I'm sorry. I know what this is, what it's *supposed* to be, but I thought it had the potential to be something more. And I thought maybe you felt the same..."

Oh, no. This wasn't how she wanted things to be with Rachel. And while she may have had some concerns about this *potentially* happening, Juliet never imagined for one second it *would* come to this. "I...don't. You're my escort."

"And that's really all I am to you?" Rachel looked up at Juliet with tears in her eyes. "Purely business."

Juliet hated this. Why couldn't Rachel be *just* another escort here? She sighed, knowing how much she could be considered a bitch right here and now. "Yes."

Rachel slid her hand out from under Juliet's, taking her bag from the island as she got down from the stool. "Okay. That's all I wanted to know."

"Rachel, I'm sorry." Juliet reached out and held Rachel by the wrist. When she turned to Juliet, the sadness in Rachel's eyes hurt her heart. "I thought that's all this was. Us...with payment."

"You're right. It was. It...*is*. I'm sorry. I shouldn't have come here this morning."

Juliet got to her feet, taking Rachel in her arms. "I should have been clearer, so *I'm* sorry. But I didn't think this was an issue for us. If it is, if we have to stop seeing one another, I understand."

"You want to stop seeing me." Rachel pulled back, sniffling as she lowered her eyes. "Maybe that would be for the best. So, I'll just go. And I don't know, if you do want to see me again, call me. You know I'll drop everything to be here for you." Rachel leaned in and kissed Juliet slowly, tears slipping down her cheeks. "Bye, Juliet. Take care of yourself."

Shocked but a little relieved, Juliet squeezed Rachel's hand as she took it, regarding her with a sincere smile. "I'm sure we'll bump into one another again. It's just...I need to get out of the habit of being with you rather than alone."

"It felt good being here with you. I thought you felt it too." Rachel turned and walked away, stopping when she heard a knock on Juliet's door. "Expecting company?"

"No." Juliet frowned. Why was she in such high demand this morning?

"Clearly, you are. See you."

Paige puffed her cheeks out as she curled her hand into a fist again. It was only nine in the morning; why the hell was she knocking on Juliet's door? Actually, regardless of the time, why *was* she knocking on Juliet's door? Yes, they'd had lunch yesterday, but that didn't give her a free pass to pop over whenever she felt like it.

You're here now. May as well knock again.

She lifted her hand, but the door opened suddenly, and Rachel walked out of Juliet's apartment.

Fuck. Paige had been interrupting. "Hi."

Rachel closed the door behind her, offering Paige one of those fake smiles again. "I wouldn't bother. She's *very tired*." Rachel winked, linking her arm through Paige's. "Walk with me."

Um...okay.

Paige stopped outside her own door, throwing her thumb over her shoulder. She had no idea where Rachel was taking her, but she wasn't going. "I'm only going to my place."

"You...live here?" Rachel snarled, and then she scoffed. "Things are beginning to make sense."

"Okay, well, I've only had one coffee this morning, so I'm not quite ready to decipher whatever you're saying yet." Paige turned and slid her key into the lock, smiling over her shoulder. "Take care, Rachel. See you around."

Rachel walked away and turned the corner, heading for the lifts further down the building. As Paige stopped and frowned, she heard a throat clearing. She looked up, surprised to see Juliet standing at her door and beckoning Paige closer. But Paige hesitated for a moment. Because Juliet was wearing nothing but a short, silk ivory robe. Her bare legs—bare thighs —were too much this morning. Paige's heart slammed hard as she swept her gaze up to where Juliet's robe barely covered her breasts. This woman was incredible.

"Are you just going to stand there?" Juliet asked, folding her arms across her chest and making her cleavage even more prominent than it already was.

Fucking hell.

"Well?"

Paige took her key and walked back towards Juliet's door. She was an adult. She could *be* an adult this morning. "Hi. Sorry for calling so early. I can come back later. It's no problem."

"You're here now. Why come back?"

"Oh, just that Rachel implied you were…indisposed."

Juliet looked over Paige's shoulder, her brows drawn together. "I'm not. But if you're happy to sit with me while I'm not even dressed, you're welcome to come in."

Heat crept through Paige as she kept her eyes on Juliet's face. *Don't look down. Fuck, don't look down.* "Sure. If you're okay with that?"

"Come on in."

Paige foolishly lowered her eyes as Juliet turned her back and walked into her apartment. The robe finished just below her arse cheeks. *Oh, shit!* Paige's eyes widened as her mouth salivated.

"So," Juliet started as she spun around.

Paige knew in that moment she'd been caught staring. Admiring. *Imagining*. Oh, it was a good job Juliet couldn't read minds right now. Because running through Paige's was pure filth.

"Would you like me to change?" Juliet laughed, but it only had Paige even more aroused than she already was. "I realise it's probably not what you expected."

"Excuse me?" Paige shook all thoughts of a naked Juliet from her mind, trying to make sense of how the hell she'd come to be in this position.

"This. *Me*. A middle-aged woman practically naked in front of you. I can change. Just give me a few minutes."

"No!" Paige practically yelled, pinching the bridge of her nose suddenly. "I love middle-aged women." *Oh, God*. Why had she just said that? Paige wanted the walls to cave in and crush her. Immediately. She shook her head and bit her lip as she looked away. *Jesus, take the wheel. Please!* "W-what I meant to say was that this is your apartment, and I'm the one who showed up unannounced."

A sexy smile spread on Juliet's mouth. "Let me make this easier. What can I do for you, Paige?"

"I-I just wanted to thank you for lunch yesterday." Paige had tried to take care of the bill, but Juliet had threatened to fire her on the spot if she dared take out any cash.

"You did. *Twice*. After lunch and last night at the bar." Juliet motioned for Paige to join her on the couch. "Let me get you some coffee, and then you can tell me the *actual* reason you're here."

Juliet didn't know the first thing about Paige, but she could read her. That unsettled her.

"Black coffee?"

Paige smiled. "Yes. Thank you. Is it okay to sit down?"

"Sure. Make yourself at home."

Paige spied the bookmarked novel on the table close to the window, grinning at what Juliet was currently reading. "Enjoying the book?"

Juliet looked up from the coffee machine, smiling. "I am. It's a favourite of mine."

"Mine, too. I think I'm on my eleventh re-read." Paige adored lesbian romance novels. She couldn't own them in paperback because of James, but she had a wide selection on her eBook reader...always prepared to switch to another if her husband was close by. "Favourite scene?" Paige asked, watching Juliet stir the coffee. Even that was sexy. *Jesus Christ!*

"Oh, the one in chapter seventeen."

Paige knew exactly which scene Juliet was talking about. Her cheeks flushed, her hands tingling as Juliet walked towards her. "The one when she's—"

"Fucking her against the table in the photocopying room?"

Oh, Lord. Paige instantly clenched her hands into fists at that, her nails almost drawing blood from her palms. Juliet didn't mince her words. "Yep. That's the one," Paige said, forcing out a breath. "So, how has your morning been?"

"It was going very well until it wasn't." Juliet sat down beside Paige, her thighs more exposed than before. She turned her body away ever so slightly, giving Paige a chance to calm her breathing. "Rachel turned up. I think I upset her."

"Really? She didn't seem upset when she was leaving. At least, not until she realised I lived two doors from you."

"I think we've just ended our client/escort relationship."

Paige wanted to pretend she was sad about that, but she wasn't. Why would she be? Juliet was potentially free of all women, and Paige was sitting in her apartment. *Yeah, because you're in a position to have an interest, right?* "I'm sorry about that."

"It needed to happen. I just didn't expect it to happen ten minutes ago. I wanted to call her and meet up. Maybe have dinner and end it on better terms. You know?"

"I can understand that. How exactly did it end today?"

"She came here to tell me she'd crossed the line. That she enjoyed being with me...and not as an escort."

Paige felt for Rachel. While escorting was her line of work, it surely happened from time to time that some got attached. Rachel was only human at the end of the day. "That must be hard for her. For both of you, actually. I see how you are with one another, and honestly...I thought you *were* together when I first met her."

"Rachel isn't who I see myself settling down with."

"But you said yesterday that you wished you could settle down, no?" Paige noted the pain behind Juliet's eyes when they'd shared lunch. As much as Juliet brushed off the past, what she'd lost out on by focusing on her career, Paige knew deep down that Juliet wished for far more. "Unless I got it wrong..."

"You didn't. And yes, I do want to settle down. But Rachel and I don't really have anything in common. She's great—really, she is, but I want a quiet life now. I don't want to be out drinking and dancing every weekend. That's the kind of person she is, and I'd never want to suppress that, you know? And then there's the fact that she's an escort."

Paige's brows rose as she exhaled a breath. "I don't know how you do it. I know I'd become far too attached just from going out to dinner. It's not something I could do. Knowing she's going to meet someone else, give them all her attention... and whatever else she gets up to."

Juliet lifted a hand. "Rachel doesn't sleep with any other clients."

"You're sure about that? You believe her?"

Juliet nodded, bringing her cup to her lips. "I do."

"Fair enough. I don't know her so..."

"I started booking her a week before my mother died. I've had a few escorts over the years; my job meant it was difficult to find a relationship, let alone hold one down. She was with me when I got the call to say my mum had passed away in her sleep. Rachel stayed, helped me through it, and then a month later, we started sleeping together. She doesn't usually sleep with *any* clients, but she must have recognised that it was what

I needed at the time. I didn't think it had changed our contract or our relationship. It just worked for us."

Paige wished she'd had someone with her when her mum passed away. James had taken the afternoon off work to be at the hospital—to show his face to Paige's adoring family—and then told her to pick herself up because her mum wouldn't want her to be miserable. To...get on with it the way everyone else does. "I'm glad you had her with you. It had to make things easier. Not being alone."

"It did. Perhaps that's why it's taken me so long to *let her go* if you will."

"Well, if you ever need someone to talk to, I'm only down the hall."

Juliet reached out a hand, placing it on Paige's knee. Her body fizzed with something she'd rarely had the chance to enjoy. Arousal. Appreciation for another woman. "Thank you. That means a lot."

"I should probably head off."

"You didn't tell me why you'd come here."

Paige lifted a shoulder. "Honestly, I just thought it might be nice to have coffee together. Outside of work, you know?"

"Well, I'm available for coffee outside of work whenever you'd like that." Juliet winked and got to her feet.

As she did so, her robe separated, exposing white lace lingerie. She took the cups from the table, smiled back at Paige, and turned her back. And thank God she had done so because all Paige could picture as Juliet sauntered away was that gorgeous woman, naked and moaning beneath her.

"I'll see myself out." On shaky legs, Paige got to her feet and made a beeline for the door. "See you tonight, Juliet."

"You will. And I look forward to it."

CHAPTER 6
DISTANT DREAMER

Paige scanned the menu in a local coffee shop, undecided as to what she should treat herself to. Today marked a week since she'd been given the job at The Hideout, and the sun was shining. What more could Paige want other than fine coffee and good weather?

Maybe she could find out Juliet's coffee order for future reference. It might be nice to turn up at work with something different. But then Paige scoffed to herself. Juliet wouldn't be interested in a specialty coffee.

Wouldn't she?

Paige was under no illusion that Juliet looked at her in a particular way, but perhaps that was just the kind of woman her boss was. Flirtatious and sure of herself. She'd already commented on the fact that she was enamoured by Paige, but she couldn't understand why. Paige was just...Paige. She hadn't done anything extraordinary in her life, and she didn't imagine she ever would. Still, that confidence that seeped from Juliet was contagious for Paige. But it only left her longing for a meaningful relationship here with Juliet. Not as a couple, Paige would never be that lucky, but good friends could work. If only that time wouldn't come when Paige had to run again.

"I'll take a large brown sugar oat shaken espresso, please." Paige handed over some cash, smiling at the barista. "Thanks."

"It'll be at the end in a few minutes."

She nodded, slowly strolling to the end of the counter. Liverpool was bustling today, with friends, family, and lovers laughing as they sat around drinking their drink of choice. One or two people sat alone, contemplating their day, but overall, it was a sight to behold. Paige didn't have the beauty of seeing this back at home. People kept to themselves unless it was to poke their noses in business that didn't concern them.

"Could I get a large brown sugar oat shaken espresso, please."

Paige frowned, side-eyeing the customer at the counter. Juliet chatted away to the barista as she paid for her drink, and then her eyes found Paige's.

"Oh, hi. Fancy seeing you here." Juliet sidled up beside Paige, grinning. "Is my coffee terrible?"

"At the bar?" Paige asked, and Juliet nodded. "No, your coffee is great."

"Then why are you here drinking this franchise coffee?"

"Because it's filled with sugar and I wanted to treat myself?"

Juliet winked, and then that laugh lit Paige up inside. "Perfect answer. The same reason I'm here."

Paige fell silent as Juliet rummaged around in her handbag that hung off her shoulder. She watched her boss, trying desperately not to grin too much. She still had an image of Juliet in her head from last week when they'd had coffee. At least she was wearing clothes this time. Although, that wasn't necessarily what Paige wanted. Juliet looked good enough to eat as she'd sat there in her robe. It also wasn't hard to imagine how she'd look out of it. *Stop!*

"What?" Juliet frowned when she looked up at Paige.

Paige's brows drew together. "Um, sorry?" Oh, God. She hadn't said that out loud, had she? Panic rose from the pit of her stomach.

"You're staring..."

"S-sorry. I was appreciating your blazer." Paige cleared her throat, aware that she was lying through her teeth. *Think of something convincing.* "The trim is lovely." Jesus. That was a piss poor attempt.

"You were appreciating my blazer?" Juliet had that playful look in her eyes, Paige's belly fluttering as she continued to watch her, her eyes now narrowed. "Thank you?"

"Welcome." Paige silently cringed at her lack of flirting game. Part of her knew she should fight it off, but being around Juliet just felt so good. Paige wanted there to be more times. "Any plans before you open the bar?"

"No. I was just going to walk down to the river and keep myself busy. You?"

Paige shoved one hand in her pocket when she took her drink from the counter. "No. Nothing planned." She took a step back, giving the other customers room to wait, and smiled. "I guess I'll see you in a few hours then."

Juliet took her own drink and followed Paige out onto the pavement. "You could join me. If you wanted to?"

"Oh, that's a lovely offer, but I'm sure you want to spend some time without me around you. You're already stuck with me every night of the week."

Juliet chewed her lip, those eyes penetrating Paige. "I could think of worse people to be stuck with."

Paige couldn't help the grin that spread on her mouth. But she really wished she wasn't blushing. Her cheeks would scorch her fingertips if she dared touch her skin. "Okay. If you're sure?"

"Very sure." Juliet lifted her coffee and motioned towards

the water visible in the distance. "Have you been down to the dock yet?"

"No, I haven't really had the time." Paige fell into step with Juliet, her worn converse a stark contrast to Juliet's heels. She didn't know how Juliet managed them all day every day, but she was impressed. Paige could bear heels when she had to, if she was dressing up for a night out, but they stayed at home otherwise. "Can you recommend any restaurants down there? I've heard there are some lovely places around."

"At the dock? Oh, you can't go wrong with whatever place you choose. It's all very good."

Paige nodded slowly, bookmarking that response should she ever be in a position to ask Juliet out to dinner. "Great. I'll have a look around one day."

"Have you thought any more about those signature cocktails? I'd love to try them sometime."

Paige had thought about them, but she was yet to get to work on them. "I haven't tested any out yet, but I'm thinking of something bold yet smooth."

"Who is this one based on? Because God knows it's not me."

"Actually, it is." Paige side glanced at Juliet, surprised that Juliet didn't see herself that way. "That's how *I* see you, anyway."

"Bold and smooth?" Juliet lifted a brow. "Paige, if you want to get into my pants, there's much easier ways than lying to yourself...and me."

Oh, Jesus. If only she could get into Juliet's pants. "See! Bold!"

"Okay, I walked right into that one," Juliet said, grinning. "But smooth? Really?"

Paige lifted a shoulder. "Sure. Why not?"

"I don't think anyone has ever called me smooth before."

"Then you're clearly dating the wrong people." Paige

followed Juliet towards a bench that faced out towards the river. When they sat down, she turned to her boss. "Speaking of dating, have you heard anything from Rachel?"

"No. Not since she left my place last week. And we weren't dating. For the record."

Paige held up her hand. "Sorry. My bad. I just feel like you two had a lot of chemistry."

"Me and Rachel? No. No way."

Juliet could deny it until she was blue in the face, but Paige saw it with her own eyes. "You really don't see it, do you? Anyone in the room can see it and feel it."

"Before we go any further, can I ask you something?"

"Sure." Paige sipped her coffee, resting her ankle on her knee.

"You *are* into women, right?"

Paige laughed. Was it that obvious to everyone, or was Juliet just seeing how Paige looked at her? "I am, yes."

"Okay. So, have you ever been with an escort?"

Ha! I wish! Even if only for the experience and to have some fun instead of being with James. "No."

"Then you have no idea. No disrespect, but you really don't."

Paige turned her body towards Juliet, resting her head in her hand. "Explain it to me then."

"Rachel is amazing—there's no doubting that. She's funny, and she's sexy, and trust me...she knows her way around a woman's body. But there's just something missing there for me. It's also awfully hard to know what's real when I'm paying her a hefty sum just to sit and drink wine with me. Escorts are very good at their job. Rachel, in particular, is *very* good at her job. Because that's what it is. A job, Paige."

"That's fucked up."

"Why? Not everyone is in a position to put themselves

through meaningless dates and whatever else. Some don't have the luxury or the time to pursue woman after woman. I was one of those women for a long time. Too long. Nobody is to blame for that, I cared too much about my career, but it's done now. I guess I just found it easier to call her up than create dating profiles online."

"Why online?"

"Have you tried to pick a woman up in a bar?" Juliet asked, laughing. "Actually, don't answer that. Of course you have. You're a bloody mixologist. I bet you have them drooling over you every night."

"I haven't been on a date since I was twenty-three."

"Because you don't need to. How many women have you been with in the last twelve months? God, to be young and free again."

"Actually, none."

Juliet scoffed. "Bullshit."

"I haven't. I don't have time to date with working." Paige hated lying to Juliet. This woman was as open and honest as they came. But she couldn't reveal who she was or the life she had. "You've seen it yourself. I work every night."

"Okay, but what happens when you meet someone at work. A colleague?"

Oh, don't even go there. Paige didn't need Juliet putting those ideas in her head. "It's never happened before, and I don't imagine it'll happen any time soon."

Juliet smirked, covering her mouth with her coffee cup. "Oh, I wouldn't be so sure of that."

Paige's phone interrupted them when it started to ring in her pocket. She removed it and silenced it when she saw Harriet was calling.

"You don't need to take that?" Juliet asked.

"No. Just a friend. I can call her back later when I'm home."

"Okay." Juliet placed a hand on Paige's knee, leaning in. "Did you want to grab some pancakes while we're here?"

That thought alone had Paige never wanting to leave Liverpool. Juliet was fun, she was flirty, and she was on the market. It was a shame Paige wasn't. She knew becoming friends with Juliet outside of work could be problematic, it was quite clear they were both interested in one another, but Paige was an adult, and she knew when to step back. Today *wasn't* one of those times. "I'd love to."

Juliet dripped chocolate sauce down her chin as she laughed, her breath hitching when Paige reached out and caught it on the pad of her thumb before it went directly to her white blouse. She stared at Paige, her body tingling when Paige slipped her thumb into her own mouth and cleaned the chocolate sauce off. "Clumsy."

"Or...preoccupied." Juliet smiled, staring down at her pancake on the cardboard dish. "What do you think of them?"

Paige's body remained far closer than Juliet expected as she said, "Gorgeous. Really gorgeous."

"Best in the city." Juliet looked back up at Paige, noting the want in her eyes. Why was Paige playing hard to get? If this day had told her anything so far, it was that they clearly had something going on between them.

"So I've heard." Paige's voice dropped a little lower, her eyes glazing over. "Or was it...best this side of the country?"

"Depends who you ask. They've been known to be an acquired taste."

Paige smirked as she shook her head. "Good thing they're absolutely my taste then, isn't it?" Paige continued walking, her head bowed as she remained a few steps ahead of Juliet. But that was okay. It meant Juliet could admire Paige without her knowing. "We should probably head back soon. I need to change before I start my shift."

"Right. Yes." Juliet snapped out of her perfect afternoon with Paige, completely forgetting it would have to come to an end at some point. "I'll probably get in a little earlier than usual. I have a stock order to put in."

Paige slowed her pace until Juliet was by her side. "I still can't believe someone like you decided to just take on a bar. Do you have any idea of the closing rate these days?"

"I think it's a case of knowing what you want and pursuing that. If you put the effort in, you can be happy with your achievements."

"And when it doesn't work out?" Paige asked, glancing at Juliet briefly. "Does that mean you fucked up, or it just wasn't meant to be?"

"I guess it depends on whether you tried hard enough to make it work." Juliet was fully aware of the cryptic conversation they had fallen into, but if this was how Paige needed to do things, so be it.

"You know what, you're right. I only see good things happening with The Hideout, and that comes down to your dedication. The place would be closed if you hadn't taken it over, and then we never would have met."

"I, for one, am *very* happy that we met."

Paige licked chocolate sauce from her finger, disposing of her tray in a nearby bin. "Me, too."

"So, about that contract I mentioned?"

"Still mulling it over. But I *will* let you know soon if that's okay?"

Juliet held up a hand. "No rush at all."

"I don't want to leave you hanging for too long. I hope you know that's not my intention. I'm just not sure what's what with me at the moment. But if I can be sure that The Hideout is the place for me, I'd love to stick around. I really would."

"Then I can't ask for anything more right now. Just let me know, okay?"

"I will." Paige nudged Juliet's shoulder and smiled. "Hey, thanks for inviting me here today. I've had a great time."

"Thank you for coming with me. It's not often I have someone to spend the afternoon with. It's been lovely."

Paige quirked a brow. "Fancy it again some other time?"

Juliet's chest expanded as Paige asked that. Unless it was Rachel, people rarely gave Juliet the time of day. "Yes. Let's make that a plan."

CHAPTER 7
GIVE ME A LITTLE MORE TIME

Paige was feeling good tonight. Positive. She hadn't heard back from James, she felt as though something had shifted within her, and she was determined to make it count here at The Hideout. It seemed to have formed too perfectly for her to consider any other alternative. Juliet wanted to offer her a six-month contract; Paige would be out of her mind to turn it down. Still, she had to be sure she was making the right decision. She didn't want to burn her bridges here with Juliet when James eventually showed up.

She sat perched on a barstool, making notes in the small handbook she carried everywhere with her. It had been a late night last night, Paige sitting up until almost sunrise scouring the internet for new recipes to introduce at Juliet's bar. She wasn't quite ready to showcase them, especially not to Juliet, but her moment would arrive.

And when it did, she hoped Juliet would be impressed.

"Paige?" Juliet poked her head around the door that led to the back of the building. Her long dark hair shone against the spotlights, pairing beautifully with the ambient lighting down in the underground bar. "Do you have a minute?"

Paige set her pen down. "Sure."

"I wasn't planning on this just yet, but I think I've found another bartender to bring into the team."

Okay, but why? Paige wanted to ask, refraining from doing so. This was Juliet's bar; she had the final say in what went on there. "Have I fucked up?"

"What? No." Juliet smiled, approaching Paige at the bar. "Far from it. But six nights a week is a lot, Paige. I'm no bartender; I don't know the first thing about the various drinks we have to offer. But you do. As does the bartender I have coming in today to meet with us."

"Six nights a week doesn't bother me. It's not like I have anything else to do." If Juliet was trying to let Paige down gently, it was time to look for something else. She didn't need to sit at home staring at the walls. What she needed was to be working.

"Still, it's a lot. She's also worked in bar management, so if I need a night off, she can be here to take care of stuff."

Paige would let it lie. Unless Juliet reduced her shifts dramatically, she wouldn't worry herself too much. What was the point? She had a job, and that was the main thing.

"I get it. You don't have to explain yourself to me. I look forward to meeting her." Paige smiled, picking her pen back up. But Juliet remained in front of her, watching her. "Was there... something else?"

"N-no." Juliet shook her head, lowering her eyes. But then she opened her mouth to speak, her shoulders sagging slightly. "It's just... Would you like to get a drink together sometime?"

If Paige hadn't been sitting on a stool with a backrest, she'd have fallen off it. "Pardon? A...drink?"

"Yes. Not here. Maybe somewhere quiet, somewhere that we can talk and get to know one another."

"W-what is it that you want to know?" Paige frowned. Juliet

asking her out for a drink surely wasn't meant the way Paige perceived it. Was it?

"No, I'm not trying to pry." Juliet suddenly seemed flustered, and now Paige was beginning to realise that she *had* been asking her out on a date. *Holy fuck*. In what world could that possibly happen? "You know, never mind. F-forget I asked." She backed away, holding up a hand. "I'll be in the office if you need anything."

"Juliet—"

The buzzer on the main door interrupted whatever the hell Paige was planning to say. But that could only be a good thing since she had no idea *what* she wanted to say. Juliet turned, giving Paige the perfect opportunity to admire her boss. She wore black, high-waisted fitted pants, a white sleeveless blouse tucked into them, and impressive heels. Paige shuddered. This woman couldn't have possibly asked Paige to go for 'a drink'.

"It's the new server." Juliet, her cheeks bright red, turned back to Paige and then eyed the stairwell. "Let's hope she's a good fit."

"Yeah." Paige cleared her throat and got down from her stool. She stood against the bar, smiling when a woman a little younger than her walked through the door.

"Hi. It's Cara, yes?"

Cara took Juliet's hand, her eyes drifting over Juliet before she'd opened her mouth to confirm who she was. "That's me. I'm *so* excited to be here. This place is fab."

"Thanks. I'll take you through to the office in a moment."

Paige watched Cara as she placed a hand on Juliet's shoulder. Could this woman be any more of an arse-licker? *Ugh*. "Sure. Lead the way."

"Well, first, this is my incredible mixologist," Juliet said, turning her attention to Paige. But Paige just lifted a hand and smiled. "Paige, this is Cara."

"Yeah. Nice to meet you."

"Mixologist? Isn't that just a fancy name for 'I can make a cocktail look cool'?" Cara shoved her hands in her pockets, giving off that cocky air Paige *hated*.

Paige pushed off the bar, laughing. "Sure. Usually said by people who can't make a decent cocktail." She winked, passing Cara by, and headed for the storeroom. "I'll be out here checking on the stock if you need me, Juliet."

Not willing to entertain someone who liked to make smart arse comments during a first meeting, Paige puffed out her cheeks and forced the heavy metal door open. Not only had Cara tried to diminish Paige's job role here, Paige had also fucked up and turned down Juliet.

Well, today is just one huge balls up!

Juliet inconspicuously watched Paige interact with Cara, her shoulders tense as Cara moved things around behind the bar. If this working relationship was going to cause issues, Juliet might have to reconsider one of their positions. It wouldn't be Paige who she pulled to one side, not in a million years, but she had to give Cara a chance. Still, Juliet was fairly confident Paige could handle herself behind the bar. She wasn't one of the best for no reason. She also had to admit she found it highly arousing watching Paige take control of her space. Because that's exactly what it was. *Paige's* space. For a long time to come, hopefully.

Paige turned her watch towards herself, saying something to Cara as she threw a thumb over her shoulder. She caught Juliet's attention from the other side of the bar, leaning over as Juliet suddenly focused on the paperwork and iPad on the table. *Almost caught!* "You want coffee?"

"If you're making some, I'd love one."

"Usual espresso, or?"

Juliet beamed a smile. "Espresso would be great."

Paige nodded, turning her back on Juliet. She'd expected the atmosphere to be a little unsettled this evening, but it didn't appear to be. Yes, Paige seemed on edge about Cara and what she was doing to her pristine bar setup, but between her and Juliet, things were calm.

When Juliet had asked Paige out for a drink earlier, she hadn't exactly expected her to agree. But in that moment, when Juliet had realised Paige wasn't into her in any way at all, she hadn't quite known what to do with herself. Being with Rachel was casual. It felt like nothing more than some friends having fun. But when she was alone with Paige, Juliet felt entirely different. She could picture them having dinner together, talking about future plans. She thought about Paige's enthusiasm in terms of being here and wanting to involve herself in ideas for the bar. Paige felt real. She felt genuine. She was interesting and intelligent, and they had things in common.

But the only thing tonight had shown Juliet was that while she was more than happy flirting in bars and whatnot, it appeared she had *no idea* how to ask a woman out on a date.

Would it always be so hard?

Paige rounded the counter with two espresso cups, placing one down on the table in front of Juliet. "I'm going to take my break now while it's quiet. I'll only be five minutes."

"Five minutes isn't a break, Paige. Five minutes is barely enough time to use the bathroom and breathe." Juliet looked at Paige over the rim of her reading glasses.

"Five minutes is all I need. I'm going to take this outside if that's okay? Could do with a bit of fresh air."

Juliet nodded. "Sure. I was going to ask if you'd like to sit here with me but of course. You do what you need to do."

Paige chewed the corner of her lip, hesitating between the couch and the exit.

"We're okay, right? What I said earlier… If I was out of line, I apologise."

Paige sat on a single chair opposite Juliet. She lowered her coffee to the table, propping her elbows on her knees as she leant in. "About the drink? Yeah, I was hoping to actually finish that conversation with you, but Cara walked in and put paid to that."

"I don't know why I even asked. Well, I do. But…it *was* out of line. I'm your boss, and you've never once insinuated that it would be something you'd be interested in. I was just chancing my luck, I guess."

Paige suddenly swapped seats, now sinking into the leather beside Juliet.

Thrilled that Paige was sitting next to her, Juliet removed her reading glasses, downed her espresso, and gave her full attention to Paige.

"I'd love to go for a drink with you, I can't quite believe you asked me, but I'm only here to work, Juliet. Liverpool is temporary for me; it's not likely that I'll be in a position to stay full-time, so yeah…I'm just here to work."

"No chance of that six-month contract then?" Juliet chose to focus on the business side of things. It seemed she was far more capable of doing that than trying to date.

"M-maybe. I don't know. I have things going on back in my hometown that I might have to deal with, so I don't want to say yes and then have to leave. I wouldn't do that to you."

Juliet placed a hand on Paige's forearm, squeezing gently. "I understand. But I hope you know that if you *did* want to stay, I'd make sure you could go home if you needed to. Sudden or planned, I'd make sure you didn't have to worry about the bar."

Paige scoffed. "I never want to go back home again, but chances are, it will eventually happen."

"For good or just to visit?" Paige seemed very secretive about her personal life, but Juliet couldn't blame her. Not everybody had their life plastered all over social media for everyone to pick apart. Paige seemed like one of the few people who didn't give in to those sorts of pressures.

"I'm...in the process of coming out of a relationship. Things are complicated, but I should go back at some point to clear everything up. To...move forward."

"I see."

Paige placed her hand over Juliet's, smiling as her shoulders relaxed. "Look, you're gorgeous. Absolutely way out of everyone's league. Please don't take my rejection as anything personal."

Paige shouldn't say things like that. It only made Juliet want her more. "Whatever you have going on, I'm here if you need to talk, okay?"

Paige nodded, that smile widening. "You know, I had no idea what to expect when I walked in here. I figured you'd be one of those 'takes no shit from anybody' people who gives nothing away, but I've been pleasantly surprised."

"Oh, I *was* one of those people. But by doing that, look at me now." Juliet sighed, slipping her hand out from under Paige's. "A bar owner with nobody in my life. And then I go and make a fool of myself by asking a thirty-year-old out on a date. I really need to take my head out of my arse."

Paige dipped her head, finding Juliet's gaze. That grey seemed silver tonight, they shone so brightly. "Hey, this thirty-year-old almost fell off her stool when you asked. Trust me, you *didn't* make a fool of yourself. But I'm not in a position to put either of us through something that likely won't go anywhere. And that's not because of you; it's because of the situation I'm in." Paige suddenly lifted Juliet's hand and kissed her knuckles. "You made my day, but now I have to get back to work before this newbie destroys my reputation."

Juliet tried to fight the feeling Paige's lips on her skin gave her. The gentle brush, the featherlight touch, it had Juliet's insides swirling. She couldn't say she'd ever had butterflies before.

"You okay?" Paige asked as she got to her feet and stared down at Juliet.

"Yes. Fine. Work with Cara for another hour and then call it a night. Join me here. Let's see what she's made of when she's working alone."

Paige's brows rose. "Okay. I can do that."

CHAPTER 8
ALONE

Paige took her keys from her back pocket, and shoved them in the front of her rucksack. She was done for the night, and now she was going to sit back and enjoy watching Cara crumble. She may have been in the bar industry, and she may have had a fancy managerial title from previous establishments, but The Hideout wasn't *just* a bar. It was an experience.

She turned out the light in the small locker room, slinging her bag over her shoulder. While she couldn't indulge Juliet via a drink…a date, she could certainly enjoy spending time with her during working hours. It didn't matter if she'd wanted to say yes—she couldn't. But she *could* admire Juliet without making it obvious. Paige had spent plenty of time over the years perfecting *that* skill.

As she headed out from the back of the bar, Cara caught her attention.

"Hey, uh, who's the woman?" Cara cocked her head towards Juliet's spot.

Great. That was Paige's night ruined. She really had been looking forward to spending some time with Juliet. "That's… Rachel. Juliet's friend."

"Friend, huh? Wouldn't mind a *friend* of my own like that."

Yeah, me too. Paige shouldn't be surprised that Juliet had changed her mind about Rachel. She still stood by the fact that they were far more attracted to one another than just escort/client. And besides, Paige *had* turned Juliet down. "I'll be around for a little while if you need anything."

"I'm sure I can manage." Cara looked Paige up and down, and then she rolled her eyes as she walked away.

Paige couldn't be bothered with an attitude like that. She wasn't here to make Cara's life difficult. She was here to help the bar succeed. Really, that should have been Cara's reason for being here too. Paige slowly walked towards Juliet's spot, her stomach lurching when she found Rachel palming Juliet's thigh. The bar may have been winding down, only two clients finishing their drinks out of sight from Juliet's spot, but was that really necessary? If Paige didn't break it up now, Rachel would be fucking Juliet on the couch in the next thirty seconds if she had her way.

But then she watched Juliet place a hand on Rachel's chest, gently insisting she stop whatever she was trying to start. *Interesting*. And then Paige read Juliet's lips when she gave Rachel a stern look and told her to stop.

"Hi, Rachel." Paige lowered her rucksack to the floor beside a chair, shoving her hands in the pockets of her jeans.

"Oh, hi. I didn't think you were here tonight."

Paige shrugged. "Always am. I was finishing up out the back."

"That's nice." Rachel sighed when Juliet shifted away from her. "So are you going home now?"

"I was supposed to be hanging out here with Juliet, but I think I'll probably get going." She eyed Juliet, saddened that she'd turned down that drink. But then the thought of having to share Juliet sat firmly at the front of Paige's mind. She didn't do sharing, so turning down that offer was probably a wise decision. "Since we're closed tomorrow, I'll see you Friday at three."

"I thought you were staying?"

"I was staying to talk business. But you look like you've got other things going on." Paige decided she would enjoy a whiskey before her walk home. She turned to the bar and ordered herself a drink. When Cara turned to the whiskey shelf, she added, "And whatever these two are drinking." She threw a twenty-pound note down on the counter, watching Cara work.

"Paige, you don't have to do that," Juliet called out.

"It's just a drink. Relax." Once Cara set the drinks down in front of her, Paige took Juliet's and Rachel's, offering them over. "Here you go. Enjoy the rest of your night together."

Rachel frowned. "T-thank you."

"Welcome." Paige nodded, her eyes briefly finding Juliet's. What she found when she looked into them shocked her. Juliet seemed disappointed that Paige was leaving. Saddened that they wouldn't be spending time together. But Paige couldn't sit here with Rachel when Rachel was obviously trying to keep Juliet's attention away from her. It was quite clear that Juliet's escort had a problem with Paige being around. "I'll see you Friday."

She turned back to the bar, sitting up on a stool as she nursed her whiskey. She stared down at the glass of amber liquid, exhaling a deep breath through her nose.

"And there was me thinking *she* was the reason you'd gone distant on me." Paige heard Rachel say, not as quietly as she likely thought she had. "I see how she looks at you, but Paige knows her place around here."

Nope! I'm not doing this.

Paige knocked back her whiskey, grimacing as she brought the glass back down to the counter. She wasn't sitting here listening to Rachel discuss her with Juliet. *Fuck that.* "Night, Cara. See you Friday."

"Yeah, see ya!"

Paige slid off her stool, took her rucksack, and glared at Rachel. "My *place* is behind that bar where Juliet has employed me to be. You have no reason to feel threatened by me being here."

And then Paige walked away, taking the stairs up to street level two at a time. She heard Juliet call her name, but she couldn't deal with this. Tonight had been a whirlwind compared to what Paige was used to. She couldn't hack the drama. And even if she could, she didn't *want* to.

Maybe Liverpool isn't going to be the quiet life you hoped it would be.

"Paige! Wait!"

Paige turned to find Juliet rushing after her down the side street.

"I'm so sorry about that. She called me to say she was outside. She had a terrible time tonight with a new client. Please, come back inside."

"I can't. I have to go."

Juliet leaned forward and took Paige's hand. "Please, you can."

"So, it's back on with you two then?" Paige pulled her hand from Juliet's. She had no idea where it had been since she'd gone into the back of the bar to end her shift. "I knew you were into her more than you wanted to admit. But…if you can be honest with her, tell her what you want, then I think you could be great together."

"N-no. We're not back together in any way at all. Client or not."

Paige laughed. "Oh, I think we both know that's not quite the truth. If I hadn't turned up, you'd be on your third orgasm by now."

Juliet's brows drew together. "Why do you care so much about what I'm doing with Rachel?"

"I don't. But I *do* care about you. So, I want you to do what's best for you. When we were talking the other day, when we had coffee at your place, you told me you didn't want to continue with her. Either that was a lie, or something has changed for you. Whatever it is, you need to decide what you want in life. Only a few hours ago, you asked me to go for a drink with you. And right now, I'm glad I said no."

"Paige."

"Because as the night has gone on, I did wonder if I'd done the wrong thing by turning you down. But seeing that, how you can just switch and change, that's not for me. Even if I was in a position to go for a drink with you." Paige walked backwards slowly, watching as that sunk in with Juliet. "And for the record, if my life wasn't so complicated… I'd have been doing far more than drinking with you by now."

"W-what?"

Paige smiled as she lifted a shoulder. "You're absolutely my type."

"Paige, wait. Come on, we can figure it out."

"We can't. But you can go back inside and figure *that* out. See you Friday, boss."

Rachel was ruining her chance with Paige. Whether Juliet's head was up her arse or not, it was true. And she couldn't handle it anymore. She wanted Paige to see her as someone she could trust, not someone who allowed their escort to control her night whenever it suited her.

She took the stairs to the bar quickly, stopping at the couch Rachel was sprawled out on. "You need to leave."

"What? Why? You said you'd be there for me if I needed someone. And I do, I need you." Rachel pouted, fluttering her eyelashes at Juliet. "Come on, baby. Sit down."

"You're fucking with my head, and I don't need that."

"Why? Because your little fantasy has run away upset? I'm not worried about her. She's only a fucking bartender." Rachel reached for her glass of wine and then sat back with her legs crossed. "I walked in here tonight, and your eyes lit up for me."

"Because I was happy to see that you were okay. You'd just called me out of the blue crying down the phone." And then Juliet realised what was happening. Rachel hadn't been in trouble; she hadn't needed a friend. She'd lied purely to get into the bar. "You didn't have any issues with your last client, did you?"

Rachel smirked as she lifted a shoulder. "I wanted to see if you'd drop everything for me, and you did."

"Yeah. Because I'm a fool. I thought you were hurt. Why would you do that to me?"

"To prove a point." Rachel got to her feet, stalking towards Juliet. "You were supposed to spend the rest of the night with *her*. And instead, you ended up with *me*. That says a lot considering you don't want to see me again."

Juliet's bottom lip quivered. "I can't do this with you. You never once hinted that you expected more from me, Rachel. Every time we were together, we *both* knew what this was. Why *now* do you want more?"

"Because I like you, Juliet. And ever since she arrived, I mean nothing to you. I wanted to see what was so special about her. Honestly, she's *nothing* compared to me."

"I'm not trying to compare. That's all *your* doing. To think I actually sat there a few days ago with Paige over coffee and told her about you. About us. How I felt bad for the way we'd parted.

She was the one who sat and listened. She didn't belittle you, she didn't judge you, she just sat and listened."

"You spoke to her about me?" Rachel asked, surprised.

"I did. Because I felt terrible. But now? Now I'm wondering why I care at all if you're going to act like this."

"Um, Juliet?" Cara suddenly spoke.

"WHAT?!"

Cara flinched as she slowly walked towards the exit. "I-I just wanted to let you know I was leaving and that I've locked up the back and the stock room for you."

"Right, yeah. Thanks, Cara." She turned to her server. "I'm sorry. I forgot you were still here. I'll see you on Friday, okay?"

"You will. Goodnight."

Juliet pinched the bridge of her nose, waiting until she heard the main door close. It slammed with a thud, her shoulders tensing as it did so. "I'm leaving now. And so are you. Get your stuff, and get out."

"Please, Juliet—"

"No. This is my business. You can't come here and make a scene like this. I thought we'd talked about this. I *thought* you understood..."

Rachel retrieved her bag and walked back towards Juliet. "I'm sorry. I'll call you. Maybe in a few days when things have calmed down."

Rachel shot up the stairs leaving Juliet standing alone in the bar. She took her phone from her pants pocket, swallowing as she brought up Paige's number. She didn't know why Paige was the first person she thought of or why she was about to call her, but she did...only to be disappointed when it went to voicemail.

"Hi, it's me. Juliet. I just wanted to apologise again for everything that's happened since your shift started today. It seems I'm a little bit all over the place since you arrived to work here, and I don't quite know what to do with myself. But that's no excuse, and you putting me in my place was the right thing. Not many would willingly do that to me, so I appreciate it." Juliet took a deep breath, pulling her hair over one shoulder as she paced the small bar. "Anyway, I have your tips here. I'll keep hold of them until I see you again. Hopefully on Friday, but if I've complicated everything and you don't want to return, I understand. Goodnight, Paige."

With tears in her eyes, Juliet lowered her phone. She couldn't be bothered to finish clearing away, so she turned out the light and moved into her office. She had no idea what to do with herself…but she had to figure it all out soon. Her life was up in the air.

CHAPTER 9
1000 TIMES

"Hello?" Paige answered a call from an unknown number, frowning when nobody spoke. "Hello?"

"I've had time to think," A voice said, immediately recognisable. She should have known James would call from an unknown number. He'd done it before. "And if you want to fix us, you need to come home."

"If *I* want to fix us?" Paige's brows rose. Paige would usually keep James calm on a call, but she was tired of his never-ending complaints. When would he take the hint that she didn't want to be with him anymore? Even if it wasn't because of her sexuality, Paige didn't want to be with a man like him. A man who beat her to control their relationship. "You're not taking any responsibility then?"

"If you hadn't decided you wanted to go on some fucking bar crawl around the UK, we wouldn't be in this position, Paige."

Paige looked out at the city, her mood beginning to dip now that James was on the line. She'd spent the morning getting some things together in her head, a little meditation to relieve the tension headache she felt coming on, and she'd felt much better for it. Until now.

"Don't ignore me, Paige. You're a fucking terrible wife."

"Then why are you so desperate for me to come home?"

James scoffed. "Because if you think you're going to make a laughingstock out of me, you're wrong. You come home, you *stay* home, and we get on with our lives."

"And when I walk through the door, what happens then? Another punch? A shove in the back? The old *you fell over my foot* again?"

"Those things happened one time. One time, Paige!" James roared down the phone, Paige's heart rate soaring as he did. Those things may have only *technically* happened once, but that was because James hurt her in some other way the next time. "You make out like you're some beaten wife, but you're not. You just don't know your place yet!"

Why did people keep talking about Paige's place in their lives? Rachel, James, who next? Why couldn't she just work and go home each day? Was it really that difficult to lead a simple life?

"You've no idea how much you hurt me, do you, James? I don't *want* to be with you anymore."

"Your mum would be so disappointed in how you're behaving."

Paige slumped against the wall in her living room. James had never used her mother in an argument before. "Yeah, well, she's not here, so what does it matter?"

"IT FUCKING MATTERS!"

Paige brought the phone away from her ear as James screeched, his voice almost breaking.

"If you're not home by the end of the month, I'm coming to get you. And I know exactly where you are, so if I were you, I'd do the right thing."

"James, I want a divorce." Saying those words had never felt so freeing, even if it was never going to happen. Paige's heart ached to be free from him. "Please, can we do that?"

"You don't want a divorce. You just need a firm hand and a reality check, love." James ended the call, leaving Paige alone as she slid down the wall and brought her knees to her chest.

She'd never felt safe with him. And that was all Paige had ever wanted. To feel safe and loved by someone. She wanted to be held and told life would all work itself out. She wanted to smile and laugh and plan a future with someone. But more than anything, she wanted to feel respected. That was it. Respect from another human being who thought something of her.

Paige swallowed. She couldn't go back to him; she wouldn't survive.

A knock on the door had her wiping tears from her cheeks. She had called the maintenance company an hour ago because her shower was running hot and cold unexpectedly. Maybe having something to focus on, meaningless conversation while the workman fixed it, would be good for her.

"Just a minute," She called out, getting to her feet. Paige rushed to the sink and splashed her face with cold water, pulling her hair up into a bun. Well, a half-bun, half-ponytail. "Coming!" She reached the door and pulled it open. "O-oh. Hi, morning."

"Hi, Paige." Juliet stood nervously out in the corridor, casting her gaze on the criss-cross carpet. But Paige understood. They hadn't really parted on the best of terms last night. "I wondered if you had a couple of minutes?"

Paige opened the door. "Sure. Come in."

Juliet smiled as she slipped past Paige, looking delicious in a pair of casual jeans and a V-neck T-shirt. Paige was well aware of the fact her boss had a great arse but in jeans? *Oh, boy.* "Thanks. I won't keep you long."

"Is everything okay? If this is about last night, I'm sorry for anything I said out of turn. I got your voicemail, but I thought it was best to let it lie. I'm not one for confrontation."

Juliet stopped at the kitchen island in Paige's open-plan living space. "It *is* about last night. What Rachel said. She was way out of line, Paige. I'm sorry."

Paige held up a hand. "First of all, I don't know why *you* are apologising. You're not responsible for what comes out of her mouth. And secondly, I really don't have it in me today to care about someone I don't know, nor do I wish to know. Rachel is into you, and I get that. Who isn't?"

"You. You're not," Juliet said, closing her eyes briefly. "But that's beside the point. I just wanted to drop by and see that you were okay. I think sometimes she forgets that she's not my girlfriend…and she never will be."

Paige would be lying if she said she hadn't kept an eye on Juliet coming home last night. And when she *had* heard the lift, she was surprised to look through the peephole in her door to see Juliet alone. "Just last week, you claimed she wasn't anything to you anymore. Last night, that was so far from the truth."

"I didn't even want her to be at the bar."

Paige held up a hand. "Juliet, I don't know why you think you have to explain yourself to me. I'm just your bartender."

"Rachel was only ever supposed to be a means to an end for me. She's a high-class escort. If I wasn't paying her ridiculous amounts of money, she wouldn't be all over me. I can assure you of that."

"I'm not convinced by that, but okay." Paige lifted a shoulder.

Then her phone buzzed in her hand. She looked down at the message, her heart sinking to the pit of her stomach.

End of the month, Paige. And then we put a stop to this

once and for all. If you don't show, I'll be at The Hideout to collect you myself!

Paige stumbled back, gripping a stool at the breakfast bar. Juliet instantly offered an arm, holding her upright. "Is everything okay?"

She pressed a palm to her forehead, smiling weakly. "Yeah. Fine. Just lightheaded again."

"Have you eaten?"

Paige nodded, lifting her shaking body onto the stool she was resting against. James was coming for her. It was time to go. "Yeah. Uh, I can only stay at the bar for another week, and then I have to move on. I'm sorry."

Juliet frowned. "N-no. You can't leave yet."

"I have to. I'll help you fill the position if you want. I'm not sure Cara is going to take you places on her own."

"But—" Juliet's voice broke, surprising Paige. "I thought you enjoyed working with me. You seemed right at home."

Paige smiled, cocking her head. "I was."

"Is this because of Rachel? If it is, say the word, and I'll make her understand. I never want you to feel uncomfortable, Paige."

"Rachel is the furthest thing from my mind. She just thinks I'm trying to get my hands on her woman, and I'm really not." Paige shrugged the hand on her shoulder away. "Please make sure she knows that, Juliet."

"I'm not *her woman*." Juliet backed away, resting against the counter. "But something is going on, and I'd like to think that you trust me. Let me figure it out with you. I don't want to lose you, Paige. You're a part of The Hideout."

"I'll never really be a part of anything. But thank you for being so welcoming. I'll miss working for you." Paige gingerly climbed from the stool, throwing her phone onto the couch. "I should start making some calls. Look for a place to visit and digs to stay at."

As Paige walked away, Juliet took her hand suddenly. "Come over for dinner tonight."

"Sounds lovely, but I can't. There's some open mic night thing on in town, and I stupidly decided to sign up for it."

"Oh, where? Can I come too?"

Paige laced her fingers with Juliet's, turning her body fully to Juliet. "I love your determination, your enthusiasm too, but no. Call Rachel and make things right with one another. Tell her what she means to you and spend the evening together. God knows one of us may as well be having some fun, and I know it'll never be me."

"But—"

"But nothing, Juliet."

Paige was going to hate her for this, but Juliet couldn't pass up on the opportunity to hear her play one final time. That voice, she'd dreamt about it once or twice since the first time she'd heard it. The pain in it, but also the peacefulness too. There was no denying that Paige was in some kind of trouble—she was constantly running away—but Juliet knew Paige would never trust her enough to confide in her. She prayed it could be different, but she had to understand coming from Paige's point of view.

Juliet was a complete stranger.

She'd positioned herself to be out of Paige's line of sight, but for she, herself, to have an unspoilt view through the small number of tables separating them. Juliet lifted her glass and sipped her wine slowly as Paige walked across the floor and took a seat behind the piano just off centre of the stage.

And then that melody reached her ears. Juliet closed her eyes, savouring the image of Paige in a world she loved.

Creative, musical, away from the inner turmoil she knew Paige felt. It was all she could do. Fantasise about Paige Harrison.

Her voice came to life as she serenaded the crowd with Sara Bareilles' *1000 Times*, the venue so quiet Juliet could hear her own heart beating. And right now, it was beating *only* for Paige and her impeccable talent. How was it that a woman she didn't know, a woman who had given her nothing whatsoever, held a special place in Juliet's heart? She could consider that she was just dreaming of a life with a significant other, but this wasn't that. No. Juliet felt Paige crawling further inside her with each moment they spent together. This wasn't Juliet desperate for *something*; this was Juliet *hoping* for Paige.

She looked around the venue, all eyes firmly on the woman behind the piano. Paige looked entirely different this evening with light makeup on and her outfit leaving very little to the imagination. But it wasn't Paige's sexuality she was focusing on. It was her undeniable beauty as she poured her heart out via song.

Juliet sunk deeper into her seat, tears pricking her eyes as she took her wine glass between her lips. If only she could explain to Paige that she—*her talent*—was worth more than she thought of herself. If only she could take this woman in her arms and promise her everything was going to be okay, that she didn't need to run from her life anymore. If only...

The song came to an end, the break in Paige's voice sending tears down Juliet's cheeks. This wasn't the woman she used to be. Never in all of her years had she sat in a bar and cried for someone. But that stone-cold heart was beginning to thaw, and it was Paige Harrison who was to blame. Not Rachel, not any of the one-night stands she'd had over the years. *Paige*.

A server passed her table, and Juliet caught their attention. She saw Paige had situated herself at the bar on arrival, and as she craned her neck, Paige was back there again...the crowd still cheering for more as Paige sat with her head hung. "Could you send a honey JD to the woman sitting alone at the bar? The one with the incredible voice. Add it to my tab."

The server smiled and offered a nod. "Sure can."

Juliet swallowed as she watched the same server prepare Paige's drink, placing it in front of her and pointing in Juliet's direction. Paige squinted as she followed his line of sight, and then the prettiest, softest smile spread on Paige's mouth.

Well, that could have gone much worse.

As Paige made her way towards her, Juliet's heart pounded furiously. Juliet's heart *never* pounded for *anyone*. She sat up straight on the couch she'd managed to snag on arrival, placing her wine on the table.

"Are you stalking me?" Paige lifted a brow.

"Well, if I am, I'm not doing a very good job." Juliet stared up at Paige, aware that she still had tears in her eyes. But Paige did too, so she didn't feel so stupid. "Did you want to join me?"

"W-why are you here?"

"I know you don't want me here, and I have no right to be here after last night, but I…wanted to experience this—*you*—alone. One final time."

Paige blushed, taking a large gulp of the drink Juliet had ordered for her. When Juliet was convinced Paige was about to refuse a seat, she suddenly flopped down beside her. "Thanks for the drink."

"Thanks for the song." Juliet nudged Paige's shoulder with her own, smiling when their eyes met. "You really should see someone about that voice. It's one hell of a talent."

Paige just stared down at her almost empty glass.

"Or, if you don't want to be in the public eye…see me about it. Because I'm telling you right now, I would pay good money to have you in the bar on the piano a few nights a week."

She heard Paige scoff beside her, but Juliet had put it out

there now, and all she could do was hope that Paige would consider it. It didn't matter what the initial conversation had been when Juliet had walked in on Paige singing. She knew deep down that Paige adored these moments. Her beautiful eyes gave it away.

"Music was *all* I lived for at one time," Paige said quietly, rubbing her thumb against the glass in her hand. "I self-taught, then I went to college, then…well, then it all went wrong, and I fell out of love with it."

"I think you could fall back in love again." Juliet shifted closer, turning side-on to face Paige. "I think you can do anything you want to do."

"Life never works out for me that way. But thank you for being here tonight. I didn't think I would care that I was here alone, but you being here…it means a lot."

Juliet lifted a hand when Paige turned to her, cradling her chin. She smiled, stroked a thumb across Paige's soft skin, and held her gaze. "I wish you didn't have to leave."

"You'll find another mixologist, don't worry."

Juliet closed her eyes, her bottom lip trembling. "But they won't be you."

When she opened her eyes again, Paige had her own closed, tears falling down her face. Juliet did the only thing she felt she could do. She leaned in, hesitating for a moment, and then pressed her lips to Paige's. She tasted sweet, her lips so full and plump. Lips Juliet would quite happily kiss all night long. Expecting Paige to pull away, Juliet was pleasantly surprised when Paige reciprocated. She gripped Juliet's bare thigh, sending a roar of arousal straight to where she expected it to be. *Oh, God.* Paige's delicate fingers on her skin had her breath catching in her throat, wetness gathering between her thighs, Juliet's nipples painfully taut.

She knew she should stop this, knew Paige was going to

realise what was happening and run, but Paige slid her tongue into Juliet's mouth, moaning when she grazed her fingernails down her thigh. Juliet's only response was to moan too, their tongues rolling against one another's. Because that exhilarating sensation that had just shot through her... Oh, she'd never felt anything like it.

"Paige," she murmured against her lips, smiling when Paige went straight back in for another kiss. "You have to s-stop doing that." She placed her hand on Paige's, stilling her movements as her hand found its way beneath Juliet's dress. Those fingers were far too close for the public. "You're killing me."

Paige frowned as she pulled away. "Fuck, I'm sorry."

"Oh, don't be. Don't ever be sorry for kissing *any* woman like that." Juliet held her bottom lip between her teeth, the taste of Paige and her bourbon still present. "*Never* be sorry."

"I...have to go. I should go." Paige got to her feet, looking around the bar. She patted her pockets frantically, checking she hadn't left anything, and rushed away. But she stopped and turned back briefly, desire overtaking the fear in those eyes. "I wish I wasn't leaving, too."

Juliet swallowed as Paige fled from the venue. Her body ached for more, to take what had just happened back to Juliet's place, but she couldn't rush after her. Juliet's knees trembled, an entirely different version of Paige now cemented in her mind. Gone was the quiet bartender she spent most evenings with. Gone was the uncertainty that permanently clouded Paige's beautiful grey eyes. And all that remained was a new Paige Harrison. One who was sexy as hell. Fuck, that woman could kiss. She could fire Juliet up in a split second. That kiss... had been the greatest kiss of her life.

Yet here Juliet was...*alone*.

CHAPTER 10
HATE TO SEE YOUR HEART BREAK

Juliet stepped into the shower, the steaming hot water soothing her back as she allowed it to cascade over her from head to toe. It was all she could do this morning to stop her from reaching for her phone and calling Paige, or worse...walking the corridor and banging her door down.

Last night had been intense. So intense that Juliet hadn't actually slept much at all through the night. She'd sat up nursing her herbal tea until the early hours of the morning, and today she was barely functioning.

She increased the water temperature a little, groaning as it lashed her skin. She needed this, something to distract her from the pain she felt when she thought of Paige. Nobody had ever touched her so gently. Nobody had ever made her lose her breath from a simple yet unexpected kiss. *Nobody* had ever kissed her quite like that before.

With Rachel, it had been hot and heavy. With Rachel, it had been pleasurable but meaningless. With Rachel, it was...a transaction. But with Paige? *Oh, God*. With Paige, it was stars exploding behind Juliet's eyes. It was her skin igniting from the slightest touch. It was something so intense she didn't know how to make sense of how she was feeling.

Unable to get Paige off her mind, Juliet lowered her hand down her stomach, moaning when her fingertips touched her aching clit. It had been swollen and sensitive since their kiss last night, but only now was Juliet so overcome with arousal that she felt able to relieve herself of the pent-up desire Paige had left her with. "Oh, fuck." Juliet inhaled a deep breath, rubbing vigorously. All she saw was Paige. All she felt was that tongue slipping against her own. Those fingers slowly creeping beneath her dress and to where Juliet desperately wanted them to be.

She felt her orgasm roaring towards the edge...but then her doorbell sounded, and Juliet paused. It could only be one person. *Paige*. She knew it was the wrong move to make when she was just about ready to come hard for the woman outside her door, but Juliet turned the shower off and grabbed her towel anyway. She couldn't pass up the chance to see Paige. Almost losing her footing on the tiled floor, she composed herself and shot to the door. But when she pulled it open, her clit aching for so much more, Rachel was standing in the corridor.

"H-hi." Juliet frowned, squeezing her thighs together. Now *was not* the time to have Rachel in her home. "Why are you here?" As unusual as this unexpected visit was, Juliet didn't actually care why her escort was there; she just wanted to get rid of her so she could slip off into the bedroom and take care of herself. "Rachel?"

"I'm sorry." Rachel held up her hands, tears in her eyes as she stepped inside the apartment. "I know you don't want to hear it because I was a complete bitch to you on Wednesday night, but I am. I'm so sorry, Juliet."

No. This couldn't be happening right now. Juliet appreciated Rachel's apology, of course, just...not right now. "I... It's okay. Really."

Rachel took Juliet's hand, kicking the door shut. "It's not. You mean so much to me, Juliet, and I've been very out of character lately."

"Come here. Everything will be okay." Juliet pulled Rachel into a hug, hating the pain she saw in her eyes. Yes, she'd been out of character, but everyone had a moment at one time or another. "We're okay. I promise." She pressed a soothing palm to Rachel's back, smiling as Rachel sniffled.

Slowly, Rachel pulled out of their embrace, bringing a hand up to Juliet's cheek. She swiped a thumb across Juliet's bottom lip, only fuelling that fire Juliet felt burning deep within. This really wasn't ideal. It was Paige she wanted standing before her. It was Paige she *desperately* craved.

"I'd recognise that flushed look anywhere," Rachel whispered, ghosting her fingers down Juliet's neck and along her shoulder. "Tell me what you need."

Juliet tried to calm her breathing, but it simply wasn't possible. Her body was far too sensitive, her mind was racing, and she couldn't hold on much longer. "W-what?"

Rachel slid a hand between Juliet's legs. The towel she was wearing fell to the floor as Rachel stroked her clit. *Oh, fuck.*

Juliet's breath caught; her knees went weak. "Rachel, s-sto—oh, shit."

"That is a *very* wet pussy. I don't think you really want me to stop at all."

"N-no," Juliet spoke breathlessly, stumbling back as Rachel guided her further into the room. "Rachel, please—"

Rachel pushed Juliet against the back of her couch, dropped to her knees, and sucked her clit into her mouth.

"Fuck." Juliet's eyes slammed shut, her head thrown back,

so overcome with arousal that she couldn't stop Rachel. She needed relief, and she needed it now. "Y-yes. Harder."

"Mm. I knew you wanted me." Rachel sucked harder, sinking two fingers inside Juliet as she hummed against her clit. "I've missed you."

Juliet fell apart, releasing around Rachel's fingers. But Rachel didn't stop, didn't slow. Instead, she kept fucking Juliet, knowing she was about to peak again. Only this time, Paige flashed through her mind, her lips sucking Juliet into her mouth. Rachel didn't exist, their arrangement was gone, and all Juliet felt was Paige all over her. *Inside* her. Shit, she was going to come like she'd never come before.

"Fuck, yes. Give it to me. Come for me again, baby."

Juliet gripped the back of Rachel's head, forcing her mouth against her. She rode hard and fast, and then she roared out as she came for a second time. "Oh, Paige. Y-yes. Take me. D-don't stop."

Rachel slowed, and then she eased out of Juliet, staring up at her where she sat back on her knees at Juliet's feet. "Did you just..."

Juliet exhaled a shaky breath, her chest heaving as she slumped back against the couch. Her hands tightened around the cushions, her knees trembling. "God, I wasn't expecting that."

"No," Rachel said as she scoffed and got to her feet. "Neither was I!"

Juliet watched with confusion as Rachel turned away, sniffling again. "Rachel, what's wrong?" She grabbed her towel from the floor and covered herself, placing a hand on Rachel's shoulder. "Hey..."

"Don't." Rachel shrugged Juliet's touch away. "Just don't."

"What's—"

"I came over because I tried calling last night and got your voicemail. I've been calling you this morning, and it just rang out. I miss you, Juliet. I came over because I wanted to see you, to *be* with you, but you..." Rachel pinched the bridge of her nose. "You're sleeping with her, aren't you?"

"Who? I'm not sleeping with anybody!"

"Paige." Rachel had a look in her eyes that Juliet had never seen before. Cold, hurt...insulted. "It makes sense now. You haven't wanted me since she turned up at the bar."

"I'm...not doing anything with Paige." Juliet wished she was after that kiss, but the hard truth was that she would never share anything more with Paige. "Why the hell would you think that?"

"Because while I had my fingers inside you, you called out her name!"

Juliet hadn't. She couldn't. Had she? *Oh, God!*

"Rachel, I'm sorry." Juliet felt dreadful. As she cast her mind back, she knew she *had* called out Paige's name.

But Rachel's body language suddenly changed. She pulled her shoulders back, fixed her jacket, and turned towards the door. "Please, don't apologise. You pay me to fuck you, Juliet. It's my own fault for forgetting that...even if only briefly."

"You got me at a bad time, that's all." Juliet took a step towards Rachel, reaching out a hand.

Rachel took a step back, followed by another. Juliet immediately noted how her shoulders lowered, making Rachel appear smaller. This...wasn't the woman Juliet knew. God, she'd fucked it all up.

Rachel cleared her throat. "You employ me. You call when you need me. You really don't need to explain yourself. More fool me for showing up."

"Why *did* you show up?"

"Maybe I just thought I could give it one last shot. To apologise and see if you had changed your mind." Rachel lifted a shoulder, taking hold of the door handle.

No, no, no. Juliet clenched the hand at her side into a fist, her chest tight. She desperately wanted to get through to Rachel, but she didn't want this to end the way it seemed to be ending. Juliet wanted it to be amicable. The least she could do here, and right now, was afford Rachel time to discuss this properly. "But...I told you we were done."

"Yet I've just been on my knees, fucking you. So, tell me, Juliet. What the hell is it that you want?"

Juliet wouldn't be spoken to like that. "Like I said, you caught me at a bad time."

"Yeah, it looked terrible. A really bad time."

Juliet sighed, motioning towards the couch. She needed to sit down, and she suspected Rachel did too. Juliet lowered herself, dragging a hand through her hair. "I...kissed her. Last night. And since then, I just feel out of sorts. On edge. I have been all night. You turned up, and I should have said no." Juliet wasn't sure she was even making any sense now. "I used you, and for that, I can never apologise enough."

Rachel crouched in front of Juliet, lifting a hand to her face. "Don't you see that I want you, Juliet? *I'm* here and she's not."

"I...need space. A lot of space. I don't know what I'm doing lately. My head is a fucking mess."

"I want to be there for you," Rachel whispered, leaning in. But Juliet turned her head and shifted further away. Juliet wrapped her arms around herself and swallowed the emotion lodged in her throat. She couldn't allow this again. Rachel had to understand. And Juliet, well... She had to stop with this hold Rachel seemed to have over her. "Juliet...baby?"

"Stop. Please, for the love of God, just stop." Juliet was beginning to grow frustrated with this now. Yes, she was in the wrong for not turning Rachel away earlier, but it didn't change anything. "I think we should *really* stop seeing one another now. We can't keep doing this." Juliet was barely able to look at Rachel. But she did, hoping Rachel would understand—would *see*—the loss Juliet also felt. Rachel had helped her through one of the most difficult times of her life; Juliet could *never* forget that support or the friendship they'd built. She sighed lightly, shaking her head. "I can't focus on anything else at the moment. I'm sorry. I hope you know that."

"I-I know."

"I'm *not* sleeping with her, Rachel. I wouldn't lie to you. I just need some space. I need to be alone. I haven't been alone since my mother died, and I think that maybe it's the best thing for me."

"I helped you through that. I was there whenever you needed me."

Juliet smiled. "I know. And I can never repay you for that. But it's time for me to figure some stuff out, and in order to do that, I need space."

"Right. *Space*. Well, I don't know..." Rachel got to her feet, smiling weakly as she stared down at Juliet. The atmosphere was calmer than Juliet thought it would be, so that was positive. "If you ever need anything, if you...ever need *me*, then you know where to find me. Bye, Juliet."

Juliet sighed, watching Rachel walk out the door, it closing softly behind her. She sat on the couch, holding her towel against her, aware that her life was about to become complicated. It always had been in some way, but that had never been because of a woman.

Never.

Until now.

Paige turned the key in the door to the bar, her hand shaking at the thought of seeing Juliet. Last night had blown her mind in many ways, but in others, it had only complicated everything. She couldn't explain to Juliet the life she had; she couldn't put it on anyone else. Paige recalled their first meeting when Juliet had asked that she leave her issues at the door. To walk into the bar tonight and expect the opportunity to explain, she wouldn't do it.

Paige had *never* kissed another woman in the years she'd been married to James, but could she even call herself a cheat? After her last few exchanges with her husband, Paige didn't plan to see him again. It wasn't a case of letting the air settle and then figuring things out with him. No, she was *way* past that. James wanted to control her, to demean her, to...hurt her. Paige wasn't going back to him, and if she ever did return, it wouldn't be to make amends.

She pushed the door open. The bar was in darkness, but the alarm wasn't set. That meant Juliet was already here, and Paige didn't have time to figure out her next step. She was going to come face to face with Juliet, and there was nothing she could do about it.

She took the stairs, sadness anchored in her stomach when she walked through to the bar. Juliet was sitting on a barstool, hunched over paperwork, just one spotlight above her head illuminating the room. Paige wanted to leave, to forget about the world and run once again, but she was better than that.

"Hey," she spoke quietly so as not to startle Juliet.

Juliet sat upright and turned, removing her glasses. "Hi."

"Are...you not opening today?"

Juliet's forehead creased as she eyed her watch. "Sorry, I didn't realise the time. It's been quite a day." She slid from her stool and turned on the lights, squinting as the room brightened. She moved back to her paperwork, gathering it in her arms. "I'll let you get on. If you need anything, you know where I am."

"Juliet?"

"Yes?" She looked up at Paige, dark circles around her eyes. Eyes that looked a little swollen. Bloodshot.

"Are you okay?"

"Sure. I'll be fine." She threw a thumb over her shoulder, struggling to keep her focus on Paige. "I should finish these invoices." Paige wanted to move closer, to hold Juliet...to touch her. She wanted to find...to *feel* that connection, with the hope of seeing the very same woman she'd met the first time she'd walked in here. God, she wanted to admire her all over again. Because this Juliet was nothing more than a shadow. How she spoke barely above a whisper. How she seemed anxious. How she couldn't even look Paige in the eye. "I'll...get to work. Bye, Paige."

"Of course. Yeah." Paige waited a moment or two, calming her nerves, and took her spot behind the bar. Where she belonged. Where she was at her most comfortable.

Still, she wished things were better with Juliet. Paige wanted to knock on the office door, she wanted to clear the air, but she was worried about the reaction...the response from Juliet. Paige had more than enjoyed that kiss last night, but then she'd fled. Typical, and *clearly* what she was best at. Fleeing...whatever the situation.

Braced against the bar, Paige dropped her head on her shoulders. Could she change the course of her life and do something different? Could she stay and fight off James? Really, he was nothing more than a bully who would be devastated if people knew what he was capable of. But that didn't mean he wouldn't try to find her. To hurt her.

Maybe it's time to call his bluff.

"Excuse me, sorry." Juliet's voice suddenly startled Paige, her heart pounding unexpectedly.

"Jesus." She stood bolt upright, pressing a palm to her chest. "Can you be a bit more obvious next time?"

"I just..." Juliet squeezed past Paige, pointing at the coffee machine as she did so. "I need coffee if I'm going to get through this shift."

"I-I can manage if you'd rather be at home. I don't mind."

"Thanks, but I'm not leaving you alone in here on a Friday night. Cara can't make it in tonight, so—" Juliet focused on the coffee machine, her usual one-shot replaced by a double. "Can I get you anything while I'm here?"

"No, thank you. I should start setting up. If it's as busy as last week, I'd like to be prepared."

Juliet nodded, clearing her throat. She'd been crying. That only hurt Paige's heart more. She hated that her life was this way. "What day do you leave?"

"I'm not sure yet. I didn't have much time to look for another place yesterday. I'll get onto it in the morning."

"Right."

"Juliet, about last night..."

Juliet held up a hand, taking her coffee and walking away from the bar. "Not right now. Please."

"Is everything okay? You seem really tense."

"I'm fine. It's just been a long day. I'll speak to you later, okay?"

"Okay. I *would* really like to talk. I don't want to leave on bad terms with you."

Juliet smiled, shaking her head. "With you? That's not possible."

Paige stifled another yawn, turning her back to do so. She had customers at the bar; it was unprofessional, but tonight, she was dead on her feet. If Juliet had been through the same sleepless night as she had, then her boss was probably napping in the office.

Whatever she was doing, it had been three hours since she'd last seen Juliet.

The security system flashed beneath the bar, the camera outside showing Rachel trying to enter the building. *Great.* Just what she needed. Juliet and Rachel flaunting themselves in front of her. Paige wasn't sure she could stomach such a scene tonight. Because as she'd stood here, once again enjoying her shift, she was quickly realising that it wasn't as simple as just walking away. She cared about Juliet too much. This goodbye was going to be harder than the others.

Nevertheless, she let Rachel into the building, setting a glass out ready for her. She was in Juliet's life whether Paige liked it or not, but soon, she wouldn't have to see it anymore.

"Hi." Paige regarded Rachel with her best smile. Fake, of course. "Large white?"

"Sure." Rachel set her clutch bag down, taking the stool at the end of the bar.

Paige had tried not to think about it, but earlier this morning, she had considered knocking at Juliet's place. She had wanted to make things better between them. That was until she watched Rachel leave Juliet's apartment, and she was glad she hadn't gone anywhere near that door. "I'll just get your drink and then let Juliet know you're here."

Rachel scoffed. "Don't bother."

"Oh, uh...okay." Paige watched Rachel as she placed her head in her hands, confused as to why she was here if she hadn't come for Juliet. "I want to ask if everything is okay, but I'm not sure it's my place to ask."

"You're right. It's *not* your place to ask."

Paige held up her hands and backed away. She had no time for attitudes this evening. She was ready to flip her shit when it came to Rachel, in all honesty. "Okay, I'm sorry."

"Except you're not, are you? You couldn't care less if she cut ties with me," Rachel lifted the glass as soon as Paige placed it down, taking a huge gulp. "Happy now?"

"Um, not particularly, no. If you're going to speak in riddles, you'll be waiting a while for me to catch on."

What the hell was this woman's problem? Paige had never spoken out of turn to her, she'd always treated her with respect, but it seemed just being here was an issue for Rachel.

"This morning," Rachel said, sitting forward on her stool, "Juliet told me she couldn't see me anymore."

"I'm sorry to hear that. If I recall right, she sort of told you the same thing last week, too, so I wouldn't worry too much." Paige wiped down the bar, scanning the room for any empty glasses. Empty glasses meant people expected refills. "And anyway, whatever her reason, I don't know what it has to do with me."

"Oh, it has *everything* to do with you. Trust me."

"Look, if you have something to say, just say it. I can't be arsed trying to figure it out myself."

"How long have you been sleeping with her?" Rachel trailed a fingertip around the rim of her glass, her cold eyes glaring through Paige. "Before you started working here? Since?"

"You think I'm sleeping with Juliet?" Paige asked quietly, aware that the bar was packed tonight. "I don't know what's going on, but I'm *not* sleeping with her. I won't even be here after next week, so you can chill out and stop accusing people of things that aren't true."

Rachel sighed and closed her eyes. "She's really into you,

Paige. I don't care if neither of you wants to acknowledge it, but she is."

Yeah, the kiss had happened, but Paige didn't think it had meant so much to Juliet. Okay, it was clear they were attracted to one another, but what exactly had she told Rachel? "And she's told you this? Because it's news to me."

"She didn't have to tell me. I may have been the one between her legs this morning, but it was your name that she called out."

Paige's heart stuttered. Juliet had slept with Rachel this morning? After kissing Paige just last night? No, Paige couldn't be involved in any of this. It wasn't the kind of life she wanted here in Liverpool. She pulled her shoulders back and cleared the waver she knew her voice would hold. Whatever was going on between Juliet and Rachel, they needed to sort their shit out. Paige could feel hurt later on, but right now, she had a job to do.

Then it dawned on her.

Juliet was fantasising about her?

That surely couldn't be true. "E-excuse me?"

"Ask her."

"I'll do no such thing. You may be quite happy coming in here and talking about Juliet's private life, her intimate life, but I'm not about to do the same thing and humiliate her like that."

Rachel frowned. "What?"

"You're angry, I get that, but coming in here and saying that...whether it's true or not, is really shitty. I may not know you very well, but I still thought you were better than that."

Rachel rolled her eyes. "Just give me another glass of wine."

Paige pressed the silent alarm under the bar that alerted Juliet. "Do you have a membership?"

"You know I don't. But that's never stopped you from serving me before."

"Yeah, well, you don't usually come in here shooting your

mouth off either, so no, I'm not serving you another drink. I can't trust that you will keep the noise to a minimum, and that's not the kind of establishment this is."

Rachel's head whipped around when Juliet came from the back and stood beside her. "It's time to go, Rachel."

"Oh, come to her rescue, have you?"

Juliet stepped closer, pushing what was left in Rachel's wine glass toward Paige. "Get rid of that, please, Paige."

Paige watched Juliet take Rachel by the elbow and guide her down from the stool. She directed her towards the exit, whispered something in Rachel's ear, and watched her leave.

With tears in her eyes, Juliet turned and kept her head down as she moved back towards the door she'd come from. She stopped at the end of the bar, glancing up at Paige. "I'm sorry about whatever she said. I'm just finishing up in the office and I'll be out to help you close up, okay?"

"No rush. I'll call for last orders."

CHAPTER 11
ALL I ASK

Paige swallowed down two paracetamol, closing her eyes where she stood at the kitchen sink. She couldn't shift this headache, and the longer it went on, the less inclined she was to get dressed today. Just the reminder of Juliet locking up the bar last night had tears in Paige's eyes. How they'd walked back to the apartment building together in silence. That wasn't what Paige wanted…but what she *did* want, she couldn't have.

As they'd slowly approached the building, she'd considered inviting Juliet into her apartment so they could talk, but it was almost two in the morning, and Juliet looked as though she was barely able to stand for another second. Paige hated that. How Juliet had struggled to work with her last night. How they'd not spoken about anything other than cocktails, or stock, or…the weather. Juliet was intelligent and intriguing. She was fascinating in Paige's mind. But Paige had somehow reduced her to a quiet introvert who preferred to lock herself away in her office.

All the more reason to pack your things up and go.

Paige groaned as she moved towards the couch. She didn't *want* to pack up and leave. She didn't want to run anymore. She was tired, and she was fed up missing out on opportunities to be happy. Because here, she *was* happy. Stupidly happy, in all honesty. Okay, life wasn't perfect, but Paige knew it could be. The Hideout was going to exceed her expectations, but she needed some time alone to consider what the right thing to do was. James would find her wherever she went. Whether she stayed here and pushed on or moved further away…he *would* catch up with her one of these days.

Perhaps being here and having friends around her would be for the best. If James knew Paige wasn't alone in a big unfamiliar city, he was less likely to intimidate her. And if Paige could show him that the friends she had were considered close friends, he wouldn't show up trying to hammer the door down with his fist. The very same fist he'd broken Paige's nose with in the past.

She shuddered at the thought.

That night had been blocked from her mind the moment it happened. She couldn't think about the man she'd married hurting her. She also couldn't deal with the fact that she'd stayed with him after it. The reason for the broken nose…Paige had been at a bar with him when friends had encouraged her to sing karaoke. She hadn't thought it would be an issue, but the moment they'd arrived home, James changed. The rage in his eyes wasn't like *anything* she'd seen from him before. Yes, he'd always had a temper, but this was an entirely different person.

James had claimed that Paige flirted with multiple men while singing that night. Paige had laughed, and that was the moment when she felt her nose *pop*. The searing pain was short-lived, mostly because of the shock of what he'd done to her. Then came the sheer sadness of the position she found herself in. Her mum was already sick by that point, so she couldn't burden her with it. Harriet wasn't the best person to go to either. So, Paige had said no more about it, hoping it wouldn't happen again.

Only it did.

Many more times.

She tugged on the cuff of the hoodie she was wearing, swallowing down the emotion lodged in her throat. She didn't deserve the life she had with James. Paige had never hurt anyone or done anything untoward. She'd never questioned who James was or the choices he made. She just went about her life and hoped it could be as easy as possible. She'd never felt as though she was in a position to be true to herself, but she could live with that if the man she'd married was half decent.

But he hadn't been. Not by a long stretch of the imagination.

A light knock on the door had Paige getting to her feet. It could only be Juliet. She may not feel as though she was ready to see her this morning, but she'd never ignore her. Juliet had done nothing wrong here. She'd simply found herself attracted to a woman she couldn't have. Vice versa for Paige, too.

Paige opened the door, aware that her face was stained with tears. "Hi."

Juliet smiled weakly, hesitating as she took a step closer. "Are you okay?"

"Yes. I think I'm getting a migraine."

"Oh, then...I can come back another time." Juliet turned to leave, but Paige caught her hand. "Paige, it's okay. You should rest."

"Did you need something?" That was a stupid question to ask, but seeing Juliet this morning had made Paige feel a little safer here. She wasn't quite ready to let her go. "I've just made some coffee."

"I wondered if we could talk."

Paige opened the door and ushered Juliet inside. "Sure. Come in."

"If this isn't a good time for you, we really don't have to do this now."

"Come in, Juliet. I'm fine, and I'll be better once my medication has kicked in."

Juliet reluctantly stepped over the threshold, exhaling a deep breath as she did so. She turned to face Paige, her eyes sweeping up Paige's body. *That* would never not feel good. "So, I know you're leaving…and I wanted to help in some way."

"Help?"

"I have a friend who lives in Gateshead. He owns one of those 'Instagrammable' places that all the celebrities drink at. I called him and asked if he was looking for a new mixologist."

Paige's heart melted. Juliet had done something selfless—something that meant the world to Paige—without even knowing why she was doing it. Still, she didn't want it to be this way.

"I don't know what's going on with you, but I want you to be safe. You're not comfortable confiding in me, and that's okay. It's my own fault for simply being who I am. I know I appear to be quite closed off, but I-I'm trying to work on that. It clearly puts women off." Juliet approached Paige, placing a set of keys in her palm and closing her fingers around them. "You're in trouble. I know the signs from years of working within the criminal justice system, but if you think moving on is for the best, then I won't try to stop you."

Paige frowned when she stared down at the keys in her hand.

"I have some property. I'd considered moving out of Liverpool if the bar hadn't taken off, but well, I'm needed here. My place in Gateshead is empty and I want you to stay there until you don't need to be there anymore. It's close to the train station and is only about fifteen minutes away from Guy's bar."

"Juliet, I—"

"You really don't have to say anything. I think we can both agree that Liverpool is not where you want to be, and I can't wish for something more when you can't even bring yourself to look me in the eye, Paige. I'm sorry about Thursday, I never should have come to the bar, but I'm glad I did. That I got to see you in that other setting. The one that makes your eyes light up when you sit behind the piano. So, thank you. It really is something beautiful."

Paige's bottom lip trembled when she lifted her head and found Juliet's eyes.

"I should go. I have somewhere to be." Juliet tried to step past Paige, but Paige blocked her from leaving. "Please, Paige. I need to go."

"Why?" It took everything Paige possessed not to lean in and kiss Juliet. She was saying all the things Paige had ever dreamed of hearing, but this could never possibly work between them. Paige had far too much going on, and she feared for Juliet's safety if she dared to entertain this for a second.

"Because…" Juliet swallowed when she studied Paige's eyes. Then she lifted a hand and placed it on Paige's cheek. That softness had Paige leaning into Juliet's touch without a second thought. Her lips parted, and for every second Juliet's hand remained, James' beatings evaporated once and for all. "I can't be alone with you anymore. Thursday has only complicated things for me. This…it's too hard for me. To want you…knowing I can't have you."

"I'm sorry."

"Don't be. It's okay. I shouldn't have been there." Juliet leaned in, kissing Paige on the cheek. "See how that migraine goes. If it's no better in a couple of hours, take the weekend off. I can manage."

"Juliet—"

"Bye, Paige. Take it easy."

Paige's forehead creased when she watched Juliet walk away, loneliness setting back in again. She didn't know where to begin with making sense of anything Juliet had just said, but she would consider that offer of taking the weekend off.

Juliet turned her watch towards herself, puffing out her cheeks when she realised Paige was not only taking the night off but not planning to tell her either. She should have been here an hour ago, but Juliet should have expected a no-show. She was beginning to wish she hadn't offered her place in the northeast to Paige; it was only encouraging her to leave. Juliet didn't want that; she *never* wanted that. What she wanted was to sit down and talk this through with Paige, to understand her reasons for leaving so suddenly. Still, she couldn't force it from Paige's mouth.

God, that mouth.

Juliet really needed to get that night out of her head. It was interfering with her sleep, her ability to eat, and it was even discouraging Juliet from being the social butterfly she was. All she wanted to do was curl up under a blanket and wish the days away.

Her phone started to ring on the desk, Paige's name surprising Juliet.

"Hello?"

"Shit, Juliet, I'm so sorry. I went to bed for a few hours to shift this migraine, and I must have slept through my alarm."

She could hear Paige rummaging around. "I'll be there as soon as I can be."

"Paige, take the weekend off. Get your head straight and come back on Monday...if you plan to still be here then."

"I will be. I haven't decided what I'm doing yet."

Juliet's heart fluttered at that admission. Was it possible that Paige would stay? Juliet knew better than to hope for that, but it was still a thought she'd allow to float into her mind occasionally. "Well, whatever you want to do, okay?"

"Juliet?" Paige spoke just above a whisper, her voice soft and soothing.

Juliet closed her eyes, resting her chin in the palm of her hand. If she could listen to Paige talk to her all night, this weekend without her wouldn't be so bad. "Yes?"

"Those things you said earlier. Did you mean them?"

"Of course I meant them. Everything I said was true."

Paige cleared her throat. "Even how you couldn't be alone with me anymore?"

Being alone with Paige was only going to lead to something she couldn't control. That kiss had ignited everything inside Juliet. "Y-yes. I'm sorry."

"It meant something to you, didn't it? The kiss."

Juliet took her bottom lip between her teeth, holding back tears. She couldn't keep crying for something she couldn't have. It was ridiculous. "It meant everything."

"It...meant everything to me, too."

No. Paige couldn't say that. She couldn't admit to feeling something for Juliet, only to leave. She couldn't say these things and walk away. "If that was true, we wouldn't be in the position we're in now."

Paige sighed. "I think I will take the weekend off. I need some time to think. Some space away from anything that could influence me, you know?"

"Whatever you need. Bye, Paige."

With a heavy heart, Juliet locked her phone and set it down on the desk. The bar was open, and Cara was out there alone. It wasn't that Juliet expected Cara to be another Paige, but she just didn't have that flair about her. She didn't show an interest in the customers or create conversation. That was likely down to the fact she was used to working in busier bars, but Juliet hoped Cara would come into her own at some point in the not-too-distant future. The Hideout was supposed to be friendly, and so far, Juliet hadn't seen that from Cara.

She left the office and took the tiny corridor to the bar area. A few familiar faces sat dotted about while Cara stood behind the counter on her phone. "Not busy enough for you?"

"Oh, sorry." Cara shoved her phone into her back pocket, beaming a smile at Juliet. "Is Paige not here tonight?"

"She's taking the weekend off. Migraine."

"Ouch. And there was me thinking it had something to do with the scene your...friend caused a few nights ago."

Juliet stepped closer, lowering her voice. "I'm sorry about that. And for how I spoke to you. It won't happen again."

"You could always make it up to me..."

Juliet's brows rose when Cara's eyes travelled down her body. "Excuse me?"

"For the other night. You could make it up to me."

"And how exactly do you propose I do that?" Juliet folded her arms across her chest, standing heavier on one leg.

"You could agree to have a drink with me." Cara lifted a shoulder.

"Why would we go drinking together?"

"Oh, I didn't mean a girl's night out. I meant 'a drink', you know?" Was Cara asking Juliet out on a date? Christ, was this how Paige had felt when Juliet had asked her the very same question?

"I'm your boss, Cara. I'm not sure why you think that would be appropriate."

"It didn't seem to matter with Paige."

Ah. Cara had not only walked in at the end of Juliet's conversation with Rachel, she'd heard the entire thing. Which meant she knew about Paige and Juliet. "Paige and I are different."

"How so?"

Juliet looked around the bar, satisfied that her clients were occupied, and turned her back on them. She cleared her throat as she stepped closer to Cara and said, "This is my bar. *You* are my staff. Don't question why I do what I do. You're here to work and work only. Got it?"

Cara held up her hands and scoffed. "Jesus. Okay. Anyone else would be happy that someone had asked them out on a date."

"I'm flattered, but no, thank you. I have a business to run, and if you want to be a part of that, stick to the job description."

Cara smirked. "Are you going to insist Paige does the same thing? I think it's only fair since we both work here."

Juliet rolled her eyes and laughed. "Grow up, Cara. Jealousy is *very* distasteful."

Leaving the bar counter, Juliet made herself busy around the clients. It was bad enough that she had Paige on her mind. She didn't need Cara and her petty behaviour too. It was Saturday night; she had work to do.

Work she could focus on instead of what was really in her heart.

Paige Harrison.

CHAPTER 12
LOVE IN THE DARK

On unsteady legs, Juliet left her office and walked into the dimly lit bar area. The Hideout had emptied, not a soul in sight, and Cara had left already. It was Monday, a quiet night overall, but Juliet felt far more tired than usual. The likelihood was that it was caused by her lack of sleep over the weekend. Whatever she did, she couldn't shake Paige from her mind. Right now, she just wanted to see her. To know that she was okay. It had been three weeks since Paige had started working at The Hideout—and she hadn't shown for her shift. Only this time, she *hadn't* called Juliet to tell her she wouldn't be available. Juliet couldn't help but feel it was personal.

She slung her satchel over her shoulder, yawning as she moved behind the bar to turn out the rest of the lights. But a figure sat on the couch, familiar perfume reaching Juliet's nose before she could panic.

It was Paige.

She sat with her elbows on her knees, her head bowed with her hands clasped. Juliet knew Paige was here to say goodbye— her body language gave it away—but she was appreciative of her coming over to tell her. She could have fled in the night, but she hadn't.

Juliet straightened herself, prepared for whatever Paige needed or wanted to say, and stopped in front of the table. "Hey."

"Poured you a drink," Paige said, looking up at Juliet with tired yet beautiful eyes. "And I figured I'd pour myself one if there's any chance of being honest with you."

Juliet nodded, a faint smile on her lips. "Whatever you need. I told you I was here for you. That hasn't changed."

Paige patted the couch beside her, cocking her head towards the empty spot. "Sit down. Let's talk."

Juliet wasn't sure she wanted to go through this. It had taken her a million years to be in a position to have a relationship, and Paige was the woman she'd set her sights on. While she wasn't spoilt and didn't expect the world, their kiss had shown Juliet just the kind of electricity they had between them. All weekend, she'd felt miserable. She hadn't wanted to leave her apartment this afternoon. Knowing Paige was leaving the bar *and* the city had really affected her. She couldn't say why, but again, it all came back to that kiss. The voice too.

Juliet wished Paige could see what everyone else likely did when they looked at her, but she was beginning to understand that Paige was leaving...and there was nothing she could do about it. She was going to miss this woman far more than Juliet would openly admit. They may have only just been learning about one another, but Juliet couldn't deny that connection, however hard she tried.

She sat down, took a tiny sip from the small glass of wine Paige had poured her, and exhaled a breath. "How are you?"

"Not good." Paige's voice trembled; her stare focused directly ahead of her. "I shouldn't have left you in the lurch this weekend. I'm so angry with myself for not calling you this morning. You deserve better than that. This *is not* me."

"It's okay. You needed space, and I understand."

"But I shouldn't need space. I don't even know you, Juliet. We've known one another for three weeks, and really, that's not a lot at all."

Juliet could see where Paige was from coming from, but she'd focused on the connection, so the fact they'd known one another for just a few weeks was irrelevant in Juliet's opinion. "Well, it's done now. It doesn't really matter."

Paige suddenly turned to Juliet, the torment in her eyes catching Juliet off guard. "I'm really sorry about Thursday night."

That wasn't how she wanted the conversation to begin. With an apology...for the kiss. Had Paige regretted it, even if she'd said otherwise on the phone? "You don't have to apologise. It's okay. I took the hint the moment you fled the bar. But I also take full responsibility. *I* kissed you."

"Oh, no. I'm apologising for *leaving*. Not for kissing you. Unless you want me to say sorry for that..."

Juliet instantly covered Paige's hand. "No. Please don't say sorry for that."

"Okay, good." Paige smiled, her cheeks reddening.

And then Juliet suddenly had the urge to say some stuff when Paige fell silent. "Look, can we start again? No Rachel in the picture. No running away. Just...start from the beginning."

Paige chewed her lip, shaking her head. "I want that, but I'm not sure there will ever be a picture *without* Rachel in it."

"Rachel and I are...not going to be seeing one another for a long while. And never again how we once did."

Paige watched Juliet, inspecting every inch of her face. Of course she would have doubts. Juliet had done very little to show Paige that Rachel wasn't going to be an issue. "Then yes. I think the beginning is the best place to start. For me, anyway."

Juliet reached for her glass, sat back on the couch, and tried to be as calm and relaxed as she possibly could. She suspected that was the version of herself Paige would need. "You should know that *nothing* can shock me with the work I used to do." She laced their fingers together between their thighs, squeezing Paige's hand. "I know you need to talk, so please, trust me."

"I'm...married."

Juliet instinctively loosened her grip on Paige's hand as immense disappointment shot through her. But she would still listen, and if Paige needed it, offer whatever help she could. She hadn't exactly lied to Juliet. Paige *had* stated she was just out of a relationship. "Okay."

"And before you sit there wondering whether I've cheated, I haven't. I'm trying to leave, but he's making it painfully hard for me to do so."

"I...don't understand," Juliet said, her brows drawn.

"You probably think I'm just shagging my way from city to city." Paige lowered her drink and dragged a hand through her hair. "But I'm really not. I *promise you* I'm not. You're the first woman, the first and *only* person I've even kissed since I married him. Feel free to take that however you want to take it."

"I'm not sure what the issue is then. If you're not together anymore, why are you so worried?"

"He's under the impression that we *are* still together. I've told him I'm not coming home; I've asked him for a divorce, but...well, it's not really working out for me. He already knows I'm here. He's coming for me."

"Coming for you?" Juliet quirked a brow, shocked by the choice of words Paige had used. "And what's he going to do when he gets here? Sling you over his shoulder and ride off on his fucking white horse?"

Paige lifted her drink again, staring into the bottom of the glass. "Nothing quite as romantic as that."

Juliet suddenly realised what Paige was saying, her blood running a little colder than she would have liked it to. She took Paige's drink from her hand, brought their hands together, and dipped her head. The look she witnessed was one she'd seen many times over the years. Usually during a domestic violence case. "You really are in trouble, aren't you?"

"Possibly. P-probably."

Juliet saw the fear flash in Paige's eyes again. The usual intriguing grey was hesitant and wary. "Tell me what you need."

"I just need him to let me go."

Juliet felt the pain as Paige spoke those words. She felt the distress and the knowledge that Paige didn't feel safe. God, she hated all of that. She lowered Paige's hands to her lap, instead bringing her face into her hands. "You're safe with me, okay?"

"But I'm not." Paige sniffled, casting her gaze on the space between them. "I've never been safe *with* him, and I never will be *while* he's around. The first time I left, when I went back, he gave me two black eyes."

Juliet wasn't prepared for this conversation. Because as she'd left the office tonight, she hadn't anticipated it. Not this. The severity of why Paige continued to run. "I'm sorry he ever laid a hand on you."

"He doesn't know I'm gay...nobody does. I feel like I'm drowning, Juliet. I don't know what to do."

"I know people who can castrate him if that's any help." That may have achieved a smile from Paige, but... "I'm serious. Never underestimate the people I know. If you need protection, say the word, and I'll make a call."

Paige held up a hand. "Can we not talk about him anymore tonight? I already have to leave again, and I don't have much time with you because of that. And I know, *I know* I'm here to talk to you, to explain, but that's all you need to know for now. I'd rather just be with you. Here, in the quiet. Can we do that? It's just...*you do* make me feel safe. And I just want to be here, where I *do* feel protected, and spend what little time I can with you. I'll never have the chance at something more with you, so this... I'd like this to be what we can have."

Oh, Juliet's heart broke at those words. Paige wanted there to be time for them; that meant far more than she could ever know. Even if she still planned to leave.

Paige leaned into Juliet's touch, her eyes closing for a brief moment when Juliet stroked her thumb across Paige's cheek. "I just wanted to tell you that Thursday was something extremely special for me. Not only did you kiss me at the end of the night, but you showed up for me. You'll never know how much that means, okay?" Paige leaned in, touching her forehead to Juliet's. "Nobody *ever* shows up for me. They're all obsessed with James and how perfect he apparently is. When it comes to me and what I want, I'm left to fight for it alone. My family and friends don't see me as *anything* unless he's around. I say family very loosely, though. Since I don't really have anyone left. Few cousins, the odd long-distance great aunt, but that's about all. My mum was the only one who ever really supported me. But even that was only based on the side of my life I chose to show her. My singing, though, she always supported that."

Juliet ghosted a thumb across Paige's bottom lip. God, she wanted to move in and kiss her, to take away the pain in her voice, but Paige needed a space to talk, and that was what Juliet would provide. "Not anymore. I'll always show up for you, Paige."

"I can't stay." Paige's voice broke, bringing tears to Juliet's eyes. "I want to, you don't know how desperately I want to be here, but I *can't* stay. When he finds me..." Paige looked into

Juliet's eyes, cold and filled with torment. "Because he always does...I don't know if I can survive it again."

"I know this must be difficult, but he cannot access this bar unless you or I let him in."

"He'll find out where I'm living. He has friends, people who have nothing better to do than whatever he asks. He probably already knows where I live. It's just a waiting game until he reaches me."

"You shouldn't have to live your life that way." Juliet tucked Paige's hair behind her ear, smiling as Paige inched closer and their lips brushed. She wanted this just as much as Juliet did. "If you'd like my help, you just let me know what you want, and I'll do anything I can to make it happen."

"You. I want you. *Wanted*...you." Paige swallowed; clear emotion lodged in her throat. "I never should have even looked at you. Or thought about you. Because I can't have you, and even though we don't really know one another, I feel as though it could have been something really good between us."

Juliet smiled, capturing Paige's lips. They tasted just as good, if not better, than the last time they'd kissed. "Does it help to know that I want you, too?"

"No. It makes it all worse."

Juliet kissed Paige again. "Why?"

"Because it doesn't matter what either of us want. I won't put you through all this shit too. I can barely look after myself."

"All I ask is that you trust me. That you believe I'm here for you. If you can do so, I promise you'll be safe with me."

Paige's eyes brightened at those words. Even if they hadn't found themselves attracted to one another, Juliet still would have done anything she could to make Paige safe. The fact that she *did* want her only made Juliet more determined to follow through on her promise.

"How?"

Juliet scoffed. "Because I've had to deal with pricks like him for most of my career."

Paige gripped the front of Juliet's blouse, pulling her impossibly close. "And why the hell would you want to keep dealing with them now that you're no longer a lawyer?"

"Because some people are important to me."

"You don't even know me. How can I possibly be important to you?"

"I've had quite a few women in my life in the past, I don't deny that, but not a single one of them has made me feel how you made me feel from a simple kiss. *None*. I can't recall a single woman kissing me like that."

"So, you're basing all of this off a single kiss?" Paige laughed, pulling back a little. "Seriously?"

"Yes. I am. Because it's that connection for me. So, I suggest you kiss me again to remind me why I'm so captured by you." Juliet cocked her head, her eyes narrowed. "Unless you changed your mind?"

Paige opened her mouth to protest but fell short of any words. She leaned in, rolling her tongue across Juliet's, gripping her thigh just the way she had on Thursday night.

"Mmm." Juliet moaned, pulling Paige against her. The response she expected from that delicious mouth. "Exactly like that."

"Y-you...you're out of your mind."

"Maybe I am, but it's nice to be out of my mind for a little while."

Paige leaned back in, shifting until Juliet was on her back, and Paige was braced above her. "Juliet..."

"What is it?" She held Paige's gaze, noting the desire.

Paige leaned down, smiling against her lips as she whispered, "I want to touch you."

"*Where* do you want to touch me, Paige?"

With a steady hand, Paige squeezed Juliet's breast, grazing a thumb against her nipple. Juliet bent the knee between Paige's legs, smirking when Paige rocked against her thigh, moaning. "All over."

"Here? Now?"

"N-no." Paige closed her eyes, her lips parted when she continued to rock back and forth. "Fuck, not here."

God, just watching this woman enjoy life for a brief second turned Juliet on like never before. She lifted her head and took Paige's bottom lip between her teeth, smirking when her breathing became laboured. "You need to come, don't you?"

All Paige could manage was a barely audible "y-yes."

"I'd love nothing more than to watch you come, Paige." Juliet forced her hand between them, struggling past the waistband of Paige's jeans. When she discovered Paige wasn't wearing any underwear, Juliet melted into the couch. "Oh, *you* are just a delight." Juliet almost came when her fingertips found scorching heat, a wetness she hadn't known was possible. Paige's clit throbbed against her fingers, the desire she had for this woman only increasing tenfold. "You feel so beautiful."

"J-Juliet, oh, fuck."

"Let go, Paige." Paige's arm shook where it was braced, her eyes slowly opening as she stared down at Juliet. "Go on. Let me feel you."

"Oh, God." Paige rocked harder; their eyes locked. When her body trembled, Paige's mouth hanging open, Juliet could only grin and watch on with sheer delight. "Fuck, I'm coming."

"Mm. For me. And what a gorgeous sight it is." Paige shook against Juliet, her arm almost giving out. When she slowed the kiss and slumped against Juliet, Paige let out the most incredible moan. "Well, I didn't expect the night to end like this."

"I-I can't believe that's just happened."

Wanting to remind Paige of exactly what had just happened, Juliet slid her hand from Paige's pants and brought her fingers to her own lips. She drew her tongue up her fingers, licking Paige from them, and sighed. "Well, it did. And you taste amazing."

CHAPTER 13
WHEREVER YOU WILL GO

Juliet closed her office door, checking the clock on the wall as she took a seat behind her desk. She had around thirty minutes before Paige arrived for her shift, neither of them knowing what today would bring. Would Paige be just as apprehensive as Juliet felt? She'd wanted to call Paige, more so to ask how she was feeling about Juliet knowing her home life situation, but she'd decided against it. After how their night had ended, Juliet wanted to give Paige some space to breathe.

Juliet laid in bed last night, truly shocked by the turn of events, so Paige had to be feeling immensely confused too. Perhaps confused was the wrong word, but...she would certainly be feeling something about it.

As she pulled herself closer to her desk, she brought up a familiar number on her speed dial.

"Yes?"

"It's me." She sat back, crossing her legs. "You may have noticed I have someone working at the bar."

"The blonde or the redhead?"

"The blonde," Juliet said, smiling when Paige and that sexy moan floated into her thoughts. "Can you keep an eye on her, please? More so at my apartment block. She's living in the same building as me. Anyone new coming and going or hanging around, I need to know. And if anything changes, I'll let *you* know."

"Will do. Got it."

The call cut out—a standard response when Juliet spoke to the guy who was already protecting her. She'd wanted to tell Paige that she also didn't lead an ordinary life, but it would have been too much in that moment. Paige was already wary of her husband finding her; to add Juliet's own worries to that situation would have surely seen Paige fleeing. Without a doubt.

With a coffee now in her hand, and her gorgeous bartender on her mind, Juliet enjoyed her first hit of caffeine since seven this morning. Juliet felt so alive today that she wasn't sure she actually needed caffeine. She was high on Paige Harrison.

"Hello?"

And there was that voice. The woman who had given herself over to Juliet last night without a second thought. There was something incredibly sexy about Paige when she let go, and Juliet couldn't wait to see that far more often.

"Juliet?"

"In here." She called out, spinning in her seat as the office door opened. "Good afternoon."

"H-hey." Paige's face flushed instantly, her eyes darting around the room. "The door wasn't locked. Someone could have broken in while you were in here."

"Oops. Must have forgotten to lock it behind me." Juliet lowered her cup, standing and stalking towards Paige. "Did you lock it on your way down?"

"Yeah."

"Convenient." Juliet curled her fingers through Paige's belt loop, pulling their bodies together. "How was your morning?"

"It was...a lot."

Juliet's brows drew together. "Why?"

"I woke up thinking about last night. About you. I wasn't quite sure what to do with myself, so I just sat there, looking out the window."

"You should have called me."

"I couldn't. I needed a minute to think. Last night *did* happen, didn't it?"

Juliet beamed a smile. It wasn't often women were speechless and shocked about her. She'd never had the chance to find that before now. "It did happen, yes."

"Right. Okay." Paige straightened the lapels on Juliet's blazer, focusing anywhere but on Juliet's face. "So, um..."

"Talk to me, Paige. Tell me what you're thinking."

"That maybe I should ask you out on a date or something? We sort of jumped right in at the deep end, didn't we?"

"I'm not worried. The deep end is the best part. That's where all the fun happens."

"Fun." Paige nodded slowly, finally lifting her eyes to Juliet's. While they sparkled, she did note the slight hint of uncertainty. "Is that what this is?"

"I'm hoping not, but why don't we just take it one day at a time? I think you need to let it sink in first." Juliet didn't want this to be fun. The connection she felt with Paige was far more than fun. But Paige did need to know if this was really what she wanted before anything else. She was the one who wasn't out. She was the one who had a bastard husband.

"Yeah. I just didn't expect it. Even as we were talking, I didn't expect it. Not for one moment. But thank you," Paige said, curling her hand around the back of Juliet's neck and pulling her into a lingering kiss. "For not judging me. For listening...a-and for what followed."

"I'll never judge you, Paige. You're going through a lot, and I'm here for you. Remember that."

"I would like to see you again. You know, outside of work."

"I'd like to see you again, too. In here, out there, wherever you want to be." Juliet feathered a fingertip across Paige's cheek, watching as her features softened and her shoulders relaxed. "Hey, you don't need to be tense around me."

"I'm just permanently tense lately. It's not you. You make me feel calm."

"I do?" A smile spread on Juliet's mouth, her heart fluttering. When Paige said things like that, Juliet felt like an entirely different woman from who she once was. "You mean that?"

"I mean it."

"Wow, well—"

Paige pressed her fingertip to Juliet's lips, shaking her head. "Don't say anything. Just keep being the woman I met, and I'll be more than happy."

"Okay."

"Can I make us some coffee before I get ready to open? I have a feeling it's going to be a busy night."

"Why so?" Juliet lowered her hand and gripped Paige's arse. And what a fine arse it was. She squeezed, wanting to devour her, but pulled away. "Sorry, I find it very hard to keep my hands off you."

Paige lifted Juliet's hand and kissed her skin, smiling. "Because I'm feeling good today. Better than I've felt in a long time. And yes, I'm finding it hard to keep my hands to myself, too."

That flash of desire crossed Paige's features. If Juliet didn't curb this now, the bar would be opening late.

"You know, I think you could be right about how busy it'll be. And today, I think I'll set up with you."

Paige's brows rose as she rolled her lips inward.

"What?" Juliet took the slightest step back, studying Paige's features.

"You...can't touch anything once I've laid it out. Okay?"

Juliet smoothed her finger up the middle of Paige's throat, squinting. "Nothing at all?"

"Well, no. I like it to be in a certain order. I know where everything is then."

"Not...even you? Can I touch *you* when you're laid out?"

Paige visibly swallowed, her mouth opening and closing.

"Last night was *very* special, Paige." Juliet drew Paige in, one arm wrapped around her, her other hand holding the back of her neck. "Watching you come undone above me. Those eyes." Juliet moaned lightly, her eyes closing. "God, it was a sight."

"I wanted to touch you," Paige whispered, her forehead pressed to Juliet's. "I *still* want to touch you."

"Don't worry. Once this night is over, you can touch me wherever you want...whenever you want."

Paige dipped her head, taking Juliet's bottom lip between her teeth. She loved this version of her bartender. The boldness, the arousal, the intensity. "I'm not sure I can wait that long."

"Try being me, knowing what that mouth is capable of."

"Another?" Paige nodded to the glass in front of Pete, one of the regulars.

"Please, Paige." He gave her a thumbs-up and went back to his conversation.

For the first time since she started working at The Hideout, she felt as though she belonged. That wasn't because Juliet had unexpectedly slid her hand down the front of her jeans last night—though it helped—it was because she felt as though she could breathe. For the first time in her life, Paige felt as though she could stand here this evening...and be who she was.

A woman who loved women. A woman who enjoyed and appreciated everything other women had to offer. A woman who, just last night, had let go without a care in the world. Because in that moment, when she braced herself above Juliet and decided to be brave, she *did* feel invincible. She felt whole. She felt...wanted.

It was a feeling Paige could never forget. It was also a feeling she never wanted to be without again. So much had happened in the last three weeks that she'd barely had time to breathe, but it was the good stuff. Not the terrible things she was used to. Running away, hiding from a life she wished she'd never gotten herself involved in. No, *this* was the beautiful part of life.

New, but oh so beautiful.

She set a French brandy down in front of Pete and then moved along the bar. It was steady tonight, but that was just another thing she loved about working here. It wasn't manic like some places she'd worked at. The pace was chilled out, nobody having disagreements or taking fights out onto the streets. It just showed that when people wanted to, they could consume alcohol safely and in a respectful manner.

Juliet was talking with customers, Paige was resting until the next person came along, and life was fucking fantastic. It didn't matter if she still had James to deal with. Tonight, she was truly happy.

A sudden wave—a need—to perform washed over her. She didn't hesitate; she didn't consider if she was doing the right thing. If Paige was beginning to realise anything, it was that The Hideout made her far happier than she thought it could. It was just supposed to be another bar in a long line of bar-hopping. But it was Juliet's support—that look in her eye when she spoke about Paige performing in the past—that had her *wanting* to do this for her. Here, tonight, Paige *needed* to enjoy her voice. She took a sip from her glass of water and moved across the bar area to the piano.

She sat down, rolling her head on her shoulders as she silently stroked the black and white keys beneath her fingertips. She felt at home behind the piano. She felt free and uninhibited. She felt...like Paige.

The first press of the keys had the bar falling silent, people shushing their partners and friends. The hairs on the back of Paige's neck bristled, but it wasn't fear she felt. It wasn't James' voice as he belittled her. No, it was Juliet's as she encouraged her and reminded her of what she was capable of.

The melody of Charlene Soraia's version of "Wherever You Will Go" played through the tiniest bar Paige had ever had the pleasure of working at, just the sound of her own heartbeat accompanying it.

And then she started to sing, her lungs not filled with air but euphoria. God, she'd missed this. The freedom to sing, to *feel*. The freedom to enjoy her voice and her talent without someone, somewhere, telling her she couldn't do it. She couldn't make it. She was a failure.

Because Paige wasn't. She may have failed at being her true self for too long, but tonight? Oh, tonight, she was a winner in every aspect of her life.

Chancing a look up at Juliet, what she found staring back stole her breath. Juliet rested against the wall to the side of the bar, her arms wrapped around herself. She wore the most beautiful smile, her huge brown eyes shining. Glistening.

She barely knew this woman, but she had so much to thank her for. The job, the self-confidence, the heart Juliet was beginning to repair. It hadn't been James who'd broken it; he didn't deserve an accolade so important. It was Paige who'd broken her own heart. By not being honest, by not living life on her terms, by running.

She was tired of running, tired of fighting, and tired of hurting. Paige was done with it all. It was time to live for herself.

When her fingers slowed against the keys, the song coming to an end, the bar remained silent. Not a breath could be heard. Okay, that wasn't the reaction she expected. And then one of the businessmen who spent every night here got to his feet and started to clap, followed by another table of men, then the table where their wives sat. Paige grinned, eyeing Juliet, who was wiping tears from her cheeks. She hated seeing Juliet cry, but if she was crying because of Paige's talent, then she had to be doing something right.

"Bloody fantastic, Paige!" One of the men patted her on the shoulder as she moved back towards the bar. "We expect more of that. Juliet! Sign this girl up right now!"

Juliet grinned and nodded, her voice trembling. "Oh, I intend to, Rick."

As Paige approached Juliet, she was suddenly enveloped by the most incredible embrace. Juliet held onto her as though she was about to run away, but Paige only wrapped her arms around her waist and held her in return. "Thank you," Paige said, nuzzling into Juliet's neck. "For bringing my voice back. For believing in me."

"Oh, Paige." Juliet kissed her temple, her lips lingering. "I'll believe in you every day."

"I'm...not running. Ever again."

Juliet pulled back, that smile spreading further. "No? You're sure?"

"I'm not sure I've ever been so certain before. But yes, I'm sure. If you think I can be a good fit here, then I'm staying."

"You *are* a good fit here. You've proved that already."

Paige's arms hung loosely around Juliet's waist, both of

them aware that they were working. "And you know, it doesn't even matter if you and I don't go any further. I'm happy here, regardless of that. But I do want to try. With you."

"I'm not sure you have to try, beautiful. You know how I feel about you."

"Can we walk home together tonight?" Paige asked, hoping the rest of the night would entail more than just walking home together.

"It depends if I'm leaving you at your door or you're following me to mine," Juliet whispered, slipping her hand into the back pocket of Paige's jeans.

"I think we both know the answer to that."

CHAPTER 14
LAST OF THE TRUE BELIEVERS

Juliet lowered her keys to the kitchen island and kicked off her heels, aware of Paige's nerves as they'd walked through the door together. While they both wanted to take this further, Juliet knew she had to be patient. She knew that Paige wasn't as open as she was when it came to letting go. Sure, Paige had let go last night when she'd come to the bar to speak to Juliet, but a lot had changed since then. Emotions were now fully involved. The stakes had well and truly been upped.

"Did you—"

Juliet was cut off when Paige rushed towards her, gripping the blouse she wore beneath her suit jacket. Their lips met with an urgency, and as Juliet stumbled back against the counter, Paige was already undoing the buttons.

"I don't want to talk anymore. I just want to touch you." Paige spoke so breathlessly that Juliet wondered if she needed a moment to actually breathe. But then she kicked that from her mind. Knowing this woman wanted her so much was doing unimaginable things to her body. "Last night..." Paige trailed her lips along Juliet's jaw, moaning as her fingertips reached Juliet's skin. "Shouldn't have happened how it did."

Juliet didn't care how it happened, so long as it did happen. And it had. Just the thought of Paige above her had sent her wild with want multiple times today.

"But this," Paige said, dragging Juliet away from the counter and through her living room. "This is the right time."

They stumbled their way towards Juliet's bedroom, Paige's back now pressed to the closed door. Juliet brought a hand up to her jaw, holding it as she looked into Paige's gorgeous eyes. "Do you have any idea what you do to me, Paige?"

Paige didn't blush, she didn't dip her head, she just grazed her nails down Juliet's stomach, more wetness gathering between Juliet's legs. "Tell me."

"Fuck, if only I could." Juliet pressed herself to Paige. She could only imagine how amazing the rest of this night was going to be. She took the hand resting on her stomach and guided it past the waistband of her pants. Paige didn't take her eyes off Juliet. No, she stared deep into her soul as Juliet guided her lower. And lower. Until...

"Oh, fuck." Paige took her bottom lip between her teeth.

"I'm not sure I've ever been so wet for anyone in my entire life." Juliet's voice was gravelly, her lips parted, and her eyes closed when Paige slowly rolled her fingertips over her clit. "Y-you, oh—"

"I can't believe I'm here with you."

Juliet chose to bookmark that, instead reaching around Paige and opening her bedroom door. They stumbled through it, just the moonlight illuminating the bedroom through the floor-to-ceiling windows.

Paige lifted her hand and feathered her fingertips across Juliet's cheek, smiling. "So fucking beautiful."

"Paige..."

Paige stared into Juliet's eyes, her hand stilling. "Yeah?"

"Thank you for trusting me."

Paige leaned in, kissing Juliet slowly, sensually. She ran her tongue across Juliet's bottom lip, and then she turned her, Juliet's legs connecting with the bed. She pushed her down to the mattress, slid her blazer from her shoulders, and took a step back.

Juliet would never tire of Paige admiring her. A thirty-year-old...hot for Juliet, who was close to fifty. Yeah, she'd never forget how Paige made her feel, even if this didn't work out.

"I don't know where to begin." Paige slipped her own jacket off, dropping it to the floor where she stood.

"How about you start by undressing for me?" Juliet rested back on her elbows, smirking as Paige lowered her hands to the button on her jeans. "I could do it myself, but I want to watch you."

Paige pushed her jeans down her legs, stepping out of them and kicking them to the pile she was making with her jacket. She looked up at Juliet, that desire intensifying in her eyes, and brought her fingers to the hem of her T-shirt. She lifted it above her head, so effortless in her movements. Her blonde hair fell back into place, that unexpected confidence Paige exuded knocking the wind out of Juliet. She couldn't wait for a fully confident Paige Harrison. It was sexy as hell. Then Juliet focused on the tattoo that began under Paige's breasts, continued down her stomach and around the sides, finishing down one hip as it trailed off at her thigh. Oh, God. Juliet was one lucky woman. "Better?"

"God, yes." Juliet stood, pulling Paige in by the waist. Her skin felt soft beneath Juliet's fingertips, the room calm. "I can't wait to taste you again."

"I'm *dying* to touch you," Paige spoke low as she gripped Juliet's backside and pulled them flush together. "Really dying to touch you."

"Well, we can't keep you waiting, can we?" The smirk Juliet

wore had Paige grinning, and as she quickly unbuttoned the rest of her blouse, Paige's eyes drifted lower.

"Fucking hell."

"I'm going to assume that's a good fucking hell." Juliet shrugged her blouse from her shoulders, adding it to Paige's pile of clothes. She shuddered when Paige ghosted a fingertip over the swell of her breast, her bottom lip firmly between her teeth.

"A very good one." Paige leaned in, replacing her fingertip with her lips. "God, you're so gorgeous, Juliet."

Juliet instinctively lifted a hand and fisted it in Paige's hair, her head thrown back as she kissed along one breast, then the other. But it was when Paige lowered Juliet's bra that her body truly came alive. Those lips enveloped her painfully taut nipple, sucking gently, her teeth grazing. "Jesus, Paige. O-oh, fuck."

Paige looked up at Juliet with hooded eyes, smirking against her skin. "You feel so good." Paige teased her fingertips along the waistband of Juliet's pants, popping the button and bringing them down her thighs. But it wasn't only Juliet's pants she was losing; her underwear was going too. "I need to be inside you." Paige frantically forced her pants the rest of the way down. The least Juliet could do was put her out of her misery and kick them the rest of the way off.

The second they were gone, Paige slowly kissed her way down between Juliet's cleavage, her stomach, until she was on her knees in front of Juliet. That would never not be incredibly arousing. Paige looked up at Juliet as she pressed her thumb between Juliet's lips, those eyes too much to take right now. And then Juliet offered a nod, encouraging Paige to take over this entire night.

"Lie down," Paige said, her voice hoarse and laced with desire.

As Juliet removed her bra and positioned herself on the bed,

Paige wrapped her hands around her thighs and pulled Juliet nearer to the edge. That tongue slid so effortlessly through Juliet's folds that she arched up, trying desperately to not clamp her thighs shut. Paige hummed her approval, her thumb teasing Juliet's clit while her tongue moved lower and towards her entrance.

Euphoric.

Paige slowly eased her tongue inside Juliet and applied more pressure to her clit. "P-Paige, fuck!"

"Mmm. You like that?"

"Oh, I fucking love it." Juliet rocked her hips when Paige dove back in, the urge to come for this woman leaving her teetering on the edge. "God, that mouth."

Paige replaced her tongue with her fingers, stood, and rested between Juliet's legs. When she drew Juliet into a kiss, Juliet's arousal covering her lips, Paige sunk two fingers inside her slowly. Paige drew back, touching her forehead to Juliet's, and whispered, "I don't want this night to end."

Juliet stroked the back of Paige's neck and smiled. "We're going to have so many more moments like this, Paige."

"Promise me," Paige said, the heel of her hand pressing against Juliet's clit. She couldn't hold on much longer; it simply wasn't possible. "Promise me that whatever happens, I'll have the chance to touch you again."

"Oh, I promise." Juliet rocked her hips against Paige's hand, that delicious sensation far more intense than it had been with any woman in a long time. "Paige, please...make me come."

Paige grinned, pushing in and out of Juliet a little faster, a little harder, so fucking deep.

"Y-yes, oh, y-yes." Juliet's entire body came alive, one hand fisting in the bed sheet, the other holding Paige against her. Her walls tightened, the sound of just how wet she was for this woman only turning Juliet on more. "I...I'm coming."

"Mm." Paige thrust harder, her own hips bucking against her hand as Juliet roared her approval. "God, I could watch you come over and over," Paige captured Juliet's lips in a fierce kiss, tongues rolling, their bodies shaking. And then Paige slowed, still teasing Juliet, as she whispered, "Where the hell did I find you?"

Juliet was asking herself the very same question. Paige had come into her life so unexpectedly that she was surely going to disappear at some point. "Don't think about that right now."

"No?"

"No, beautiful. It's my turn to really taste you. But I have a question."

"Fire away." Paige propped herself up against Juliet.

"How...do you feel about toys?"

As Juliet watched Paige's features change, she didn't wait for a response. When her eyes lit up, they told Juliet everything she needed to know.

"Oh, it's time for you to get completely naked."

Paige woke to the sound of the coffee machine grinding beans, the scent of Juliet enveloping her in the most soothing of ways. While this may feel unusual for her, waking up in another woman's bed, Paige wasn't going to let it freak her out. Because that could easily happen if she allowed it to, without a doubt.

No, this morning, she was going to enjoy being here...and whatever else came with dating Juliet Saunders. She didn't *need* to overthink. She didn't *need* to worry about the future. The here and now was what mattered today. Just Paige and Juliet, doing their own thing...together.

She stretched her body the length of the bed, grinning—and groaning—when it slowly started to come alive. Paige couldn't say she'd ever partaken in marathon sex before, but she planned to do it a whole lot more now that she'd been introduced. Juliet, the way her hands stroked Paige's skin so deftly... phew, that woman knew what she was doing.

With the smell of coffee growing stronger, Paige reluctantly sat up in bed, the sheet wrapped around her, shoulders exposed. Did she have to leave this bed today? Could she at least stay here until midday? The apartment she was renting was great, amazing given the fact that it was right in the city centre, but Juliet wasn't there. Her presence wouldn't linger or her perfume. No, Paige wanted to be here for as long as Juliet would have her today.

Paige considered climbing from the bed, but Juliet came sauntering into the bedroom wearing that sexy smile Paige adored. "Mornin'."

"Good morning," Juliet said, placing a cup of coffee on the bedside table next to Paige. "Sleep well?"

"What little sleep I *did* get, I slept very well." Paige lifted her coffee, wrapping her hands around the cup and bringing it to her lips. Even Juliet's coffee was perfect. "Don't worry, I'll get out of your hair soon."

Juliet slid into bed, unfortunately wearing her robe. But that could only be a good thing in Paige's mind. It meant they would actually make it to the bar later. "You're welcome to hang around here for as long as you want. I have no plans before I open the bar."

Paige shifted closer to Juliet, craving that warmth and security. "Thanks for having me over last night."

"Oh, no. Thank *you*." Juliet turned her face, kissing Paige on the temple. "How are you feeling this morning?"

"About what?"

"Everything, I guess." Juliet slid further down the bed, resting against the headboard. She held her coffee in her lap, the silence of the room calming. "Mostly us, but everything else, too."

"I'm feeling good. About us. Everything else is just a lot."

"Understandable."

"It's hard to know what to do and when to do it, you know?" Paige felt incredibly lucky to have someone like Juliet by her side. Someone who didn't demand she be open about who she was. Someone who didn't beat her to make themselves feel better. "I want *so much* to just tell everyone about leaving James, about who I really am, but then the coward in me prevails, and I talk myself out of it."

"Your safety is what I'm concerned about more than anything. When the time is right, you'll come out, but until then...I just want you to feel safe, Paige. Because the rest doesn't really matter. Not to me, anyway. You have me regardless of who knows the truth."

Until when, though? Paige wanted to ask. She couldn't expect Juliet to keep their relationship quiet forever, nor would she ever want her to. But she appreciated what Juliet was saying. "I don't want to hide anymore."

"I know." Juliet took Paige's hand on top of the sheet, squeezing it. "But let's just go slow with all of this and not worry about it."

Paige would love nothing more than to forget James existed and enjoy her life, but it really wasn't that simple. The thought of him creeping up unexpectedly was enough for Paige to *always* watch her back. Even when the truth came out, she knew she wouldn't fully settle. Stepping away from her marriage wasn't going to be so cut and dry. "I really wish I didn't have to worry about it. But you're right. I *do* just want to enjoy being here with you."

"Then we should do that. Enjoy one another."

Paige lowered her coffee cup to the bedside table, turning

back and snuggling into Juliet. "We should. Because if I've realised anything since I came to Liverpool, it's that I never want to leave."

"Oh. Any particular reason why?" Juliet asked, holding Paige against her.

"One or two reasons. Mostly...a certain woman." Wrapped up in one another, Paige offered a contented sigh, sinking further into not only Juliet's bed but the world she was slowly creating with her. "Maybe I'll tell you all about her someday."

CHAPTER 15
I WON'T LET YOU GO

"I like what Juliet has done with the place."

Paige turned at the sound of a voice, smiling when a well-suited man stood on the other side of the bar. "Yeah, it's great."

"And you're the new mixologist, I assume?" He held out his hand, and Paige took it.

"That's me. Paige. You are?" Paige drew back her hand, taking a bar towel as she wiped down the oak between them.

"John. Long-time member. Just arrived back from a month-long golfing trip to Alvor in Portugal. There's just something about *this* place, though, that keeps me coming back."

"Well, we're very happy to have you here." Paige threw a thumb over her shoulder. "What can I get you?"

He rubbed his chin, perusing the bottles behind Paige. He seemed like a nice guy, respectful and polite. "I'll just take a scotch for the time being. Your choice."

Paige quirked a brow. "Macallan? We have a lovely 12 double cask in at the minute."

John winked, pointing to Paige. "I like you. You make good choices. I'll take a double."

Paige prepared John's drink, sitting it on a napkin in front of him. He placed a £50 note down and turned to walk away. "John, your change!"

"Keep it, love."

Paige stared down at the £50 note in her hand, her brows raised. She rung up the cost of the whiskey on the cash register and then shoved the change into her tip jar. At this rate, she could buy her own apartment in the next couple of years. She could live off the tips alone.

The security system flagged, a smile spreading on Paige's mouth when she watched Juliet let herself into the bar. Could she re-watch the footage when she needed to? When she wanted to admire Juliet? That woman was something else. And as Paige had opened up to her last week, it was in that moment that she'd really noticed it. Paige...was *so* into Juliet, and there was no denying it. Now, she had to decide what to do about it. She was yet to contact James and call his bluff.

She cleared her throat when Juliet stepped into the bar, watching her move with so much grace. She lifted her eyes to Paige, wearing that gorgeous smile, along with a tailor-made black suit. "Hi."

"Hey," Paige said, a bar towel slung over her shoulder. She felt Juliet's eyes on her, her stare burning through her as it travelled down her body. Juliet...was checking her out. *Oh, God. Stop!* Paige wasn't sure she'd ever get over those looks. How it made her feel. "Can I get you a drink?"

Juliet practically draped herself against the bar as she sighed. "What would you recommend?"

"Sex on the bar?"

Juliet smirked. "It's been a while. I may be a little rusty."

Paige brought a glass up and placed it down on the counter. She found Juliet's eyes again, watching her intently. She loved the flirtatious side they had with one another. It only made the sex hotter at the end of the night. "Maybe...you need a hand with it."

"You and I would be perfectly capable between us, no?"

Paige almost choked on the saliva she'd just swallowed. "Behave yourself!"

Juliet rounded the bar, taking a bottle of red wine from the shelf. She lifted a glass and set it down next to the glass Paige had placed down, then stepped up behind Paige. When Juliet lowered her lips to Paige's ear, her body pressing Paige to the counter, her legs almost gave out. "I prefer the real thing over the drink. So, unless *that* was what you were offering, I'll take the wine." Juliet remained behind Paige, smiling against her ear, her breath hot. "If you change your mind, don't hesitate to come find me."

Paige gripped the counter, her lips parted and her eyes closed. *Fuck.*

And then Juliet was back on the other side of the bar, looking at Paige as though she'd just imagined the entire thing. "I, uh...small or large wine?"

"Make it a large. And pour yourself one. You're ever so tense tonight, Paige."

The way in which Juliet said Paige's name sent a shiver down her spine. It was practically a moan as it slid from her gorgeous lips. "I'm fine. Don't know what you're talking about."

"Mm. Maybe *you* need that sex on the bar. Take your own advice."

Oh, Juliet was bold. But if she thought Paige wouldn't bite back, she was sadly mistaken. God, she'd never turn down banter. "I'm a little like you in that I prefer the real thing, too." And then Paige turned her back and moved to the other end of the bar. She rearranged her whiskey selection as she slotted the bottle of Macallan back in place, feeling that burn of Juliet's stare once again. She may have been throwing it back at Juliet, but as she stood here—wet just from the sensation of Juliet's lips on her ear—she meant it.

Oh, she meant it...and then some.

Juliet should have been closing up for the night, yet here she was, sitting in the barely lit bar on the couch. Paige had shocked her with her response earlier. She wasn't usually so open around The Hideout, but Juliet couldn't help herself. Walking into the bar tonight, Paige had stolen her breath. She wore her usual fitted pants and white shirt, only this time, the shirt was a little tighter—her cleavage exposed—with a black bra visible through the fabric. Juliet had always been weak for a woman who knew how to dress, and Paige was absolutely one of those women.

She squeezed her thighs together, trying desperately to push the image as far from her mind as she possibly could. She had no idea if Paige was available to come back to her place tonight, and if Juliet was being brutally honest with herself, she didn't want Paige to feel suffocated. This was a huge adjustment for her; Juliet had to remember that before her own libido.

Still, she had no idea where they stood with one another. While it was frowned upon to get into any sort of relationship with Paige—she *was* her employee—Juliet had never been one for that particular rule. If she found herself attracted to a woman, regardless of the situation, she always made sure they were aware of it.

Because all it took was that one person to feel the same way. And the rest could be history.

Juliet didn't have time to hang around, waiting for something to drop in her lap. She didn't have the weeks and months to ponder what her ideal woman was. If that connection was there...it pulled Juliet in. And with Paige, that connection was electrifying. She'd felt it as she'd pressed herself to Paige. She knew it when her entire body tingled as she sloped off into the office. And she was certain of it when she'd *almost* slid her hands down the front of her pants thinking about Paige just an hour ago.

She was entirely captivated by Paige Harrison.

"Okay, I'm done out the back. Need a hand with anything before I leave?"

Juliet allowed her gaze to sweep up Paige's body, her eyes landing exactly where she wanted them to. "I...don't know. *Do* I need a hand with anything?"

Paige blushed, lowering her eyes. "You have to stop that. You're going to get me into trouble one of these days."

"Trouble?" Juliet quirked a brow, her arm resting along the back of the couch. God, Paige was unexpectedly hot. She'd seemed quiet at first, but now in her sixth week at the bar, she'd only come out of her shell more. And if the outfits—along with the intense sex—were anything to go by, Juliet would be a very happy woman for the foreseeable future. "Why don't you pour yourself a drink and tell me *all about* this trouble..."

"Oh, I'd *love* to. Trust me, I would. But it's almost one in the morning."

"Okay, but tell me one thing before you head off."

Paige lifted a shoulder. "Sure. What's up?"

"Am I way off the mark, or did you dress for me tonight?"

Paige laughed, a pure delight to Juliet's ears. "You're right on the mark."

"That's all I need to know." Juliet nodded slowly as she reached forward for what was left of her wine. "Thank you for another stellar performance behind the bar."

Paige dragged a hand through her hair, one hand in her

jeans pocket. "I think we can both agree that *your* performance was far better than mine."

"You're good for me." Juliet tipped her wine glass in Paige's direction. She narrowed her eyes. "Yeah. *Really* good for me. We're going to make a great team."

"Maybe. Who knows."

"I'm usually a very good judge of character. So, me. *I* know."

"Did you...want to walk home together? Y-you don't have anywhere to be?"

Juliet knew Paige was still hesitant about Rachel now and then, but she'd been the farthest thing from Juliet's mind since the night she'd slid her fingers through Paige's wetness. That spoke volumes in terms of how she felt about her escort. It really *had* just been business. Whereas Juliet trembled at the mere thought of Paige beneath her.

"No. I'm all yours. Let me get my bag. I'll just be a minute."

Paige remained relaxed as Juliet approached her, shoving her other hand in her pocket and leaning heavier on one leg. "Sure. No rush."

Juliet stopped in front of her, drawing a fingertip across her wrist. "Whatever is happening here between us, know that I'm in." Juliet dipped her eyes momentarily to Paige's cleavage, her hands desperately wanting to touch Paige in the most intimate of places. "*Entirely* in."

Paige pressed her body to Juliet's, smiling into a kiss. "I think we both know what's happening here, don't you? And I think it's time for you to collect your stuff so we can leave. I have...things to take care of."

"Mm. That's the right answer." Juliet stepped away and made a beeline for the office. When she grabbed her bag and reached to turn out the lamp, her phone vibrated in her back pocket.

Blonde guy. Directed him away from the building. Tried

to gain access via a different apartment number seven minutes ago.

Juliet swallowed, gathering her thoughts for a moment or two before she faced Paige again. She didn't want her to know that someone was watching over her, and she didn't want her to know that someone had tried to get into the building.

Can you pick us up? I'm locking up now. If she asks, you're a cab driver.

I'll be outside in three minutes.

"Juliet?" Paige called out, jangling her keys in her hand. "The sooner you get out of the office, the sooner I can be taking care of all your stresses."

"Relax. I'm coming." She beamed a smile as she locked the office door and made her way back to Paige. "I decided that since I couldn't wait too long, I've booked us a cab."

Paige gripped the front of Juliet's blouse and dragged her into a heated kiss. When she pulled back, their noses brushing, Paige moaned. "Who the hell knew I'd end up with someone like you when I got here?"

"Oh, I hoped. From the second you walked down those stairs."

Juliet felt the vibration in her back pocket. It would be her guy telling her he was outside.

"Come on. Let's get out of here."

Paige stepped out of the lift hand-in-hand with Juliet as they strolled down the corridor. She wasn't sure they'd make it to Juliet's apartment, and since Paige's was nearer, it made sense to stay the night there. "Let me find my key."

Juliet stroked a palm up Paige's bicep, resting her head on Paige's shoulder. These were the moments Paige hadn't realised she needed. Another woman holding onto her. Wanting to be with her. "Let's go to my place instead."

"But mine is right here."

Juliet smiled as she cocked her head towards her own apartment. "And mine is right there."

"Fine. Okay. But is there a reason you don't want to come into mine?" Paige was thinking too deeply into this, but Juliet really didn't seem to want to step foot inside Paige's place. "Juliet?"

"I think we need my bed. I have...the view and *stuff*. You know—"

Paige held up a hand, cutting Juliet off. "Fine. You win."

It didn't really matter where it happened. Tonight, Paige just wanted to get her hands on Juliet's body again. She wanted to touch Juliet in all the ways she'd dreamt of since the last time.

She followed Juliet two doors down, stepping inside her apartment in no time at all. Juliet was just as eager as Paige was. Thankfully. But then Juliet suddenly turned around, a slight frown present. "Do...you have a picture of your husband?"

Not where Paige expected their night to go. "Um, on social media, yes."

"Can you send it over to me?"

Paige rested against the back of the couch, her legs crossed at the ankles. If Juliet wanted a picture of James, she'd better have a good reason for it. "Because?"

"For the bar. I don't know what he looks like, and I don't want to accidentally give him access if I mistake him for a new client."

Paige smiled. That made complete sense. And it wasn't something she'd already thought of herself. She took her phone from her pocket, scrolling through her social media profile to find a recent one with James. Would over 12 months ago suffice? "Is this one clear enough?"

Juliet took Paige's phone from her, studying the image. "Yes. Perfect. Would you mind if I airdrop it to myself?"

Paige held up her hands as she started to turn away. "Not at all. Do what you need to do." She shed her jacket, rolling her head on her shoulders as she relaxed into Juliet's space. "Last time I was here, I didn't realise how good the view was at night. Preoccupied, you know?"

Juliet smirked. "Trust me, I paid for these views. It doesn't come cheap."

Paige approached the window, sighing when she shoved her hands in her pockets and watched the lights on the river. But then blackout blinds started to lower down each and every window in Juliet's apartment, disappointing Paige. "Hey! I was enjoying that."

"I'm sure I can help you enjoy yourself far more if you come over here, Paige."

Yeah, Juliet definitely could. Paige eyed Juliet across the open space, her skin tingling when Juliet pinned her with her own stare. "God, you're fucking gorgeous."

"Right back at you," Juliet said, holding out a hand and encouraging Paige closer. "Maybe we should take this into the bedroom."

"No maybe about it."

As Juliet turned and guided Paige towards the bedroom, her phone pinged in her hand. Juliet looked down at it, visibly swallowing.

"Is...everything okay?"

"Y-yes." She offered Paige a non-convincing smile and cleared her throat. "Could you give me a few minutes? I'll be right back."

"Yeah. Of course. I'm the one gate-crashing your night."

"You *are* my night." Juliet held Paige by the waist, kissing her. Her tongue dragged along Paige's bottom lip, her body trembling. "Won't be a second. Get comfy...*and naked*."

Paige's smile spread impossibly wide as she watched Juliet walk away.

Of all the cities Paige had visited, this was the only city where she'd wanted to stay. Perhaps it was the company, maybe the people, but Paige knew without a doubt that she had to figure out life at home so she could be truly happy here. Juliet meant far too much to her for someone to come along and take it all away.

Paige turned around and admired Juliet's bedroom. It was bright white, spacious, with a huge bed that looked out onto the river.

"And you're sure it was him?"

Paige frowned, stepping back towards the door. She shouldn't listen to Juliet's private conversations, but Paige was constantly on edge, so it was hard not to.

"Let me get another picture, and I'll send that over, too. I know you're sure, I understand that, but I need you to be *absolutely* certain. If he shows up here, I don't know what he's capable of!" Juliet whisper yelled, but Paige heard every word. "Don't leave your spot all night. I'll pay you double."

She ended the call, cleared her throat, and turned back to the bedroom. But Paige was already watching her, a startled look now on Juliet's features.

"Sorry about that. Old client."

Paige nodded slowly. "I'd like to think you're an honest woman, Juliet. Actually, I'm counting on that. Please don't lie to me."

"I...I'm not."

"So you're telling me that was an old client on the phone? One who sounds a lot like they're in trouble?"

"It *was* an old client. And no, they're not in trouble. They... keep an eye on things for me when I ask them to."

"An eye," Paige said, leaving the bedroom and slumping down on the couch. "And what or who are they keeping an eye on?"

"You."

Paige wasn't doing this. She didn't want the woman she was with to have to protect her. She didn't want Juliet getting caught up in any of this. That wasn't the relationship she desired. Not at all.

She looked up at Juliet with tears in her eyes. "I think I'm just going to head back to my place." Paige stood, taking a step closer to Juliet and placing a kiss on her cheek. "I know you mean well, but this isn't how I want things to be."

"Paige, wait." Juliet held Paige in place with an arm around her waist. "It's just for your own peace of mind. Please, don't leave."

"That may have been the initial reason for it, but James is here, isn't he? I heard you on the call. He's in Liverpool."

Juliet lowered her eyes. "Yes."

"Then I need to go."

"How does he keep finding you, Paige? Liverpool is a big enough place for it to take him a while. You don't just work at some generic bar in the city."

"I don't know. The only person who knew I was here was my best friend." Paige allowed that to sink in. Harriet had told him. "And now I realise what I've just said."

"Do you think maybe you could call your best friend and tell her it didn't work out here? That you've moved on again?" Juliet guided Paige back to the couch, sinking down into the leather with her. "It's worth a shot."

"I can try. She'll believe me if I tell her I've left Liverpool."

"He...tried to access this building tonight while we were at the bar. He doesn't know who I am or that you know anyone in this building, so I really need you to stay here with me until we know he's left the city."

Paige sighed. "I'm so tired of this. I just want to live my life."

Juliet pulled Paige to her, holding her close. "I know. And soon, you'll do exactly that. Hopefully in this city. With me."

"One day at a time, okay?"

Juliet squeezed Paige's thigh lightly. "Oh, of course. Yes. I'm getting ahead of myself."

"I say one day at a time because you may not even like me in a few weeks. I certainly expect that. There's nothing exciting about me, Juliet. Unless you're into women who like to run."

"No, I'm not. But I *am* into you." Juliet shifted on the couch, cupping Paige's cheek. "And I know I'm only going to like what I see more and more as I get to know you."

"I hope so." Paige smiled weakly. It would be a dream come true to fall in love with someone like Juliet. Someone strong and confident in their abilities. Someone who had a firm knowledge of who she was, what she wanted, and how she proceeded with that. But Paige had a long way to go in terms of figuring herself out. "I'll just get some things from my apartment, okay?"

"I'll...come with you."

CHAPTER 16
IN MY OWN TIME

With her phone in one hand and coffee in the other, Paige stood at the window and looked out over the river. Juliet had suggested last night that the blinds remain closed until they could get rid of James, but Paige wasn't willing to allow Juliet to be a prisoner in her own home. She'd avoided the area of the living room that looked out over the city, so there was nothing to worry about.

Juliet had been great last night, but Paige wished their night hadn't ended how it did. She would have much preferred to be waiting on Juliet's bed—naked—not discussing the fact that her husband was in Liverpool. And as she stood here this morning, she wished Juliet was pressed against her. Kissing her. Touching her.

But she wasn't, and Paige had things to take care of.

She unlocked her phone, sipping her coffee as she brought up Harriet's number. Juliet had put the idea in her head last night, so here Paige was, hoping she could kick James off her trail.

"Hello?"

Paige smiled. She had to consider whether Harriet was the

'mole,' but if she was, Harriet wouldn't have told James about her location if she knew about their home life. "Hey! How the hell are you?"

"I'm good. Tired and ready for the weekend, but good. How's the job going in Liverpool?"

"It's not," Paige lied. "I'm moving on. It didn't work out for me there."

"Really? I thought you liked it at The Hideout."

And there it was. Just what Paige had suspected. "I don't remember telling you the name of the bar."

"Oh, no. I...looked it up. It might be membership only, but it's not as secret as it wants to be."

"It's not marketed to be secret. It's not some underground criminal ring, just a private bar."

Harriet laughed. "Well, it doesn't really matter what it is anymore if you've left."

Paige dragged a hand through her hair, staring down at her coffee cup. "Yeah. You're right. So, anyway, I just called to let you know that I'm moving on. Scotland this time."

"Paige, why are you moving further and further away?" Paige heard the concern in Harriet's voice, but her best friend could relax. So long as she continued to stay away from her hometown, she would be perfectly fine.

"Got to go where the work is, my friend. Scotland has a lot to offer. I think I might head to one of those tiny islands. Live a life of solitude."

"You do realise you have a husband at home, don't you? Considering you've been married for five years, you seem to forget that."

Paige scoffed. Harriet had no idea. "Trust me, James *doesn't* let me forget."

"It's just that I'm worried about you. You didn't even come home for your wedding anniversary, Paige. I know you've been through a lot with your mum passing away, but maybe it's time to stop running from your problems and go home to be with James. He misses you."

Paige instantly frowned. How would Harriet know what James was feeling? And why was Harriet using her mum to guilt her into going home? Paige had lost her mum over eighteen months ago; she'd dealt with it. Or was this James putting ideas in Harriet's head as to why she refused to come home? Likely, given the fact that James wouldn't reveal the true reason. "Are you in regular contact with him or something?"

"No, but I see him most Friday nights at the pub when I finish work. You know, they have a vacancy there."

"At the Forest Arms?" Paige's brows lifted. Was Harriet suggesting she work at their local and only pub? Not in a million years. "They always have vacancies there. What does that tell you?"

"That it's fate?" Paige heard the hope in Harriet's voice, but it didn't change anything. She was done with living that life. Now that she was here, enjoying her time with Juliet, she couldn't possibly revert to what she'd once subjected herself to. "Paige, are you there?"

"I am, but I have to go. My cab is here, and my train leaves in thirty minutes."

"You're really going to Scotland?!" Harriet shrieked.

"I'm really going to Scotland. I'll call you once I've found a place to live for the time being. Take care of yourself."

"Y-yeah. You, too."

Paige lowered her phone, exhaling a sigh of relief when Harriet cut the call. She didn't have time to sit around lying to people, nor was it how she wanted to do this, but Paige needed more time to enjoy her budding relationship with Juliet before she left Kent behind once and for all.

"Everything okay?"

Paige turned, smiling at Juliet where she stood in the kitchen. "Sure. Harriet thinks I'm leaving for Scotland."

"She believes you?"

Paige shrugged. "There's no reason she wouldn't. She's always gone with it in the past. She was shocked that I'm going so far away, but it's not Harriet I'm worried about. It's James who needs to believe the story."

"Paige, I know this is incredibly difficult for you. The position you're in. But don't you think it may be easier to come out and lay it all on the table rather than continuing to run?"

"I'm not ready yet." Paige hoped Juliet could understand, that she wouldn't start to back off, but it was a possibility Paige had to consider. "It's not even the coming out part I'm worried about. That...I can't *wait* to do. It's everything else. Speaking to him face to face, being around him when I need to get my things from the house. The confrontation."

"I know." Juliet crossed the floor and opened her arms to Paige. She kissed her forehead and smiled. "Whatever you think is best. I just don't want you to continually torture yourself about this."

"You want the truth?" Paige pulled back, a brow lifted. When Juliet nodded, Paige wrapped her arms around her waist. "This, what we're doing...I don't want to lose it yet."

"We won't—"

"Hear me out." Paige held up a hand. "I've always known I was gay. *Always*. But this is the first time I've actually put myself first and enjoyed being with another woman. Yes, there were dates in the past, but they rarely moved past a few. Because I couldn't commit to anyone without either keeping them a secret or coming out. And I just wasn't ready for that. My mum... she wouldn't have approved. But that's okay. I had to focus on her, her health issues. And then I met James through my mum's friend at work. Her son. Mum was so excited I was dating him, and I just wanted her to be happy. She wasn't always going to be around, we knew she wouldn't live a long life, so for the time that she was here, I just wanted to make her happy."

"That's a very selfless thing you did, Paige."

"Because she was my mum. And while people would probably criticise me for not coming out or criticise her for not approving, we had the most amazing relationship. She loved me so much, and I don't know, maybe she would have been okay with my sexuality…but I wasn't willing to risk it. That may make me a coward, but at least she passed away still loving me."

"I don't think it makes you a coward at all. You did what worked for you, and that was your decision. How you lived your life is nobody else's business."

"Maybe so, but look at me now. Stuck with an abusive husband I'm constantly running from."

Juliet brushed Paige's hair from her face, regarding her with the most beautiful smile. "Look, there's no rush to do anything here. If we have to keep things strictly between us, or as best as we can, given the fact that we work together, I'm okay with that. I just want to enjoy being with you…without seeing that constant look of fear in your eyes."

"I'm sorry. I'll try harder to relax."

"You don't have to try harder to do anything, Paige. You're perfect in my eyes."

Paige found that hard to believe. Juliet was surely just trying to keep the peace here. But that wasn't the relationship Paige wanted. If Juliet was unhappy with anything, Paige needed her to communicate that. It would make life easier for everyone involved. "I'm not perfect, and I never will be."

"But to me, you are. Can you accept that?"

Paige laughed. "Doubtful, but if it makes you feel better, sure."

"You know what makes me feel better? Being with you like this. Spending my morning drinking coffee with you, and talking to you, just...being with you. Because I've also never had this before. And I really don't want to imagine losing it. Losing *you*."

Paige would like to believe that this would all work out well in the end, but if James continued to prowl, that may not be the case. Still, she didn't want to think about that right now. She wanted to enjoy Juliet, too. "Let's hope it doesn't come to that then."

The last thing Juliet wanted to do this afternoon was leave her apartment. It had taken her long enough just to peel herself from her bed, Paige lying next to her, very naked and very sexy. But she had some business to take care of. Thank God it was Thursday so neither of them had to work. Juliet may be in good shape, but Paige was making up for lost time...and it was beginning to show.

She finished her coffee, placing her cup in the sink as she fixed the cuff links on her shirt. Paige could stay back at the apartment and relax. If James was still lurking, they didn't want him to know that Paige and Juliet knew one another. While he was unaware of that, he was less likely to gain access to the building and Juliet's apartment. And he was less likely to come to the bar if he believed that Paige had moved on. Seeing them together would only encourage him to stick around.

Juliet knew of men like James. She knew they rarely stopped with their stalking and desperation. The best thing she could do was not be seen with Paige. That was terrible, considering the morning they'd just had, but it was for Paige's safety. Everything would come good in the end. Juliet was a firm believer in that.

"Hey," Paige said, resting against the doorframe of Juliet's bedroom. "Are you sure you don't want me to come with you? Maybe we could get some lunch while we're out."

Juliet's eyes travelled Paige's entire body, just the sheet from her bed covering that delicate skin. "No. Stay here and do nothing. You've been on the go since you came to Liverpool. Have an *actual* day off. I need to call into the bar for some invoices while I'm out."

"I'll get dressed and go back to my place."

"You won't. You brought clothes over last night. Just...relax and take your time. Make this place your own. Take a shower and do whatever you need to do."

Paige pushed off the doorframe, slowly walking towards Juliet. If she kept looking at her that way, Juliet would never leave. "Thank you. For being great."

Juliet lifted a hand to Paige's cheek. "It helps when the woman in your life is perfect."

Paige leaned into Juliet's touch. "I'm really not. Don't set your expectations so high with me. But I am genuine and honest. That means something, right?"

Juliet drew Paige into a slow kiss. When she smiled against her lips, her thumb stroking Paige's cheek, Juliet simply nodded. "It means *everything*."

"I feel good about this with you. All I ask is that you give me time to get it right. I've hidden who I am for so long that it doesn't seem possible for me to be me. I love your confidence and the fact that you're out and proud. I don't want to put a downer on that, so if it's going to be too much for you, I completely get it. Okay?"

Juliet appreciated that, but it wouldn't change anything.

Paige was who she wanted in her life, and Paige, it would remain. "I'm forty-nine. I'm not the kind of woman who has to have someone on her arm. I'm also in no hurry to push this. I want *you* to know when the time is right."

Paige lifted her eyes, that gorgeous grey showing a slight hint of green. "The time was right this morning for me. Touching you, I just..." Paige pressed her hand to Juliet's that rested against her cheek. "Being with you means so much, okay?"

"I know. I felt it."

Paige regarded Juliet with a shy smile. "I really wish you didn't have to leave yet."

"I'll see you in a couple of hours. I'll probably be back by the time you've put some clothes on."

"Maybe I won't put any clothes on." Paige lifted a shoulder, a slight smirk present on her lips. "See how I feel."

Juliet pressed her body to Paige's, the sheet wrapped around her the only thing stopping Juliet from slipping a hand between Paige's thighs. "Oh, I'd look forward to that."

"I'll see you soon. Text me when you get to the bar."

Juliet's brows drew together. "Why?"

"So I know you got there safely."

Oh, God. This was serious. Nobody ever insisted Juliet contact them when she arrived anywhere. Paige was truly adorable. "I'll call you." She leaned in and kissed Paige, lingering for a moment as their noses brushed. "If you need anything, I'm only on the end of the phone."

"Go. I'll be fine." Paige stole a final kiss, resting against the wall as Juliet strode towards the door. "See you soon."

"You will."

Juliet left her apartment, rushing towards the lift before the door could close. She checked her watch. It was right on time for Mrs Faustino—who lived at the other end of the corridor—

to arrive home. She didn't make it a habit to keep an eye on everyone who lived here, but she did like to know who was coming and going on her floor. Juliet couldn't be too careful.

Exhaling a breath as the lift took her down to the ground floor, she gathered herself, knowing that this wasn't going to be plain sailing with Paige. While James was around, nothing would be easy.

The lift doors opened, Juliet cleared her throat, and then she made her way towards the electronic door at the entrance to the building. As she pushed it open, a man came rushing towards her. "Hold the door, please."

Juliet looked up, recognising him immediately. She forced the heavy hydraulic door closed as quickly as she could, remaining in front of it. "Sorry. No can do."

"What?" James' eyes bulged, his large frame almost towering over Juliet. But she wasn't intimidated. She'd worked with some of the worst of society. James was a pussy cat in comparison. "Why not? I'm only visiting a friend!"

"In that case, you'll have no issue entering the correct way. By buzzing your way in."

"I bet you're fun at parties!" He scoffed, taking a step back. Then he removed his phone and frowned at the screen. He scrolled, eventually smiling. "I'm looking for 319."

"319 is...empty." How *the hell* did James know Paige's apartment number?

James shook his head. "Nope. My friend is staying there. Paige."

Friend. Huh. Considering Paige was his wife, James didn't want Juliet to know that. That only further proved he had something to hide. "Paige," she said. "Blonde hair? Around 30?"

"Y-yeah. That's the one."

"She left this morning." Juliet remained composed as James' features changed. He wasn't happy; that much was clear by the way the vein in his forehead started to throb. "I only spoke to her briefly, but I bumped into her when she was moving out. Something about Scotland?"

"Scotland?"

Juliet nodded, shifting her handbag higher up her shoulder. "That's what she told me. But I don't know her so she really could be anywhere. All I can tell you is that she's no longer here."

James scratched at his beard, anger no longer present, just defeat. He puffed out a breath. "Right, well, thank you."

"No problem. Have a nice day." Juliet remained in front of the door when James didn't move. "Something else?"

"Oh, no. I...need to wait for a cab."

Juliet gently placed a hand on his elbow, guiding him away from the door. "Well, you can do that *outside* of the secure gates. Gates you shouldn't have been able to access in the first place."

"What do you care where I wait?"

"I live here. Forgive me for wanting to keep the security tight. I didn't pay a fortune for the place so strangers could stroll around the corridors."

Juliet knew exactly what James was up to. He was waiting until Juliet was out of sight so he could try his luck at getting inside again. Well, not today. Not on her watch.

"If you see her, could you tell her James was looking for her?" Tears welled in his eyes as he cleared his throat. "It's been a while since we got the chance to catch up. I really hoped I'd catch her here."

"Sure. But from what little conversation I did have with... Paige, was it?" James nodded. "She has no intentions of coming back here. Maybe try calling her instead. I'm sure she'll let you know where she is if she wants to meet up with you."

"Yeah. Thanks. I'll try that." James turned and walked away, his shoulders hunched.

Juliet took her phone from her pocket, bringing up her 'guys' number. When the call connected, her nostrils flared. "Where the hell are you?"

"Getting coffee. Why?"

"Why? I don't employ you to get fucking coffee! I employ you to watch my back."

"Jules, relax. You told me last night that you wouldn't be working today. I assumed you'd be at your place unless I heard differently."

"Well, I'm not. And the woman I asked you to keep an eye on? Her abusive husband has just almost gained entry to the building. Luckily it was me leaving when he tried to get in."

"Shit. I'm sorry. I'll be there in three minutes."

Juliet ended the call, her mind reeling. She didn't want to imagine what could have happened if Paige had been in her own apartment and James had managed to get inside. It only left her heart pounding.

She brought up Paige's number. The last thing she wanted was to keep her in the dark.

"Hi. Missing me already?" Paige teased.

"Of course. But that's not why I'm calling. I...bumped into James. Outside the building. I wanted to tell you and not keep it from you. Relationships based on lies never end well."

"James is here?" The fear in Paige's voice didn't go unnoticed by Juliet. "I should go. Leave the city. He won't leave until he finds me."

"Paige, I told him you'd moved out. Said you'd left for Scotland."

"I...have a bad feeling about this. And it shouldn't fall to you to protect me."

Juliet smiled weakly, taking a seat at a bench on the pavement. "You've never had anyone to protect you before, have you?"

"No."

"Well, now you do. I won't let him hurt you, Paige." Juliet meant that with every fibre of her being. Paige may be new to her life, they may not have had the deep and meaningful conversations yet, but Juliet knew she'd still protect her with her life. The pull was undeniable, the connection palpable. This woman, before too long, was going to mean the world to her. "I'm serious. I give you my word."

"I have some decisions to make," Paige said, her voice breaking. "I need to decide what to do for the best."

"Let me run to the bar and grab the things I need, and then I'll be back. Do not go to your apartment. Stay in mine. I'll be thirty minutes. Not a second longer."

"Okay."

"And Paige?"

Paige sighed. "Yeah?"

"We're going to fix this. I...don't want to lose you."

CHAPTER 17
KISS ME

The silence in Juliet's apartment was to be expected this morning. Paige was on edge, Juliet didn't know what to do for the best, and as she glanced out of the window, Henry was still outside. He'd been there all night, but that was exactly what Juliet paid him to do. To watch her back. And her apartment. And her car...the bar...anywhere and anything that was related to Juliet needed eyes on it. Because if she dropped her guard, God only knew what could happen. Someone had already tried to access her car three weeks before she retired, but she had full faith in Henry and his abilities. She wouldn't pay just anyone.

As she sipped her coffee and turned away from the window, Paige was watching her from the bedroom door. "Mornin'." She yawned, tiptoeing across the tiled kitchen floor. "Can I get some coffee?"

"Have a seat. I'll make you some."

Paige flopped down on the couch, yawning again. She hadn't slept much last night; Juliet had felt her toss and turn in the night.

"Looks like someone needs to go back to bed for a while."

Paige waved a hand, resting her head back on a cushion and closing her eyes. "I'll be fine. It's just taking me a minute or two to wake up this morning."

"Do you want to talk about it?"

"Honestly, no. I just want him to leave me alone. Is that really too much to ask?"

Juliet offered a weak smile, handing Paige a large cup of strong, black coffee. "You'd *think* it would be simple."

"He just..." Paige groaned, bringing her hands up to her face. "I'm trying not to think about what would have happened if you hadn't been there at the main entrance. Okay, he wouldn't have thought to come here, but if I'd been at my apartment...well."

"Mm. I see where you're going with this." Juliet snuggled down beside Paige, covering them both with a blanket. "Maybe you need a day outdoors. The countryside. I know the perfect picnic spot that nobody else uses."

"Sounds amazing, but you're forgetting the small matter of your business."

Juliet grinned. "Bar is closed today. I've sent an email out. Emergency maintenance."

"You...shouldn't have done that." Paige turned her body towards Juliet's, their legs tangled beneath the blanket. "But thank you. I'd love to spend the day with you."

"We all need a day off now and then. I really should look into employing someone to take care of the place so we can be off together more often. I know we have Thursdays, but it's still a lot. Surely you agree?"

Paige leaned in, her coffee cup resting on her thigh, and kissed Juliet. "I don't care where I am so long as I get to see you. If that means working six nights and watching you from across the bar, so be it."

Juliet's skin prickled at those words. Paige, when James

wasn't interfering with her day-to-day life, was an absolute joy to be with. Okay, she was a joy to be with whatever the situation, but when Paige was like this…snuggled up and seemingly happy, Juliet adored it. "But if we could get an extra day off?"

"I can think of *many* activities to replace work." Paige slid her hand along Juliet's thigh beneath the blanket, smiling into another kiss. "But for now, we should drink our coffee and get ready for this picnic you mentioned. Can't remember the last time I got out into the countryside."

"You're going to love this place. It's off a dirt track, and it looks out onto a lake."

Paige sighed, resting her head on Juliet's shoulder. "Sounds really nice. And it means we get to spend some extra uninterrupted time with one another."

Yes, it did. And Juliet couldn't wait for that extra time with Paige. "I'd really like that."

"So, tell me about this guy who watches your place." Paige turned in her seat, the soft leather interior of Juliet's car hugging her. "Is someone threatening you?" Paige didn't want to imagine that possibility, but there had to be a reason.

"I…yes. It was suggested that I should watch my back by the family of someone inside. I had him sent down. I'm not sure how it would have gone if I'd lost the case. I was representing the lesser of two evils."

"Just a little fish, though, right?"

Juliet cleared her throat. "Not quite. Are you familiar with Shay Fitzgerald? Drug lord and murderer?"

Paige's heart sank. She knew exactly who that was. The whole country knew his name. "Y-yes."

"Well, him. He got sixty years without parole. His brother is trying to take over his empire for him and seems to think I should be the one in the firing line. If they hadn't hired such a poor defence lawyer, then maybe he'd have got off."

"Yeah, but then look at the trouble he could still be causing if he *wasn't* inside." Paige couldn't recall all of Shay Fitzgerald's crimes, but she would never forget the news article about him being responsible for a house fire that killed a woman and her four children. That story had stuck with Paige for a long time. "You did the right thing."

"I know. I just wish I didn't have to bring work home with me." Juliet tightened her grip on her steering wheel, pulling off the main road and onto the dirt track she'd mentioned. "If that's going to be an issue for you, Paige—"

"It's not."

"But if it does become one, you'll tell me? You have enough of your own stuff going on without mine coming into it."

Paige reached out a hand, grazing her nails across the back of Juliet's neck. "You think some scumbag is going to scare me off? No chance. His brother is probably all mouth."

Juliet puffed out her cheeks, her brows lifting. "I certainly hope so. For my sake."

"Anyway, today is about us. Not all the dickheads we seem to have in our lives. So, I don't want to talk about anyone else until we're at least heading back to the city."

"Fine by me."

"Do you come out here often?" Paige peered out the windscreen, taken aback by the gorgeous lake ahead of them. The area Juliet was pulling up in was secluded, surrounded by trees, not a house or another car in sight. "Please tell me you used to come here when you needed time to yourself."

"Time to myself?" Juliet cut the engine and turned in her seat, a look of shock on her face. "What's that?"

"Har-har!"

"I'm serious. You're the first person I've brought here in years. And by years, I'm talking at least fifteen. I didn't have time to breathe, let alone enjoy picnics by a lake."

"Then we should make sure you can have that time in the future. It's important that you look after yourself. Nobody else will do it for you."

"Not even you?" Juliet stuck her bottom lip out.

Paige grinned. It would be an honour to look after Juliet if things went well for them. It really would. "You know I will. That's not something you ever have to wonder."

"That's an odd feeling for me," Juliet explained, unfastening her seatbelt. Paige did the same, waiting until Juliet wanted to expand on that comment. "I've never had someone to spend time with. To share my home with. Someone to enjoy dinner with and conversations like this."

"I hate that."

"It is what it is. I focused on my career for far too long. But look what I have now." Juliet reached a hand across the console, squeezing Paige's knee. "I think it was worth the wait."

Paige dipped her head, her cheeks heating rapidly. "You're going to make me cry. Stop."

"This is very much the unknown for us both. Life at home wasn't happy for you, and I know just by the look in your eyes when we're together like this that it's foreign to you, too."

Wow. Paige had no idea Juliet could read her so well. "You're right. This is all new for me, too. We didn't do anything like this. There was never a day out or any excitement."

"I'm sorry you had to put yourself through a marriage to make other people comfortable."

Paige lifted a shoulder. "Like you say, it is what it is."

"Come on. Let's have a closer look at the lake." Juliet opened her door, smiling over her shoulder at Paige. "Maybe we could take our first selfie together."

Every time Juliet said something like that, Paige wanted to melt in her arms. She grabbed her phone from the side of the door and rushed around the front of the car. Her arm landed around Juliet's waist as she pulled her closer, no worries on her mind for once. That was another weird feeling. Not worrying. But being with Juliet meant Paige rarely worried.

"Hey!" Paige lifted her phone and snapped a photo as she caught Juliet off guard with a kiss. She brought up the picture and smiled. "I think that is the perfect first picture, don't you?"

Juliet took Paige's phone, studying the image. And then she sighed, handing it back as they slowly approached the edge of the water. "It really is."

"The number of times I sat at home, across the room from him...just wishing I wasn't stuck, you know?" Paige shoved her phone in the pocket of her shorts, raking a hand through her hair. "I've never complained, I've never asked for anything, but being stuck there and knowing that coming out would probably mean the end of my life...I'd never felt so alone. It's a horrible feeling."

Juliet turned to Paige, wrapping her up in her arms. Paige pressed the side of her face to Juliet's chest, allowing the embrace to really make her feel.

"The thought of you being there and miserable hurts my heart, Paige." Juliet kissed Paige's hair, holding her close. "And I'm going to do everything I can to make sure you're safe and that you never have to worry about him again."

Paige lifted her head, her gaze piercing Juliet. "I really hope this can work out for us."

"Tell me what you want. What you see in your future..."

"Honestly, nothing too grand." And that was the truth. Paige just wanted to be comfortable in her own skin while loving someone unconditionally. "A calm home. To be comfortable financially. To not worry about what people think of me.

And to have great sex. That's about it. I've missed out on so much great sex that it actually pains me to think about it. Like, imagine if I died tomorrow. I'd have spent all of my twenties having the worst sex of my life. But at least I'd be leaving this shitty earth knowing I'd had the chance to touch you, and taste you, and be with you."

Juliet's eyes filled with tears. "You're not going to die tomorrow. But you *will* be having some great sex before then. I can promise you that."

"Oh, yeah?" Paige quirked a brow, knowing that Juliet was easy to tease. "Then you'd better control yourself until we get back later."

"Who...said anything about later?" Juliet walked Paige backwards until she was pressed to the bonnet of her car. Paige swallowed, her mouth opening and closing, but she had no idea if Juliet was playing games in this moment. "Well?"

"I, uh...I mean."

Juliet smirked as she drew Paige into a kiss, her body pressing against Paige. "I thought you wanted to have great sex?"

"I-I do. But...here? *Now?*"

As one hand slid up the inside of Paige's thigh, her body responded without a second thought. It didn't matter that they were in the middle of the countryside. Paige was always going to give Juliet whatever she wanted. They could have an audience, and she wouldn't be overly concerned.

"You seem...I don't know." Juliet cocked her head, dragging her nails higher. "A little tense, maybe?"

"I just didn't think I'd be in *this* position today." Paige closed her eyes, the sensation of Juliet's fingers doing unimaginable things to her body. "F-fuck."

"We can change position if you'd prefer that."

Paige grinned, wrapping a hand around the back of Juliet's

neck and kissing her with eagerness. Whether they had deep and meaningful sex or raw and raunchy, it really didn't matter. When Juliet's lips were on Paige's, when her tongue glided against her own, Paige felt grounded. As though she was supposed to be here. Because it felt normal and natural to be with another woman. It felt real. The only real thing Paige had in her life.

"Paige?"

Paige shook herself out of the thoughts whirring around her mind. Juliet was here...and she wanted Paige. She could never deny her that. "Sorry. I was busy thinking about how much I love kissing you."

Juliet grinned against Paige's lips. "Hold that thought. And *do not* move."

Paige felt the loss immediately when Juliet stepped away and rushed to the boot of her car. What the hell was she doing? She should have had her hand down Paige's shorts by now! "Babe?"

"Wait! Don't come around here."

Paige frowned, the tone of Juliet's voice encouraging her to stay right where she was. "Okay, but like...what are you doing?" Paige took her phone from her pocket, bringing up the selfie they'd taken, and changed her wallpaper. Home *and* lock screen. It was no hardship to see Juliet and those gorgeous eyes every time she picked up her device. None whatsoever. "Is everything okay?" Paige was growing impatient now, but before she could call out Juliet's name again, she was right in front of her. "You good?"

"Oh, I'm far better than good." Juliet had an unfamiliar look in her eyes. "You really want to enjoy yourself and be adventurous?"

It was all Paige desired. "Absolutely."

Juliet took Paige's hand and lowered it between them. She

guided it between her legs, smirking when it dawned on Paige what was happening.

"Y-you want to do this here?" Paige throbbed at the mere thought of Juliet using a strap-on, but really...in the countryside? Where some poor unsuspecting dog walker could bump into them? "What if—"

Juliet pressed a finger to Paige's lips. "Trust me, nobody is going to come by."

"I...is it inside you?" Paige's body begged to know that answer, whether she was wary or not.

"Mmhmm."

She grabbed the strap through Juliet's pants, tugging gently. The pleasure that rippled across Juliet's face was a sight to behold. It had been so long since Paige had used any toys. She couldn't risk James finding them back at home, and there had only been one woman in the past who she had trusted enough to go that far with. Paige recalled how she'd felt that night, away in a hotel with a woman she'd been dating on and off for a few months. It was nothing serious, Helen had known Paige wasn't in a position to be in a relationship with her, but it didn't matter. And as she stood here now, Paige knew this was one of the most intimate moments she could share with someone else. She tugged again.

"Oh, fuck." Juliet's eyes closed as she pulled her bottom lip between her teeth. "That feels—"

"Oh, I can imagine how it feels," Paige whispered, leaning into a kiss. "I'm not even wearing it and just knowing it's inside you," Paige said, pausing as she searched Juliet's eyes. "God, I'm wet for you, Juliet."

Juliet slid her hand past the waistband of Paige's shorts, gathering her arousal on her fingertips. That grin she wore, dirty but so beautiful, only encouraged Paige to rock her hips.

"Paige, I want to fuck you."

Oh, shit. Those words...Juliet's voice.

"I want to fuck you and make you feel so good that you'll forget you ever had another life."

Paige wanted that. God, she needed it.

Juliet slowly teased Paige's clit. "May I?"

"Y-yes." Paige pressed her back to the bonnet of Juliet's car, her knees shaking as Juliet worked her up. "M-make me yours. Make me...forget."

"Is that what you need? For me to make you mine?"

Juliet didn't need to fuck Paige into oblivion to ensure that. No, this woman was firmly in Paige's life now. And Paige could sit around going over all of this in her head, but what was the point? Juliet wanted her. She wanted Juliet. So what if this was moving fast. Perhaps moving fast was exactly what Paige needed. God only knew how long she'd suffered being someone else.

Paige brought her hands to Juliet's face, stroking a thumb across her cheek. "I only want you. You don't have to worry about that."

"Yeah?" Juliet swiped her thumb across Paige's bottom lip, cocking her head. "All mine?"

Paige's heart tightened. This woman was going to mean so much to her. "All yours."

Juliet guided Paige away from the front of her car, kissing her as she tugged the driver-side door open. She slid her hand back between Paige's legs, moaning into Paige's mouth. "God, you're soaking, Paige."

Paige smirked against Juliet's lips. "I wonder why." She tugged the toy that was sitting snugly inside Juliet. "Every time I do that, your knees tremble, don't they?"

"Y-yes." Juliet closed her eyes, rocking her hips slowly. "Paige, you're killing me."

"Where do you want me?"

Juliet brought her hand to Paige's jaw, holding her still. "I want you bent over my seat."

If this had been anyone else, Paige would have wondered if that would leave her too exposed. But with Juliet, it was all she wanted to be. Exposed and open. Paige turned around, shivering when Juliet pressed her body to Paige's. She felt that wandering hand reach around her waist, and then those slender fingers parted her lips once again.

Juliet brought her mouth to Paige's ear and whispered, "I really want to be inside you."

Paige shuddered at those words, her body throbbing when Juliet pressed a hand between her shoulder blades, encouraging her to bend over. Paige rested on her elbows, her mouth hanging open when Juliet removed her shorts and underwear.

Juliet smoothed her palm over one cheek, then the other, and moaned. "You're really fucking beautiful. I hope you know that."

Even as Paige rested here, half naked and bent over Juliet's front seat, those words meant so much. Intimacy came in all kinds of forms, Paige knew that, but how could something so raw and dirty be coupled with the most beautiful words...and still feel so damn good? So meaningful?

Juliet crouched, spreading Paige's lips from behind and taking a long, slow lick up the length of her sex. Paige's arms wobbled, and her head dropped low between her shoulders. "Oh, f-fuck."

"You taste so good." Juliet tasted Paige again, humming her approval as she dragged her nails down the back of Paige's thigh. "And you feel ready for me."

Paige was ready. More than ready. The moment Juliet was inside her, this was all going to be over. Juliet may not know it, but her teasing was just as hot as the act itself.

"Are you, Paige?" Juliet got to her feet and smiled when Paige looked over her shoulder at her. "Ready for me?"

"Yes."

She lowered her head again, her lips parting when Juliet teased her with the tip of the toy. She wanted to force herself back, to slam against it, but hearing Juliet moan as she continued to tease Paige was only making her wetter. How was that possible?

"Spread your legs a little more."

Paige complied, widening her stance. Never in a million years did she imagine she'd be here doing this today. Or any day. But Juliet made her feel incredibly comfortable in any situation. And if Paige was being honest with herself, these kinds of moments were what she'd dreamt of.

"Fuck, you're perfect." Juliet teased Paige once again with the tip of the toy, smoothing her hands over her hips and holding onto her lower back. Slowly but so surely, she eased the toy inside Paige, filling her.

"O-oh." Paige's eyes closed, her hands clenched into fists against the leather interior of Juliet's car. "Y-yes. So good."

Juliet pulled back, only to sink deeper this time. "Tell me what you want, Paige."

"More," Paige whispered. "All of it."

Without responding, Juliet filled Paige as much as she possibly could. And with each move, every thrust, Paige's breath caught in her throat. "Fuck, I can barely move inside you."

Paige tried to relax her body, to enjoy this moment without holding back on her orgasm, but she couldn't. The moment her body swallowed the toy, the second Juliet really got going, Paige was going to come harder than she'd ever come before.

"Relax, gorgeous." Juliet's soothing voice had Paige doing

exactly that, her knees almost giving out when Juliet thrust hard and fast. "Mmhmm. That's better."

"Juliet, I-I..." Paige clenched her jaw, gripping the seat. "Fuck, I need to come."

"Already?"

Paige may not be able to see Juliet, but she felt her smirking as she asked that question. What could Paige say? Her girlfriend was too hot for her to handle.

"Y-yes."

Juliet slowed her thrusts, running her palm up Paige's back beneath her T-shirt. That settled her, kind of, her body no longer on the brink of exploding. "You don't know how wet it makes me seeing you like this, Paige. There's something incredibly sexy about seeing you let go and enjoy yourself."

"Yeah?" Paige grinned as she chanced another look over her shoulder. The look she found in Juliet's eyes only had her on the edge again. This woman...she genuinely wanted Paige. *Mind. Blown.*

"Fuck, yes." Juliet thrust hard. "Keep your eyes on me."

Paige wasn't sure that was possible.

"And don't come."

Okay, that was never going to happen. But for Juliet, she would try. She'd do anything for the woman deep inside her. Juliet bent her knees and thrust deeper. "J-Juliet." Paige's eyes fluttered closed, but that only had Juliet stopping suddenly.

"What did I say?"

"I-I can't." Paige whimpered, earning her a squeeze of the arse cheek. But that only opened her up more to Juliet, and as she watched Juliet, her lip between her teeth as she pushed deeper, it took everything within Paige to hold on for a moment longer. "Please."

"Oh, Paige. I don't want to ever stop fucking you." Juliet watched herself as she fucked Paige hard and fast.

"P-please, let me come."

Juliet forced her hips against Paige, her own breath ragged. "Fuck, you're too much." Juliet moaned with each push of her hips, her nails digging into Paige's skin. "But so good."

Paige's thighs shook when Juliet reached a hand around her, her fingers finding Paige's clit. "Oh, shit. F-fuck."

"Come for me, Paige."

Paige released around the toy buried inside her, roaring her approval when Juliet thrust, short and sharp, her own orgasm rolling through her. "Yes. Just like that." Paige trembled as she tried to hold herself up, and then she felt Juliet slump against her, panting. "Oh, God."

Paige groaned when the toy slid out of her, but then complete euphoria took over her. Nothing could ever compare to this moment. Letting go, living life on her terms, nobody could take this from her, whatever happened next.

Juliet stepped back, helping Paige to her feet, and turned her against the car. "Paige." She noted how Juliet shuddered as she released the toy from inside herself.

Paige shook her head, silencing Juliet with a kiss. Her hands found Juliet's neck, her nails grazing her skin. "Thank you."

Juliet frowned as she touched her forehead to Paige's. "For what?"

"Making me feel so fucking good."

"I wouldn't want you to feel any other way when you're with me." Juliet grinned, suddenly bending down and taking Paige's shorts and underwear from the floor. "Maybe next time, you can lose the underwear. It's really not necessary."

CHAPTER 18
YOURS

O*ne month later...*

Paige stretched as she yawned, tiptoeing barefoot into Juliet's living room. While she loved being at the bar, she loved Thursdays even more. It meant they had a day and night off together to do absolutely nothing. Only this morning, Paige wanted to run something by Juliet. Paige had called Harriet while Juliet prepared a pot of coffee ten minutes ago. She hadn't gone into too much detail about the real reason for her call, simply stating it was a quick catch up. When Paige had asked if Harriet has seen or spoken to James recently, her best friend had told Paige that James was out of the country for the weekend. Harriet and James had shared a drink together mid-week, and she recalled the brief mention of a new business venture in Paris, but Paige hadn't paid too much attention to the ins and outs of it all. The fact he wouldn't be there meant Paige had the perfect opportunity to do something she had been considering for a week or two now.

She wanted to go back to her hometown and get her belongings. To say a final goodbye to the village once and for all. She had nothing there. Why bother holding onto a place that made her miserable? She'd considered not returning at all, but Paige needed to do this. If she didn't go back and retrieve her things, she would feel as though she was still running. But she didn't want that anymore. No, she wanted to be here with Juliet. In Liverpool.

"Mm. Good morning," Juliet said from across the kitchen. Her smile was bright and white, that long dark hair pulled atop her head. "You look radiant."

"It'll be the athletics of last night. Orgasms always make my skin look better." Paige crossed the space, holding Juliet from behind. "You smell good. Did you shower without me?"

"I did. You looked too comfortable sleeping. I didn't want to wake you."

Paige pouted, turning Juliet in her arms. When Juliet pinned her with that stare, those dark brown eyes constantly stealing her breath, Paige weakened for this woman. "Do you have a minute while I speak to you about something?"

Juliet pulled back, holding Paige by the elbows. "Sure. What's up?"

"I'm leaving Liverpool on Saturday for the day. Would you mind if I didn't work the bar? I'll speak to Cara, and make sure she's good with working the shift alone."

"Of course. Going anywhere nice?"

"I, uh...home. Well, to Kent. To collect my stuff." It wasn't home. It never would be.

Juliet's features changed instantly. Fear clouded her eyes. "Why would you possibly want to go back there?"

"It's just something I need to do. For my own sanity."

"Then I'll come with you." Juliet straightened herself out, a determination in her eyes. "No point going alone when I can be with you."

Paige pressed a hand to Juliet's chest, smiling. "While I really appreciate that, I'd like to go alone. I only plan to be at the house for ten minutes while I shove my stuff into a bag. I'll mostly spend my time on the train. And if I'm back in time, I'll come straight to the bar to help you close up."

"Paige, I really don't like this."

"I know, but James won't even be there. I've spoken to Harriet. He's out of the country this weekend."

"And if he's not?" Juliet lifted a brow, one hand squeezing Paige's hip. "If you go home and he's there?"

"I'll know if he's there before I even make it to the front door. If his car is up the drive, I'll turn around and come back here. To you." Paige leaned in, kissing Juliet. They may have only been together for six weeks, but in those six weeks, life had truly flourished. And knowing that James wasn't hanging around the city anymore, Paige felt far calmer than she had in all her time running away. "Because that's where I really want to be. With you."

"Promise me?"

Paige's brows drew together. "Promise you that I'll come back?"

"That, and promise me that you'll be okay. That you won't step foot in that house if he's there. I need you to promise me that, baby."

When Juliet called her that, Paige's insides swirled. She knew what this was. She was in love with Juliet Saunders, but it wasn't time to announce that. It was far too soon. And Paige knew that if she did say those words, she couldn't take them back. She had to be one hundred percent sure. *Who am I kidding? I know I'm in love with her.* "I promise you that I'll be back here by Saturday night."

"I can close the bar. If you want me there with you, I'll close the bar without a second thought."

"You won't. This is your business, and you've already closed once for me. I won't let you do that again."

"Paige, are you sure this is a good idea? I don't want to stop you from doing whatever the hell you want to do, but I also want you to be safe."

"Everything is going to be fine. Maybe I'll call Harriet once I arrive. See if she wants to meet up for coffee. Trust me, if I thought he would be there, I wouldn't be going."

"But you think Harriet is feeding him information, don't you?"

Paige nodded, aware that Juliet had every right to worry. While Paige was wary of Harriet and any information she shared, she would play it carefully. She didn't believe her friend was sharing information maliciously, but still, she wouldn't call Harriet until she had collected her belongings, making it far easier to hop on a train suddenly if Paige felt she needed to. "I do. But he's not in Kent, so that won't matter. Because I won't be there long enough for him to come back and find me at the house. It's going to be fine, babe. Really, it is."

Juliet lowered her eyes between them. "Okay. If this is what you want to do."

"Hey, look at me," Paige said, lifting Juliet's chin with the tips of her fingers. "It's going to be okay. You *know* I wouldn't go back there if I knew he'd be around. He's going to Paris. But this is our day off together. I'd rather be here with you, not thinking about him, so that's what I'm going to do."

Juliet's lips curled into the most beautiful smile. "All day and all night?"

"All day and all night, gorgeous."

Juliet turned Paige, pressing her to the counter. "You're all mine?"

"All yours."

"You mean so much to me, Paige. The thought of anything happening to you..." Juliet sighed, choosing to not go any further with her line of thinking. But Paige understood. She, too, had those same fears when it came to Juliet and her safety. "Just come back, okay?"

"I wouldn't want to be anywhere else."

Juliet slid a hand down Paige's stomach, inside the split of her robe, and grinned against her lips. "Good job I love having you here then, isn't it?"

"Oh, it is." Paige moaned when Juliet trailed kisses along her jawline and towards her ear.

"Since we have nowhere to be today, maybe we should head back to bed."

As she zipped up her hoodie, Juliet stopped and watched Paige inconspicuously for a moment. The more time they spent together, the more at ease Paige appeared to be. Okay, they hadn't ever really been awkward with one another before they decided to get together, but Paige seemed different. How she made herself at home here in Juliet's apartment...God, Juliet loved it. She'd always dreamt of finding that woman who was comfortable in silence. Someone who helped themselves to the cupboards and the TV channels. It didn't seem like much when Juliet thought about it—especially now that she *did* have it—but this had been her dream. Someone like Paige.

"Can I help with anything?" she asked as she approached the kitchen. "You've been cooking for the last hour."

Paige glanced over her shoulder and smiled. "No. I'm good."

"There must be something I can do."

"Sit and talk to me." Paige lowered the gas on the stove and pulled out a stool. "I love it when you dress down, by the way."

Juliet frowned, looking down her body at her comfy jeans and hoodie. What could possibly be loveable about this Juliet?

"Don't look so surprised. You look good in anything."

Juliet waved a hand, laughing. "Okay, what is it you're after?"

"Does there need to be a reason for me to compliment you?"

Huh. Juliet didn't suppose so. But she would admit to not being familiar with this. Wooing women—*escorts*—in a fancy restaurant she could do, but this? In the comfort of her own home, where she was far more exposed? No. This was new. "No. I guess not."

"You just seem much more relaxed at home, you know?"

"Hard to be anything other than relaxed when I have a beautiful woman in my kitchen cooking dinner for me."

Paige turned and narrowed her eyes, a slotted spoon in her hand. "Okay, now it's *you* who sounds like they're trying to get something..."

"Not at all. Just being honest."

"Then I'm glad we can both be honest with one another. That's important to me." Paige turned her back and carried on making dinner. "I've never really had that honesty and trust before. Either I wasn't being true to myself, or I couldn't trust the people around me. But I don't feel that way when I'm here with you."

"I'm glad you feel at ease here."

"Me, too. Life has been...a lot since my mum passed away." Paige cleared her throat, but Juliet had already caught the emotion lodged there. She didn't often speak about her mother, so perhaps now was the time to delve a little deeper. If Paige wanted to, of course. "It was after she died that James really changed."

"Can I ask what happened? With your mum?"

Paige nodded, continuing with dinner. "She was an alcoholic. Always had been for as long as I could remember."

"I'm sorry."

"She had her demons, and she chose to silence them with vodka. But you know what? She always put me first. She wasn't an angry drunk, and she didn't lash out at people. She just...sat alone all day, every day, drinking. We were so close, and I tried to get her help so many times."

"Alcohol is difficult. The number of cases I've worked where the root cause of the problem relates to alcohol is too many to count. It often plays a part in people's lives, unfortunately."

"It's why I became a mixologist," Paige said, turning to Juliet as she rested against the counter. "I'm well aware that a lot of people have a healthy relationship with alcohol, and I wanted to be one of those people. I wanted to see the side of it that didn't ruin lives. I wanted to learn about the technique and the flavours that could be put together to give someone a positive experience. The average alcoholic isn't sitting at home whipping up cocktails most of the time. They're on the hard, raw stuff. Or the cheap stuff. You know?"

"I think it was a good idea for you to change how you see alcohol. You could have either hit the bottle yourself or come to resent it. Instead, you made a career out of it."

"I...didn't want to end up like her. I loved her so much, but once I found out she was drinking a large bottle of vodka a day, I knew she wasn't going to recover. She did try, but in the end, it killed her."

"Trying killed her?" Juliet frowned.

"Yep. She decided one day that she'd had enough." Paige brushed a tear from her jawline, managing the smallest smile. "She thought she could detox herself, but she was so dependent on the drink that she needed to be in hospital for something like that. She'd called and told me she wanted to get off the drink, that she was embarrassed and wanted to see me having kids. I told her not to stop suddenly and that we'd get the specialist help she needed, but I went to see her a few days later, and she was already detoxing. She'd cut out all alcohol completely. She looked terrible." Paige paused, sniffling. Juliet heard the pain in her voice, leading her to wonder if she'd actually had the chance to grieve for her mum. It didn't feel as though she had. "Nine days later, she died in hospital."

Juliet slid from her stool, wrapping Paige up in her arms when she started sobbing. "I'm sorry."

"H-he wouldn't even give me time to be sad. He told me everyone knew it would happen and that I should deal with it and move on." Paige buried her face in Juliet's neck, her body slumped.

Juliet could only hold Paige and give her whatever time she needed to process. It was one thing to lose your mother in your twenties, but to be forced *not* to grieve... That was something else entirely. Juliet rarely hated anyone, but if she ever came across James again, she was likely to stand on his balls until he turned blue.

"And he was just so sickly sweet at the funeral or whenever people came to visit me. But I knew deep down what he was like. I hated sitting in rooms with him and my family because they all gave him the attention that he craved. Always asking about his job and congratulating him on his success...while looking down their noses at me. The reason I didn't work was because *he* wouldn't allow it, but they didn't know that. They just looked at me as though I was some lazy fucker who lived the high life. I would have rather been homeless without a penny than live with him for a moment longer. I just..." Paige pulled back, her eyes swollen. "I didn't feel strong enough to leave. Until I really couldn't stay any longer, anyway."

"You're out now. And I'm going to ensure you make up for all the time you've lost."

Paige gazed back at Juliet. "You have no idea how much you mean to me."

"I do." She kissed Paige's forehead, lingering. "I really do."

Holding onto Juliet's waist, Paige leaned in and kissed her, smiling as her tears dried. "Can I finish making dinner for us, and then we'll just relax?"

"I'd really like that."

Juliet didn't need to be out on the town to enjoy herself. No, she would rather be here, holding Paige while they got to know one another better. She'd spent her life aching for these moments. Now that she had them, she couldn't let them go.

CHAPTER 19
PROMISE ME

"I have to say, Paige. That new whiskey you brought in is very good." John tipped Paige a £20 note, lifting his glass and winking as he turned his back and walked away.

She stared down at it, still confused as to why the people in this bar tipped so well. It wasn't as though Juliet was paying her a terrible wage. Actually, it was above the minimum for the country.

"Hey, John!"

John turned, frowning.

"Thank you." Paige shoved the twenty in her tip jar, wiping down the back of the bar area. She liked to keep things polished and looking fresh, and here at The Hideout, it was required. It wasn't your average dive bar. No, it was classy...a little like its owner.

"Are you cleaning again?" Cara sidled up beside her, laughing. "Does she pay you extra or something?"

"She?" Paige quirked a brow as she side-glanced at Cara. "*She* has a name, and *she* is your boss. Have some respect."

"God, you two are so fucking uptight." Cara trailed a finger up Paige's forearm, grinning as she leaned in. "You really need to lighten up."

Paige spun around, standing toe to toe with Cara. "And if *you* touch me again, I'll have you fired for sexual harassment!"

"Everything okay here?" Juliet appeared out of nowhere.

"Yeah. Fine." Paige cleared her throat, stepping around Cara. "Cara here seems to have an issue with cleanliness. I was reminding her that it takes all of five seconds to wipe down an area."

Juliet nodded, her eyes narrowed as she looked between Paige and Cara. "Mm. I did keep meaning to bring that up. Thanks for reminding me."

"It's fine. I'm sure she'll remember for next time, right?" Paige glanced back at Cara. She seemed shocked that Paige hadn't flipped her shit on her. But Paige didn't need to. She was certain Cara was aware of the consequences now.

"Y-yeah. Sorry. I'll keep on top of it in the future."

"Very well." Juliet followed Paige out from behind the bar, catching her hand. "Can I have a word with you for a few minutes?"

"Sure. If you think Cara can manage alone?"

Juliet smiled, cocking her head towards the office. "I'm sure she'll be fine. Come into the office for a minute."

Paige wondered if she'd done something wrong. Juliet never called her into the office. "Um, yeah. Is everything okay, babe?"

"Oh, of course." Juliet ushered Paige into the office, closing the door behind her. She took an envelope from the desk, handing it over. "Take that with you in the morning."

"What...is it?"

"Some cash. To see you over. I don't want you to have to worry about anything, and I'd rather you just use cash. You know, in case he finds you based on where you use your card."

Paige smiled. "That's why I only use cash now. It's a bit of a pain in the arse when I need to buy something from a cashless place. Quite humiliating too when I walk out empty-handed."

Juliet reached into her handbag on the desk, removing her purse. She took out multiple cards, checking them. "Take this. It's one of my credit cards. I'll text you the pin. Keep it on you, even when you're back, and then you don't have to worry about being caught out in a cashless shop."

Paige held up a hand, pushing it back towards Juliet. "That's really lovely, but I'm fine. I don't need it. I just check now when I go into a shop that they accept cash."

"Paige, please."

"Really, I'm fine. I have plenty of cash. You can take this back too." She thrust the envelope back at Juliet, but she wouldn't accept it. "Babe, come on. Don't make me take this."

"Don't give it back to me." Juliet lifted a shoulder. "Keep it for an emergency. You never know when you might need it."

"But I won't need it. I know I won't."

Juliet sighed, pinching the bridge of her nose. "If you don't take it, I'm coming with you."

"W-what? You're bribing me?"

"If that's the only way to make you take it, yes. You could miss the train or anything and need to find a hotel for the night. There could be a multitude of reasons why you can't get home. At least if you take this cash, I'll know that you have the means to put yourself up somewhere for the night."

Paige nodded, aware that Juliet was worried about tomorrow. "Fine. I'll take it. But expect me to give it back to you tomorrow night when I get back."

"That works for me." Juliet took Paige's hand, pulling her in. "I don't want you to go, Paige."

"But I have to. I need to leave that place behind once and for all. If I don't, I'll never feel free. It's just...something I have to do."

"I know."

"Now, I need to get back out there before Cara pisses off one of the clients with her attitude."

Juliet reluctantly let go of Paige's hand, nodding slowly. "If you must."

"Oh, I don't want to. I'd rather stay locked away in here with you. But if you want to keep the reputation of this place, I should be out there with her."

"Something was going on when I came out there just before. Had she said something to you?"

Paige shrugged. "She was just trying her luck. Nothing to worry about."

Juliet scoffed. "Trying her luck?"

"Yeah. Been there before. Never ends well for the other person." Paige winked, leaning up and kissing Juliet. She wore sexy heels tonight, meaning Paige could just about reach those delicious lips. "Don't worry. I'm all yours."

"Damn right you are!"

Juliet stood back, watching as Paige mingled with clients. She was going to miss working without her tomorrow, but she fully believed that Paige knew what she was doing. She'd witnessed that fear in her eyes at the thought of James finding her. Paige would *not* go back to Kent unless she was certain she'd be safe. She wasn't stupid, and Juliet had to trust that this was going to be okay. If it went wrong somewhere along the way, she could only be there for whatever Paige needed.

Her girlfriend turned back towards the bar, that smile wide and those eyes gleaming. "Hey, do you mind if I hop on the piano for a quick song, babe?"

Juliet's heart beat a little faster. She would never deny that opportunity to Paige. "Please do. And don't ever ask such a question again. That piano *belongs* to you."

Paige rounded the bar, stepping as close to Juliet as she possibly could. She laced their fingers, grinning as she whispered in her ear. "This one is for you, gorgeous."

"It is?"

"Of course it is. All for you."

Juliet wanted to pin Paige to the nearest hard surface, but she had to remain professional. Her clients knew she was in a relationship with Paige, they were all very supportive, but she wouldn't go overboard with public displays of affection. "Then I can't wait to hear it."

Paige offered her a slow kiss, nothing too intimate, and smiled against her lips. "I'm going to miss you tomorrow."

"Don't. I'm trying not to think about it."

"Be back before you know it." With a final chaste kiss, Paige stepped away from Juliet and made a beeline for the piano.

Juliet sighed, mostly content, and watched her girlfriend get situated behind the keys. God, this was overwhelming. She'd never had anyone she called a girlfriend before. But that only made this all the more special. It only meant far more than it usually would to Juliet.

Paige stroked her fingers against the keys, the bar falling silent when Paige closed her eyes and sang the opening line of Beverley Craven's "Promise Me". Her voice immediately sent a shiver down Juliet's spine, her eyes focused on Paige's wrists and fingers as they moved so effortlessly. Was this woman really hers? Juliet, tonight, couldn't quite believe it.

Paige's eyelids fluttered open, and she stared directly at Juliet. Every line, every word, every breath...Juliet felt her own breath begin to labour. And then the tears started to well, Cara's presence beside her suddenly.

Juliet zoned out from everyone around her, only Paige

visible as she serenaded her with the most beautiful vocal her ears had ever had the pleasure of hearing.

"Wow," Cara whispered beside Juliet, leaning in a little more than she would have liked. "Paige has a set of lungs on her."

"Yes, she does. And if you don't close your mouth and just listen very soon, you're fired." Juliet brushed a tear from her cheek, offering a gentle smile in Paige's direction. Her girlfriend winked at her, and it was in that moment that Juliet wanted to get to her knees and tell Paige she loved her. That she needed her. That...they were going to be amazing together.

But she wouldn't.

Paige wouldn't want to hear that neediness from Juliet. It wouldn't be meant as neediness, but it was surely how it would be perceived.

"Can I take my break?" Cara asked.

"Yes. Go. Take as long as you want." Juliet didn't want to hear Cara's voice for another second. It was all Paige. And Paige it would always be. "And for future reference, you don't speak to me when Paige is on piano, okay?"

"You two are obsessed with one another."

No longer willing to entertain Cara, Juliet turned her body and stopped in front of her mediocre bartender. "I don't know who you think you are or who in the world you think you're talking to, but if you want to keep this job, you'll tone down the smart-arse comments. Got it?"

"Whatever."

"Pardon?" Juliet lifted a brow, fully aware of what Cara had said yet daring her to repeat it.

"I said okay. It's just...what does she have that I don't?"

"It's not about what one or the other has. Paige and I are together. If you don't like that, the exit sign is illuminated and clear for you to see." Juliet threw a thumb over her shoulder, directing Cara towards the green exit sign. "The choice is yours, Cara. Don't let me stop you from leaving."

"I...need this job."

"Then I suggest you get on with what you're employed to do."

Cara wrung her hands, bowing her head. "I'm sorry. What I said was uncalled for."

"It was. But I'll let it go if you're willing to understand that you work for me...and that's that."

"I do. I'm sorry."

"Take your break. Maybe get some fresh air. You're a good worker when you put your mind to it."

Cara smiled as she took a step away. "Thanks, Juliet. I am sorry."

Juliet followed Cara as she backed up, narrowing her eyes. "Just one other thing..."

"Y-yes?"

"I *am* watching you. And it's not your work I'm watching. It's those hands. I find them anywhere near Paige again, and you *will* be out of a job."

"I...uh, it won't happen again. You have my word." Cara held up her hands, genuine remorse in her eyes. But Juliet would still keep an eye on her. She didn't know her well enough to take Cara at her word.

As Cara left the bar, Juliet muttered, "Damn right, it won't." And then she turned her attention back to her beautiful girlfriend on piano, the song coming to an end.

Paige stood, taking a slight bow as everyone cheered and clapped. She wore that usual blush when she was being praised, but Juliet loved a blushing Paige. It was far more adorable than she would ever admit. She watched Paige slowly head back to the bar, visibly swallowing as her eyes met Juliet's.

"That was..." Juliet held out a hand, beckoning Paige closer. "God, you don't have any idea how beautiful that was."

Paige shrugged, taking Juliet's hand. "Just some fun, remember?"

"You're still sticking with that? *Really?*"

Paige smiled. "It's easier to stick with that. Because that way, I can't be disappointed when it never comes to anything. Which it won't."

"How can you be so sure?"

"Because I'm not good enough for it to be anything more. And I hate being the centre of attention. It works here because I feel as though these people are my friends. In bars for open mic night isn't so bad because I'll never see those people again, so their opinion doesn't really matter. But anything other than that, no thank you."

"That's a shame." And it really was. The world needed to hear Paige's voice. Her talent was up there with the best of them. "But I won't push you. So long as *I* get the pleasure of hearing your voice, that's good enough for me."

"I'll sing for you any time of day. You know that."

Juliet's heart thundered at that. Perhaps she could find space at her apartment for a piano. The thought alone made her shudder.

"What's got you grinning?" Paige frowned. "Babe?"

"Oh, nothing. Just thinking about you singing privately for me."

"Clothed or unclothed? Because I know that's where your mind went to."

Juliet laughed, pulling Paige in close. "You know me better than I know myself. How is that possible?"

Paige held onto Juliet's waist, those hooded eyes staring up at her. "I don't know. But from the moment I met you, I felt as though we just clicked right into place. Which is a strange feeling for me because I've never really felt connected to another person. Not like this, anyway."

"I know what you're saying. Because I feel the same way. But it feels good, doesn't it? To be so at ease around someone who means so much to you..."

"It really does. And once I'm back tomorrow night, I'm going to start looking for a place more permanent. An apartment that I can call my own. Perhaps look into mortgages once I'm sure I'm comfortable financially."

That knowledge, knowing Paige was serious about making a permanent move to Liverpool...Juliet didn't quite know what to say.

"If you think that's something I should do?"

"Paige, I'd really love it if you stayed." Juliet's voice wavered ever so slightly, her days far more emotional than they used to be before Paige walked through the door to The Hideout. "God, I'd be so happy."

"Then I'm going to do that. Because here, I feel wanted. And needed. And so stupidly happy."

"I want you to be happy. And I want to be a part of that happiness."

Paige kissed Juliet, turning and resting against the bar with her. "You're the reason for my happiness."

CHAPTER 20
HOLD ON

CONTENT WARNING

Just go home. It's going to be fine.

Paige had been telling herself that since she'd boarded the seven o'clock train this morning. Juliet had insisted she drop her at the station, but Paige had needed to walk. To clear her mind and to prepare herself for going inside her old home. Paige had briefly considered the idea of James coming back while she was here, but that was just her anxiety trying to get the better of her. Juliet's guy hadn't mentioned any sightings of James, and other than a message two weeks ago, Paige hadn't heard from James at all. Even that message hadn't been much. Just a simple text to say that he hoped Paige was happy doing whatever she was doing and that he was going to give her space. She hadn't responded. Mostly because she knew it was just James' way of striking up a conversation with her. He'd sent the very same message in the past.

She took her phone from her pocket, bringing up Harriet's number. They should get coffee together while Paige was in

Kent. After today, she wouldn't be returning. *Get your things first, then call her.* Paige locked her phone and crossed the street. She was just thirty seconds away from stepping through the home she lived in with James. He owned it. She didn't. He paid the bills. She didn't. He said what colour scheme they'd have... and Paige would like it.

Breathing a sigh of relief when she found no sign of James' car, she quickly took her key from the inside pocket of her coat and slid it into the lock. Paige glanced around once or twice, hoping the neighbours didn't catch sight of her, and then she slipped inside as inconspicuously as she possibly could.

Get your stuff and get out.

She wouldn't exactly hang around to take anything she didn't absolutely want or need. Paige didn't have anything she could put into that category anyway, though. James had always made this place feel cold and uninviting, so it wasn't hard to detach from this house. As she shoved her key back into her pocket, she heard a noise upstairs. Her heart pounded at the familiar creak of the floorboard on the landing, her mouth dry as she gazed up the stairs.

"P-Paige."

Oh, God.

It wasn't James who'd come to greet her. No, it was Harriet wearing nothing but a pair of James' boxers. Paige turned her back quickly. "I... What the fuck is going on here?" Paige couldn't care less that Harriet was almost naked—it was the fact she was here at all. Was she house sitting for James? God, Paige hoped so. The thought of Harriet being in bed with James had Paige's blood running cold. Then the idea that he was here too had tears almost brimming in her eyes.

"Shit. I'm so sorry. Please don't leave." Harriet's voice cracked, but honestly, Paige was beginning to realise that she was relieved by...whatever was going on here. No, she was *ecstatic* that she had walked in to find Harriet. Because it meant that she wouldn't be alone with James while she packed up her things if he was here. It also meant James didn't have a leg to stand on when she had divorce papers sent out to him. "Paige, I'm sorry."

"Why are you here? Are you...sleeping with him?"

Paige was entirely confused when she heard Harriet sniffle.

"Why did you tell me he was away this weekend?" Was Harriet in on this? No, she couldn't be. She was just oblivious to the fear Paige felt when she was in this house. "Harriet?"

"You asked if I'd seen him lately. I didn't want you to think... or *know*, rather, that this was going on, so I told you he was away." Harriet's voice trembled. "I am sorry."

"Any chance you could put a T-shirt on or something?" Paige slowly turned around, keeping her eyes firmly on the hallway floor. "And then maybe we could talk?"

They wouldn't talk. Paige had nothing to say. She just needed Harriet not to run out the door before Paige was finished here. Quite frankly, she couldn't care less about the fact her best friend was sleeping with her husband. Why would she? It made Paige's life a hell of a lot easier.

"You know, I think I'll just leave. It's probably best if I leave."

Paige looked up at her best friend, no longer interested in the fact she wore practically nothing. "Oh, I don't think so."

"Paige, it was a mistake. James loves you."

"Please, stay. I'm sure we can figure this all out." Paige really would say anything in this moment. "Everything is fine. *Really*. I'm not mad at you."

"You're not?"

"No. I've been a terrible wife lately. I guess I can't blame him." Paige's stomach rolled at those words. She didn't believe a word that came from her mouth, but Harriet didn't know the first thing about her marriage with James. She started slowly up the stairs. "Maybe you could make the coffee while I get something I forgot last time I was home?"

"Y-you're not staying?" Harriet frowned, her arms folded and covering her boobs. "You can't leave again; it'll devastate him."

"What's going on, babe?" James came from the bedroom, his eyes suddenly wide. "Paige, you're home."

"I'm here, yes." She glared at James, glad that Harriet stood between them. "Harriet is going to make a brew while I get something from the spare bedroom. I won't be long. Maybe you could give her a hand?"

"Uh, yeah." James scratched at his beard, confused by the situation this morning. "Sure, yeah. I can do that."

Paige made her way towards the spare bedroom, but James gripped her wrist. Tight. "Good to have you back." Harriet wouldn't have caught it, but Paige did. The look in James' eyes. "Really good."

Paige regarded James with a smile, her throat impossibly dry. She didn't dare speak. The last thing she wanted was for James to hear the fear in her voice. He thrived on fear and pain. "Yeah. It is. I'll have a coffee with two sugars."

She made herself busy in the spare room, quietly taking a hold-all from the bottom of the wardrobe and shoving whatever clothes she could into it. She didn't need much, not really. She was making plenty in tips that would see her over if Paige needed a few new outfits. And while she wasn't paying rent, that could only work in her favour too. The cash Juliet had given her last night was safely in a hidden pocket in her jacket, but Paige didn't plan to dip into it. It wasn't Juliet's job to fund her, and so long as everything went to plan, Paige wouldn't *need* it.

Glancing around the room as she checked the drawers, she blew out a breath, satisfied that she had everything she needed.

Anything that had belonged to her mum—jewellery and whatnot—had been pawned a while ago. They hadn't needed the money. It was just another way for James to hurt Paige. Insisting that it was meaningless and of no sentimental value. But truthfully, those things had meant so much to Paige. It was all she had left.

You don't have time to sit around reminiscing.

Paige lifted the hold-all and quietly left the spare room. She crept down the stairs and placed the bag close to the door, then moved towards the kitchen. If she just took a couple of deep breaths, she wouldn't feel so anxious. James would never lash out while Harriet was here. But when Paige finally plucked up the courage to go *into* the kitchen, Harriet wasn't there. Just James, resting against the counter with his legs crossed at the ankles.

"Where's Harriet?"

James smirked. "She's gone. Told her we needed some time together to sort out all this shit you've caused."

I've caused? Paige wanted to add but didn't. "Right, well, can you just give me a minute to use the loo, and then we'll have that talk?"

"You could have had a piss while you were upstairs!"

"I...didn't realise you wanted to sit down and talk right this second. I'll be a minute, that's all."

James pushed off the counter and slowly walked towards her. "Well, go on. Fucking move yourself."

Paige inhaled a deep breath and turned back out of the kitchen. Thank God she'd thought ahead and left her bag at the door. She eyed it, moving closer, and grabbed the door handle as soon as she was within reach.

But her heart sank when the handle didn't turn. James had double-locked it.

"Going somewhere?" he asked from behind her.

"N-no." Paige felt the tears already forming in her eyes. She tried to focus on the positive steps she'd taken. She tried to remember Juliet's calming smile. But it all blurred into one. In this moment, she couldn't even recall what Juliet smelt like.

She felt James behind her, his breath on her neck, and then his hand came up and gripped the back of it, tightening further and further. "I don't know what the fuck you think you're doing, but you won't make a fool out of me again!"

"James, please." Paige wanted to scream, to call out to anyone who may hear her, but as she lifted her hands to hopefully brace on impact, she was too late. She felt her face hit the door...

And then everything turned black.

Juliet checked her watch for the fifth time in three minutes. She continued to pace in front of her bedroom window, her apartment cold and lonely since Paige left six hours ago. She knew she shouldn't worry, Paige was certain James was out of the country, but Juliet had a bad feeling. So bad that she almost got into her car two hours ago and drove down south. It would take her the best part of six hours on a Saturday, but then she remembered that the last thing Paige would want was Juliet showing up at her door if James *was* there.

But...Paige wasn't answering her calls. Or her texts. She was showing as online via her social media messenger service, but that didn't necessarily mean anything.

Juliet lifted the piece of paper Paige had left her earlier containing the address she was going to. Juliet knew what she should do, that she should already be on her way to the small village in Kent, but her heart told her not to. Her heart...told her it wouldn't be a good idea.

Only her law head was saying otherwise. The lawyer in her was telling Juliet that she should have already made a call to the police. No, the lawyer in her was saying that she never should have let Paige go alone. How fucking stupid could she be to allow that? If anything happened to Paige, this would be solely on Juliet. Because she hadn't stood her ground, she hadn't begged Paige up until the very last second, she...hadn't gone too.

But her respect for Paige and the fact that she'd asked Juliet not to go with her sat at the forefront of her mind. She couldn't do something Paige had asked her not to. Then she had to consider if Paige had left her old address behind in case Juliet needed it. God, why was it so fucking difficult to know what to do for the best? Juliet hated feeling this way.

Her phone flashed in her hand, Juliet's stomach rolling as she looked down at the screen.

Please don't call me again. I'm okay.

Juliet frowned. Surely Paige hadn't sent that message to her. It seemed so...lifeless.

I just want to know that you arrived okay. You said you'd text when you got there and had a rough idea of the time you'd be coming back. J x

Juliet swallowed as she stared down at the screen. She never should have let Paige leave the city.

I made it here. Not sure of the time I'm leaving yet. Getting things together.

On shaky legs, Juliet lowered herself to the edge of the bed. Paige seemed out of character, but Juliet had to consider whether her own mind was just jumping to that conclusion. If Paige was busy packing, she wouldn't have time to stand around texting Juliet.

Will you call me when you leave the house? J x
Yeah.

Juliet swallowed, tears filling her eyes as she stared down at the one-word response. She wanted to insist she drive down to collect Paige, but she'd never go for it. Still, she found herself asking anyway.

If I leave now, I could be there before dark. J x

No! Don't come here!

Okay. But if you need me, you'll tell me, won't you? J x

I'm fine. I'll be fine. Go to work and I'll see you when I see you.

Juliet brought her phone to her ear, her hand shaking as she waited for the call to connect. "Hey, I need you to do something for me."

"Sure. What is it?"

"Paige Harrison. Find out anything you can about her. Where she frequents. Generally down in Kent. Any family? Friends? That sort of thing." Juliet needed to find Paige. She had no idea where to look, so she hoped Henry could help.

"Everything okay, Jules?"

Juliet swallowed down the lump in her throat. "I don't know. I hope so. Whatever you find, however minute, let me know. I'll be leaving for the bar in the next hour."

"You got it."

The call ended, leaving Juliet with nothing other than her racing thoughts. Thoughts she didn't want to have, thoughts she didn't need, thoughts...that made her want to throw up.

Paige didn't want Juliet to involve herself, and she had to respect that. But it didn't mean she couldn't have some information on hand if she needed it. Because as she sat here, alone and scared for her girlfriend, Juliet suspected she *was* going to need it.

Her phone buzzed in her hand.

"Yes?"

"Did you say Harrison?" The deep voice she'd relied on for the last several months strangely comforted her.

"Yes."

"No record of a Paige Harrison. At least, not one that matches up with your Paige."

Juliet smiled. *My Paige*.

"Try...Dunbar." Paige was married to James Dunbar, so she surely had to be in the system under that name. "And if she shows under that name, find out her maiden name too. It's clearly not Harrison."

"Got it. Leave it with me."

"Thanks."

Juliet lay back on the bed, still wearing her robe from this morning, and calmed her breathing. If she didn't, she was going to have a panic attack. Because the longer she waited to hear from Paige, the more that fear grew.

And then her phone vibrated.

She brought it up to her face, tears spilling down her cheeks.

Done. I'm out. I just need some time to get myself together, and then I'll call you. Give me a few days. Maybe a week. I don't know. I just know that I can't see you right now. I'm sorry. Paige x

Juliet sat bolt upright, her heart hammering. Part of her was thrilled that Paige had managed to get her stuff and get out, but the rest of her had dread sinking to the pit of her stomach. Paige wasn't coming back today? Or this week?

And then another message came through.

I'm probably way off the mark here in thinking you'd even want to hear this, but I love you. If I don't make it back, just know that I love you. It doesn't even matter that you don't feel the same. I just had to say it. I don't want

anything to happen and I never have the chance to tell you. You mean the entire world to me. Paige x

If Paige never had the chance to say it... What the hell did that mean? Juliet should have been grinning from ear to ear at the mere thought of Paige loving her, but instead she was dissecting the rest of the message.

Please come back to me, Paige. I love you, too. J x

CHAPTER 21
ALL FOR YOU

"You better have something for me, Henry." Juliet rested against the piano as Henry eyed her, then Cara. "Oh, she's fine. Don't worry about Cara being here. We're only doing a stock take." It was Thursday; Juliet didn't need to be here. But it beat sitting at home.

"You know how this goes, Jules. I need you alone."

Juliet nodded, pushing off the piano. "Cara, can you…make yourself busy elsewhere for a few minutes?"

"Sure." Cara threw down a bar towel and left the room, but Juliet lifted it and folded it just the way Paige would have. It wasn't hard to keep things tidy for when Paige returned, and she would remind Cara of that once Henry had left.

"So?" Juliet turned back to Henry, anxiety swirling around in her belly as it had for the last five days. Only the longer this went on, the more it grew. She hadn't actually eaten anything substantial in the last three days, but she was used to running on fumes from her law days. "Please, tell me you have something?"

"Maiden name is Ashburn."

Juliet dropped into her spot, running a hand through her hair.

"This is really affecting you, isn't it? You look terrible, Jules."

"Thanks. I appreciate you reminding me." Juliet rolled her eyes, sinking back into the couch. She offered a seat to Henry, but he held up a hand and refused.

"I called in a favour or two. Some of the guys I used to work with still have connections. Paige is in Birmingham. I checked for relatives around the area, but she appears to be an only child, mother deceased. No record of a father."

"She's in Birmingham." Juliet nodded slowly, repeating what Henry said and giving it a moment or two to sink in. She knew Paige wouldn't have stayed in Kent once she'd collected her things, and for the first time, she finally felt as though she was getting somewhere this afternoon. "And when was the last time you checked her location?"

"Oh, this information came via a friend an hour ago. Latest ping on her phone was," Henry paused, checking his watch. "Seventy-one minutes ago."

"I need to find her, Henry. I think she's in trouble."

Henry did take a seat this time. "What kind of trouble, Jules?"

"Husband trouble. Domestic violence case."

Henry squared his shoulders and cleared his throat. "So, you'll be wanting a visit to Kent, I assume? I can ask one of the guys to handle that, or I can go myself, but then it leaves *you* vulnerable."

"I don't care about me right now. If I don't find Paige, if I don't keep her safe, I'll pray whoever wants *me* dead finds me."

"Jules, I'll handle this. When have I ever let you down?"

Juliet lifted a brow, a faint smile playing on her lips. "You really want me to answer that, H?"

He grinned. "No, probably best if you don't. But you know I

have your back on this. Say the word, and I'll pay the bastard a visit."

"I just want to find her first. Can you help me do that?"

"Already have."

Juliet frowned. Was Henry talking about the information he'd already gathered and shared or was he holding something back for dramatic effect? "Talk to me, Henry."

"Paige is staying at a three-star hotel in the very centre of the city. Maybe she wants to blend in, I don't know."

Juliet shot to her feet, taking her coat that hung over one of the barstools. "What hotel? And how the hell did you find her? I told her to *only* use cash."

"She has a credit card in her maiden name. Clever if you ask me. It rarely has any activity on it, but she checked in two nights ago and is booked in for a total of four. It's definitely her. Security camera picked her up going in." If Paige had only been there for two nights, where the hell had she been before that? Jesus, this was too much for Juliet's brain to take this morning.

"And coming out?"

Henry shook his head. "No sign of her coming out so far."

Juliet placed a hand to her chest and closed her eyes, praying her emotions remained buried deep down. Paige was hiding, she was alone, and she was scared. Even if she didn't want to be with Juliet anymore—and that was the impression Juliet was getting—she couldn't leave her there. It didn't matter that the last message she'd received was Paige telling Juliet she loved her. It didn't matter that she saw a future with Paige. What mattered at the moment was that Juliet could push all of that to one side and be a friend...nothing more. It clearly wasn't what Paige needed right now.

"I...need to close up. I know she doesn't want to see me, but I can't sit here knowing she's out there alone."

"Do you want me to go and get her?" Henry asked, genuine concern in his eyes. "I can leave now..."

"Thank you, but no. I should be the one who knocks on her hotel room door."

Henry smiled. "I understand. If you need me, call me. I'll follow you to a point so I'm close by."

"Okay, thanks. I need to go home and change. Make myself look a little more professional."

Henry frowned. "Professional? What for?"

"How else am I supposed to gain access to her hotel room number?"

Henry reached out and squeezed Juliet's shoulder, smiling. "You're a clever woman, Jules. It's a pleasure working for you."

With her knees pulled up to her chest, Paige sat in the corner of her hotel room. She'd spent the last three hours down here, perched under the window, just playing music on repeat through her earphones. While she listened to music, she wasn't in her own head. While she wasn't in her own head, she couldn't miss Juliet.

Because she did. She missed Juliet more than she thought possible. When she lay in bed each night, she longed for those protective arms around her. When she sat staring at the wall every day, she prayed she could one day return to Liverpool. It felt like home. The people, the buildings, the happiness. Liverpool had it in bucketloads. It felt like her place to be. When she stood in front of the three graces, it took her breath away. Liverpool was where she wanted to be, but she didn't know how to leave this room anymore. It had become her place of safety. Before she arrived here, everywhere else had felt too close to her old home.

James hadn't contacted her. He would be out there keeping a watchful eye, no doubt about it. But Paige *had* to run on Saturday.

Once she'd come around, curled in a ball on the hallway floor, she quickly realised James had locked her in her house again. Paige had managed to break the double-glazed window in the back kitchen and climb out. She didn't know how, it must have been the adrenaline that helped in some way, but she'd fled, and that was all she cared about. James hadn't been home, he didn't like to stick around when he'd beaten her in the past, but he remained cocky in his ability to restrain Paige. Or so he thought, anyway.

And now, here she sat. Alone, tired, and fed up with life. Just last night, she'd stared down at her screen, at Juliet's number, and sobbed until she'd fallen asleep. But sleep hadn't lasted very long. Another resident had been quite rowdy coming back to their room, and it had put the fear of God in Paige. She'd gone into such a deep sleep that the sound out in the corridor had scared the life out of her.

Her playlist switched to a new song, fresh tears falling down her thighs where her head rested on her knees. "All for You" by Cian Ducrot played through her earphones, his gravelly voice and heart-wrenching lyrics tearing Paige in two.

This song...could have been written for her. For Juliet. For the mess their relationship was in. Paige knew what she wanted in her heart, but Juliet didn't need all of this. She was a mature, professional woman who'd once had one hell of a reputation throughout this country. Paige, battered and bruised, wasn't worth a single thing in her life. Juliet would argue that wasn't true, but Paige couldn't put her through all of this. *Nobody* wanted to go through this.

Paige...didn't want to be here anymore.

Not in this hotel room.

And not on this planet.

She swallowed, her ribs aching from her position, but refused to move. The same song started to play again, continuing to destroy Paige from the inside out.

But the sudden feeling of a presence in the room had Paige's hair standing on the back of her neck. James...had found her.

This was it. He was going to end this once and for all. Paige rocked back and forth, her hands gripping her ankles. If she could will it all away, maybe James wouldn't notice her. Maybe he'd see how worthless she was and realise the fight wasn't worth scratching his knuckles for.

A hand on her shin had Paige's breath caught in her throat, her instant reaction to try to crawl backwards. But the wall was there, and she couldn't crawl up the wall. Her head shot up, eyes wide, knowing she had nowhere to go, but it wasn't James staring back at her.

It was a retreating Juliet.

Paige placed a hand to her chest, her deep breathing only causing further pain to her ribs. God, he'd really put some effort into the blows he'd inflicted.

"I'm sorry," Juliet said as she moved away as far as she possibly could. "I'm sorry, I shouldn't have come in, but you didn't respond when I knocked, and I..." Juliet sat back on her knees in the middle of the room, her bottom lip trembling. "I had to let myself in. I had to see you were okay."

Paige just stared. Dumbfounded that Juliet was in her hotel room with her. And then the realisation that Juliet could see the state Paige was in dawned on her. She turned her face and her body away, focusing her gaze on the wall. "I'm fine. S-so you can go."

A strangled sob from Juliet had tears falling down Paige's face, but she couldn't do this. She couldn't bring herself to look Juliet in the eye.

"Paige," Juliet whimpered, the fear in the room palpable. "Can I... May I..." She paused and sniffled. "Can I come closer?"

"What for?" Paige pressed her temple to the wall, her eyes closed.

"To check you over. To...hold your hand. Just...to be there for you."

Paige chewed her bottom lip, trying to calm her emotions. But Juliet being here and wanting to see that Paige was okay was just bringing out more emotion. More tears. More pain. "I... I'm okay. Really."

"Baby, you're not." Juliet's voice broke. Paige could feel her inching closer, but she didn't want her up close and personal. Because then she would see the black eyes, the bruised jaw, the split lip. "Paige, please?"

"I tried to leave," Paige spoke barely above a whisper. "I had my bag, and I thought Harriet was still there. But she wasn't; he'd asked her to leave. And then...I don't know. He smashed my face against the door and knocked me out." Paige swallowed, finally turning to Juliet. Only Juliet wasn't in the middle of the room anymore. She was on her knees in front of Paige. "I...thought he was going to kill me."

Juliet reached out a hand, softly placing it over Paige's. "I'm sorry I wasn't there for you."

"I knew it was coming. Once I realised the door was locked, I knew it was coming. I had my back to him, and all I was trying to remember was your face. I needed the last thing I ever saw to be your face. But I couldn't. I couldn't see you, I couldn't feel you, I couldn't smell you. I'd just left you that morning, and I couldn't remember what you looked like."

Juliet didn't say anything. She shifted until she was beside Paige, her own knees brought up to her chest. "Paige, I...need to hold you."

Paige turned her face to Juliet, noting the shock in her eyes immediately. Paige knew how she looked. She wasn't surprised by Juliet's reaction at all. "I'm in pain."

Juliet whimpered at those words, the back of her head pressed against the wall, her eyes closed. "This is all my fault. I should have been here. And now..."

Yeah. Now what? Paige thought.

"Now I don't know how to make this right. How to fix you."

Paige slowly reached her hand over and touched it to Juliet's knee. "I'm going to be okay." Maybe she would, and maybe she wouldn't. But Paige had to at least put that out there so one or both of them could feel better about the situation.

"Will you come back home with me?" Juliet settled her hand over Paige's. "Right now, with me, back to my place."

"I...yes." Paige studied Juliet's profile, a tear as it slowly glided down her cheek. She had no idea what was to come in the weeks ahead, but she knew she didn't want to stay in this hotel room alone. "If that would be okay?"

Juliet turned, her eyes swollen and red. "I don't want you anywhere other than with me."

While Paige adored hearing those words from Juliet, they couldn't mean anything. She loved this woman, she had no issues with saying that out loud, but Paige couldn't stay in Liverpool long-term. Once James had regrouped, he'd be out there looking for her again. Paige couldn't risk one final showdown with him. She simply wouldn't survive.

"Would you like me to help you up off the floor?" Paige noted that hesitation in Juliet's eyes, but she got to her feet and held out a hand. "I know you don't want me too close, but I just need to help you up."

Paige smiled as Juliet carefully helped her up from the floor. She slowly put an arm around Paige's waist, the uncertainty in Juliet's touch causing an ache deep in Paige's heart. "Thank you."

"Maybe you should rest while I get your things together. A nap could be good for you. We can leave after you've taken your next lot of medication. I'll go downstairs and get you a bite to eat."

Juliet turned to leave, but Paige reached out and took her hand. "Don't go. Please."

"O-okay."

"Will you lie with me? I haven't been sleeping very well."

"Sure." Juliet helped Paige onto the bed, kicking off her heels as she rounded the foot and took the comforter that was folded on the chair. She climbed onto the bed beside Paige, covering her up carefully. "How's that?"

"Perfect, thank you."

Juliet lay down, staring up at the ceiling, but Paige couldn't take her eyes off her. She really was the ideal woman. Damn, she was going to miss this.

"Juliet?"

"Mm?" She didn't turn to Paige. She just focused above her, tears slowly working their way down her cheeks.

"I do love you."

Juliet inhaled a deep breath, her eyes closing as she puffed out her cheeks. "Get some rest. Your body needs it in order to heal."

CHAPTER 22
TO BE LOVED

"How are you feeling?"

Startled by the voice coming from the open bedroom door, Paige grimaced and turned to face Juliet. "I've been better."

They'd been back at the apartment for just over an hour, and Paige had decided to take Juliet's spare room rather than share a bed with her. It wasn't that she didn't want to, but doing so would be a mistake. It would imply that Paige was staying, that she wasn't worried about the day when James came barrelling through Juliet's door. Sharing a bed with Juliet would only make this far more difficult than it needed to be.

"Can I get you something to eat? I was going to cook, but I think it's best if I just order in."

Paige shook her head, limping across the room to her hold-all. "No, thank you. I'm not really feeling up to eating."

"Understandable." Juliet cleared her throat, moving towards Paige. "Can I help you unpack?"

Paige lay a hand on Juliet's wrist as she reached into the hold-all, stopping her. "I'm just going to leave it as it is for now. It's been a long day, you know?"

"Then...can I hold you?" That glint in Juliet's eyes didn't go unnoticed by Paige, but it only broke her heart.

Paige shook her head. "It's best if you don't."

"Why?"

"Because it's going to make all of this so much harder."

"Make what harder?" Juliet frowned, but she reached out a hand and gently touched Paige's face. "I want to help you. Please, let me do that."

"I'm...leaving."

Juliet's face paled. "I...what? Leaving?"

"I'm leaving England."

Juliet's shoulders slumped as those words sunk in. "I... thought you loved me."

"I do," Paige said, shifting gingerly in her spot. Juliet caught the wince but hesitated as she reached out an arm to help Paige. "But it doesn't change the fact that I can't stay in this country any longer. He's going to kill me."

"You think I'd let that happen?"

"I admire your confidence, and I adore how strong you are, but even you can't stop him. And I'm not risking him finding me with you and hurting you. If he ever laid a hand on you, I *would* kill him."

"Do one thing for me then, please?"

"W-what?"

"Stay here while you recover. And then, even though it hurts me to say this...I'll help you leave. I'll help you to get to anywhere in the world you want to be. I'll make sure you're safe."

"Why would you do that for me?"

Juliet closed her eyes, her cheeks damp as she exhaled a calming breath. "Because I love you, and I'd never ask you to stay if you didn't feel safe with me."

Paige lowered her eyes, that feeling of being loved bittersweet. It wasn't that she didn't feel safe with Juliet, she felt entirely safe in her arms, but it wasn't the same kind of safety when James was still out there. And it wasn't about Juliet not being capable. It was down to the fact that Paige couldn't take another beating. Because if she did...she could guarantee it would be her last.

"I've waited all my life for you, Paige. Your personality, that beautiful smile, that infectious laugh. It may be early days, but I know you're the one I've been waiting for. When you float off into your own world behind that piano, I want to run away with you. When you sleep beside me, just hearing your gentle breathing makes me feel safe in not only my own home but my skin. That's just how you make me feel. Happy. Pure joy. And while I never want to lose that, I want you to do what's best for you. So, please, stay here, and I promise that when you've recovered, I won't ask you to stay."

Juliet's face had devastation written all over it. But Paige understood because she felt that same way.

"I just..." Juliet shook her head, sighing. "Can I kiss you one last time?"

Paige could barely see through her swollen, tear-filled eyes. But she knew she couldn't leave without kissing Juliet.

"I want so much to kiss you, to hold you, but if you don't feel comfortable with that, I understand."

Paige leaned in, mindful of her split lip, and kissed Juliet. It wasn't the type of kiss she wanted to be sharing with her, but it was all she could manage. Juliet placed the gentlest hand on Paige's cheek, her body shaking as she sobbed against Paige's lips.

"I'm sorry it wasn't a better last kiss, but I'm in pain."

Juliet somehow managed a smile, but Paige saw right past the mask. "It was a perfect last kiss." Juliet brushed the back of her hand across Paige's cheek and stepped back. "I'm sorry. I... shouldn't have done that."

"It's okay. Your hands are nothing like his hands." It hurt so much to see Juliet like this, almost broken, but Paige knew this was for the best.

"Can I get you some medication?"

"I'm not due any for another hour. I've been piggybacking paracetamol and ibuprofen."

"I think you may need something stronger. I'll see what we have." Juliet held up a hand. "Sorry. What *I* have."

Paige may be the one choosing to leave, but this wasn't going to be easy for her either. They may not have spent a lifetime together, but it felt as though they had. This was going to be an adjustment for the time she remained in the country. "Thank you for being there for me."

"I would have been with you on Saturday if you'd told me where you were staying. You wouldn't be in this condition if I'd come with you in the first place." Paige frowned when Juliet clenched her jaw, anger flaring in her eyes. "I should have been there."

Paige watched as Juliet paced around the room, likely not knowing what to do with herself. "Juliet, I didn't want to see you while I looked like this."

Juliet nodded slowly. "It's just...I feel like you took that chance to be with you out of my hands, and now you're just going to leave, and that's the end of us. I'm having a hard time comprehending what I've done to deserve that. Just last week, you were planning to find a place here. You wanted to be with me, and now...I'm losing you."

"You've been perfect. Really, you have." Paige tried to reach out a hand, but Juliet moved further away. "Juliet."

"I can't. I'm sorry. Seeing you like this, but not being 'allowed' to help you or care for you...it doesn't feel right. *I* don't feel right. This wasn't how I thought it would go when I got you back."

Got you back. Oh, Paige's heart was close to breaking once and for all now.

"If I'd known you were coming, I'd have asked you not to."

"I know. That's why I couldn't tell you I knew where you were. Because I needed to see with my own eyes the condition you were in. I didn't want to imagine the worst, but I lay in bed for those five nights that you were gone, unable to sleep worrying about you. But now that you're here, I feel as though I don't have any right to worry about you."

"Of course you do."

"Still, it won't change anything, will it? I mean, you're adamant you're leaving?"

Paige sighed as she lowered herself slowly to the bed. "Y-yes."

"Then from this moment on, I need to only be a friend to you, Paige. That may sound awful, I feel dreadful for just saying it, but I can't have you here with me and pray that you'll see I'm worth it, only for you to leave and I'll never see you again. I'm not cut out for that. You may think I am, that I'm this stoic ex-lawyer, but I have a heart, too. *Unfortunately.*"

"I understand."

Juliet's eyes darted around the room as she wrung her hands. Paige couldn't bear to see Juliet like this. Looking as though she felt useless.

"Do you need to go to the hospital? I'm sure you've already been to the police station, but maybe a check-up would be wise."

"I don't want to speak to the police. I just want to leave and never see him again. Forget all about this mess I got myself into." Paige had gone over it all in her head for every second of the day recently, but she came back to the fact that she didn't want to make a police statement. Paige didn't have the energy to go through a trial. Juliet wouldn't like that at all, more so not the lawyer in her, but it was Paige's decision. And her decision was final. "A divorce would have been enough, but there's no chance I'm going to get that from him. It would require him admitting defeat."

"While I think you're making a mistake not going to the police, I'm not going to make you do anything you don't want to do. But I am going to ask you once more if you'll please stay here with me until I know you're better."

"You're sure you don't mind?"

Juliet smiled, cocking her head. "It would be nice to spend whatever time we have left together. Even if only to have you around the place. I won't overstep, I'm aware of what's happening here, but I would like to have you here until you've made some decisions on where you'll go."

"Okay."

Juliet crossed the room, taking both of Paige's hands as she sunk to her knees in front of her. "I'll never regret anything more than not being there with you. And if you hate me for that, for not pushing harder when you wanted to go there alone, then I accept that this is on me. I'm so sorry, Paige. I'll never forgive myself."

"I chose to go there alone. You have nothing to be sorry for."

Lowering her eyes between them, Juliet squeezed Paige's hands. "It doesn't feel that way."

"Just having you here with me now...it means the world to me. And deep down, you know how much I appreciate it."

Juliet shifted and took a seat beside Paige. She really wished things could be different, that she could be confident that James was finally done once and for all, but Paige couldn't risk it.

"For the shortest time, I felt so happy with you, Paige. You made me realise that there was so much more to life than just existing and working. You...made me feel something deep down. I had a purpose again that extended beyond my career. And I know that you'll move on from Liverpool and forget all about me, but I'll never forget about you. Remember that, okay? Remember that when you're falling in love with someone, when you're building a life and a home with them, even just while you're enjoying your first coffee of the day...that *you* made me so unbelievably happy. You're more than capable of planning out a whole new life, and I'm excited for what your future holds."

Juliet lowered Paige's hands into her lap and stepped away. She heard the sniffle, she watched as Juliet's shoulders slumped, and then she felt an immense loss as Juliet glanced back at her with tears in her eyes.

"Thank you, Paige."

"F-for what?"

"Showing me that I can be loved." Juliet smiled half-heartedly, her eyes closed briefly. "And for the most beautiful last kiss."

CHAPTER 23
FOREVER

Juliet watched Paige sleeping from the doorway to her spare room, anger ferociously bubbling away deep inside her. Paige's beautiful face was swollen, those eyes she'd dreamt about while Paige was gone deep purple, now beginning to yellow. The last twenty-four hours had been hard; Juliet didn't know what to do for the best, but if she knew one thing for certain, it was that she was going to lose Paige in the coming weeks. She'd witnessed the determination in her eyes last night as she told Juliet she was leaving.

She wanted to try. She wanted to show Paige she could have a meaningful, happy life here in Liverpool. But who was Juliet to do that to her? She had no right to beg Paige to stay, and she wouldn't. She...*couldn't*. Juliet meant it last night when she told Paige she'd help her leave. It was the least she could do given the situation they were in. Maybe some would criticise Juliet, insisting this wasn't *her* situation, but Paige was her responsibility in some way...and she'd failed her. God, she'd let her down like she didn't know it was possible.

Juliet turned away, brushing a tear from her jaw. She couldn't face the day when Paige left for good. She'd grown far too attached to wave her off and wish her well. Still, she couldn't sit and dwell on that moment. She had far more important things to take care of.

Needing to talk this through with someone, she lifted her phone and moved down the hallway into the kitchen. Paige would be sleeping for a while longer yet, and even if she wasn't, it was quite clear the relationship they had now. So Juliet would give her some space, time to process the last week, and unless Paige specifically asked that Juliet be around, let her be.

She puffed out her cheeks, bringing up a number she hadn't called in many months. When the call connected, she couldn't help but smile.

"Well, if it isn't the woman who pissed off and forgot I existed!"

"Hannah, hi. How are you?"

"Friendless now that you've buggered off! But otherwise good."

Juliet rested against the kitchen counter, closing her eyes. She'd gotten out of the habit of staying in touch with her ex-escort turned employee, but it was really good to hear Hannah's voice. "Is there any chance you can get out of the office for an hour?"

"I'm not working today. So, yes. I can meet you. Save me from this mountain of laundry and tell me where. I'm sure Edie and Caz have some kind of competition going to see who can wear the most clothes in a single friggin' day!"

Oh, how Juliet's heart ached for something so trivial. "Count yourself lucky that you can even complain about that."

"Still nothing in the stars for you then?"

If only. She'd had it...and now she was losing it. Juliet cleared her throat. "If I send you the address, can you be there soon?"

"Sure. Is it in the city? I'll drive in now."

"Yes. I'll text you the address." Juliet took her bag from the breakfast stool and scribbled a note to Paige, leaving it on the counter. "I'm leaving my place now. And Hannah?"

"Yeah?"

"Thanks for this. I really appreciate it."

She felt Hannah smiling down the line. But that was Hannah, always happy even if life threw shit at her. "No problem, boss!"

Juliet ended the call and sent off the address, glancing down the hallway once more before she left her apartment. And then her phone started to vibrate in her hand as she stepped into the lift. "Henry, hi."

"How are things this morning, Jules?"

"Paige is sleeping. *I'm* seething. I may be in prison by the end of the day!"

Henry sighed. "Bad, huh?"

"Are you outside?" Juliet asked, stepping out of the lift and heading for the exit. Her mind flashed back to the moment she'd met James here, her stomach turning at the mere thought of his face.

"I am. Usual spot."

"I'm coming out now."

Juliet had opted for jeans and a pair of Converse today, the thought of dressing up the last thing on her mind. She'd barely made it out of bed this morning, let alone picked out an outfit. As the rain pelted her, the wind howling as she rushed across the car park, the electronic gates opened, and she jogged across the street to Henry's car.

"You couldn't have timed that any more poorly." Henry laughed, handing Juliet some napkins from the side of his door. "You look like a drowned rat."

"If you say something about my appearance once more, *you'll* be disappearing, my friend."

"Talk to me. Tell me what you two need."

"You don't know anyone who can run a bar for me, do you?" Juliet was joking, she had a very specific kind of clientele at The Hideout, but she would be lying if she said the thought had never crossed her mind. One day off a week wasn't what she had in mind when she'd taken early retirement.

"Dabbled in bar work myself over the years." Henry lifted a brow, tapping his fingers against the steering wheel. "Look, Jules, if you need to be at your place with Paige, the bar can take a backseat. I'm sure people would understand."

"To be honest, the bar is the only thing that keeps me sane at the moment. I know where I stand with that place."

"I get that."

"So," Juliet paused, aware that her next words could really fuck everything up. "I need you to pay a visit to the guy at this address." She handed over a piece of paper that had James' address written on it. "I don't want anything too heavy, but you don't leave that house until he agrees to a divorce."

"And if he doesn't agree easily?"

"Kneecaps. Nothing more." Juliet was disappointed that she'd just said those words, but Paige was more important than anything else in her life. If James needed to be scared...beaten into giving her the divorce, he was getting off lightly. If Juliet had her way, she'd have insisted Henry end James without a second thought. But she had to think about Paige. The comeback on her. She couldn't live with herself if something went wrong and Paige was arrested. Juliet didn't care if she was, though. She'd take this one on the chin if it meant Paige was safe. "I mean that, Henry. Nothing more."

"Got it. And it'll be my pleasure."

"You're a good man. But now I have to go because I have a meeting at the bar. Stay here until you can get cover."

"What about you?" Henry's brows drew together. "You won't have anyone watching your back."

"At this point, I no longer care about any threats made against me. I'm about to lose everything anyway, so what does it matter?"

"What's going on?"

"Paige is leaving." Juliet stared out of the windscreen, tears blurring her vision. "And there's nothing I can do to stop her. I *wouldn't* do anything to stop her. She...God, she's in a bad way, H. Black eyes, possible broken ribs, bruising all over her." Juliet almost didn't stomach that, but she fought back the urge to empty the contents of her stomach. "I wasn't there to protect her, and now she's leaving."

"That's not on you, Jules. It's on that shithouse husband who beats women."

Juliet smiled weakly. "Maybe so, but I should have known. I should have made her listen. I...should have been there with her."

"Everything will work itself out in the end. It always does."

Juliet placed her hand on the door handle, nodding slowly. "I hope everything works out for her how it's supposed to. She deserves far more than this. Let me know when you're leaving for Kent. Don't go until someone is watching this place."

"Got it. Take it easy, Jules. I'll call you."

"Well, I didn't expect to meet you in a place like this." Hannah whistled as she came down the stairs. "You do realise I'm not your escort anymore, don't you?"

Juliet smiled from the darkened corner of her spot in the bar. "I'm aware. But this isn't a business call. It's...a friendly call."

Hannah frowned when Juliet's voice broke. "What's going on? And why the hell are you sitting here in the dark?"

Juliet slid a coffee towards Hannah, urging her to sit down. "I took the liberty of assuming I still knew your coffee order. But since I don't seem to be able to get anything right lately, I'm probably wrong."

"Any coffee is good coffee for me today." Hannah slowly sat down beside Juliet, her brows drawn together. "Please don't be offended, but you look like shit. Is everything okay?"

Hannah was the only person who would get away with saying such a thing to her. And that was purely down to the fact that she knew Hannah was right. When Juliet had reached the bar, she'd been shocked when she looked in the bathroom mirror.

"Honestly, no." She ran her hands down her thighs, puffing out her cheeks. "How's Caz and Edie?"

"Yeah, they're good. Edie is excelling in school, and Caz loves the headteacher job. She's come into her own since she took it. I'm so proud of her for doing something for herself, you know?"

Juliet's bottom lip trembled at that. She'd give anything in this world to feel even an ounce of what Hannah felt with her partner and daughter. "I'm happy it's all worked out for you."

"Really? Because you don't look it." Hannah reached for her coffee, sitting back on the couch. "Is that why you stopped calling? Because it all worked out for me?"

"God, no. I've been busy getting this place set up and whatnot."

"I...don't follow."

"Oh, I own this. Early retirement wasn't really working out for me. I was bored to fucking tears."

"Wow. I never once pinned you for a bar owner. But hey, if it makes you happy, that's great."

"It did. For a short time. I mean, the place makes a lot of money, but...everything else is falling apart."

"Juliet Saunders' life does *not* fall apart." Hannah laughed, and shook her head. "What happened? Did your nail technician cancel your appointment, and now the end is nigh?"

Juliet's mind flashed back to a time when Paige was behind the bar. Her smile and how it lit up the place. Her gentle but sexy voice as she spoke with clients. God, she'd never look at this place the same way again. Perhaps if Paige had joined further down the line, she would feel different about being here without her, but she hadn't. Paige *was* The Hideout. Tears brimmed in Juliet's eyes, her chest tight. "No."

"Juliet Saunders also doesn't cry, so what the hell is going on?" Hannah shifted closer, placing a hand on Juliet's knee. But that supportive touch only had Juliet sobbing into her hands. "Juliet?"

"I had it. Almost, at least."

"H-had what?"

"What you have. She started working here the night I opened. Paige. Mixologist."

Hannah smiled when she noted that look in Juliet's eyes. But it was hard not to show how fond of Paige she was.

"We flirted from the get-go. She was just so easy-going with a great personality. You know, the kind of person you want to bump into every day?"

"Mm. I know how that feels."

"Then I found out she'd rented a place in my apartment block. Two doors away."

"If that's not a sign, I don't know what is." Hannah sighed, clearly enjoying where this was going. But Hannah had always told Juliet her time would come. She was certain of it. "Did you date?"

"We...kind of skipped the actual dating stage." Sitting here now, Juliet was beginning to wish she'd taken Paige on a real date. God, she'd done everything entirely wrong. "But sure, we dated in our own way. We were happy."

"And now you're not?" Hannah frowned, holding up a hand. "What could have possibly gone so wrong that it's all turned to shit?"

"Paige isn't out. But that wasn't the issue, not at all. She had a complicated life back in Kent, and I found out she was married."

Hannah's eyes widened. "O-oh. Let me guess, she's gone back to her wife?"

"Husband, and no. Not quite how you'd imagine. She was on the run from him."

"Ah. I see." Hannah lowered her eyes, offering the smallest smile. "That has to be tough."

"It was. Really tough for her. But to cut a long story short, she went back to Kent last Saturday. She wanted to collect the last of her belongings. James has been threatening to come and get her. She was led to believe that he was in Paris...that he wouldn't be at home—"

"But he was."

"Y-yes." Juliet's voice trembled, her nails digging into her knees. "I think she has broken ribs, but she won't let me take her to the hospital."

Juliet heard the light gasp from Hannah, and she felt the uncertainty now hanging over them.

"She won't go to the police or seek any sort of treatment. Her face... She looks like she's been mauled by a dog."

"She may not want to do those things, and that's entirely her decision, but she has you. And I know you're going to take care of her and give her anything she needs."

"She doesn't want me, Hannah. She comes here to work, sits at that piano, and plays...and I'm just in awe of her. Before all of this happened, I'd do anything for her...and I still would. But she doesn't want me. She's leaving."

"Oh, Juliet. I'm sorry."

"I-I don't know what to do. I feel like I'm falling apart, and I know that when she leaves, I'm going to lose the best thing to ever happen to me. But I guess I should have known it wouldn't work out. We've only known each other two months, and I know that's ridiculous of me to even feel something for Paige, but I feel *so much* for her."

"It's not ridiculous. I knew I was in love with Caz the night I met her, Juliet. When we know, we know. But I think that given what she's been through, it's going to take time. For her to heal, and for her to realise that she doesn't need to run away."

"I wish she'd never told me she loved me." That was a dreadful thing to say, but Juliet meant it. The pain of losing Paige was going to be bad enough without bringing love into it. "I wish she'd told me she hated me and never wanted to see me again. That I was no good for her. That...this was my fault."

"Why would this possibly be your fault?" Hannah shifted forward on the couch, dipping her head to meet Juliet's eyes.

"Because I let her go alone. Because I didn't protect her. Because I'm incapable of being responsible for anyone but myself."

"That's bullshit, Juliet. You can't be responsible for somebody else's hands. Or words. Caz still has days when her own past comes back to haunt her, but she knows what she has with me and that I'm *always* there if or when she needs me. Paige, in time, will know that she has you, too."

"I'm scared to be alone with her. Since she came back with me yesterday, I'm terrified to be alone with her. Because I want to hold her so much. To promise her that everything will be okay. But she doesn't want that."

"Juliet, you're one of the strongest women I know. You do so much for everyone else, and it's time you focused on yourself and what you want. If you want Paige, you tell her you want her. You open up and have that conversation with her. You make her understand that while you don't want to see her leaving, you can give her the space she needs to work through what's happened. And if that means she decides to stay or comes back in six months' time, so long as she knows you'll be there waiting, you really can't do any more than that. Trust me, I know *exactly* how you're feeling."

"I don't like feeling this way. I wouldn't wish it on anyone."

"But feeling this way means you know you have so much to lose. If you didn't feel so torn up about it, you'd simply let her go and move on with your life. Believe me, I tried not to care when Caz repeatedly pushed me away, but look at us now."

"What you have can never be matched. I see exactly how Caz looks at you. That woman would lay down her life for you."

"And you wouldn't do the same for Paige?"

"Oh, I would. Ten times over." Juliet swallowed. "I've...sent someone to pay her husband a visit."

Hannah smirked, nodding slowly. "Well, maybe it'll teach him to keep his fucking hands to himself."

"She only wants a divorce. She doesn't want any fuss, any trial, just a divorce."

"Mm. If he knows what's good for him, he'll sign those papers the second he sees them."

Juliet's phone buzzed on the table. She lifted it, smiling.

Could I take a quick shower, please? x

Juliet swallowed down the emotion lodged in her throat, texting Paige back.

You're welcome to do whatever you need to do, Paige. No need to ask. J x

Thank you x

Juliet scoffed, locking her phone and throwing it down on

the table. "I think she's scared to even be with me. We've been sleeping together, been together, for the last six weeks, and she's texting to ask if she can use the shower."

"It's going to take time for her to feel like herself again. It's also going to take time for you to feel as though you don't need to walk on eggshells. It doesn't happen often, but there are still times when Caz asks permission to do something. Or worries that she's said or done the wrong thing and that I'm going to fly off the handle about it. But in time, things get easier. For both of you. It's all about her knowing you're there for her. It's about understanding and patience." Hannah dragged a hand through her hair, that familiar smile warming Juliet ever so slightly. "But she *will* be herself again, I know it."

"I hope so." Juliet exhaled a slow breath, sitting forward on the couch. "I know it's over for us, but I'd hate to see her struggle coming out of this."

Juliet got to her feet, squaring her shoulders as Hannah followed her. Hannah tugged her hand, turning Juliet to face her. "Hug?"

"Yes. Please."

She hadn't known how much she needed to be held, but Hannah's arms around her, supportive and understanding, really did help. It meant she had someone she could confide in. Someone who understood what she was going through. Someone who cared.

"Thank you," Juliet said, pulling back and holding onto Hannah's forearms. "And thank you for coming over when I needed you. It means a lot."

"You're my friend, Juliet. Don't forget that."

CHAPTER 24
RUN TO YOU

Paige slowly made her way around Juliet's kitchen, her laptop open on one end of the island while she prepared lunch at the opposite end. Juliet had left her a note this morning to say she had things to take care of at the bar, so Paige would make life easier for her by feeding Juliet before she went back to work later. It was Friday; the bar was always full on Fridays.

Paige had tried to apply makeup before she got in the shower earlier to see how she'd look so she could return to work, but the makeup did absolutely nothing for her. It didn't take away anything she saw when she looked at herself in the mirror, so now she would have to let Juliet down once again by telling her she was unable to work tonight. It wasn't ideal, Juliet needed all the hands she could on a Friday, but hopefully, she'd understand. Having said that, if she wanted to replace Paige at The Hideout, Paige would accept that. She was giving herself four weeks to recover, and then she would be gone. It made sense to hire a new mixologist sooner rather than later.

Sighing and disappointed that she could no longer call

Juliet hers, Paige sniffled and carried on chopping salad. As she sliced into a red onion, Juliet's apartment door opened.

"Hi."

Juliet slowly closed the door, staring back at Paige.

"Everything okay at the bar?"

"Yes. I was meeting with an old friend. I came back because I had a few hours to spare. But if you need some space, I can go out and find something to do."

"This is your apartment. If anyone is leaving, it's me."

Juliet applied the extra security lock on the back of her front door and lowered her bag. "You're safer here."

Paige gingerly lifted a shoulder, focusing on the salad. "I'm not sure he has the energy to go another round yet. I'd imagine his knuckles aren't in the best condition." Paige sprinkled the finely sliced red onion over the chicken salad in the bowl and slid it along the island. "Lunch is ready."

"You made lunch?"

"For you, yes. Saves you eating crap from the nearest cafe you can find before you go back to the bar later."

Juliet sniffled, shaking her head. "Thanks, but you didn't have to do that."

"I can't sit here looking at the walls. If I keep busy and moving, I don't hurt so much."

"How are you feeling today?"

Wow, that was one hell of a question. How was Paige feeling? She wasn't sure she could answer that. But she'd try. Juliet deserved that at least. "Like an idiot for ever thinking I'd be safe to go back there."

Juliet remained at the opposite end of the island.

"And I know, I know you warned me, but please don't give me the 'I told you so' speech."

"I would never." Juliet frowned.

"But I'm sure you're thinking it. You'd have every right to be."

"Actually, I'm thinking about *you*. How you're feeling, if you're in pain, and whether you need anything. I haven't once thought that it was your own fault for going back. What he did to you is solely on him, Paige."

"But I walked right into it. I'm a fucking idiot. It makes no difference how we look at it."

Juliet sighed, dragging a hand through her hair. Paige couldn't help but notice how dressed down she was; still, she looked beautiful. "What's this?" Juliet lifted the piece of paper next to Paige's laptop. And then it sunk in. "You've already decided where you're going?"

"Possibly. I'm undecided between Spain and the Netherlands."

"Both are beautiful." Juliet's voice broke as she regarded Paige with an indecisive smile. And then her eyes met Paige's. "You're sure this is what you want?"

"I think it's the safest option for me. And you."

"Me?"

"I don't want him to hurt you, too. That's probably played more of a part in my decision to go than anything else."

Juliet crossed the kitchen, stopping in front of Paige. She knew how much Juliet wanted to hold her, to be with her, but why put one another through the pain of that? Juliet lay a gentle hand over Paige's that pressed against the counter. "Paige, I'm only going to say this once, and what you do with that is your own decision." Juliet exhaled a breath and closed her eyes briefly. "If you're only going because you're worried about me, don't be. I want you to be here with me, you know that, so please...if you think that maybe you see a future with me, consider staying. Or coming back."

"Coming back?"

"Yes. I...had a little guidance from a friend at the bar. And they were right in what they said. That you need time and space. Believe me when I say that I can give you all the time and space you need. If you need to go so you can clear your head, I get that. But I'll be here waiting for you. Ready to love you when the time is right for *you*. Forget about me and what I want, but know that I'm *always* going to be right here." Juliet took Paige's hand, stroking her thumb across her knuckles. "Because I am ready, Paige. God, I'm *so* ready to love you."

Paige chewed her bottom lip, tears sitting on her eyelids. She turned her hand and laced her fingers with Juliet's, kissing her skin. "You are the most incredible woman I've ever laid eyes on, but you don't need this shit in your life. Nobody does. Why choose someone like me when you can have the entire pick of women out there? Why bother to get tangled up in all of this, something even I don't want to be a part of, just for me?"

"Because I love you."

"Love isn't always enough, Juliet. When he comes through that door one day, and he will, when he hurts you...you won't love me then. You'll despise me. And you'd have every right to."

"He's not coming, Paige."

Paige scoffed. How the hell could Juliet possibly know what James was capable of? She didn't know him, she hadn't lived with him, he hadn't beaten her unconscious...yet.

"Juliet, I have to go. I'm sorry."

Paige's phone vibrated on the counter, thankfully ending this conversation. Paige hated seeing that sadness in Juliet's eyes. She hated knowing that a woman so strong was close to falling apart because of her. Paige wasn't worth the tears. Not really.

I'll sign divorce papers.

Paige stumbled back, her phone clattering to the marble, and brought a hand to her mouth.

"Paige, what is it?"

And then Juliet's phone started to ring in her pocket. She glanced at the screen, answering the call, only this time, it was on loudspeaker. "Henry, hi."

"All taken care of, Jules. The bastard isn't as cocky as he thinks he is. Your Paige should have received a message from him. I brought out the baseball bat and the weasel offered her the house, too. Little prick didn't even try to beg. He's nothing more than a bully."

"Thanks, Henry. Come into the bar tonight, and I'll see that you're right."

"No need. It was my pleasure. And please, tell Paige I hope she's feeling okay. He won't be bothering her again. He knows what'll happen if he so much as breathes in the same city as her. Catch up with you tomorrow."

Paige stared at Juliet as the line went dead, a range of emotions swirling in her belly. She'd sent someone to threaten James? But why would she do something like that?

Because she loves you.

"You may hate me even more now than you did before that call, but I couldn't sleep at night knowing he'd done this to you. I'll have someone prepare divorce papers for you, and then we'll get you that flight."

Juliet turned and walked away, her phone gripped tight in her hand. The bedroom door closed, a muffled sob breaking through it, but Paige couldn't quite get her head around what Juliet had done for her. If she wasn't in such a bad way, Paige would have run after Juliet, but truthfully, she needed a moment to understand what had happened.

That one call had potentially just changed Paige's entire future, but first, she needed to do something she should have done a long time ago.

Hey! Can you come to Liverpool this weekend? Paige x

She wouldn't respond to James; she had no reason to. The next time he would hear anything from Paige would be via a lawyer.

Sure. I know we need to talk. I just hope we can figure it out and remain friends. Harriet x

Trust me, you did me a favour. I'll get you into the bar I'm working at, and we'll have that talk, okay? Paige x

Perfect. I'll get the train in tomorrow. Call you when I arrive for the address. Harriet x

Paige placed her phone down and moved into the living room. She would give it a little while, and then she would try to tempt Juliet again with the salad. And then maybe they could talk about what the hell had happened today.

Sat quietly in the corner of the bar, Juliet scanned the room, stifling a yawn. She'd managed to nap for an hour earlier, but after the call from Henry about James, she was yet to look Paige in the eye. Yes, she'd snuck out of the apartment long before the bar was due to open, and now she was barely able to remain awake. This wasn't the future she'd expected when she said goodbye to her law firm eight months ago. Sleepless nights over a woman. Crying silently in the bathroom and avoiding talking to anyone for this entire night. No, Juliet hadn't expected any of this.

She lowered her head to her hands, her elbows resting on her knees. While she loved Paige and wanted to be with her in the future, Juliet was beginning to wonder if being single was easier. When she didn't have to worry about other people, life was far less complicated. And knowing that she couldn't encourage Paige to stay, well, that just ate away at her constantly. Still, Paige could make her own decisions. She could follow her own path. One that was heading in the opposite direction to Juliet.

You never should have got involved with her.

That wasn't a reflection on Paige, not at all. But at forty-nine, Juliet had to consider if anyone would ever really fall in love with her. She'd struggled to find that in the past, and as she sat here this evening, she knew that would continue into her later years.

Aware that this wasn't the place for contemplation, Juliet lifted her head and inconspicuously wiped away tears from her jaw. They were the last of them. It was time to pull herself together, help Paige move on, and then get on with her own life. There was no more she could do than that.

She lifted her wine glass, sipped slowly, and watched Cara grant someone access to the bar. Tonight wasn't as busy as previous Friday nights, but it was pleasant. Fewer customers meant less conversation. That was exactly what Juliet needed tonight. Minimal socialisation.

But then Paige walked into the bar, her head down and with sunglasses on. Juliet frowned as she took a seat facing her, wondering why the hell Paige had even ventured out this evening.

"I know I'm probably the last person you want in here tonight, I'm drawing attention to myself, but I tried calling and you didn't pick up."

"I'm sorry. My phone is in the office. Is everything okay?"

Paige looked over both shoulders, removing her sunglasses as she faced Juliet again, her head slightly dipped. "Would it be okay if Harriet came here tomorrow night? I'll pay for a membership or whatever I need to do, but I'd rather be in public with her."

"I...yes. But you don't need to pay for a membership."

Paige nodded, then swallowed. "Would you be there with

me when she arrives? I have some things I need to say to her, and I'm not sure how well it's going to go."

Juliet would be there for whatever Paige needed. Night or day. "I'll be here."

"Okay, thanks. So…" Paige managed a smile, that split lip scabbed and swollen. Anger only rose from deep within Juliet again. Whenever she thought about what Paige had been through, she wanted to trash the place. "I-I think maybe we need to talk."

"About what?" Juliet's stomach sank. Had Paige finalised her plans for when the time came to leave? Juliet wasn't sure she wanted to know.

"Me. This. *Us*."

Juliet chanced her luck, reaching a hand forward to Paige's. "You don't have to do this, Paige. I know where we stand with one another, and I'm okay with that. Whatever you see in your future…that's what matters."

"Everything is a mess. And I don't want it to be that way for us. You're scared to be in a room with me, and I'm scared to even contemplate the future. We're better than that. We…were happy."

Oh, they were. They were so happy for the shortest time. "But you're going, Paige. I can't pretend that's not happening because it is."

Paige slumped back in her seat, exhaling a deep breath. "What you did for me…getting the divorce," Paige paused, offering a painful smile in Juliet's direction. "I wasn't expecting that."

"It was all you wanted. To be free. Soon you will be. And for the happiness you've given me since we met, it was the least I could do."

"I know, but for you to take matters into your own hands like that, I'm not sure how to repay you."

By not leaving me, Juliet wanted to blurt out. "By living your life on your terms. That's how you repay me, Paige. By being happy and fulfilled and being the exceptional woman you are. That's *all* I want from you. To see you happy."

"I'm not going to be, though...am I?"

"You will be. I know it. And living in a gorgeous country somewhere, you really can't ask for more."

Paige stared at Juliet, a tear working its way down her cheek. "I won't be happy without you."

Juliet opened her mouth to speak, but Cara came up behind Paige and placed a hand on her shoulder.

"Thought you were sick?"

Paige tumbled out of her chair, practically running through the table between them, and sunk to the floor at the side of Juliet's couch.

"Paige." Juliet slid to her knees, hiding Paige from the clients in the bar. "Baby, it's me. You're okay."

Paige shook, protecting her face with her hands. Juliet heard her sobbing, her heart breaking all over again for this woman.

"Paige, it was just Cara. I'm sorry; I should have tried to warn you that she was about to interrupt us. Baby, please..." Juliet's voice trembled, her own emotions spilling out. She placed a gentle hand on Paige's knee, soothing her palm over it. "Come on. Let me get you into the office. You need to be alone where it's quiet."

Paige suddenly wrapped both hands around Juliet's forearm. "No. Don't leave me."

"I won't. But you can't stay down there." Juliet glanced over her shoulder to find a shocked Cara watching on. "Make yourself useful and get me a large whiskey."

Cara rushed away, and as Juliet turned back to Paige, she found Paige watching her.

"Is everyone looking at me?"

Juliet smiled. "No. They're all too busy caring about themselves."

"You're a terrible liar." Paige's hand still shook, but the fear in her eyes was beginning to lessen. "God, I feel like an idiot. I just...I didn't expect her to come up behind me like that. I'm so sorry."

"Don't dare apologise. She's getting you a whiskey and then you're coming into the office with me." Juliet helped Paige up from the corner, one arm around her waist. "Did you hurt yourself?"

"No. I'm okay."

Juliet turned to Paige, their bodies touching, and brushed her hair from her face. "Did you still want to have that talk?"

"Yes."

"Come on. Let's get out of here." Juliet guided Paige through the bar, taking the whiskey from the counter as Paige snuck off into the office. She eyed Cara. "Sorry about that."

"What the hell was *that* about? And why is Paige's face smashed in?"

Juliet pinched the bridge of her nose. "If you could keep that to yourself, I'd appreciate it."

"D-did you—" Cara's eyes widened. "Did *you* do that?"

"What?" Juliet didn't know whether to laugh or cry at that accusation. "No, I did not!"

"Then who the hell did?" Cara stepped closer to Juliet, poking her head around the bar and trying to catch a glimpse of Paige.

"It's not for me to tell. But Paige is okay. She'll *be* okay." Juliet knocked back the whiskey she held for Paige, motioning for another. "Sorry, can you refill that, and I'll have another, too. Something tells me I'm going to need it."

Cara refilled the glass and filled another, clearing her throat as she pushed them towards Juliet.

"Are you okay out here while I check on Paige?"

"Oh, sure. Yeah, I'll be fine. Quiet night anyway."

Juliet noted Cara's shaking hand where it rested on the bar. She'd probably had the fright of her life when Paige flung herself from her seat. "Pour yourself one of those, too. And again, I'm sorry about that."

"It's fine. Check on Paige. She needs you."

CHAPTER 25
POINTLESS

Paige watched Juliet from the other side of the kitchen, the air still thick with uncertainty. It didn't matter that Paige had spent the night at the bar with Juliet; everything still felt off compared to the days before she left for Kent.

They'd decided not to have the talk back at the bar. Paige was too shaken up, and Juliet hadn't wanted any interruptions. So, here they were…staring one another down with a huge distance between them.

"Are you sure you want to do this now, Paige? It's one in the morning, and you should be resting."

"I…want to do it now. I'm not sleeping anyway so what does it matter?" Paige hadn't settled once since she had left Liverpool. Mostly because she was in pain but also because she didn't seem to be able to sleep alone. She'd become so used to having Juliet's arms around her in the night, being alone felt not only miserable but unfamiliar.

"Okay, if you're sure."

Paige stepped around the island and moved towards the whiskey Juliet kept out on a side table. She took two glasses and filled them, turning back and handing one to Juliet. "Who is Henry?"

Juliet stared down at the whiskey. "I told you who he was. An old client."

"If we're doing this, I need the truth. You're the only person in my life that I trust, so please, be honest with me."

Juliet nodded, smiling weakly. "Join me on the couch?"

Paige followed, itching to reach out and take Juliet's hand. But she didn't. She wasn't sure where they stood with one another yet. Paige had spent the afternoon and early evening making some decisions based on the last twenty-four hours—that call—and by the end of this night, she hoped to be on far better terms with Juliet.

"Henry is an old client. That's true. But he's been under the impression that he owes me for many years. Ten, to be exact."

"For what? Getting him off an assault charge or something?"

Juliet scoffed lightly. "No, but I can see why you'd think that."

Paige watched Juliet expectantly. She wanted the entire truth. If this was ever going to work, they had to be open.

"I've known Henry since I was seventeen. We went to school together a *million* years ago, and we always kept in touch. Twenty years ago, I got a call from him. He needed representation."

"What did he do?"

"He was mixed up with the wrong people. His sister's ex-husband, to be precise. Keira was his world. They'd lost their parents when they were kids, and he protected her fiercely. Always had. Anyway, long story short...Keira fell in love with one of the bosses in the criminal underworld. Drug dealer for most of Europe. She was young and naive. We all thought she couldn't see past the fancy watches and expensive cars he bought her."

"I've never understood people like that. People who know what their partner is getting up to, the pain they're causing by dealing drugs, but living off the money."

"At one time, I agreed. But everything wasn't as it seemed. He was abusive. He threatened to kill her if she left. And trust me, he would have in a split second. In the grand scheme of things, it seemed easier to stay and play the happy housewife than risk her life."

Paige sipped her whiskey. "That'll teach me to assume."

"Oh, no. You have every right to feel whatever you feel." Juliet placed a hand on Paige's knee, stroking her thumb against the denim. "Henry found out about it. He went crazy when he found out that Marcus had been beating his sister up. To protect Keira, Henry took on a job working for Marcus. Drug runs across Europe and county lines here in the UK. He knew the mistake he was making, those kinds of people are *always* being watched by the authorities, but he felt as though he could see Keira more often. Working for Marcus meant seeing her in the flesh rather than talking on the phone."

"He sounds like a great brother."

"Someone managed to get word to him that the police were planning to raid Marcus' place in Spain and a few known properties here. He called me and gave me the heads up. Told me he didn't plan to deny any of it, so long as Marcus got put away for a long time."

"Did you even want to defend him? I know you have a job to do, but defending a drug dealer?"

"I understood why he'd done it. And yes, I'd told him how stupid he'd been, but he couldn't see past being there for Keira."

"Fair enough. I get that, I suppose."

"While Henry and Marcus were awaiting trial, Henry asked me if I'd check in with Keira. He wanted to be sure she was okay and was planning to leave the house she lived at with her husband. Henry gave me the address, and I took the afternoon off to visit. It was out in Cheshire."

Paige noted how the atmosphere in the room changed. Juliet swallowed, knocked back her whiskey, and exhaled a breath. "As I was approaching the private road, a 4x4 came speeding out at the junction. Something felt off, but I was on edge already because of the location I was going to. The last thing I wanted was to be sitting having coffee with Keira if the police turned up."

Paige listened as Juliet's voice changed. How it trembled.

"The front door was open when I got there. I knocked, but it was deathly silent around the place. So I went looking, and I'm glad I did. I found Keira on the kitchen floor with multiple stab wounds. Most turned out to be superficial, but one was bleeding a lot. Thick red blood. They'd tried to cut her throat but got spooked when the alarm system malfunctioned and started to go off. I found that out later."

"Fucking hell. W-why would someone do that?" Paige's blood ran cold at the thought of Juliet being faced with something so horrific. "What did you do?"

"Applied pressure to her neck with my blouse until the ambulance arrived. I'll never forget that look in her eyes. The fear." Juliet brushed a hand across her cheek, glancing briefly at Paige. "It was the very same look you had in your eyes when I found you at the hotel."

Paige chewed her lip. She may have been shocked and terrified when she realised Juliet was there, but she wouldn't have wanted anyone else to come through that door. Juliet was her safety. "I'm sorry."

"Keira survived because I arrived when I did. Marcus is still inside now. And Henry did his ten years. He's been out for another ten but always kept in touch and insisted I call him if I ever needed anything."

"So, Henry looks out for you because you saved his sister's life." Paige nodded slowly, understanding fully how Henry would want to be around for Juliet. "Did they find out who attacked Keira?"

"Rival drug gang. They saw that Marcus had been weakened and wanted to prove a point that they could get to his wife."

"That's...I don't even know what to say."

"I know that I may have done the wrong thing by sending Henry to James, but I didn't know what else to do, Paige. I've spent my career defending and protecting people. Granted, it hasn't been the right people, but still. It's just in my instincts to fix things. Knowing I couldn't do anything to help you, knowing I'd failed to protect you...I didn't know what else to do." Juliet lowered her glass to the table with a shaking hand, sighing. "I know that sending Henry has completely fucked any chance of there being an us, I've inadvertently managed to be perceived as a violent person by doing so, but I don't regret it. If it means you can move on with your life and not look over your shoulder every minute of the day, then I'd do it again in a heartbeat. I just...I saved Keira, a woman I didn't know very well at all, but I failed you. I lost you. The woman I love."

"Juliet."

"No. I *need* you to listen to me." Juliet took Paige's hand and held it tight. "You deserve to be happy, Paige. What he did to you, how he's treated you in the past, nobody deserves that. And maybe you asked me not to go with you because you knew I couldn't protect you, I don't know, but that's something I have to live with. Seeing you this way, the pain you've been in, I couldn't not try to at least get you the divorce. I'm hopeless when it comes to anything else that you want or need, so I had to get you what I knew could change your life. And believe me, it will. You can go anywhere and do anything you want. You can be *you*. That makes me happier than anything else." Juliet dragged a hand through her hair, a slight smile on her lips. "Well, *almost*. But we are where we are…and you're going to be okay. You're going to be amazing. That's the only thing that matters to me."

"Thank you," Paige said, barely above a whisper. "I can't believe you did that for me."

"I've come to realise that I'd do just about anything for you. And I'll keep to my promise of helping you leave. I'd never go back on that. So, where's it going to be? Spain or the Netherlands?"

Paige studied Juliet's dark eyes. The tears that sat on her eyelids. The pain behind that smile she wore.

"I'll cover your flight; you don't have to worry about that."

"Juliet…"

Juliet swallowed, that soft hand stroking Paige's skin so delicately. "Yes?"

"I don't want to be in Spain or the Netherlands."

"Well, there's no immediate rush to decide. I'm not exactly going to kick you out of here."

"I want to be here. With you."

Juliet's forehead creased. "What?"

"I…want to build a life here in Liverpool, and I want you to be the biggest part of that life."

"Y-you want to stay?"

Paige smiled, her scabbed lip pulling as she did so. "I'd really like to try."

Juliet covered her face with her hands, sobbing as Paige placed a hand on her shoulder.

"Hey, come on. Please don't cry. I don't like seeing you cry."

"I really thought I was going to lose you." Juliet brought her hands away from her face, tears streaming down her cheeks. God, this woman had never looked so vulnerable as she had these last few days. "I couldn't imagine you staying. I didn't think I was worth it for you."

"Oh, you're worth it. You're far more than worth it. Believe me."

"Paige, when I told you I loved you, I meant it. I wasn't just telling you what you wanted to hear."

Paige shifted closer to Juliet, groaning a little. She really wished she didn't still feel so sore almost a week on. But in time, and with Juliet's embrace, she *would* feel better. It was onwards and upwards from this point forward. It *had* to be. "I know. You wouldn't have done any of this for me if you didn't."

"It's taking a little time for me to understand what's happening here. I'm not sure I'm convinced that it's possible to just fall in love with someone so easily, but it really has been easy with you, Paige. I feel as though I've known you my entire life."

"I know, babe. Me, too."

"You really are extraordinary," Juliet said, cupping Paige's cheek. "I hope you know that."

"You make me believe that I can be who I am."

"And you make me believe that I can have a beautiful future."

"Will you still be there with me tomorrow when Harriet comes in? I'd like to introduce you to one another."

Juliet's eyes lit up. "I'd love to. Does...this mean you're going to come out?"

"I am." Paige cleared her throat, sitting back on the couch as carefully as she could. "There was something else I needed to tell you, too."

"O...kay."

"When I got to Kent and let myself into the house, Harriet was there. She's been sleeping with James."

"You're joking!"

"I'm not. And as you can probably guess, I'm not mad at her either. But I do have to tell her the truth about my marriage with him. I'd never forgive myself if she decided to have a relationship with him and he hurt her."

"That's very big of you, but then again, it's not as though you were still in love with him. If anything, she's probably done you a favour in some weird, messed-up way. Because she kept him busy when he could have been seeking you out."

"Yeah. I suppose that's something to thank her for. But...I'm worried that she's going to stay with him."

Juliet nodded slowly, sipping her whiskey. "Yes, that's not ideal. Having said that, she's going to have more information once you've spoken to her. All you can do is hope she makes the right decision for herself."

Paige chewed her lip, staring down at their entwined fingers. There was only one way she could ensure Harriet's safety in the long run...as well as any other woman James came across. "Juliet, I think I've changed my mind."

"About what?"

"G-going to the police. I want to press charges. It's the only way I'll be able to live with myself. You know?"

Juliet exhaled a long breath, placing what looked like a relieved hand to her chest. "Oh, thank God. I didn't want to push you to do that, but I'm glad you are. He *cannot* get away with this, Paige."

"I'll go to the police station tomorrow morning. Make a statement or whatever it is that I need to do. I'll tell them everything."

"I'm so proud of you, baby." Juliet reached out a hand,

placing it gently to Paige's cheek. The soft touch, the careful caress, it only made Paige fall more in love with Juliet than she already was. "I love you, and I'm with you every step of the way."

"I...couldn't do it without you."

"Then let's get that bastard together."

CHAPTER 26
TRUE COLOURS

Juliet fidgeted behind the bar, the place looking a little strange since Paige wasn't working. She couldn't get used to Cara having Paige's tools in the wrong order, the wrong place...just Cara. She couldn't get used to her. There was something that felt off with her. She'd tried it on with Juliet, she'd tried it on with Paige, and something just didn't appeal to either of them about her.

But when she needed extra hands, at least she could rely on Cara. Even if that was because Cara thought she had a chance with Juliet and helping out was scoring points, Juliet could live with that. She'd never tell Paige she was struggling without her. Paige had far more important things on her mind. Between James, their relationship, and the thought of seeing Harriet today, Juliet knew Paige was struggling to make sense of everything in her head.

They were still sleeping in separate rooms, but Juliet was okay with that. Paige needed space to process. To breathe. She needed Juliet...but not in an intimate setting. Not right now. And while Paige had told Juliet that she was staying, Juliet still wasn't sure how to approach Paige. Her biggest fear was saying or doing something that could have Paige teetering towards the edge. She wasn't stupid; she'd seen just how fearful Paige was last night when Cara innocently placed a hand on her shoulder. Juliet couldn't make the same mistake. Trust and support were paramount in the coming weeks.

As she turned the coffee machine on, Juliet heard the key in the lock of the main door. She smiled, knowing it was Paige, but she still found it difficult to see her in the state she was in. That beautiful face marred with bruises and cuts, those soft lips hurting. But Paige's eyes had some life back in them, and it was her eyes that Juliet had fallen in love with. Paige's eyes told a million different stories. Still, they'd got the ball rolling this morning by going to the local police station. Paige had seemed nervous upon entering the building, but by the time they'd left —Paige getting a lot of past trauma off her chest—Juliet saw her in a different light. She seemed invigorated in some way.

"Hey." She leant against the bar, the counter separating them. "Did you get here okay?"

"I did. I walked."

"Paige, I told you Henry was outside to give you a lift."

Paige shoved her keys in her pocket, taking a step closer. "I needed to loosen up. I'm okay, and the walk helped to clear my head. Today has been *a lot*."

"I know. But you've done the right thing," Juliet said, taking two coffee cups from the stack beside the machine. "Have you heard from the police yet?"

"No. They were passing the information on to whoever they needed to in Kent. And they said they'd be in touch once they had something for me. I doubt they'll rush themselves. They never do with domestic violence cases."

Paige didn't have to tell Juliet that. She knew the statistics, the likelihood of a conviction, and the rigmarole of the whole process. Unless they got lucky and James admitted it all, this could be a long, drawn-out journey. Paige yawned, her eyes watering as she sighed. "Still not sleeping?"

Paige lifted a shoulder slowly, approaching the counter. "Last night was better, but no. It's not great."

Juliet wanted to offer to stay with Paige, even in the spare room if that was more comfortable for her, but she didn't want Paige to feel obliged to say yes. "Well, you know where I am if you need someone in the night."

"I know. I just think we both need some space right now. Please don't hate me for that. It's not about you, I promise."

Juliet couldn't hate Paige if she tried. This woman, however broken she may be, made Juliet stupidly happy. "Don't ever think I hate you. Whatever you need right now is fine with me. I just don't want you to lay awake through the night if it's as simple as climbing in beside me. We don't even have to acknowledge that you're in the room if that's not what you want." Juliet reached a hand across the counter. "Consider it. Or remember it, at least."

Paige leaned forward and kissed Juliet's hand, a familiar sensation fizzing in her belly for the first time in over a week. "I will. Thank you for being so amazing."

Juliet scoffed. "Far from it, believe me."

"Can you...come around to this side of the bar for a few minutes?"

Juliet refrained from frowning, but she did wonder what Paige could possibly need. "Sure. Is everything okay?"

"You said something to me on Thursday night," Paige said, shedding her jacket to expose her beautiful arms in her short-sleeved T-shirt. She threw her jacket over the back of a chair and rolled her head on her shoulders. "About how I probably think you're a stoic ex-lawyer without a heart..."

"I'm sorry."

"Don't be. If that's how you feel, speak your truth." Paige

took a step closer, surprising Juliet. Her body heat was comforting, but Juliet still itched to reach out and hold Paige. "I know you have a heart." Paige placed a palm to Juliet's chest and smiled. "You don't show it much to the outside world, but with me, you've been nothing short of amazing. Even before all of this happened."

Juliet dipped her head. "Paige."

"I'm serious. From the moment I met you, I knew you had a heart. It didn't matter what I'd seen online...the people you'd defended in the past."

Juliet's brow did furrow this time. "I don't understand."

"The day I came here for the interview, I told you I recognised your name. That was because I'd looked you up before I came to Liverpool. Someone from my previous job knew parts of my past and gave me your name. They knew I was leaving and travelling further north."

"O-oh." That was news Juliet hadn't expected.

"But that's not why I came here. You told me to leave my issues at the door, and that's what I've tried to do. To the best of my ability, anyway."

"Baby, no. If you went back home and dealt with this alone because I said that to you, I'm sorry. So sorry." Juliet's heart sank. Paige had gone to Kent alone because of that initial conversation. It didn't matter if she said differently—Juliet knew it was the truth. God, she felt terrible. And unworthy of another chance.

"No, that's not what I'm saying. I just...knew who you were because I'd looked you up. But you'd retired, and I didn't have the balls to do anything about James anyway."

Juliet placed her hand over Paige's that still sat against her chest. "Oh, you've got balls. Look at how amazing you were giving that statement this morning."

Paige lifted her other hand and pressed a finger to Juliet's lips. Juliet's eyes closed, her heart fluttering. "Let's just wait and see if anything comes of it." She offered Juliet the smallest kiss to the lips, and then she stepped back and turned on her heel. "Sit down where I can see you."

"Pardon?"

"The stool to your right should do the trick."

Juliet pulled herself up onto the stool, crossing her legs. And then Paige took a seat behind the piano. The thought alone of Paige singing to only Juliet had her ears pricked. "Are you—"

"I'm going to try. I don't know how well I'll do since it hurts to breathe deeply, but I'm sure as hell going to try."

"Paige."

Paige didn't respond. Her fingers teased the keys, that beautiful sound something Juliet didn't think she'd hear again.

Oh, God. It was Paige...here in the flesh.

Here...to stay.

The melody of *"True Colours"* played around the empty bar, the sound amplified since they were alone. Juliet didn't take her eyes off Paige, and Paige didn't take her eyes off Juliet. She smiled as she reached the chorus, a slight blush present on those pale cheeks. While Juliet loved to see Paige's shy side, she focused on her voice. Raw, pained, but so delicate.

The entry system flashed above the door. Juliet quickly shot down from her stool and checked the CCTV screen. She assumed it was Harriet, and as she checked her watch, the time confirmed it. She quickly released the lock and returned to her stool. She didn't care who it was. Paige was singing to her, and she wouldn't have *anyone* interrupt her for another second.

Harriet slowly descended the stairs, watching from the doorway as Paige put her heart and soul into her song. *Incredible* didn't quite do it justice. They eyed one another, smiling to acknowledge the fact they were in the same room, and then they both focused on Paige again as the song came to an end.

Clearly worn out from her performance, Paige slumped against the piano, her arms resting on the top, her head resting on her arms. Juliet rushed from her seat and placed a careful hand to Paige's shoulder. "Are you okay?"

"Yeah." Paige didn't lift her head. "Just need a minute."

"Okay, well...Harriet is here."

"Yeah, I know." Paige shook her head against her arms, the sound of her exhaling a long breath audible.

Juliet sat on the edge of the bench next to Paige, pressing a soothing hand to her lower back. "You take a breath, get yourself together, and I'll make her a drink, okay?"

Paige turned her head ever so slightly, her teary eyes staring back at Juliet. She smiled the slightest smile and whispered, "I love you."

Juliet leaned down, barely able to touch her head to Paige's. "I love you, too."

She cleared her throat and got to her feet. Paige would speak to Harriet in her own time. The least Juliet could do right now was be accommodating to the woman who'd been fucking Paige's husband behind her back. Regardless of what Harriet knew, it was still a shitty thing to do to a best friend. "Hi."

"Um, hi. Is...Paige okay?"

Juliet regarded Harriet with her best professional smile. "Of course. She's just a little worn out from all those amazing songs she sings here."

"S-she's singing here now?" Harriet frowned. "Wait, I'm confused. She told me she'd left her job here and gone up to Scotland."

Juliet opened her mouth to speak, but the bench Paige sat at suddenly screeched across the floor. Both Juliet and Harriet's heads shot up, focusing on Paige.

"Yeah. I had to tell you that. Because while you were sleeping with my husband, I was trying to escape him." Paige came closer to the main light above the bar, stopping in front of Harriet and shoving her hands in the pockets of her jeans. "I don't know what's going on with you two, but I'd suggest you call it off."

Harriet gasped, her hand smacked to her mouth. "Paige! What the hell has happened?"

Juliet wanted to cut in, to help Paige in some way as her bottom lip trembled, but Paige must have sensed exactly that and held up a hand.

"What do you think has happened, Harriet?"

"I-I don't know."

"Your beloved James...the guy who everyone adores...beats the shit out of me any chance he can get."

Harriet stumbled back, gripping the stool closest to her when Paige lifted her T-shirt and exposed the bruising around her ribs. Juliet hadn't seen this before; she'd only heard Paige tell her about the bruising, the police too. She hadn't gone into the room when they took pictures of her injuries this morning, opting to give Paige space and privacy. To see it so unexpectedly knocked the wind right out of her.

"Paige—"

Paige glanced in Juliet's direction. "No. She wants to know what's happened, so I'll tell her." Paige cleared her throat, lowering her T-shirt. "James is under the impression that I'm to stay home and live my life as a housewife. No job. No hobbies. Just existing."

"What?" Harriet scoffed.

"Yep. And as you can see, he doesn't like that I have my own life or my own mind. So, he beats me."

"Hang on! Are we talking about the same person here?"

Paige barked a laugh. "Oh, yeah. The very same person. Sweet and innocent James beats women." Paige took a calming breath, closing her eyes as she gathered herself. "I only went back there because you told me he was in Paris. If you'd just been honest and told me you were seeing him, I could have prevented all this. I wouldn't have stepped foot inside that fucking house if you'd told me the truth!"

Juliet knew Paige didn't blame Harriet for her injuries, that was entirely on James, but her lies had contributed to Paige making the decision to go back. Paige had discussed that with her last night when she was going over it all in her head again. Paige had tried to blame herself—something Juliet had quickly nipped in the bud—and then she'd mentioned Harriet. But why *wouldn't* Paige trust her best friend when she told her James had left the country? Paige had then gone on to wonder if Harriet was in on this, but it appeared James was very good at hiding their home life. Harriet was in the dark as much as everyone else when it came to James' true intentions.

"I don't care if you're fucking him, I really don't, but when your lies lead to this happening, *that* I care about."

Harriet let out a strangled sob, her eyes studying Paige's face. "Paige, I'm so sorry. I had no idea."

"Why would you?"

"Because I'm your best friend and we're supposed to talk about stuff like this." Juliet heard the anger in Harriet's voice, but she'd keep an eye on that. The first hint of this getting out of hand, Juliet would remove her from the bar. Harriet may be shocked, but she wouldn't have Paige upset. "Why didn't you tell me?"

"Because you're all fucking obsessed with him!"

"That's not true." Harriet sighed, lifting herself onto a stool and offering Paige the other. "Please, sit down."

"I've never felt as though I've been in a position to tell you about it. Whenever we meet up, you want to know about him. His career, how he's doing. Why would I come to you with this when you've been telling him where I am?"

"If I'd known this was going on, I wouldn't have told him *anything*, Paige. I hope you know that."

"Look, it's done now. And I haven't asked you to come here so I could talk about him. He's not worth my breath."

"O...kay."

"I'm in love. The most amazing and stupidest love."

Harriet's brow rose. "Must be serious."

"It is, yeah. Very serious." Paige smiled fully for the first time since she'd gone back to Kent. "Because they're all I've ever dreamt of. They protect me and love me and show me that life can be incredibly fulfilling. And you know, when this all happened with James, they were willing to let me go if it made me happy."

Harriet cocked her head, smiling. "I'm happy for you, Paige."

"They encourage me to perform. Nobody in my life has *ever* encouraged me. Except for Mum, but when she died, my voice died with her. Because she was the only one who ever had any faith in me. Everyone else told me I wasn't good enough. They belittled me and sneered at me when my passion was all I wanted to pursue. Until now."

"Paige, we just didn't want to see you get hurt. The music industry is a tough business."

"But it wasn't about the music industry. I never once said I wanted to be professional. Not even close to anything that resembled being professional. I just loved sitting down at the piano. But it was never good enough for you lot back at home. In *Kent*. But that's not home. This is home. Liverpool." Paige reached across the bar and took Juliet's hand. "Right, babe?"

"Yes, beautiful."

Harriet looked between them, and then her eyes landed on their entwined fingers "What's going on here?"

"What do you *think* is going on?" Paige laughed as she shook her head. "Isn't it obvious?"

"I mean, yeah…but what? You're gay now?"

"Always have been. I've just never felt supported enough to actually tell you or anyone else back in the town."

Harriet lowered her eyes, toying with the tassel on her bag. Was the lack of support Paige had received beginning to sink in? Juliet certainly hoped so. Harriet seemed like a nice enough person; surely, she could be open-minded and supportive of her best friend. "I'm sorry, Paige. I had no idea you felt this way."

"Now you do. And you can feel however you want about it. It's not really an issue for me anymore. But I wanted to speak to you face to face and let you know how my life would be from now on. You have the choice to stay or walk away."

"W-walk away?" Harriet's bottom lip quivered as she spoke those words. "You think I'd love you less because you're gay?"

"I'd hope not, but I've always prepared myself for that possibility…"

"God, no! Never. You're my best friend, Paige. If you'd told me sooner, about your sexuality *and* about James, I would have helped you however I could."

Juliet's heart settled at that admission. While she could understand Paige's unease at being forthcoming, it seemed they'd simply got their wires crossed. Nothing more. "I'd like to cut in, if that's okay?"

"Sure, babe. Say whatever you need to say."

"Well…" Juliet paused, smiling. "I just wanted to introduce myself more than anything else. I'm Juliet. The owner of The Hideout…and Paige's partner."

"It's really lovely to meet you." Harriet smiled fully, genuine and lovingly.

"You've travelled all the way down here. You're welcome to stay for the evening."

"Oh, I'm not sure Paige wants that."

Paige suddenly sat upright on her stool, straightening herself out. "I'd...like to catch up, if you can stay?"

"I wasn't sure of the plan, so I booked a hotel room for the night."

"Okay, great. I'm going to be working but I'd love it if you could stay around, and I'll grab you whenever I can?"

Juliet cut in again. "That's a lie. She's not working." She looked pointedly at Paige. "You're in no fit state to work. Spend the evening with your friend. Drinks are on me."

"Juliet, no. I've already missed a week of work. I need to get back."

"If it's cash you're worried about, you should know me better than that by now."

"It's not even about the cash. I just don't want to let you down, babe."

Deciding to be bold, Juliet rounded the counter and stopped between Paige's legs. She brought her hands to her face, no sign of hesitation from Paige, and leant in, kissing her gently. "You've never let me down. Please, spend time with Harriet, and then we'll get you fit for work again. I'm still waiting on that signature cocktail."

CHAPTER 27
CALIFORNIA KING BED

Paige stared down at the whiskey in her hand, chewing the inside of her mouth. She didn't know what to say now that she was alone with Harriet, but at least Harriet had decided to stay and listen. At least she hadn't run out the door hating Paige. Even if she had done that, Paige couldn't say she would have been particularly bothered, but knowing she had one other person in her corner made a huge difference to her future.

"Paige?"

She turned her head, glancing at Harriet where she sat at the other end of the couch. "Yeah?"

"I'm so sorry."

Paige offered a half-hearted smile. "It's okay. Nobody is to blame. I chose not to speak up, and that's on me."

"I know, but you also didn't feel as though you could speak up, and that's on me." Harriet shifted and placed a hand on Paige's shoulder. "How long has this been going on?"

"The beating?" Paige asked, noting the sadness in Harriet's eyes. "Since we got married. It got worse when my mum died.

He…didn't like me having a life. He didn't like that I had friends or that I wanted to sing, or…anything at all."

"He always spoke so highly of you." The anger in Harriet's voice was clear to Paige. "He always played the concerned husband. Fucking bastard!" Harriet hung her head. "I…felt sorry for him. He came across as being so upset and distraught, a-and I felt sorry for him. When he made a move one night outside the pub, that's the reason I went home with him. Because I'm so fucking stupid that I felt sorry for him."

Paige couldn't help but feel for Harriet. James had always been very convincing when it came to most things in life. Hadn't she been fooled by his lies for long enough? "Look, I get it."

"I was misled by him."

"Of course you were. He did that as well as keep up the façade in the past because he wanted me to feel like I had nobody to turn to. And it worked—look at me now. If I'd spoken up in the past, maybe it wouldn't have reached this point. If I'd left him, or better yet never married him in the first place, I could have been happier a long time ago. But by him being sweet and innocent around everyone else like butter wouldn't melt, I felt alone."

"I wondered why I hadn't heard from him all week. I assume he's been arrested?"

"No. I didn't call the police. Once I came around, I just got my stuff and got out. Juliet tried to convince me to go to them, but I didn't want to. I…don't want to see him ever again."

"I understand that, but don't you think he deserves to be held accountable for what he did to you?"

"Last night I changed my mind." Paige lifted a shoulder, sipping her whiskey and then setting it down on the table. As she sat back and turned to face Harriet better, she cleared her throat. "They took a statement from me this morning. Documented my injuries."

"Good. I'm glad you made that decision," Harriet said, rubbing at her forearm. "I can't believe he led me on like that. Or that I *ever* found him charming and attractive."

"Is that all?"

Harriet lowered her eyes. "No. I can't believe I went behind your back and had an affair with him."

Paige had wondered when Harriet would acknowledge what she'd actually done. While she didn't hate her for it, she was still in the wrong for sleeping with James. "If I just didn't love him, I'd say you're welcome to him. But he's dangerous, Harriet. He's bad news."

"Yeah. I'm beginning to realise that." Harriet finished her glass of wine, sitting forward and inching closer to Paige. "You don't think he's still going to come looking for you, do you?"

As Harriet asked that, Juliet sauntered past the table and smiled at Paige. "No. Juliet took care of that. Because she's amazing, and I don't know how I ever got so damn lucky."

"Took care of it?"

Paige grinned, no longer caring about her split lip. It was healing, and so was she. "Yeah. Sent someone to spook him. But I don't want to say any more than that because I don't want to get anyone into trouble. Especially not someone who helped get me out of my situation."

Harriet lifted a hand. "Then say no more."

"The police may want to speak to you. Probably not. But...if they do, will you just be honest about anything they ask? If you've ever had a bad experience with him or something felt off, just say it. You never know if it could help me down the line."

"Of course. I'll be honest about anything they ask. I really haven't seen that side of him, though. *Thankfully*. But you know I'll never speak to him again."

Paige wasn't surprised that Harriet hadn't seen James' violent side. It just seemed to be Paige that James had an issue with. Which was a shame, really, because she wasn't a bad person. She didn't deserve to be beaten up for something so trivial like what she chose to listen to on the radio.

"And when you go back tomorrow, don't tell him you've been here if you see him. I don't want him to know that you know anything. It gives him time to get his story straight then."

"You have my word that I won't do *anything* to jeopardise this for you."

Paige caught a glimpse of Juliet again. She couldn't take her eyes off her. "I do love her, you know."

"I…know. This may be a new Paige to me, but I see the difference in you. Your body language is entirely different. Even though you've just been through hell with James, you seem more relaxed here. But not like 'normal' relaxed. Relaxed within your own body."

Paige was glad Harriet had noticed that. Because she felt it. With Juliet, she felt everything she'd never felt with anyone else. "You have Juliet to thank for that. She's the one who allowed me to be myself from the moment we met."

"How *did* you meet? Was it really via the interview for this job or did you know her before then?"

She could understand why Harriet would ask that question. Paige hadn't been in Liverpool for long enough—some may say—to fall for Juliet, but she knew what she felt in her heart. She didn't care if people thought she was moving too fast. What she cared about was the fact that they felt comfortable and they fit well together. To hell with anyone else. "Yeah, we met when she interviewed me for the job. I'm so happy she took me on. Not only because it gave me the chance to know her and stuff but because I love this place. It's really my kind of vibe."

"I'm glad you're happy here, Paige. I really am."

"Me too." Paige slowly stood up, taking their empty glasses from the table. "Another?"

"Go on. If you're feeling up to it, I'll have one of your fancy cocktails."

Paige looked around the bar. Juliet wasn't anywhere to be found. "Okay. If I'm quick, I'll be able to make you one without Juliet telling me off."

"Don't go out of your way to make it, Paige."

Paige lifted a shoulder. "I want to. It's where I'm most comfortable."

Paige threw her head back laughing, aware that she should be taking it easier than she was. Her pain had been manageable, so she hadn't needed to medicate today, and that was just as well since they were practically drinking the bar dry. She'd likely regret it in the morning, but Paige enjoyed not worrying about what was coming in the next hour or the next day. Since James had agreed to the divorce, she'd felt entirely free.

She watched Juliet as she allowed someone entry to the bar, her eyes shifting to the entrance as the heavy door slammed shut at the top of the stairs. She felt Harriet's eyes on her, trying to get a read on Paige's thoughts, but she wasn't worried about who was coming into the bar. Juliet was so on the ball that it was comforting.

A tall, well-dressed man straightened his suit jacket as he landed inside the small space. She'd seen him in here on many occasions, but he usually sat out of view, nursing a single drink all night. Then she realised she recognised him as their cab driver from several weeks ago, too. Paige instantly grinned. It was Henry. She just knew it when he smiled in her direction and offered her a single nod. Paige turned to Harriet, lifting her glass and sipping her whiskey slowly. "Can you give me a few minutes?"

"Sure."

"Thanks." Paige approached Henry, placing a gentle hand on his shoulder as he reached the bar. "Hey, Henry."

Henry turned, a glint in his eye when he smiled at Paige. "Paige. Great to *finally* get to meet you." He eyed Juliet, but she simply scoffed and walked away. "Charming."

"I...just wanted to say thank you for...you know."

Henry nodded. "Don't mention it. Anything for Juliet. She was worried about you."

"I know. And she had every right to be. But seriously, thank you so much for taking care of things. You don't know me, and I didn't expect anyone to put themselves on the line for me. Least of all someone I've never had the chance to speak to before. But that changes now. Anything you want when you come in here is on me from now on, okay?"

"No. That's not necessary."

Paige squeezed Henry's shoulder. "It is. You saved my life."

"But—"

"Do as the lady says, H." Juliet stopped on the other side of the bar, giving Henry one of her stern looks. "If Paige wants to take care of things in here while *you* take care of things out there, you agree to it. Okay?"

Henry held up both hands. "Fine. I'm not going to fight with two of the strongest women in Liverpool. I'll just do as I'm told."

"Good man." Juliet winked, taking a bottle of Scotch from the shelf. "Usual then?"

Henry grinned as he pulled himself up on a stool. "Good woman."

"Hey, babe." Paige leaned forward, beckoning Juliet closer. When her girlfriend did so, Paige immediately planted a kiss on her lips. "Just wanted to say that you look really good behind the bar."

Juliet wrinkled her nose. "Really? I'm not enjoying it much. I smell of whatever alcohol I keep spilling."

"That's okay. I *love* sleeping next to someone who smells like a brewery."

"Is that so? Does that mean you'll be sleeping next to me tonight?"

Paige adored that look in Juliet's eyes. It was a look that said 'please come back to me.' Nobody had ever given her that look before. Love, that's exactly what it was. A crazy amount of love.

"Would you like that?"

"Oh, Paige, I'd *love* it."

"Then I'll be there." Paige placed a hand over Juliet's that sat on top of a beer pump. She didn't know why beer pumps were even installed in the bar. Nobody drank the stuff. "All night. With you."

"Thank you. Now, get back to Harriet, and I'll be over soon to catch up while I can."

"I'd really like that. I want her to know you, you know? I want her to see how proud I am to have you in my life."

Juliet turned her hand over, lacing their fingers. "I love you."

Paige's stomach somersaulted. She wasn't sure she'd ever get used to hearing those words come from Juliet. "I love you, too."

Juliet stared up at the ceiling, listening to Paige as she pottered about in the bathroom. She'd dreamt of this moment since the morning Paige left for Kent, and now it was happening. Paige would be sleeping *safely* beside her. If Juliet had realised anything recently, it was that she wanted to protect Paige and keep her safe with every fibre of her being. It didn't matter if Juliet got hurt; it didn't matter if Paige fled. She just wanted her to be safe.

She turned her head towards the bathroom door when it opened, smiling at Paige. "You doing okay?"

"Yeah. I'm shattered. I'm glad I decided to stop drinking when I did. Harriet could have gone all night, but she always could drink far more than me."

Juliet pulled back the cover, watching for any signs of hesitation from Paige. She almost breathed a sigh of relief when she didn't find any. "Come on. Get some sleep."

Paige slid into bed, unexpectedly moving as close as she possibly could to Juliet. "Thank you for being patient with me."

"Never thank me for something like that. You've been through a lot, and I wanted you to have the space to process your thoughts, your emotions. It's been a difficult time for you."

"And you," Paige whispered, draping an arm across Juliet's stomach, her head resting on Juliet's chest. "I know you pretend that you're okay, but I saw it in your eyes that night at the hotel. I'm sorry I worried you."

"If I wasn't worried, I would consider whether I truly loved you."

Paige stroked a thumb across Juliet's skin, her stomach muscles contracting as she did so. "Thank you for coming to get me. I know we've been over this, but really, I didn't know what to do for the best."

"I'll *always* be there for you, Paige. If...you want to be with me, that is." Juliet hated feeling vulnerable like this. She'd never been in this position before, unsure about how to deal with a relationship she was in. Yes, that was quite sad on reflection, but she was here now...as was Paige, and she couldn't have chosen a better woman to fall in love with. "You do want that, don't you?"

Paige tilted her head slightly, her eyes flickering shut. "I don't want to be anywhere else. Only here with you. And The Hideout. That place means a lot to me."

"It means a lot to me too since you walked through my door. I'm not sure it would be what it is without you. I certainly wouldn't enjoy being there so much."

"No?" Paige smiled one of those weary but beautiful smiles. "You really like me being there?"

"I *love* you being there, Paige. I think we're going to do very good things with the place." Juliet dipped her head and kissed Paige's forehead. "But right now, I want you to just rest and get plenty of sleep. The bar isn't going anywhere, nor am I, so I want you to take your time and only come back when you're ready to."

"I want to come back as soon as I can. I hate sitting around."

Juliet slid further down the bed, making herself comfortable as she wrapped Paige up against her. "You'll know when you're truly ready. Until then, I want to see you in nothing more than your sweats while you lounge around here looking gorgeous."

"Goodnight, Juliet."

With a sense of love sitting in her chest, Juliet flicked the switch to the side of her, sending the bedroom into total darkness. She smiled, inhaling Paige's scent, and whispered, "Goodnight, baby."

CHAPTER 28
XO

"Good morning, beautiful."

Paige smiled against her pillow, a gentle arm carefully draped over her hip. "Mornin'."

"Coffee?" Juliet asked, her voice husky and soft. That arm remained in place, the warmth of Juliet's body keeping Paige anchored.

"Soon. Stay like this with me." Paige gripped her pillow, shifting further back against Juliet. She didn't want to start her day yet. She didn't want to think about work or cocktails, or anything other than this woman beside her. "You're always so snuggly in the morning."

"And you're always adorable in the morning."

Paige smiled again. This was a stark contrast to the life she had before she met Juliet. She couldn't think about losing it. "I'll take adorable considering the state of me right now."

"You're gorgeous. That'll never change." Juliet pressed a kiss to Paige's shoulder, just a tank top covering her upper body this morning. "I'm taking you out for lunch today."

Paige gingerly turned in the bed, her brows drawn. "Why?"

"Because I want to and because I love you." Juliet said that so casually that Paige had to take a moment. Nobody ever took her for lunch simply because they wanted to. James never had. Even on the morning after their wedding, he'd gone to play golf with his friends. That was a red flag in itself, looking back. "Is that okay?"

"More than okay. Thank you." Paige nuzzled into Juliet's chest, wanting to get another short nap in before she finally rose. But her phone started to vibrate on the bedside table, disrupting that wonderful idea. She groaned and reached behind her. "Hello?"

"Mrs Dunbar, this is PC Radford—"

"I...it's just...Paige." She cut in, the idea of being a Dunbar for a moment longer causing her stomach to roll. "If that's okay?"

"Of course. My apologies." The police constable cleared her throat. "I'm calling to inform you that we picked James Dunbar up this morning. He's been out of town for a couple of days."

"Yeah, he works out of town sometimes." Paige sat up against the headboard, running a hand through her hair. "Did he tell you he didn't do it?"

"Actually, he came clean the moment we explained why we were there. That's helpful when it comes to what happens next."

"O-oh." Paige hadn't expected that. She never thought James would admit to beating her up. And now, as she sat here, she didn't know how to feel about it. "S-so what happens now?"

"An immediate injunction has been put in place. We'll question him, gather the necessary information, and then contact the Crown Prosecution Service for further instruction. Unless something changes and he decides to plead not guilty, this should be a lot less distressing for you."

An unexpected weight lifted from Paige's entire body at

those words. The aches and pains she'd suffered from since the attack lessened. Her body no longer held monumental amounts of tension. "If he does agree to plead guilty, do I have to be there? In court?"

"No. That won't be necessary."

Another weight lifted. "I can't believe he admitted it. He's probably going to change his mind. It seems too easy."

"You'd be surprised how many abusers suddenly realise that they're not as in control as they think they are when the police come calling. He sat in the back of the car looking like a lost child. He didn't say a word."

"Oh."

"Abusers forget that their lives are mostly ruined once we catch up with them. You should be proud of yourself for coming forward."

"Yeah, uh...sorry, I'm just a bit shocked by this call."

"You've done the hard thing, Paige. Leave the rest up to us. I'll be in touch when I have more information."

"Thank you. Bye."

Paige lowered her phone, staring at the closed bedroom door directly ahead of her. She felt Juliet shift beside her, mirroring her position where she sat against the headboard, but Paige had nothing to offer just yet. She needed that call to sink in for a few minutes before she could begin to make sense of it.

"You don't have to repeat any of that. I heard it all." Juliet took Paige's hand above the cover, giving her that silence she needed. But the silence only allowed Paige the opportunity to think too deeply into it, tears spilling down her cheeks.

"Come here." Juliet wrapped an arm around Paige, holding her. She placed a gentle hand on her upper arm, soothing her skin where she caressed it. "It's going to be okay. That officer was right. You *have* done the hard thing."

"I didn't think he'd admit to it. Why *has* he admitted to it? Does he want me to believe that I think he's gone away? That he's guilty? I know he's going to plead not guilty when the time comes and he's found himself a lawyer."

"The most important thing is that you're safe, Paige. Let the police do their jobs, and you focus on building your life from this point forward."

Paige's bottom lip trembled as she pulled out of Juliet's embrace. "Why did he do it, Juliet? Why did he repeatedly hurt me? I don't understand."

"Baby..."

"And why haven't you hurt me? Why haven't you left me black and blue like he has?"

Juliet's face paled at that question. "Because I'm not an abuser, Paige. Because I love you, and I want there to be a future for us. Because...I'm not him."

"I know that. God, I didn't mean to even suggest that you were, but...I don't understand people like him. If he didn't love me, he only had to tell me, and I could have left." Paige's mind started to work overtime. "And then now I'm wondering if this is all my fault? If I'd just gone to the police sooner, I wouldn't be in this mess."

"I don't understand."

"You heard that officer. He admitted to what he'd done without a second thought. Does that mean if I'd been stronger, it wouldn't have come to this? Have...I allowed him to do these things to me?"

Juliet got to her knees beside Paige, dipping her head to meet her eyes. "No. Don't *ever* think you're responsible for this in any way at all. This is on him. All of it. He chose to raise his hands. He chose to hurt you!"

"I wish I'd been stronger," Paige whispered.

"You *are* strong, Paige." Juliet took Paige's hands, squeezing them when Paige lowered her eyes. "Baby, look at me."

Paige couldn't. She didn't know what the hell was going on, but she couldn't look Juliet in the eye. She was far too embarrassed.

"Paige."

She slowly lifted her head, fresh tears rolling down her face. "Y-yeah?"

"It was all him, okay? Everything he did, he made the decision to do it. Every word, every step he took, every…time he touched you." Juliet's voice broke, her own emotions close to surfacing. "If I've learnt anything since we met, it's that you have the most beautiful soul. God, nobody makes me laugh the way you do. Nobody makes me feel whole and loved and cared for…the way you do."

"You mean that, don't you?" Paige searched Juliet's eyes, smiling. "I can actually feel how much you mean it."

"Of course I mean it," Juliet whispered, chancing a kiss. "I mean everything I've ever said to you, Paige."

"I love you." Paige toyed with Juliet's fingers where they rested in her lap. "I don't know how my life has turned out this way, but I know that I love you."

"I love you, too."

"Okay, what do you fancy for lunch?" Juliet fixed her earrings in place, watching Paige from across the room.

This morning hadn't been as plain sailing as Juliet hoped it would be, but James had been arrested, and that was the most important thing. She wouldn't tell Paige, but a weight had been lifted from Juliet's shoulders. Knowing the police were taking care of James and that Paige could now start to enjoy her life, the *biggest* weight had fallen from Juliet. Because Paige was her world, and anyone who tried to stand in the way of that would be dealt with in one way or another.

"Maybe the place we first had lunch together?"

Juliet slid her heels on, running her thumbs along the inside of the waistband of her high-waisted pants. "Perfect. I'll book a table now." She reached for her phone and brought up the website. "Done."

"Hey, uh..." Paige chewed her lip when she crossed the space, lowering her coffee cup into the sink on her way. "I was thinking that maybe this could be a date?"

Juliet's stomach fluttered at that. Paige could consider this anything she wanted to. But yes, a date was perfect. It would be their first official one. But the first of so many. "A date it is."

"Obviously, we don't have to make a big deal out of it..."

Juliet reached out a hand, pulling Paige to her. "If I want everyone in this damn city to know that you and I are dating, then I'll do that."

Paige blushed, mindlessly playing with a button on Juliet's blouse. "I've never done this."

"Neither have I. At least, not for a long time."

"Well, no." Paige lifted a shoulder. "But you go out to dinner with escorts and stuff, so you're used to being out in public with another woman."

Ah. Juliet understood what Paige was saying now. "I see. Well, we can do this at your pace, okay?" She lifted Paige's chin, giving her a knowing look. "If you need to play this as though we're just friends, then I won't be offended. Just until you find your feet, you know?"

"I'm looking forward to it," Paige said, lacing her fingers with Juliet's. She guided them towards the door, taking her satchel where it hung. "Do you have everything?"

Juliet laughed. That question could go many ways. "Yes. I have everything."

"Then let's go."

Paige stood out in the hallway while Juliet locked up, looking gorgeous in her fitted jeans and thigh-length black, open shirt. Paige did casual far better than any other woman Juliet knew. "You look really good today, by the way."

"Thank you." Paige took Juliet's hand as they caught the lift going down. She coolly rested back against the mirrored carriage, not letting go. "I feel more like myself here."

"Good." Juliet had already noticed very small changes in Paige since James had agreed to the divorce. The fact he'd been arrested had thrown her slightly, but on the whole, Paige's difference in attitude—even body language—was visible. "You seem different."

"Yeah? I'm glad you noticed. I wondered if it was just me who saw it."

"I see *everything* you are, Paige." Juliet turned her back on the doors, stopping painfully close to Paige. "And I love every last inch of you."

"You..." Paige's eyes closed when Juliet's breath washed over her lips. "I don't know how I got so lucky."

"We found one another when we were supposed to. I firmly believe that." Juliet had never felt connected to another woman the way she felt connected to Paige. While she may have had that instant attraction, it hadn't been long at all before she found herself wanting to seek her out at any given opportunity. And then there was Paige's voice. God, the things it did to Juliet, she couldn't comprehend. "Do *you* believe that?"

"I do." Paige feathered her fingertips along Juliet's jawline. "I knew the moment I met you that you were special."

"I'm not special, but I am madly in love with you, Paige."

Tears brimmed in Paige's eyes, that smile spreading slowly as their foreheads touched. "Thank you for everything."

"Anything for you."

Paige held the door for Juliet as they left the restaurant, smiling when Juliet leant in and kissed her cheek. It had only been lunch—something they'd done *many* times together—except everything was different today. Juliet hadn't let go of Paige's hand as they strolled through the city; she hadn't once hinted that they were only friends. In the past, that had been Paige's experience. Not wanting to appear too intimate with other women for fear of someone she knew catching her. But now? Paige hadn't known how freeing it would feel to hold another woman's hand in public, but it had been.

"What did you have in mind for the rest of the afternoon?" Juliet sat an arm loosely around Paige's waist as they walked down towards the dock. "Maybe a cocktail?"

"Yeah. Why not?" The click of Juliet's heels had Paige beaming as they rushed across the busy street, reminding her how incredibly lucky she was to be in this relationship. "Hey." She stopped them on the pavement, turning to Juliet. "Thanks for lunch."

"Anytime."

Juliet's bright white smile had Paige's insides fizzing. It always did. And when Juliet looked at Paige as though she was the be-all and end-all of everything, her old life moved further and further to the back of her mind.

"I love you," Paige said as she studied Juliet's eyes, her perfect nose, that flawless skin. "So much."

"I love you, too." Juliet placed a hand on Paige's chest,

moving in for a kiss. Paige didn't decline; she couldn't possibly. "I've been waiting a long time for you, Paige."

Paige's brow furrowed as she pulled back. "What do you mean?"

"I always knew or felt as though I was waiting for something special. And you're it."

Paige's cheeks heated as she swallowed, but still, she understood. Perhaps that was what she'd been waiting for too. Maybe, *just maybe*...Paige hadn't turned up in Liverpool until she was supposed to. Until Juliet had the bar. Things happened for a reason, and Paige was beginning to wonder if this all came about when it was supposed to. "I think I've been waiting for you, too."

As Juliet's hand slid to Paige's, their fingers entwined, Juliet blinked back tears. "You make me so happy. Thank you for being perfect."

"Juliet! Paige!"

They turned at the sound of a familiar voice. When Rachel hurried towards them as fast as her heels would allow, Paige groaned inwardly. What did this woman want? Hadn't she shown up enough since Paige had come to Liverpool?

"Hi, Rachel," Juliet spoke up, squeezing Paige's hand. "How are you?"

"Good. *Busy*. How are you both?"

Paige offered her best smile. "Great!"

"I'm glad to hear that. I...wanted to come to the bar to say hi to you," Rachel said, her gaze flitting from Paige to Juliet. "To apologise."

Juliet lifted a hand. "Really, there's no need. Neither you nor I was innocent towards the end. The past is the past."

Paige watched their interaction; that chemistry she once claimed they had was no longer present. Rachel seemed shocked by Juliet's response, frowning as she switched between them both. "I-I appreciate that."

"I'm happy to see you're still here, Paige. Still working at The Hideout?"

"Oh, yeah. Absolutely. Wouldn't want to be anywhere else."

"I have to admit, you look great behind that bar. I think it's going to be a brilliant venture for you both."

The hand that held Paige's shifted. Juliet's arm was back around her waist. "You're right. She does look great behind the bar. She looks even better behind the piano, though. You should come by one night when Paige isn't working. The Hideout wouldn't be the same without her in it."

"Oh, I'd love to." Rachel nodded eagerly. "If that would be okay with you, Paige?"

"Sure. The more the merrier." She had no reason to worry about Rachel coming to the bar. Paige knew exactly what she meant and what she had with Juliet. The connection was unbreakable. Besides, Rachel seemed genuine in her apology. Paige could spot her games a mile off. "Maybe next Monday? Does that work for you, babe?"

"Next Monday is perfect. Always a quieter night, so we could probably have a drink with you."

"I'll be there." Rachel smiled as she checked her watch. "I'm sorry, but I should head off. I have an appointment."

"Take care, Rachel. It was great seeing you." Juliet quickly leaned in and hugged Rachel.

Rachel offered a small wave as she turned and left. Paige watched her walk away, feeling nothing other than happy. Rachel's heart was in the right place, Paige was sure of it, and so long as she remained on the right side of friendship, she would never deny Juliet or Rachel that. Paige wasn't the kind of person to hold grudges when it wasn't necessary.

Paige puffed out her cheeks. "That went well."

"Much better than I expected it would."

"Now, I was thinking we could save the cocktail until later... and go onto the dock for some of those pancakes we had that time?"

Juliet squeezed Paige's hip as they turned away from the city and towards the fresh air down at the water. "I'd love that. I always think about that day."

"You do?"

Juliet nodded. "Of course. It was the day I realised just how much I wanted you."

CHAPTER 29
ROOTS

O*ne month later...*

Opening her mailbox, Juliet grabbed the excess number of envelopes the postman had forced inside and locked it again. She'd spent enough time this morning going over invoices and stock; she really didn't have the energy or the attention span for more paper in her life. She shuffled through them—mostly rubbish—until a large manilla envelope caught her attention. With 'FAO Paige Ashburn' scribbled in the top right-hand corner, Juliet rushed into the lift. She knew exactly what this was—something her girlfriend had been waiting weeks for.

The finalisation of her divorce.

Juliet didn't want to appear too happy; this was Paige's marriage coming to an end. It didn't matter if she knew Paige was ecstatic to say goodbye to James or not; it was still shitty circumstances to be in. For anyone, regardless of the reason behind it.

The lift dinged, and as Juliet stepped out on their floor,

she stopped for a moment and composed herself. She would hand over the papers, and then she would head to her own apartment. Paige had moved back into 319 last week, but Juliet understood her reasoning for it. Paige wanted to do this right. She wanted to learn about Juliet, and vice versa, without rushing into living together. Juliet didn't mind whether Paige stayed or not, but it was early days, and having their own space had been a wise decision to make on both their parts.

She knocked gently, hearing movement behind the door. Juliet waited a moment or two—Paige was still wary about answering the door—and then the chain was removed, the lock was turned, and the door opened. "Hi, babe. I didn't expect to see you yet. I thought you were at the bar?" Paige stepped aside, inviting Juliet in.

"I've been there. While there was a lot for me to take care of, it wasn't as much as I thought. So, I got in and got out as quick as I could. Figured I'd give Henry a few hours off while I'm home."

"Good idea. Coffee?"

Juliet stopped in the middle of Paige's living room, the manilla envelope clutched in the hand that hung loosely at her side. "No, I probably shouldn't. I'm...going to head to my place and wait to hear from you."

Paige's brows drew together. "O...kay. Is something wrong?"

"Not at all. But I do have something for you, and I wanted to give you a little while to yourself while it digested, you know?"

Paige remained confused as she dried her hands on a tea towel. "What do I need to digest?" And then fear clouded her eyes. "Wait, what's happened? Has Henry seen something we're not going to like?"

"God, no." Deciding she wanted to put Paige out of her misery, Juliet handed the envelope over and kissed Paige on the cheek. "Your divorce correspondence. If you need me, I'll just be at mine, okay?"

Paige stared down at the envelope in her hand. "O-okay."

"Hey." Juliet lifted Paige's chin and smiled. "I'm so incredibly proud of you, baby. And I love you. Let this sink in, and then if you want to come to mine, the door is open."

Paige smiled in return, leaning in and kissing Juliet. "Expect me there soon. I don't really have anything in here that needs to sink in."

With a caress of Paige's cheek, Juliet offered her a single nod and stepped towards the door. "I'll put the coffee machine on. See you soon."

"Babe?"

Juliet turned in the hallway. "Yes?"

"Lock the door when you get to your place. Please."

"I will."

"Promise me?" Paige watched Juliet expectantly. "I know you think you're safe once you're inside the apartment block, but promise me?"

"Paige, I promise." Juliet placed a hand to her chest, her head cocked ever so slightly. "Now, you do what you need to do and I'll see you when I see you."

"I'll have a sugar in my coffee."

Juliet smiled as she closed the door, breathing a sigh of relief. She hadn't known what Paige's reaction would be, but it couldn't have gone any better. Now she just had to wait patiently for her girlfriend to join her. They had a few hours together before work got in the way, but a few hours were far better than nothing at all.

As Juliet closed her apartment door, she felt someone pushing on it. "I told you I wouldn't be long." Paige grinned as Juliet allowed the door to swing open. "So, how was the bar?"

"Quiet. Full of paperwork. The usual."

Paige locked the door and took a step closer to Juliet. Her arms sat safely around Juliet's waist, relaxing her further. "I don't know how many times I have to tell you that I'll come in with you and help."

"And I don't know how many times I have to tell you that you already do enough for me."

"So?" Paige lifted a shoulder. "That's what I'm here for."

Juliet adored it when Paige said things like that. It meant they were a team...a partnership. "Okay, I'll tell you what. You can come in with me tomorrow on our day off and work on that signature cocktail while I finish the invoices. Deal?"

Paige grinned. "Deal."

"Now, tell me about your day. You were still sleeping when I left your place this morning." Juliet hoped Paige wouldn't always have a 'her place'—she'd much prefer a 'their place'—but this was working well.

"I woke up about ten minutes after you left. I had a call."

"Oh?"

"From the woman whose apartment I'm staying in. She… offered me a twelve-month contract. I decided to take it on the spot. It came with a reduced rent, and I couldn't turn it down. It means I don't have to look further afield and be too far away from you. Having said that, if you'd rather I looked elsewhere—"

Juliet cut Paige off with a heated kiss. She didn't dare allow her to finish that sentence. Paige was going to be close by; she couldn't ask for anything more. "I'm so happy you'll be staying in this block."

"She did say I could stay there free, but I want to build my life, and I want to do that without a free ride, you know?"

"I do know." Juliet lifted a hand to Paige's cheek. "That's very honest of you. Anyone else would have taken the free apartment. But that's just one of the things I love about you,

Paige. Your honesty and your willingness to better your circumstances. You know I've got you, no matter what, but yeah…you're something special."

"I just want to stand on my own two feet. And it's only twelve months, with the option to extend if I want to."

Juliet chewed the inside of her cheek, wondering whether she could be bold and throw something out there. To hell with it; she wanted Paige to know exactly what was on her mind. "Well, maybe when the twelve months are up…we'll be here together."

"Y-yeah?" Paige pulled back, studying Juliet's eyes. "I know it's what I want down the line, but yeah. That would be really nice. Providing nothing goes wrong before then, anyway."

"I don't think it will. You and I are going to grow together, okay?"

Paige grinned as a shiver worked its way down her spine. Was she really about to have this life? "It's all I want."

Exhaling a contented sigh as she watched Juliet across the room, Paige wiped down the bar and collected the empty glasses from the counter. The Hideout was packed tonight, with more clients signing up for memberships in the last few weeks. Juliet had initially worried that it could become too much or that there wouldn't be enough space, but Paige had quelled those fears immediately. This place was a success, and the sooner Juliet realised that, the sooner they could watch it grow into something special.

This was so far removed from Juliet's comfort zone that she couldn't help but admire the woman she'd fallen for, but Paige understood Juliet's concerns. She didn't know anyone else who would go from being a top lawyer…to a bar owner. And not just any bar. But a bar like this? No. A bar like this took determination. It didn't matter if it had already been successful before Juliet took over. What mattered was that it was thriving far more now that she was here.

"You want to call last orders?" Juliet sauntered towards the bar, a grin spread on Paige's mouth as she did so. "I don't know about you, but I'm ready for bed."

"Sure." Paige turned and rang the bell beside the whiskey collection. "Once everyone has been served, I thought I'd hop on the piano."

Juliet rested her elbows on the bar, her head cocked slightly. "I could never say no to that."

Paige dipped her head. There was just something about the way Juliet looked at her that had Paige blushing profusely. But that was Juliet, and her smouldering stare was something Paige was beginning to get used to. *Thankfully*.

"I...had something I wanted to ask you. I know we've had this kind of conversation before, and I *think* I know the answer, but I'm bringing it up again, anyway."

Paige nodded slowly. Where was Juliet going with this? "Okay."

"Please agree to perform here a few nights a week. I *know* people desperately want you to." Juliet had a pleading look in her eyes that Paige hadn't quite seen before. Was it that *she* was desperate for Paige to perform...or was it really the clients in here? "Baby, please?"

"I...uh...okay." Paige supposed she didn't have anything to lose by agreeing. Juliet would never humiliate her by asking her to perform if she thought it was a terrible idea. Yes, Paige knew she could sing, but that didn't mean she truly believed she was good enough for a permanent spot here. She *had* to trust Juliet with this. "If you think it's a good idea?"

"A good idea? Oh, Paige. When will you realise just how good you are?"

"I...know I'm *good*, but there's far better out there."

Juliet laughed, brushing that comment off with a wave of the hand. "Nonsense. You're amazing."

"You have to say that."

Juliet quirked a brow. "Actually, I don't. I'm not in the habit of lying. Especially to someone I love."

Paige's heart melted at that. This woman didn't have it in her to appease people for the sake of it. "Okay."

Juliet's eyes widened. "You...really mean that? You'll do it?"

"Sure." Paige turned her attention back to the counter, wiping down the already pristine wood. She didn't want it to become a big deal. It was only a song and a piano.

But Juliet suddenly rounded the bar and pulled her into an embrace. "Thank you. So much."

"Babe, it's fine. No need to thank me. It probably won't last very long."

Juliet held Paige at arm's length. "That's rubbish, and you know it. Now, get on that piano, and I'll take care of anyone who needs serving."

Paige lowered the cloth in her hand, clearing her throat as she reached for her glass of water. She sipped slowly, not a hint of anxiety present. *That* was how she knew she was exactly where she was supposed to be.

With her shoulders pulled back, she approached the piano and took a seat on the bench. That first stroke of the keys ignited Paige in a way it never had before. *Complete*. That's how she felt. Complete, safe, and incredibly loved. By Juliet and *only* Juliet. She glanced up at her girlfriend as she started to sing the first line of Grace Davies "Roots", the slightest smile curled on her mouth.

Juliet observed her, her lips parting as Paige held her gaze. She slowly lowered the glass she was drying, her own stare not wavering. Juliet wrapped her arms around herself, those dark eyes teary. That was the beauty of this place. It was so intimate that you could make out every emotion on each individual face. Juliet was no different, and Paige was beginning to realise that the 'stoic ex-lawyer' couldn't hide her emotions. Just the reminder of Juliet ever saying that to her had tears welling in Paige's eyes. There was nothing stoic about Juliet Saunders at all.

As the song came to an end, not a single breath could be heard. Paige knew that was positive these days and not what she'd assumed in the beginning. Silence meant shock...not a terrible performance. She smiled and got to her feet, heading straight back to the bar.

Cara offered her an approving nod as she passed her by, but then Paige frowned when Juliet suddenly made a beeline for her office. "B-babe?" Paige rushed after her, following Juliet inside and closing the door. When she turned Juliet, her cheeks were stained with tears. "What's up? Why are you crying?"

"You are...*extraordinary*." Juliet held Paige's face, and then she studied every last inch of it. "I never knew happiness like this could exist, Paige."

"Me neither." Paige sniffled. "I didn't think someone like *you* existed."

"This feels overwhelming at times, probably more so for you, but I don't ever want to imagine losing any of this. You. The bar. Anything my life has become."

"We won't lose it, babe. I'm so happy here."

Juliet held Paige against her, kissing the top of her head. While Juliet held her tightly, Paige still felt that relaxation in her body. "I love you, Paige."

"I love you, too."

CHAPTER 30
THE NEARNESS OF YOU

*J**uliet is going to enjoy this.* Paige thought, smiling as she brought the cocktail shaker above her shoulder, the sound of ice against the metal music to her ears. She'd become so used to the sound that once grated on her that it was rhythmic. Entrancing. It was all she knew and where she was comfortable. She set the shaker down, allowing the cocktail a moment to settle, and picked out a martini-style glass. It was a classic Brandy Alexander, only it would be named the Brandy Juliet on the new menus when they were printed this weekend.

Juliet had no idea Paige was working on this today, but if Paige had realised anything in the last few months, it was that Juliet wanted her to feel at ease here and to take control of the bar area. Paige thrived off the responsibility. She had also come to learn that Juliet preferred her food and drink on the sweet side. This was going to be right up her street.

She rolled her sleeves up further, removing the cap from the shaker as she poured slowly. The sweet and creamy liquid decanted into the glass, *almost* as smooth as the woman it was named after. Being alone at The Hideout while she was left to her own devices had become a common occurrence since the police had picked up James, that fear all but non-existent now. She didn't wonder if he was going to come through the door; she didn't watch her back if she popped out to pick up some lunch. No, she didn't fear the consequences anymore.

And today, James was up in court.

Paige had tried not to think about it too much, she couldn't change any outcome of whatever he did or didn't face, but she was expecting a call fairly soon. She just hoped she heard the news before Juliet got back from meeting with their new local gin supplier. Whenever Paige mentioned James' name, the fury in Juliet's eyes was clear as day. She didn't want Juliet to feel that anger; he wasn't worth it.

Armed with a straw, Paige dipped it into the cocktail and placed her thumb over the opposite end. She brought it to her lips and dripped it into her mouth, almost moaning as that silky smooth liquid coated her tongue. Yeah, Juliet was going to devour this the moment she got back. Paige turned her watch towards herself, nodding. She had a few minutes before Juliet would walk through the door.

Since she had the perfect opportunity to play, Paige slid the cocktail glass towards the other side of the bar—ready and waiting for its taster—and moved towards the piano. She lifted the lid, exposing the keys, and gently caressed each one from right to left. The sound sent a shiver down her spine, her skin prickling with goosebumps, a now familiar smile spread on her mouth. Never in all her life did she imagine being in this position. Happy, in love, and with the ability to play whenever the mood took her. *This is the life.*

Paige heard the lock on the main door, but she chose to continue. She wasn't playing anything in particular, simply exercising her fingers, but Juliet wouldn't complain. She watched, waiting for Juliet to appear in front of her...only when she did, Paige's heart slammed hard. Juliet stood in the doorway, holding her satchel loosely at her side. She wore a navy-blue pencil skirt with a white silk blouse tucked in, her knee-length navy-blue overcoat resting over her shoulders. Paige chose not to focus on the sexy heels. They only distracted her from everyday life.

Sheer. Perfection.

The melody of Nora Jones "The Nearness of You" came to her instantly, and as Paige blended fully into it, clearing her throat, Juliet dropped her satchel and rested back against the wall. Legs crossed at the ankles, arms folded across her chest. This woman was fully in control of Paige without even knowing it. But it wasn't the same control James had once held. No, it was a sexy, smouldering control that had Paige weak at the knees every minute of the day.

She wanted to step up and claim Juliet's lips. She wanted to lavish the delicate skin she knew hid beneath her clothes. God, what she wanted...she *could* have. Until forever.

Juliet mouthed, "you're so beautiful," as Paige pinned her with her stare. Those dark eyes held Paige's, unwavering with each word, and as Juliet pushed off the wall and approached Paige, her fingers faltered against the keys. Juliet stood behind Paige, bending down as she whispered, "keep going," low in her ear. Paige shuddered, that hot breath stroking her face. She wanted to keep going, but knowing Juliet was close by made it painfully hard to do so. Just the scent of Juliet's perfume had Paige's blood pumping faster. Her hands shaking.

When her voice eventually trailed off, the melody following, Juliet kissed Paige's neck and smiled against her skin. "Hi, baby."

"Hey."

"You smell really good today." Juliet straddled the slight space behind Paige on the bench, wrapping her arm around Paige's waist. "And I've missed you."

"How did the meeting go?" Paige had no idea why she was asking or why she cared. She felt Juliet's breasts pressing against her back...that's what she should have been focused fully on.

Juliet moaned lightly when she brought her hands to the front of Paige's shirt, gradually unbuttoning it. "I don't think that's important right now. Do you?"

"N-no." Paige shuddered when Juliet's soft palm caressed the swell of her breast, her fingers ever so slowly slipping inside her bra. "Babe..." Paige groaned, her nipples painfully taut. "Oh, fuck."

"Mm. You feel good. Do you need me?"

"I always need you." Paige allowed her head to rest back on Juliet's shoulder, her eyes closing. Juliet pinched her nipple, sending arousal directly to her core. God, this woman and her hands. "I just didn't expect this kind of welcome."

"Touching you," Juliet murmured, kissing Paige's neck. "Giving you the attention you deserve...it's *all* I want to do, Paige." The tip of Juliet's tongue carefully made its way up her neck, teasing her earlobe before Juliet took it between her teeth. "All I want is *you*."

Paige delighted in the sensation of Juliet all over her. Because that's what this was. A craving to always want to be close to one another. No other could ever make Paige's body demand something so intense, but Juliet? Oh, Juliet didn't have to even try. This... It all came so naturally and so effortlessly to them both. "I-I finished your cocktail."

Juliet's other hand made light work of the button on Paige's pants, quickly sliding past the waistband of her boy shorts, those soft fingertips stroking Paige's clit. "Perfect. I'll need it to quench my thirst once I've tasted you." Juliet tugged her hand from Paige's underwear, bringing her fingers to her lips. "You know I can't get enough of you." She moaned as those slender fingers entered her mouth, Juliet's full red lips sucking gently. "God, *never* enough."

"Babe..." Paige had no idea what she wanted to say to Juliet, her mind working overtime as she watched Juliet smirk in her direction.

"Yes?"

Paige strained her neck, capturing Juliet's mouth. She tasted herself, smiling into a deeper kiss, and gasped against Juliet's lips when her fingers returned to where Paige craved them. "I fucking love you." Paige clenched her jaw, lifting her hips and gaining a little friction.

"Mm. You know what I love? Feeling you, touching you, knowing how wet you are. Because it's all for me. Every last piece of you is all mine, Paige."

Juliet lowered her hand further, sinking two fingers inside Paige. Her breath caught, the pressure of Juliet's palm against her clit far more intense than she'd expected. "Fuck, yes."

"I've been thinking about you since you left my place this morning. I've been thinking about all the things I want to do to you." Juliet curled her fingers inside Paige, pressing her palm a little harder to her clit. "From the moment I met you, I've dreamt about fucking you in this very position. It's that voice of yours. It does so many things to me."

"Y-yes." Paige slowly rolled her hips in rhythm with Juliet. God, she was always so close to the edge when Juliet was inside her. "P-please, babe."

Juliet squeezed Paige's breast, sucking on her neck and smirking. "Please what?"

"Fuck. Please make me come." Paige forced herself against Juliet's hand, rocking back and forth. She needed so much more of this woman, but right now, she needed to come. She wanted to feel that ultimate high she only ever felt with Juliet. "I...is the door locked?"

"Mmhmm." As Juliet confirmed that, her eyes changed. Devilish. Smoking fucking hot. "Get up."

Huh? Get up? But...Paige was far from finished.

As Juliet slid her hand from Paige's pants, she got to her feet, waiting for Paige to do the same. The look in Juliet's eyes told Paige she wasn't willing to wait very long, so she stood on shaky legs, exhaling a slow breath.

Juliet nudged the bench out of the way, stepped painfully close to Paige, and cupped her cheek as she whispered, "Turn around and bend over."

Those words, Juliet's tone, fuck...Paige wasn't sure she could move. If she did, she would surely come. The wetness she felt pooling in her underwear was nothing new lately, but did Juliet really want to do what Paige was imagining? *Holy shit!* She turned, braced her forearms against the top of the piano, and bent at the hip.

Juliet stepped up behind her, pressing herself to Paige, and slowly pushed her pants and underwear down her thighs, over her knees, before they dropped to her ankles. "Paige, baby..." Juliet smoothed her hand across Paige's lower back, dipping it lower. "I want you so much."

"You have me."

"Oh, I know." Juliet eased two fingers back inside Paige, hitting deeper than before. Paige couldn't help but push back against Juliet, needing everything she had to offer. "Mm. You like that."

"Fuck, yes I do." Paige gripped the edge of the piano top, bending further. "More, babe."

Juliet obliged, easing a third finger inside. It was in that moment that Paige knew just what her future looked like. Every moment with Juliet was exhilarating. Every minute was filled with more love than those before. Juliet Saunders...was her entire future.

"Fuck, Paige. I want you to come for me." Juliet's ragged voice as she thrust hard and fast had Paige's knees trembling. "Let me hear you. I want to feel you." When Paige's walls squeezed Juliet's fingers, Juliet moaned. "Mm. Just like that."

Paige fell apart, releasing around Juliet, shaking when she didn't slow. God, was this heaven on earth? It certainly felt that way. "Y-yes. Oh, fuck!"

"More. I want more from you." Juliet dropped to her knees behind Paige, lapping up everything Paige had to offer. Paige's walls forced Juliet's fingers out, but her lips were on Paige's clit not a moment later. Sucking and teasing. Coaxing everything they could.

Paige shuddered, toppling over the edge again, only this time it was far more intense. She gripped what she could of the piano, her upper body pressed to the wood. "Shit, babe. Fuck!"

"Mm. You always taste so fucking good."

As Paige's shoulders relaxed, she pressed her forehead to the cool wood. She needed to catch her breath, but she also needed to feel Juliet. God, she wanted her like she'd never wanted anything else in her life. "B-babe."

Juliet encouraged Paige up from her position. Paige tugged her pants back up, her hands trembling. But then Juliet took her in her arms. That sultry facade fell away, leaving Paige with the most genuine and loving embrace. "Are you okay?" Juliet whispered, kissing Paige's temple.

"Yes." She nuzzled her face into Juliet's chest, sighing. "Where the hell did that come from?"

"I told you I'd been thinking about you all day." As Juliet stroked her fingers through Paige's hair, Paige's phone started to ring on the bar counter.

Paige couldn't possibly answer the call right now. She needed to get her breath back. "Can you get that for me?"

Juliet pulled back, holding Paige at arm's length. "You're sure? I...don't usually answer your phone."

"Yeah, and you don't usually walk in here and fuck me against the piano either." Paige grinned at the reminder, her body overly sensitive. "Fuck. How the hell am I supposed to sit behind there tomorrow and pretend nothing happened?"

"I'm sure you'll figure it out," Juliet said as she reached towards the counter for Paige's phone. "Hello?" She frowned. "Oh, hi. Just one second." Juliet handed Paige's phone over. "It's the police."

Page's stomach rolled. "Hello?"

"Paige, hi. I've just come from court. James has been sentenced to eighteen months, suspended for two years."

"R-right, um...so what now?"

"There is another injunction in place. He also has to pay the court fees along with compensation to you. Don't worry; you won't have any contact with him. And if he does contact you or you see him around, you're to call the police immediately, and he will be taken back into custody where he *will* face jail time. Any breach of his conditions, and he'll be recalled immediately. Given the fact that you live a long way from one another, any sighting of him would likely be suspicious. He has no reason to step foot in Liverpool."

"No, I know."

"I know you said you're staying in Liverpool, that you have a permanent job there, but I do want to ask if you're okay? Settled? Do you have anyone you can lean on with this latest development?"

"Yes." Paige took Juliet's hand, entwining their fingers. "My girlfriend is here with me."

"Perfect. Well, if I need anything else from you, I'll call. You'll receive paperwork in the coming days that go into more detail about his charges and conditions. But Paige?"

Paige swallowed. "Yeah?"

"It's time to move on now. Rebuild your life."

"Thank you, PC Radford. For everything." Paige cleared her throat, keeping her emotions in check. PC Radford was right. It was time to move on entirely. "Take care. Bye."

Paige stared down at her phone as she ended the call, her brows drawn together. James…was out of her life? Looking back, she never for one second thought that would ever happen. It didn't seem possible that she would ever be free, let alone in love with someone like Juliet. Honestly, she couldn't comprehend the idea that Juliet even saw her as someone meaningful in her life.

"Baby?" Juliet lifted her hand, gently placing it to Paige's jaw. Their eyes met. "It's over."

"I-I know."

"Are you okay? Do you need a moment alone?" Juliet cocked her head, regarding Paige with an understanding smile. "Whatever you need. You say the word."

"No. I don't want to be alone. One thing I've never needed since I met you is to be alone."

"Then maybe we should sit down for a moment…" Juliet guided Paige towards the bar, pulling out two stools. "Come on. Sit down. I'll make us coffee."

"Oh, I don't think so." Paige reached for the stem of the martini glass, sliding it towards them. "Try this."

Juliet brought it to her lips, smelling the drink before she sipped it slowly. Her eyes widened as she brought the glass away from her mouth, and then she moaned. "Oh, my! That is delicious."

"You like it?"

"It's so smooth," Juliet said, sipping again. She rolled her eyes this time, setting the glass down. "God, I'm going to have to be careful with those. I'll be on my back within minutes."

Juliet narrowed her eyes, grinning. "Or was that the plan all along?"

"Babe, I don't need to ply you with alcohol to get you on your back." Paige leaned in, kissing Juliet. They moaned together, the taste of Juliet's lips sending Paige's mind into a spin. "You know that."

"Fuck, I know."

"Now, should I send the new cocktail list to the guy who is printing the menus? Does this one satisfy you?"

Juliet cradled Paige's chin in her fingers, leaning into a gentle kiss. "Anything your hands touch satisfies me, Paige."

EPILOGUE
I GET TO LOVE YOU

Paige blew out a breath, shoving her hands in her pockets as she stared at the few boxes in the middle of the living room. The upside to living in and leaving *this* apartment was that she didn't have to traipse all kinds of stuff across the city, but she would miss it in some way. It had been the place where she felt most comfortable in the weeks and months after filing for divorce. Of course she would rather be with Juliet, but Paige had always been quite content with her own company. She wasn't sure that would ever change. It was a shame her mum hadn't felt the same when it came to not needing attention or conversation. Thankfully, Paige hadn't followed in her mother's footsteps when dealing with loneliness. She didn't hit the bottle. No, she thrived off her alone time more often than not.

She reached for her phone where it sat on the kitchen counter, and checked the time. She had promised Juliet she would be out of here by midday, so she would spend a few moments reflecting on the last year of her life before she began the next chapter. A chapter that could only be filled with further happiness and love. A chapter that she would write *herself*, not one that was written for and thrown at her. If the last twelve months had taught her anything, it was that being with the right person and living the truest version of herself would always be the correct path to take. Paige had never felt so comfortable in her own skin.

Her phone pinged in her hand.

Are you still coming here for midday? J x

Paige smiled. They were practically joined at the hip these days.

Yes. I've just finished packing my last tiny box. I can come now, if you want me to? x

No! Don't come here yet. I'm in the middle of doing something. J x

Paige frowned as she read the message. What could Juliet possibly be doing just twenty minutes before she was due to arrive? And *why* was she doing it alone?

Need a hand with whatever it is you're doing? x

Again, no. It's a surprise. J x

Paige lowered her phone and moved towards the window. Juliet's view was so much better than this, but she did enjoy the slight hint of river if she pressed her face against the glass and strained her eyes. It wasn't much, but for the last year, it had been hers. Rented, sure, but this apartment had been the first place Paige felt she could call home. A home that didn't come with the possibility of James banging the door down. A home that was warm and inviting. A home that had seen some beautiful memories already made with Juliet.

A thud out in the hallway startled her, and as she moved towards the door and spied through the peephole, she saw two men in what looked like removal uniforms standing with their hands on their hips. She brought her phone up again, texting Juliet.

Are those removal guys at your place? What's going on? x

Nothing.

And then Juliet started to respond.

Yes. They're here. DO NOT leave your apartment! J x

Okay, what the hell was going on? Paige didn't want Juliet hauling things around to make room for her few measly boxes. It wasn't necessary at all.

Are you moving out before I move in? x

Not in a million years. I'll see you at midday. Not a moment sooner. I love you. J x

Paige's heart thrummed a little harder, and a grin spread on her mouth.

I love you, too x

Feeling more at ease, Paige lowered herself to the couch and flopped back. She was done with waiting to kiss Juliet, so the sooner she'd finished doing whatever she was doing, the quicker that could be happening. Okay, she didn't spend monumental amounts of time in this apartment anymore, but she had come back here alone last night so today would be more exciting. Sad, but true. And Juliet had agreed it would make the moving-in process exciting too. She may have that hardened shell, but Juliet Saunders was *the* biggest softie underneath it all.

Paige sighed. Right now, she wanted to have her arms wrapped around that big softie.

Now, and until forever.

Juliet frantically tidied her apartment, sweeping the wood flooring around where her new delivery sat. It had been touch and go in terms of even getting it through the door, but she would have succeeded one way or another. She didn't quit, especially not with something so special now sitting in pride of place. Paige was going to be beside herself when she saw it. At least, that was what Juliet hoped for in terms of a reaction.

She shoved the brush into her cleaning cupboard, pulling the creases out of her T-shirt. It was Paige's T-shirt, but whatever. Juliet often found herself wearing her girlfriend's clothes lately.

"Babe?" Paige called through the door as she knocked. "Can I come in now?"

"Oh, uh…one minute." Juliet peered at the door; It was still locked. She did a quick double check around the place, satisfied that everything was where it should be. "Coming!" She rushed across the open space, unlocking the door and exhaling a breath. When she opened it, and Paige stared back at her looking bemused, Juliet could only smile. "Hi."

"Hi. Is…everything okay?" Paige stretched onto her tiptoes and tried to look over Juliet's shoulder. "Babe?"

"Everything is fine," Juliet said, leaning in and kissing Paige. "I know you said you didn't have much, but is this really all you've got?" She scanned the three small boxes on the floor and the suitcase beside them. Paige travelled *very* lightly.

Paige lifted a shoulder. "This is me."

"Even after spending an entire year in that apartment?"

"Yep." Paige peered over Juliet's shoulder again. "Can I come in, or are we staying out here until further notice?"

"Oh, of course. Sorry, I've been busy getting things ready."

Paige stopped as Juliet took a step back. Again, that confused look clouded her gorgeous eyes. "What exactly have you been doing? If you've done something really lovely, I'm probably going to cry."

"You won't. It'll be fine. Come on." Juliet took Paige's hand. "Close your eyes as you come inside." Juliet quickly shoved Paige's boxes with her foot until they were inside the apartment, wheeling her suitcase in behind them. "Don't open them until I tell you to, okay?"

"Okay."

Juliet felt Paige's uncertainty. God, she hoped this went to plan. "R-right, um." Juliet wrung her hands together, blowing out a nervous breath. Maybe Paige would hate what she'd done. Maybe this was a terrible idea. "Y-you can open them now."

Paige cracked one eye open, shock evident when she opened the other. "O-oh. I-I..."

"Do you like it?" Juliet hesitantly placed a hand to the small of Paige's back. She was hard to get a read on this afternoon. "Baby?"

"You...got this for me? I don't understand. Why would you do something like that for me?"

Juliet smiled, turning to Paige. When she brushed Paige's hair from her face, those greyish blue eyes teary, Juliet cocked her head. "Because I love you, and I want you to continue doing what makes you happy."

"Juliet," Paige said, her voice breaking. "This is huge. This gift...it had to cost you a fortune."

"It doesn't matter what it cost me if it makes you happy. Does it? Make you happy?"

Paige nodded slowly, a smile present even if she sniffled as it curled on her lips. "You're amazing. And supportive. I don't know what I'd do without you."

"That's what we're about, though, right? Supporting one another. I don't ever want you to feel as though you can't do what you love. And if you ever want to take it further, you know I'll be right by your side, cheering you on."

Paige's eyes flitted from Juliet to the baby Grand piano taking up space in the window. She inched towards it, taking Juliet's hand as she did so, and grinned. "I...can't believe this."

"Believe it, Paige. Believe in yourself."

"Can...I try it out?" Paige asked hesitantly.

Juliet only squeezed her hand and let go, encouraging Paige to take a seat on the bench. "God, I wish you would." Juliet swallowed down the emotion lodged in her throat. Paige was a sight sitting in her window, her hand slowly smoothing over the top of the piano. "You look perfect sitting there."

Paige looked up at Juliet with tears in her eyes. "And you look perfect standing there."

Juliet blushed, smiling as she cast her gaze on the floor. Paige was all that mattered to her in life. To know she'd done this for her, and Paige appreciated it, Juliet couldn't explain how it made her feel. For the first time in all of her days, she could stand here right now and say that she was the happiest woman in the world. She had someone by her side who didn't expect the world from her. She had someone she curled up with in the night who just wanted to be loved. She had...everything.

"Can I sing for you?" Paige asked, breaking Juliet from her wonderful thoughts.

Smiling and taking a seat at the kitchen island, Juliet nodded and exhaled a calming breath. There was something about Paige, her voice, and a piano that had Juliet's heart racing time and time again. Every note, every breath, it was as though Juliet was hearing Paige for the very first time, over and over again.

Paige's voice floated around the apartment, sending a shiver down Juliet's spine when she recognised the lyrics. Paige was serenading her with Ruelle's "I Get to Love You". *Oh, God.* Juliet's heart expanded, her palms clammy as Paige stared back at her, those fingers working so effortlessly as they feathered over the keys.

There would never be a moment when Juliet *wasn't* madly in love with Paige Ashburn.

She sniffled, brushing a tear from her cheek when Paige

smiled. But that voice continued, those eyes brightened, and Juliet's breath caught as she bit back a sob. The intensity of the love she felt for Paige was all-consuming. It was a knock you off your feet kind of love. It was a forever promise. It was…them. *Just* them, together.

The song came to an end, but Juliet could only gaze into Paige's eyes, her tears continuing to gather along her jawline. Paige got to her feet and crossed the space, brushing her knuckles gently against Juliet's jaw. "Please don't cry." She wiped them away, stepping between Juliet's legs. "Hey, come on. This is a tear-free home."

"Then you need to stop singing such beautiful songs," Juliet said, whimpering as she smiled. Her arms wrapped around Paige's waist, and as she pulled her in painfully close, their foreheads touched. "You're incredible. Every last thing about you is just…I don't know. I love you beyond words, Paige."

"I love you too, babe. But you know I hate seeing you cry."

Juliet cupped Paige's cheek. "Because in the past, crying hasn't been a positive thing for you. But for me? God, I've waited my entire life for someone who can make me cry with happiness."

Paige regarded Juliet with a shy smile. "Yeah?"

"The best decision I've ever made in my life was to leave my career. The only thing I'd ever really known. Because it brought me to you. The happiness you give me. The love I feel. These tears…they're *nothing* to worry about, Paige."

"You don't know how happy I am that I didn't leave when I said I would. Or how stupid I was for ever thinking I couldn't trust you."

"Baby, you've been through so much. I never expected your trust from the beginning. But now, now you know I've got you. That I'd never do anything to hurt you." Juliet stroked her thumb across Paige's bottom lip, leaning in and replacing it with her mouth. God, Paige's lips were a dream. And that gentle moan…oh, it would always hit the spot for Juliet. "Should we begin unpacking your belongings?"

Paige smiled against Juliet's lips. "Sure. It'll take all of five minutes."

"Perfect. That gives me much more time to undress you slowly while I worship every last inch of your skin."

"B-babe." Paige shook where she stood between Juliet's legs.

Juliet grinned as she pulled back, a brow arched. "Yes?"

"You have to stop saying things like that to me." Paige had a now familiar look in her eyes. One that Juliet enjoyed seeing daily. "You know exactly what you're doing."

"You're right. I do. But isn't it fun?" Juliet winked as she slid from the stool. One arm remained around Paige as she kissed her softly. "I know it's *a lot* of fun for me."

"M-me, too."

Satisfied that she'd worked Paige up exactly how she wanted to, Juliet's arm fell from around her waist as she headed for Paige's boxes. "Well, then we should get these out of the way. We have a home to create together."

Helplines

UK: 0808 2000 247
US: 1.800.799.SAFE (7233)
Canada: 1.888.833.7733
Australia: 1800RESPECT (1800 737 732)

It may be difficult to pick up the phone and seek advice. It may also not be safe to do so. Countries around the world offer a chat service amongst other options. If you feel unsafe or you are in immediate danger, please chose the option best for you.

Hey, you! You've got this!

SIGN UP TO WIN!

Sign up to my mailing list to be the first to hear about new releases, and to be in with a chance of winning books!

www.melissaterezeauthor.com

DID YOU ENJOY IT?

Thank you for purchasing The Hideout.

I hope you enjoyed it. Please consider leaving a review on your preferred site. As an independent author, reviews help to promote our work. One line or two really does make the difference.

Thank you, truly.

Love,
Melissa x

About the Author

Oh, hi! It's nice to see you!

I'm Melissa Tereze, author of The Arrangement, Mrs Middleton, and other bestsellers. Born, raised, and living in Liverpool, UK, I spend my time writing angsty romance about complex, real-life, women who love women. My heart lies within the age-gap trope, but you'll also find a wide range of different characters and stories to sink your teeth into.

SOCIAL MEDIA

You can contact me through my social media or my website. I'm mostly active on Twitter.

Twitter: @MelissaTereze
Facebook: http://www.facebook.com/Author.MelissaTereze
Instagram: @melissatereze_author
Find out more at: www.melissaterezeauthor.com
Contact: info@melissaterezeauthor.com

Also by Melissa Tereze

Another Love Series

The Arrangement (Book One)

The Call (Book Two)

Before You Go (Book Three)

Mrs Middleton Novels

Mrs Middleton

Teach Me (Co-write with Jourdyn Kelly)

Vanessa

The Ashforth Series

Playing For Her Heart (Book One)

Holding Her Heart (Book Two)

Other Novels

Discovery

The Stepmother

Behind Her Eyes

At First Glance

Always Allie

Breaking Routine

In Her Arms

Forever Yours

The Heat of Summer

Forget Me Not

More Than A Feeling

Where We Belong: Love Returns

Naked

Titles under L.M Croft (Erotica)

Pieces of Me